JANE ISAAC

In the Shadows

Legend Press Ltd, 51 Gower Street, London, WC1E 6HJ
info@legendpress.co.uk | www.legendpress.co.uk

Contents © Jane Isaac 2023
The right of the above author to be identified as the author of this work has
been asserted in accordance with the Copyright, Designs and Patents Act
1988. British Library Cataloguing in Publication Data available.

Set in Times.
Print ISBN 978-1-91564-389-6
Ebook ISBN 978-1-91564-390-2
Cover Design by Rose Cooper | www.rosecooper.com

Jane Isaac studied creative writing with the Writers Bureau and the London School of Journalism. Jane's short stories have appeared in several crime fiction anthologies. Her debut novel, *An Unfamiliar Murder*, was published in the US in 2012, and was followed by six novels with Legend Press: *The Truth Will Out* in 2014, *Before It's Too Late* in 2015, *Beneath the Ashes* in 2016, *The Lies Within* in 2017, *A Deathly Silence* in 2019, and *Evil Intent* in 2022.

Jane lives in rural Northamptonshire with her husband, daughter and dog, Bollo.

Visit Jane at
janeisaac.co.uk
or on Twitter
@JaneIsaacAuthor

To Nab
My best friend, first reader and greatest champion, who
retired from the police in 2022 after 25 years' service.
This one is for you x

CHAPTER I

The barrel of the rifle pressed against his thigh as he clutched the holdall close. He surveyed the ivy snaking up the concrete floors of Victoria Car Park. It was 10.51 pm.

An hour earlier, this area would have been clogged with people spilling out from the nearby theatre. The thick scent of exhaust fumes filling the air as vehicles revved and reversed. Horns blasting at drivers rudely pushing their way into the queues waiting to exit and head home after a long performance. Now it was quiet. Tranquil.

The night was overcast: a dull moon covered by a film of cloud, not a star in sight.

Moths fluttered around the light bulb as he entered the stairwell and began his ascent, pausing to glance in at each floor as he passed. A handful of vehicles on the second. A motorbike on the third. Not a pedestrian in sight.

The top floor was empty, the stillness only broken by a swooping bat overhead. He checked the stairwells located beside the lifts at either end of the floor, the only areas illuminated, the rest in darkness. Examining the two cameras, he was relieved to find the lenses still broken. The likelihood of anyone venturing up here at this time of night was remote, but still, he pulled the hood of his sweatshirt further down his forehead until it peeked across his brow before walking across to the barrier, lowering the bag to the floor, and peering down at Swan Street below. A woman scurried across the road and disappeared around the corner, leaving the cobbled street empty in her wake.

The dull thud of club music drifted upwards.

He scanned the low line of buildings opposite: the boutique with its illuminated front, showcasing this summer's trendy new outfits. The shoe museum encased in darkness. The café on the corner, a roller shutter pulled down over its door. The silhouettes dancing in the latticed windows of O'Malley's bar, the source of the pulsating beat.

This was Hampton's cultural quarter, mostly housing a mixture of cafés, shops, and museums. The theatre at the top of the hill, the cinema around the corner. Generally quiet by 10.30 on a Friday night – the hardy taking the short walk to the bars in the town centre that stayed open until the early hours. But a small contingent chose to stay and finish their evening in O'Malley's, an old-fashioned bar that had attracted a cult following due to its weekend DJ nights.

He could imagine the scene inside the pub now. Wet bar cloths. Dirty stools. The jazzy carpet filled with the stench of stale beer, barely visible under the weight of young bodies jigging to the music. Underclad women with sweat trickling down exposed cleavages. Drunken guys ogling them.

He tore his gaze away, lay the bag on its side and slid out the rifle, cradling the weapon like a new baby. There was something special about an AK-47. The smell of the gun oil, the ridges of the magazine, the cordite aroma that hung in the air after firing. He pulled out a bean bag, placed it on the concrete ledge, rested the barrel on top and took his time to line his sights up with the chipped black doors of O'Malley's.

A taxi cruised down Swan Street and pulled up at the corner. He watched it hover, the engine turning over, the 'for hire' sign unlit, indicating it was booked. Another followed, parking behind.

It was 10.59 pm – adrenalin flushed through him as he took another look at the bodies, swaying to the beat inside. Easy, carefree. Oblivious to the fact that some of them were about to die.

CHAPTER 2

Ashleigh held back Nia's hair and watched her cast the contents of her stomach into the toilet.

'Eww!' Cass said from behind. 'How many bottles of Cherry Sourz did you down?'

Head still in the pan, Nia was in no position to answer. She retched and produced another deluge of pink fluid.

Ashleigh flinched and closed her eyes. Wrinkling her nose at the acrid smell of sick hanging in the air, trying her best not to heave.

Nia vomited again. Ashleigh opened her eyes and averted her gaze towards the red-painted walls, the gilt-edged mirrors above the white sinks. The black and white tiled flooring of the pub toilets was starting to make her head ache.

'She'll be fine in a minute,' Cass said to Ashleigh. 'You know what she's like. Just needs to get the worst out of her system.'

Poor Nia, she'd always been the same. In their early teens when they'd started dabbling with alcohol – pinching Cass's parents' vodka out of the drinks cabinet after school. Mixing liberal quantities of the spirit with their lemonade or coke. It was always Nia that slurred her words after a few mouthfuls, giving the game away. At college, when they moved on to alcopops, she threw up after a couple of bottles. She'd never mastered alcohol in volume, and her mid-twenties had done little to improve her tolerance.

Nia groaned and rested her head on the toilet seat. Ashleigh let go of her hair, leaned over, and pulled the flush, wincing at the splatter of vomit on the cubicle walls. She grabbed a handful of loo roll and passed it to her friend. 'How are you feeling now?' she asked.

Nia sat back on her heels and wiped her mouth with the tissue, a sheen of sweat glistening on her forehead. 'Better.'

'See, I told you,' Cass said.

But she didn't look better. She looked like she needed a large glass of water, a couple of paracetamol and her bed. This was Ravendale Primary School's excuse for a Year 3 teacher. Hopefully, none of her students' parents were in the bar tonight.

'Help me get her out of here,' Ashleigh said to Cass, stepping over Nia who'd slid onto her side and was now pressing her cheek to the cold floor.

Grabbing an arm each, they manoeuvred Nia out of the toilet cubicle and into the main area in front of the sinks, propping her up against the far wall. Spots of pink vomit stained the front of her white shirt. Cass grabbed a wad of paper towels, ran them under the tap, and dabbed at the marks.

Nia pushed her away with the back of her hand.

The door to the ladies' toilets flapped open, and a woman entered. Face scrunching disapprovingly, she pinched her nose as she moved into the cubicle furthest away from them.

Nia glanced in the mirror. 'I look like shit,' she said, rubbing the leaked mascara from beneath her eyes.

'It's not that bad,' Cass said. 'Wash your face. You'll be as good as new in no time. We could go on to Carter's if you like. We haven't been to a casino together in years. It'll be like old times.'

Ashleigh glanced at her watch. 'My taxi will be outside in a minute.'

'Cancel it. Come on. It's my birthday!'

'It's not your birthday.'

'Well, it's like a birthday. Come on, Ash. I bought a new outfit and everything.' She lifted her arms and gave a shimmy that sent her silver dress swishing around her thighs.

Ashleigh felt a twinge of guilt. This was their big night out, celebrating Cass's return from her travels in Asia. 'My last night of being a student,' she'd said. With a gap year, a master's degree, and access to her parents' seemingly unlimited pot of cash, she'd stretched her student years into her mid-twenties. Though Ashleigh couldn't envisage her party-girl best friend donning a suit and getting a regular Monday to Friday job in a top law firm. It just wasn't her.

Nia belched and lurched over the sink.

'I think we'd better take her home.'

'Oh, not yet. The night is young!'

Ashleigh laughed. 'It's nearly closing time. Come on, give me a hand.'

'One, two, three.'

Nia wrestled them off. 'I'm okay now. I'll be fine.'

But she wasn't fine. She took one step and immediately went over on her heel.

Ashleigh caught her before she fell, took hold of her arm, and guided her out of the toilets. People were gathering in the foyer beside the exit now, a steady stream preparing to leave the pub.

'I'm going to catch the last few tunes,' Cass said.

'They're finishing up.'

'The music's still playing, that's good enough for me. You go. Might see if I can prise Eve off the guy with his tongue down her throat.'

'Nice!' Eve was an old friend of Cass's who'd joined them in the pub. 'I'll see you in the morning then,' Ashleigh said to Cass.

Cass didn't answer. She was already squeezing through the crowd, back towards the bar. She passed a guy Ashleigh didn't recognise jigging shoulders with his friends, lifted her arms and wiggled her hips. Ashleigh couldn't help chuckling. They'd started at seven with pre-drinks. Lord only knew where Cass got her energy from.

The pub was thick with bodies pressing against each other in their quest for the exit.

'Come on,' Ashleigh said to Nia, doing her best to clear a pathway through. 'Let's get you home.'

The night air gushed around them as they stepped onto the street. Nia stumbled again. Ashleigh swung her friend's arm around her shoulder. She could see the taxi straddling the corner of the street, less than fifty yards away. In a couple of minutes, they'd be inside and on their way home.

'Hey!'

Ashleigh looked back, craning her neck towards the voice. It was Cass, pushing her way through the crowd, holding up Nia's bag as if it was a winning lottery ticket. 'She left this at the table.'

'Jesus.'

Ashleigh was just leaning across, reaching out her fingers to grasp the bag when the first crack pierced the air. She automatically ducked. The bag slipped to the floor. Another crack followed. A series of pops. The crowd swayed. Screams splintered in her ears. She stumbled, struggling to stay on her feet as bodies thudded to the ground around her. Cass disappeared. For a split second, terror gripped Ashleigh, then the sound dulled. Elbows dug into her; a knee caught her groin, another her stomach, winding her. Nia grew heavier as Ashleigh fought to keep them upright.

A surge from behind. Nia was tugged from her grip. The sound returned as Ashleigh desperately battled through the bodies crashing together to get to her friend. Yelling. Shouting. Screaming. She couldn't lose Nia; the poor girl would be trampled if she fell to the floor.

A shove from the side. Ashleigh slipped and glanced down for a foothold, eyes widening at the ribbons of red trickling through the gaps between the cobbles, when a blow to the side of her head sent her off balance. The ground shifted. Faces blurred. Her legs disappeared from beneath her. And the world turned black.

CHAPTER 3

DCI Helen Lavery wiped the corner of her mouth with her napkin, dropped it to the table and looked across at Superintendent Jenkins. The contrast between his thick grey hair and dark eyebrows was softer, less severe, under the restaurant's low lighting. She smiled to herself. If she'd been told three months ago she'd be having dinner with him in a classy restaurant she'd have scoffed. An intensely private man, Jenkins had been her boss for over a year and, until recently, she hadn't known he had a partner called David or that he lived on The Elmtrees, an exclusive development overlooking the river Weir on the southern tip of Hampton. That was until his partner fell ill, and she'd been required to cover his job while he took a career break to nurse David back to health. A career break that was now over.

'Are you all ready for Monday?' she asked.

Jenkins placed his cutlery together neatly on his plate. 'I think so. I've started going through my emails, catching up.'

'You're supposed to be on leave. You don't officially start back until after the weekend.'

'Maybe not. But I want to hit the ground running. Now that David's in remission, I need to get back into things.'

Helen surveyed the man before her. Despite visiting him at home while he'd been away, meeting his partner, gaining an inkling of his life outside the police, conversations between them were still awkward and stilted at times.

'So…' He sat back in his chair and viewed her across the table. 'I could do with an update.'

'I thought you'd been looking at your emails.'

'On the stuff that isn't written down.' He crossed his legs and tucked his hands in his lap. This was beginning to feel more like a work meeting than two colleagues catching up socially.

'Like what?'

'I hear Chilli Franks's trial is scheduled to begin in a couple of weeks.'

Helen shifted in her chair at the mention of the local organised crime gang leader currently on remand. A man who'd made threats against her family when her father had put him away for twelve years in the 1990s after throwing acid into an assailant's face. Threats Chilli had renewed when Helen apprehended him herself earlier that year. Threats he'd tried to carry out. Helen rubbed her left eye; the bruising had long since disappeared, but it still ached under artificial lighting.

'And I also hear you've declared a personal relationship with an extended member of Franks's family.'

She shifted again. News spread fast. After the arrest, Chilli's stepbrother, Davy Boyd, had moved back to Hampton from Spain to run Chilli's legitimate businesses. He brought his family with him, and when his son, Zac, started at the same school as her youngest, Robert, the boys had struck up an immediate friendship. A friendship Helen was forced to declare.

'I'd tread carefully there,' he said. 'There's bound to be press interest in the upcoming trial. The force won't welcome any adverse publicity, especially given his history with your family.'

'It's a passing acquaintance,' she said, far more flippantly than she felt. 'They're in the same class, they share friends. I doubt they'll even be spending time together when the trial starts.' She shrugged. 'Teenage friendships can be so fickle.' That was what she was hoping for, though a voice deep within screamed otherwise. Because they weren't just acquaintances, they were best friends. Best friends who spent almost every waking hour together. And it wasn't just herself she was deceiving. She still hadn't found a way to tell her youngest son about her professional relationship with Zac's uncle.

'Excellent, then we understand each other.'

Helen struggled to curl her mouth into a smile, grateful for the arrival of the waiter, a slim, grey-haired man in dark trousers and a matching bow tie. She fleetingly wondered how he managed to keep his white shirt clean with the dirty plates he balanced precariously on his sleeve.

'Can I get you the dessert menu?' the waiter asked.

They shook their heads.

Jenkins had insisted on Sacks, Hampton's most exclusive restaurant – he wanted to thank her properly for keeping his work seat warm. But with exclusivity came delays. He could only secure a nine-thirty table booking, and the ensuing service had been insanely slow. It was now well after eleven, and a pudding at this late hour didn't hold much appeal.

'I need to get back,' Helen said. 'Mum's picking up Matthew, my eldest, from a friend's party. I want to make sure he's still sober. He's got work in the morning.'

Jenkins rolled his eyes. 'Teenage boys, eh?' He turned to the waiter, still hovering at his side, and requested the bill.

Helen's phone rang, dancing across the table top. 'It's the control room,' she mouthed. 'I'll take it outside.'

She weaved through the tables to the exit, a rush of balmy evening air engulfing her as she stepped out and answered, 'Chief Inspector Lavery.'

'Ma'am, this is Inspector Carrington. Are you in town?'

Helen looked over her shoulder, as if someone was watching. 'I am.'

'There's been an incident outside O'Malley's pub on Swan Street. A shooting.'

'What?' Gun crime was incredibly rare in Hampton. When it did occur, it was usually drug-related, gang on gang, on the estates, away from the busy centre. A shooting in town on a Friday night, when the pubs were at their busiest, was unprecedented.

'A mass shooting at closing time,' the inspector continued. 'The street was full.'

'Any casualties?'

'Numerous. Looks like a sniper.'

'Christ!' Helen knew O'Malley's well. She'd broken up a fight there, one of her early calls as a rookie. Arrested three men for affray and received an attractive split lip in the process. An old-fashioned bar situated down the road from The Royal Theatre, it hadn't changed much in the ensuing ten or so years, and she could only begin to conceive the horror, the terror in the street. People panicking, running in all directions.

'What about the shooter?'

The inspector's voice was low. 'Not apprehended.'

Her eyes darted up and down the street. 'You mean they're still loose in the town centre, armed?'

'From initial accounts at the scene, the killer was out of sight. They made off before anyone saw them. We're clearing the area, setting up roadblocks. We could really do with a senior investigating officer down there to oversee everything.'

'Of course. I'll be there in five minutes.'

A bolt of panic hit her as she ended the call. Matthew. He'd been at a friend's house this evening, only a few streets away from O'Malley's. *Numerous casualties.* Her heart thumped in her chest as she tried his mobile, chewing the side of her lip anxiously with each ring. The thought of her sixteen-year-old lying injured at the side of the road, or possibly worse, induced a shiver that ran right through her. The voicemail clicked in. She called off, dialled her mother.

'Hi Mum, where are you?' she said without preamble.

'At home. Just got back with Matthew.' Air instantly expelled from Helen's lungs.

'There's something going on in town,' her mother said. 'The traffic was a nightmare.'

'Are both boys there?'

'Yes. They're in their rooms. Why, is everything okay?'

Helen fought to keep her voice even. No sense in frightening anyone until she knew what they were dealing with. 'There's been an incident in the town centre, that's all. I've been called to attend. I just wanted to check you were all safe.'

'Ah. I take it you'll be late?'

'I will. Don't wait up. I'll see you in the morning.'

The restaurant door opened as Helen rang off. It was Jenkins.

'I've just heard,' he said, holding up his phone.

'I need to get over there,' she said.

'Right. I'm coming with you.'

CHAPTER 4

Grit flew through the air as Helen and Jenkins made their way through Hampton's windswept dusty streets, the elements seeming to emulate the panic. Non-stop sirens rang in their ears. They reached Hampton High Street to find the traffic snarled to a stop, thwarted on their journey out of town by the roadblocks. Motorists climbed out of cars, flooding the pavement. More hazards to weave through. It was almost as if the world was conspiring against them.

By the time Helen caught sight of The Royal Theatre in the distance, lined with police cars and ambulances, almost eight minutes had passed, every one of them pressing down on her. They rounded the corner beside the theatre and reached the blue and white police tape flapping in the wind.

Swan Street looked like a warzone. Streetlamps illuminated what could only be covered, crumpled bodies in puddles of light. Paramedics in green coveralls moved around. A woman in a black dress sat on the kerb, her head in her hands, beside one of the dead. A uniformed officer was helping a man across the road, his white shirt covered in blood. More blood gathered in the gaps between the cobbles. Helen counted the mounds on the ground, covered in blankets. One, two, three, four... She thought about Matthew again and shuddered. O'Malley's Friday DJ nights attracted Hampton's young men and women – late teens, early twenties, out for a few drinks, a dance to their favourite tunes, and the sight of so many dead chilled her to the core.

They were just flashing their warrant cards at the officer guarding the cordon when a rich Yorkshire accent bellowed across the street. 'Hey.'

Helen looked up, surprised to find Pemberton, her sergeant on homicide and major crime, approaching. 'What are you doing here, Sean?' she asked, barely able to take her eyes off the street.

'It was DS Turner's wedding anniversary. I swapped with him to do the detective night car.' He brushed a hand over his bald scalp, and looked around. 'What a night to switch. I was around the corner at a suspected burglary. Arrived within minutes of it happening.' He shook his head, forlorn. 'I've never seen anything like it. The carnage, the panic. Eleven casualties at last count. Four deaths.'

Jenkins swept a hand down the front of his face, dragging the skin with it.

'The street was chaotic when I arrived,' Pemberton said. 'People dazed. Trampling over the injured.' Another headshake. 'We moved everyone back into the pub while we searched the immediate area.'

The lights in O'Malley's, a Tudor-fronted building located halfway down the street, burnt into the night. A jagged crack ran through the window of the boutique beside it. The shoe museum on the other side was encased in darkness. Helen could see several people huddled in O'Malley's. A man in the window holding a compress to his head. A woman in a blood-stained shirt, hunched and crying, being comforted by another woman. The green coveralls of paramedics treating the wounded.

'Do we know the location of the shooter, or shooters?' she asked. They couldn't rule out there being more than one.

'We think so.' He pointed at Victoria Car Park at the bottom of the hill. 'The spray of bullet holes across the front of the pub indicates they came from that direction. When we searched, we found bullet casings on the top floor. Looks like a high calibre rifle.'

'What about those responsible?'

'No sign. We've set up roadblocks and cordoned the area. As soon as more officers arrive, we'll start house to house. But any perpetrators will be long gone. The weapons disposed of too if they've got anything about them.'

'Okay, get a guard on the car park and call the CSIs in to examine it,' Helen said. 'Let's call in the Operational Support Unit to search the adjacent buildings to ensure there weren't shooters placed at numerous sites, and get the helicopter up to overview the scene, look for anything untoward – fleeing suspects, injured people nearby.' While the likelihood of capturing the offender nearby was slim, she had to cover every eventuality.

Pemberton nodded.

'Any vehicles still inside the car park?' Jenkins asked.

'A few scattered about. It won't be difficult to trace the owners through the number plates.'

A high-pitched wail interrupted them. It was the woman in the black dress, still sitting on the kerb. They all rushed towards her.

'Can I help?' Helen asked, scanning the area for a paramedic.

A strangled sob spluttered from a face buried in hands. She shook her head. Sheets of dark hair bouncing around her shoulders.

Helen lowered herself to the kerb beside her. From what she could see, the woman didn't look injured. But they were inches away from a covered corpse, and if experience had taught her anything, it was that shock was almost as dangerous as a life-threatening wound.

She introduced herself. 'You're safe now,' she said gently. 'It's going to be okay.'

The woman lifted her head to reveal a mascara-stained face. Wide glacial eyes. A line of blood ran down the side of her cheek from a small gash at her temple.

'That cut needs attention,' Helen said.

The woman widened her eyes further. Sad and desperate.

She sucked in a sob, then nuzzled into Helen's shoulder like a poorly child. Helen pulled her close.

Time ticked by. The others moved away. The streetlamp flickered in front. Helen's shirt and shoulder grew wet from the woman's blood and tears as she cried herself out. She stroked her back soothingly and gazed across at the ivy-clad walls of Victoria Car Park. Only last week, she'd brought her mother to see Madam Butterfly at the theatre and parked on the fifth floor. It had twelve floors altogether. Two pedestrian entrances, one at each end, both serviced by a stairwell and a lift. Separate entrances and exits for vehicles. Cameras were positioned on each floor – all footage they needed to examine – but what struck her was the location. Straddling the corner, obscuring some of the access areas from this viewpoint. If this was the only location, the killer or killers could have snuck out unnoticed while the aftermath played out in Swan Street.

Unlike the pubs in the town centre, O'Malley's shut at eleven. Those responsible chose to strike at closing time and selected a location with several exits for a quick getaway. It suggested careful planning.

Pemberton had done all the right things. Preserved life as much as he could by moving people out of the street, out of danger. Preserved the scene by cordoning it off, searching the immediate vicinity. But mass shootings were incredibly rare in the UK. Rifles of this magnitude were either illegal or restricted, and the scale of this murder was unlike anything they'd encountered before.

A paramedic stepped out of the pub, crouched beside the woman, and peeled her from Helen's clutches. All the while talking to her calmly, soothingly.

Helen rejoined the others back at the cordon. Jenkins with a phone glued to his ear. Pemberton waiting beside.

'Let's lock down the scene,' she said to Pemberton. 'Get contact details of everyone in O'Malley's before they leave. And call out counter-terror.'

'You think this is a terrorist attack?' Jenkins said, ending his call.

Helen looked out into the darkness. 'It's too early to say, but I'm not taking any chances.'

CHAPTER 5

Tony Kendrick, detective superintendent of the regional counter-terror unit, was a tall, slender man with close-cropped grey hair, razor-sharp cheekbones, and pale bespectacled eyes.

'This was a meticulously organised attack,' he said, undoing the button of his navy suit jacket. 'The pub was hit at closing time when people were spilling out onto the street. Those responsible had access to weapons – possibly semi-automatic, high calibre rifles – and had staked out the area for a well-placed firing position.'

They were back in headquarters, the incident room full to bursting. Helen leaned up against a radiator beside Pemberton, cradling a coffee, desperately trying to warm up while phones rang incessantly in the background. Detectives and support staff, pulled from their beds to assist, filled the chairs. Others perched on the edges of desks; some had formed a line at the back. Chief Constable Adams stood at the front beside Jenkins, listening to Kendrick's summary. It was 3 am. Helen had never seen the chief at this hour, let alone in the homicide and major incident suite, his presence an indelible reminder of the gravity of the situation.

'You are thinking terrorism?' Adams said.

'We can't rule it out, though it's early days. No group has claimed responsibility yet.'

The chief's face fell.

Helen understood his disappointment. A terrorist inquiry trod a different route than a traditional homicide investigation. In traditional cases, there was usually a link somewhere in the victim's family or friends, their background, work, or hobbies. If they worked the case and found the link, it led them to the killer. Terrorists were strangers to their victims. Kendrick's squad utilised counter-terror intelligence and worked closely with national and international security agencies, identifying and monitoring potential threats.

Plus, Hamptonshire was a small force. A crime of this magnitude would require an abundance of legwork, placing pressure on already strained budgets. They'd have to beg, borrow, and steal from neighbouring forces. Counter-terror was funded centrally and well-cushioned, and they needed those resources. Very soon, the eyes of the world's media would be on them, scrutinising their every move.

But this wasn't about budgets or money or resources. It was about people. About fast-track actions. Delivering death messages to loved ones, updating the injured, ensuring the safety of Hampton's wider population.

'I'd suggest a coordinated approach,' Kendrick said. 'Two senior investigating officers. Until we know what we're dealing with.'

'That's fine by me,' Helen said. She listed what actions had been put in place so far to lock down the scene and preserve evidence. 'Officers are contacting the families of injured parties,' she continued. 'I'm told each of the dead have driving licences or credit cards on them, so tracing their nearest and dearest shouldn't be too difficult. One small mercy. I'll arrange for my detectives to get out to see the next of kin tonight.'

A heavy silence filled the room. Last night, families had gone to bed in the belief that their loved ones were safe and well. Only to be woken, hours later, to be told they'd faced a tragic death. One minute they were there, the next gone, like sand slipping through fingers. And if the death message wasn't bad enough, they'd still need to walk the long corridor of the morgue. Wait in the anteroom as their broken and torn loved one was wheeled in, covered with a sheet. Formal identifications tugged on any copper's heartstrings, but when the victims were young, it was both emotional and heart-wrenching.

'We're pulling CCTV footage from the area, both council and private, whatever we can get our hands on,' Helen said. She turned to the chief. 'We do need to discuss a media strategy, sir.'

'Absolutely. I'll get the press office to work on an urgent statement. Keep it general, appeal for any witnesses, and I'll visit the scene myself in the morning, give another statement there.'

'Right,' Kendrick said. He looked at Helen. 'If your team could concentrate on victimology – interviewing the survivors, taking first accounts, that would be helpful.'

'What are they doing then?' Pemberton whispered.

The chief jumped in before Helen could respond. 'We can certainly start to build up a list of those present. Perhaps you can supply officers to go through the mountain of CCTV footage. Until, as you say, we know what we are dealing with.'

Kendrick looked taken aback. 'Of course. I'll make the arrangements.'

'Are you aware of any local terror groups capable of planning something on this level?' the chief asked.

'There are a couple of pockets we are looking at.' He held the chief's gaze, clearly not wishing to say more in wider company. Counter-terror officers were well known for their reticence in sharing intelligence.

'He's no idea.' Pemberton again.

Helen snorted, but there was something else bothering her right now. Something tapping at the side of her brain. Why would a terror organisation come to a small midlands town like Hampton when they could go to one of the big cities and make a far greater impact? It didn't make sense.

CHAPTER 6

Daylight swept into the hospital room. Noah jolted forward in his chair, blinked and checked his watch. He must have dozed off.

He glanced across at Ashleigh, his dear fiancée, lying in the bed beside him, eyes gently closed, and recalled the shock when he heard the news report last night about a shooting at O'Malley's. The gut-wrenching anxiety when he couldn't reach Ashleigh by phone. The frenetic scenes in A&E when he arrived. Trolleys of injured, bloody individuals filling the corridors. Strained and stretched staff battling to prioritise the numerous casualties crashing through their doors. The overwhelming relief when he was told she was alive.

It had taken a while to find Ashleigh in the panicked knot of families. She'd been moved to one of the side rooms, placed under observation until a bed was available on a ward. He'd tried to talk to her as she drifted in and out of sleep, but she was woozy from painkillers, disorientated. A couple of hours passed as he followed her around the hospital while she was assessed. Sitting alongside anxious relatives nibbling their nails in the waiting area in radiography while she was X-rayed. Back to A&E, and eventually to this room on a ward. All the time, fighting sleep while willing her to wake and be well.

She'd taken a hard knock, possibly butted by someone in the struggle, and was unconscious when the paramedics found her in the road. A bullet had clipped her arm; a superficial tissue wound, the doctor had said. Probable concussion too. A bruise like a raincloud covered her forehead. They'd patched her up, pumped her full of painkillers. Nurses had bustled in and out of the room at regular intervals throughout the night to monitor her blood pressure and do her observations. But she was still here. Alive. The rhythmic sound of her breaths comfortingly reassuring.

As she lay motionless, save the rise and fall of her chest, he could see fragments of the teenager he'd fallen in love with after they'd found themselves sitting together in history class in Year 10. The shy girl with the messy brown curls who'd asked him to read the whiteboard because she'd forgotten her glasses. Curls that became groomed as they navigated their teenage years. Glasses that were replaced with contact lenses as they moved into their twenties. Features that had matured into a soft elegance.

His eyes grew watery. He stood, stretched out his back, and opened the curtains. It was almost 8.30 am. The phone call to Ashleigh's mother in France in the middle of the night, to tell her that her only daughter had been a victim in a suspected terrorist attack, was one of the hardest things he'd ever had to do. He couldn't put it off, couldn't delay it until morning. News of a mass shooting in the UK, a country with strict gun laws, would spread across the news sites like fire in a hay barn. And when they discovered it had happened in Hampton, where their daughter resided, they'd be racked with panic.

Ashleigh's mother's voice had quaked as he'd tried to reassure her that her daughter was one of the lucky ones. Convincing her she was going to be all right when he couldn't yet be sure himself. The doctors were still monitoring her and she was awaiting a CT scan to check there weren't any further problems. Her parents were already beside themselves with worry, talking about coming over to see her. No sense in heaping more anxiety onto an already brimming pile, and he didn't know anymore himself. There wasn't an officer in sight to quiz about the incident, and the doctors and nurses couldn't tell him anything.

He reached for his phone and googled 'shooting in

Hampton'. A stream of results appeared, including reports from CNN and Reuters. International media – word was getting out fast. He clicked on a local article from *The Hampton Herald* and skimmed the piece. Eleven casualties. Four dead. Three critical. The saliva in his mouth disappeared.

Back at the main search, a fresh piece popped up from *The Guardian*. The death toll had risen to five. He looked back at Ashleigh. Oh, how he wished he'd offered to pick her up a little before closing time, as he often did when she went out with friends. But she was always telling him she needed her space, and this was her big reunion with her friends, their special night. He didn't want to intrude.

He almost missed the flutter of her eyelids. It happened so quickly, within a couple of seconds, then was gone.

'Ash.' He leaned forward, staring at her, willing her to open her eyes. The twitch stopped. Maybe it was a nerve.

He eased back into his chair, turned off his phone, was slipping it into his pocket when he noticed it again. A definite movement. This time her eyes opened and blinked several times. Blood veins threading across the whites as they darted around the room.

'Ash?' he said, placing his face close to hers.

'Noah.' Her voice was barely a whisper.

'You're in hospital. You're safe,' he said gently. 'Do you remember being brought in last night?'

'No.'

'There was an incident in Swan Street. You took a bang on the head.' He reached out, brushed her hair away from her face tenderly. 'You're okay. You're going to be fine.'

Her face was a picture of confusion. Eyes still darting from side to side, unfocused as if she was reaching for a memory.

'Outside O'Malley's,' she said.

He nodded.

'I remember being there. Cass is back from Vietnam. We went out to celebrate. Nia was there too.' She lifted her head, craned her neck towards the door. 'Are they here?'

'No. It's just me.'

'Oh.' She rested back into the bed.

'Can you recall what happened?'

'I remember leaving the pub. And then… it's all a bit grey, foggy. Did I fall?'

'No, Ash.' He paused to swallow, unsure of how much to say. He didn't want to distress her, but it was all over the news, he couldn't keep it from her. 'There was an attack, a shooting.'

Ashleigh's face became taut, the sinews in her neck tightening to narrow lines. She immediately looked at her left arm, ballooned in bandages. 'Was anyone else hurt?'

He took a breath. 'Quite a few, I'm afraid. The hospital's still processing them.'

'What about Cass and Nia?' Her eyes widened, staring back at him.

'They haven't released names yet. I can go and ask…'

He was interrupted by the door opening, a nurse bustling in. 'Hi, Ashleigh. I'm Tilda. It's good to see you awake.'

'My friends,' Ashleigh said. 'They were with me last night. I need to find them.' She reeled off their names, and the nurse said she'd see what she could find out, then set about checking her pulse, taking her blood pressure, firing a list of questions at her – how was she feeling, did she have pain?

'I need the toilet,' she said.

Noah said he'd wait in the corridor and moved out, closing the door behind him. It was busier there. The central admin station was yards away; doctors and nurses came and went.

He reached for his phone, searched the internet again. More news updates graced the screen. A piece from the BBC naming the dead.

He swallowed, dry and hard, and opened the article. He'd lived in Hampton for seven years; it was possible he knew some of them. Ben Windsor, 24, an accountant. Dominic Yardley, 22, an insurance broker. Their names accompanied by photos. Ben was slim, with blond hair swept back from a suntanned face. Dominic dark with pointy features and dressed in a suit, his expression filled with ambition and opportunities he'd now never realise. An empty trolley trundled past. Noah nodded to the porter, looked back at his phone, scrolled down, and froze. Nia Okeke, 23, a primary school teacher. Nia – Ashleigh's scatty best friend. Trepidation needled him as he scrolled again. Cass Greenwell, 23, a law graduate. No accompanying photo. The fifth victim's identity was still undisclosed.

A lump the size of an egg filled his throat. This was worse than he could have imagined. Ashleigh, Nia, and Cass had been inseparable at school. He could picture the girls now, calling for Ashleigh in the mornings, rucksacks bouncing off their backs as they trotted to meet him on the corner. Standing in a line being photographed in their ballgowns for prom. They'd gone their separate ways through university but, unlike him who'd lost touch with most of his schoolmates, they'd retained their closeness.

The door hinges squeaked as Tilda emerged from the room. 'You can go in now,' she said to Noah. 'She's doing well.'

Noah straightened, trying to walk normally, as if nothing had happened. Though even the sight of his fiancée sitting up failed to curb his misery.

'Noah, what is it?' Ashleigh said.

He lowered the phone, still in his hand, opened his mouth and closed it again.

'Noah, you're scaring me.'

Indecision pummelled him. This wasn't the time. She was recovering from a head injury, still in shock. But he couldn't lie to her. Better to come from him than a stranger.

'It's Nia and Cass.'

'Oh, no. Are they injured too? How badly?'

'They didn't make it, Ash. I'm really sorry.'

CHAPTER 7

A gust of wind billowed Helen's jacket as she walked through town at 7 am the following morning. Low-slung clouds filled the sky, blocking any ounce of sun and making for a grey day. She reached the outer cordon of the crime scene, surprised to find a crowd of reporters and onlookers had already gathered, despite the early hour. Thankful for another line of police tape – the inner cordon – where screens had been erected, hiding the scene from hungry eyes.

Helen stopped to read the messages on a couple of bunches of flowers left at the side of the theatre. *Tragically taken too early. Always in our hearts.* The first of many she suspected over the coming days and weeks.

Dark shadows sat beneath the eyes of the officer guarding the area. A couple of reporters dashed towards her as she climbed over the tape and held up her warrant card. A microphone was thrust in her face.

Someone from behind called, 'Has anyone claimed responsibility?'

'No comment,' she said, placing up a flat hand, avoiding eye contact. The chief would be speaking to the press at the scene in a couple of hours. She wasn't about to usurp him.

She signed into the log, took a moment to thank the officer for his dedication and check when he was being relieved from duty, then headed down the road to O'Malley's. Crime scenes looked different in daylight. She needed to see it, get a feel for the location, its position, the movements of the killer or killers, without the carnage and panic of yesterday evening.

Beyond the screens, Swan Street looked markedly different this morning. Firefighters had been out and sluiced the road, and without the ambulances, the CSIs crawling around, the dead and the injured, it looked empty. Barren.

The door to O'Malley's was closed. Blue and white police tape stretched from corner to corner in a cross. Helen looked up at the forensic markers littering the far end of the exterior wall. Bullet holes. Twenty-four in total. Some deep, direct hits. Others shallow, from redirected or ricocheted shots. Bullets that had been carefully dug out of the brickwork and the soft wood of the window frame by CSIs working through the night. They needed to account for as many as they could and send them to ballistics for examination.

She turned to view Victoria Car Park diagonally opposite. On quieter evenings, many a theatre-goer parked there and popped into O'Malley's for a quick drink before a performance, preferring its laid-back style and cheaper prices to the upmarket wine bar at The Royal. A search of surrounding buildings had narrowed down the shooter's location to a single site on the top floor of the car park. The positioning of discarded shells pointing towards one weapon, possibly one shooter. The very idea that this could all be the work of one individual was off the scale.

Helen crossed the road, stepped over more police tape, and entered the car park. The ground floor was quiet, empty. She moved into the stairwell beside the lift, glancing into each floor as she passed. A collection of cars on two. A motorbike on three. Vehicles parked at the time of the shooting. Owners who had already been traced and eliminated.

On the top floor, she checked the stairwells beside the lifts at either end of the floor. Took her time to examine the smashed lenses of the two cameras. Whoever had done this, whoever had opened fire on a group of individuals leaving a pub at closing time, had clearly taken great care to ensure they wouldn't be identified.

The top floor was open to the elements. A light rain started to fall as Helen crossed the concrete towards a tented area in the corner, covering numerous yellow forensic markers.

She walked to the wall and peered over the top. A roller shutter was pulled over the door of the café opposite. The boutique window was cracked like a road map, the front door of the museum firmly shut, O'Malley's quiet. None of them would be opening today.

She glanced at the forensic tags across the floor. The killer had bolted, leaving the bullet casings behind. Ballistics would use recovered bullets and casings to identify the weapon and track whether it had been used in other crimes, but whoever did this didn't care. Which meant ballistic evidence was unlikely to give them away.

Why here? she thought. What was the commonality in O'Malley's last night that drew the killer to that venue?

CHAPTER 8

Ashleigh stared up at the hairline cracks in the ceiling. How could Cass and Nia be dead when only yesterday evening, less than twelve hours earlier, they'd been laughing, dancing, drinking together? She could almost see them getting ready in her flat last night. Curling Cass's hair, painting Nia's nails, just like old times. Times they'd never repeat. A tear slipped into the well beneath her eye, burning the raw skin. She'd collapsed into fits of sobs after Noah had delivered the news to her earlier. Cried and cried until her chest ached and her throat was raw. Tears that she couldn't stop. Tears that still traced her cheeks when Tilda had called in for her next check and when the consultant later visited with his team of medics. Cocooned so tightly in her grief, she'd barely heard what they had to say. And, as they left, the disbelief crept in. Perhaps there was a mistake. Maybe the news article had confused things, or Noah had read it incorrectly. But… writing a column for the local newspaper for the last few years, she'd grasped enough of the inner workings of the media to know that couldn't be so. Printing names in the press meant the police had gone through the formal identification process with the next of kin. They had erased all doubt.

Memories of their last night together haunted Ashleigh like a song on permanent replay. Nia in the toilet cubicle, sitting back on her heels, sweat trickling down her cheeks. Cass raising her hands to the roof, wiggling her hips as she disappeared into the crowd in O'Malley's. That was Cass – brimming with bravado and confidence. Never one to care what others thought. The recollection tugged at her heartstrings. Because everything ended there. All the plans they'd made, all the events they'd joked about, all their future memories, ground to a halt. They'd never be bridesmaids at each other's weddings, never celebrate their children's birthdays together, never holiday together when they grew old. All those earnest promises shattered. Nia and Cass had been present at almost every life event she could think of. Her eighteenth birthday party, the celebratory night out when she finally passed her driving test after the fifth attempt, the first live performance of the band she'd briefly played keyboard in when she was at uni. They'd even muscled in on her graduation party, even though they didn't have tickets. When her parents moved to France to set up a business running holiday gites, Nia and Cass had rallied around, the sisters she never had. Messaging and calling, a rod of support. When something good happened, she celebrated with them. When things went wrong, they talked it through together.

How could she only have superficial wounds when they were lying in a morgue?

Noah shouldered open Ashleigh's door and steadied the steaming coffees he was carrying, interrupting her thoughts. 'I just saw the nurse. Your CT scan is scheduled for this afternoon.'

'Thanks.' She took the cardboard cup he offered. Even the idea of coffee made her stomach roil, but he was being sweet and kind and doing his best, and she didn't want to appear ungrateful. She took a sip, flinching as the hot fluid burnt her lip. Noah looked worn out. Little wonder. Lord only knew what time he had arrived last night and how little sleep he'd managed. 'I don't mind if you want to go home,' she said. 'Get some kip. It's not like I'm going anywhere.'

'I'm not leaving you on your own.' He leaned in close, his lips brushing her cheek in a tender peck, then gently pressed his forehead to hers, closing his eyes a second, before he drew back. 'The police are outside. Do you feel up to talking to them?'

Ashleigh recoiled. She really didn't feel like talking to the police, going over the scant details she recalled from yesterday evening. But she couldn't put it off forever. Maybe it was best to get it over with. She gave a brief nod and watched him put down his coffee and disappear. The door clicked closed behind him. She could hear him talking in the corridor outside in low tones. Telling them about the shock, her loss. Warning them not to distress her further. Playing the role of the overprotective partner.

Ashleigh pressed her head into the pillow. So many lives lost, so many changed irreparably. It was like a recurring bad dream. One that she couldn't wake from. Who the hell could be responsible?

* * *

'Let's double check the timings. When exactly did you leave O'Malley's?'

Ashleigh looked up at the tall officer with the chestnut bob tucked behind her ears, shirt sleeves rolled up to her elbows. What was her name? She'd introduced herself and her colleague when they'd entered the room, but Ashleigh couldn't for the life of her remember their names. She looked across to the other detective, head dipped as he typed her answers into an iPad. She had no idea how long they had been there – it felt like hours – with their questions of who she'd been out with, what time she'd arrived, who she'd spoken to in the pub, who she recognised by name, what time she'd left. Now her head hurt, and her brain was weary.

'Closing time. Eleven. There was a crowd of people waiting to leave. I was taking Nia…' She felt her chin quiver. Bits were coming back to her now. Little snippets of information, flashing in and out of her brain, as if someone was flicking a light on and off. 'Nia was ill. I was helping her down to the taxi.'

'Did you go outside beforehand?'

'No, I was in the pub all evening. From about 9.30.'

'Not even for a cigarette or to get some air?'

'I don't smoke. I spent the last half an hour or so in the toilets with Nia. She was sick.'

A swift nod.

'What actually happened to my friends?' Ashleigh asked.

The officer exchanged a look with her colleague.

Ashleigh glanced from one to another. 'Please! I need to know.'

The officer looked uncomfortable. 'Cass Ingram was pronounced dead at the scene. It's believed she died instantly.'

No details. No specifics. Was that because they were too horrific? She recalled Cass's blonde tresses flying through the air as she raced to catch them up. Then imagined them sprawled across the cobbles, mingled with blood. 'And Nia?'

'The same.'

'I don't understand. How come I survived? Nia was right beside me.'

The officer looked uncomfortable. 'I'm not at liberty to go into detail.'

If she closed her eyes, concentrated hard, Ashleigh could feel Nia's heavy body propped against her. The sweet smell of her Chanel Coco perfume tainted with vomit.

'Are you sure you didn't see anyone, perhaps in the buildings or the car park on the other side of the road?' the officer asked.

Ashleigh shook her head absently, filing away the question in the cabinets of her mind to be considered later when she had space to piece together the flashbacks. This was the second time they'd asked a question about the location. They seemed to be focusing on the opposite side of the road.

'Why those buildings?'

'Pardon?'

'Why are you asking about that side of the road?'

'The injuries sustained suggest the bullets may have been fired from that direction.'

So, the gunman was on her left as she walked down Swan

Street. Like Nia, who'd been propped up against her. Who'd taken the bullets. Almost like a human shield...

Strong nauseating pain welled inside her like a tsunami. She reached for the nurse's button, pressed hard.

'Ash, are you okay?' She could hear Noah's voice in the distance, then the officer speaking, but couldn't decipher the words. The room whirled like a roundabout, faster and faster. The very thought that the position of her friend's body had saved her...

'Excuse me,' another voice snapped. A face peered in close. Ashleigh fought to steady her vision.

'Ashleigh. It's Tilda. How are you feeling?'

Another twinge of pain. She clamped her eyes together until it faded. 'I can't breathe.'

'Right, everybody out,' the nurse said. 'This girl needs to rest.' And with that, Tilda emptied the room.

CHAPTER 9

A stream of people spilled out of the pub and into the road, the jabber of conversation merging into a din. A pair of women, arms wrapped around each other's shoulders, heads touching, belted out the chorus of 'Bohemian Rhapsody' at the top of their voices. A man in the background waved a beer bottle at a friend who peeled off from the crowd and disappeared into the darkness. It was a happy, contented sight. Good-spirited people saying their goodbyes, moving off after a night out.

The crack of the first bullet sliced through the air. A sway of ducking heads as a stream of more bullets – pump, pump, pump – followed. Screams filled the area. Bodies falling, running, trampling those on the ground in the melee. The camera lens tipped askew, then juddered.

Helen pressed pause on the video and turned to the sea of weary faces in front of her: detectives, police officers and support staff. Her usual team and others the chief had drafted in to bolster numbers. It had been a long night and, with a body count of five and several still in a critical condition, there would be no let-up over the weekend.

'Right,' she said. 'This footage, *O'Malley's Shooting, Hampton*, was uploaded to YouTube by SecretSender1438a two hours after the incident last night.' She turned to Pemberton. 'We can see from the angles that the video was filmed from the ground, and whoever uploaded it started filming before shots were fired. See if the techies can trace them. They may have been alerted to something, or they may even be an accomplice. And get the footage copied as evidence, then taken down, will you? I don't care who we need to speak to, the victims' families certainly don't need those images shared with the world.'

'Okay.' Helen shaded her eyes from a sudden ray of Saturday morning sunshine streaming into the room and faced the wider audience. 'A public appeal has gone out for sightings of anybody in the vicinity carrying a bag or something that may conceal the weapon either before or after the incident. Counter-terror are liaising with ballistics to get more details on the weapon and viewing camera footage in the vicinity for sightings of those responsible. We need to concentrate on building up a list of all those present last night, taking witness statements, and doing background checks.'

'Do they think the attack was provoked by someone present?' Helen followed the voice to DC Steve Spencer, a mature detective at the back of the room. He scratched the parting in his salt and pepper hair as he spoke.

'There's nothing to suggest that at present, we just need to cover every eventuality until we know more. The sergeant and I are meeting with counter-terror in an hour to see where we are. What I do know is that no group has claimed responsibility yet. So, for the moment, we treat this as a multiple murder enquiry. And we start with victimology – I want to hear of anything and anyone of interest.'

She turned to the photos displayed on another noticeboard beside her. Shiny, smiling snapshots of vibrant men and women. Photos supplied by bereaved families during their darkest hours. A stone-cold silence filled the room as she moved down the line, calling out individual names, tapping each picture in turn. Names made the crime personal and, right now, personal was what Helen needed her team to focus on. Yesterday, these victims were all beating hearts. Young people going about their business. She could almost see them driving to work, going to the gym, getting ready for a night out with friends. Blissfully unaware that their lives were about to be extinguished. 'We have six more injured, two of them still critical,' Helen said. 'Where are we with the victims' families?'

A short, impish-looking woman with spiky black hair raised a hand from the side of the room. DC Rosa Dark was the youngest detective on Helen's team, and one of the most enthusiastic. 'We've spoken with each of the next of kin, and carried out formal identifications,' Dark said. 'From what we've gathered so far, two of the deceased were friends, the others appear unconnected.'

'Thanks, Rosa.' Helen turned back to the room. 'Anything from house to house?'

'Nothing of interest,' Pemberton said. 'CSI have sent over copies of their early photos.' He glanced back at the noticeboard. Distant pictures of crumpled bodies on cobbles were pinned beside the map alongside bloodied close-ups of the dead. Stills taken from the YouTube footage. It was a macabre sight, even for the strongest of stomachs. 'We've asked for an urgent preliminary report, though given the size of the scene, it's unlikely to be available quickly.'

'Keep on top of them, will you? The chief wants everything thrown at this case.' Helen ran her gaze down the list of injured pinned beside the photos. 'Okay, what do we know about the pub?' she asked.

'O'Malley's' Friday DJ nights generally attracts the late teens, early twenties,' Pemberton said. 'The victims and injured parties we've traced so far were between nineteen and twenty-five.'

Only just starting their adult life. Helen inwardly flinched. 'What about the owners?'

'Paul Stilson and David Camberra,' Spencer piped up. 'A gay couple, both in their forties, not known to us. Stilson and Camberra bought O'Malley's five years ago.' He paused as he checked his notes. 'It was run-down when they acquired it. They spent a ton on refurbishment and built it up with DJ and theme nights. It's got a reasonable rep these days. Apart from the odd affray, we're barely called there.'

'Right, let's find out about Stilson and Camberra. Their

background, their connections, how they funded the refurbishment, who their families are, who they associate with.'

Helen chewed the side of her lip. An hour's train ride from London, Hampton was known as a cosmopolitan, inclusive town. Episodes of hate crime were rare. But they couldn't afford to ignore the possibility that the shooting was aimed at the owners.

'All right, we'll need to break into teams,' she continued. 'One to build up a picture of each victim. All the usual – friends, family, background, recent movements, and associations. Anyone they'd argued with recently.' She looked around the room. 'Rosa, can you organise that?'

The young detective nodded.

'We'll also need another to focus on the survivors, injured and uninjured, anyone present, in case they were the intended target or shared some connection. Find out what they witnessed yesterday evening. Sean.' She looked across at Pemberton. 'I'll leave you to nominate someone to draw up a list we can work through there.'

Pemberton agreed.

'The phones have already started ringing,' Helen continued. 'We'll need to set up shifts, cover them around the clock. Counter-terror have purloined rooms 23 and 24 downstairs, you'll see them moving around. Support them with whatever equipment they need.'

'One final thing,' she said, glancing back at the noticeboards. 'This investigation is going to be high-profile – reported on every television screen, every news site. The world's media are already on our doorstep. So, you speak to no one. Everything we talk about, everything we discuss, stays in this room unless Sergeant Pemberton or I say so. Is that clear?'

CHAPTER 10

Superintendent Tony Kendrick ran a hand over his balding pate. 'In a terror attack of this nature, I would have expected a group to come forward and accept responsibility by now.'

Helen was back in the conference room, sitting around the end of the long table flanked by Pemberton on one side and Superintendent Jenkins on the other. Kendrick sat opposite, his laptop flipped open beside him, the screen angled just outside Helen's view.

Jenkins frowned at Kendrick. 'I'm not sure what you mean.'

'Someone representing a group would have spoken up quickly, keen to gain maximum publicity. We can't rule out a lone wolf, someone not officially linked with an illegal organisation, a staunch supporter, or a smaller, less organised group. Though I would have thought they'd still have come forward – to draw attention to their cause.'

'Okay.' Jenkins stretched out the word. 'What are you saying?'

'I'm saying, this is an unusual situation. Like nothing I've faced previously in my twelve years in counter-terror.'

Jenkins massaged the red blotches gathering above his shirt collar. With the chief still at the crime scene and no assistant chief constable – theirs had moved to another force a week earlier and they were awaiting a replacement – Jenkins had not only started back from his special leave early but also been tasked with chairing a meeting about the largest mass-homicide Hampton had ever faced, and the stress was starting to show. 'I don't need to remind you that this case is gaining national and international media attention,' he said, levelling Kendrick's gaze. 'The Prime Minister has changed his schedule to visit Hampton at one o'clock today.'

Helen raised a brow. Prime Minister Rawley had never set foot in Hampton, not to her recollection.

'He'll be expecting an update on the inquiry,' Jenkins said to Kendrick. 'What intelligence do you have of proscribed groups operating in our area?'

'We are aware of some illegal activity,' Kendrick said. 'A footprint of Combat 18 – a neo-Nazi group. We know there's also a pocket raising funds for extreme Islamic organisations like ISIS. We're currently gathering intelligence.'

Gathering intelligence. It sounded like they had nothing.

'The bullets and shells were couriered to the labs in Birmingham last night,' Kendrick continued. 'I have to say, it's the weapon that really concerns me. Historically, terror incidents in the UK rarely involve firearms.'

'Yeah, because they're difficult to get hold of and attract attention,' Pemberton said. 'But we know they are out there. Our own force infiltrated a network of illegal firearms trafficking earlier this year.'

'I'm aware of that,' Kendrick said curtly. 'It just feels like something is off here.'

Helen slid a piece of paper out of the file in front of her. 'During the last twelve months, we've had eleven shootings in Hamptonshire,' she said. 'Nine of them concentrated on the estates in Roxten, a run-down suburb on the north of the county. The shootings were mostly drug-related, gang against gang. Small fry compared to some of the bigger towns and cities. The point is, the weapons used were usually shotguns – licensed weapons stolen from nearby farms. We did have one fatal.' Helen did her best to hide her flinch. 'A police officer with an illegal handgun. A Baikal.' As she spoke the words, Helen could feel herself back in the cellar, facing the nose of the gun. She blinked the memory away. 'You have the details about that case. As the sergeant says, the firearms were seized months ago. The perpetrator, Chilli Franks, is on remand awaiting trial. But a semi-automatic rifle… We've never seen anything like that before. We asked our source handlers to reach out to their informants in the field, to check if anyone has requested a semi-automatic rifle of this nature, and nothing has come back.'

'I'll put out feelers for intelligence nationally,' Kendrick said. 'We can't rule out the possibility that the weapon was sourced elsewhere—'

'Or that the killer came from elsewhere,' Pemberton interjected.

Helen almost missed the contemptuous stare Kendrick threw her sergeant. He clearly wasn't a fan of being interrupted. But what surprised her even more was Pemberton holding his gaze; it was rare to see him so riled.

'Okay,' Jenkins said, looking up from his notes, seemingly oblivious to the exchange. 'We continue to explore all angles until we know otherwise. What do we know about the venue?'

'O'Malley's estimate there were approximately three hundred people in the pub last night, including staff,' Helen said. 'We've currently got first accounts from forty-four survivors, none of which are known to be connected to the criminal fraternity, and none who witnessed anything unusual in the vicinity beforehand. In terms of the victims – we have three women, two men. One black, four white. Nothing to indicate a specific motive at this stage, if indeed these five were targeted. With regard to the wider crowd, there was a mix of ethnicity present. If it was a spray and pray, so to speak, there's no direct lead there either.' She went on to talk about the pub owners.

'What about CCTV nearby?' Jenkins asked when she'd finished.

Kendrick clicked a button on his laptop. A map of Victoria Car Park graced the screen at the end of the room. He reduced its size to show Swan Street in relation to the surrounding area and walked over to the screen. 'We've checked the cameras around the car park. The one on Swan Street was working, but the one that covers the entrance around the corner, on Markham Street, was broken. We think that was the killer's access point. If they left via that exit, their route would take them along Markham Street,' he said, running the end of his pen along the map. 'A number of residential side streets lead off Markham Street. We've found nothing on the council footage – it looks like a few of the cameras on the route were also tampered with – so we are working on the assumption that the killer disappeared into one of those side streets. My team are now pulling CCTV from local businesses and residents nearby.'

'Any sign of the weapon?'

Heads around the table shook.

Jenkins's cheeks billowed as he let out a long sigh. 'Does anyone have any good news for me to pass on to the chief?'

He was interrupted by a knock at the door. A detective Helen didn't recognise, clearly one of the counter-terror crew, walked in. 'The ballistics report is just in,' he said. He handed a buff file to Kendrick and left the room.

'Bloody hell,' Pemberton whispered to Helen. 'That was quick.' They usually waited several days for results from the labs, especially on a weekend, and that was if they paid a premium to fast track the results.

Helen didn't respond. She was watching Kendrick open the file and read through a series of highlighted paragraphs.

'It's confirmed,' Kendrick said. 'Twenty-six bullets were recovered from the scene so far, twenty-four from the pub, two from the ground nearby. Thirty casings were left in the car park. Seemingly, they were all from one weapon, an AK-47.' He glanced back down at his notes. 'No record of it being used on another reported crime.'

Jenkins swiped a hand across his forehead. If the firearm had been used in another case, they could have tracked back, possibly traced its origin and who it was sold to. Sourcing it for this one incident bottomed out another potential lead.

'Right, the chief constable has cancelled all leave for the foreseeable future. We need everyone on this, and we need to continue with a coordinated approach. The chief asked the public to be vigilant this morning, put out a fresh appeal for sightings, and said we are following up on several leads. But that won't hold the press at bay for long.' He looked from Helen to Kendrick. 'I need an arrest from you guys, and soon.'

Helen looked past Jenkins as he gathered his paperwork together, and gazed out of the window. It wasn't the media that bothered her. She churned over historical UK mass shootings in her head. Thomas Hamilton in Dunblane. The Hungerford massacre. The Cumbria shootings. And something stood out. The murderers killed themselves at the scene. In fact, in most incidents she could recall of this nature, the perpetrator was either apprehended immediately or killed themselves, a martyr to their cause. This killer was still running loose, and they had no idea what their motive was or even where to start looking for them. Which meant they could strike again at any time.

CHAPTER 11

The roads were clear as Helen and Pemberton drove west across town to Hampton Mortuary. It was almost lunchtime. Triangles of brightly coloured bunting fluttered above them in the light wind. This was meant to be carnival weekend. Right now, the pavements should be packed with families watching a kaleidoscope of coloured floats rolling through High Street. Yet, apart from a couple rushing along hand in hand, a man vaping in a doorway, and a woman piling her kids into a car at the side of the road, it was quiet. The mayor had spoken with councillors and organisers and announced a postponement of the carnival on local news sites. Even the prospect of a ministerial visit couldn't coax out residents. Extra officers, loaned from the Met and neighbouring forces, would start arriving later today to parade the streets, a public reassurance exercise, but – Helen's stomach twisted – she couldn't see their presence improving matters. They needed a breakthrough in the investigation, and fast.

'What was going on between you and Kendrick back there?' Helen asked, snapping back to her sergeant.

Pemberton shook his head. 'He's an arrogant arse. What's with all the cloak and dagger stuff? A pocket, a footprint… He's not bloody 007.'

He had a point. Kendrick had said plenty at the meeting earlier, yet little of any substance. She'd been expecting details, theories, prospective targets. Instead, he'd reeled out a pocket raising funds for extreme Islamic organisations, and a footprint of Combat 18, no specifics, and what bothered her most was that no group had accepted responsibility for the incident. Surely the attack was related to a terror cell. It had to be. Because the alternative, the very idea that this was some deranged individual on a personal mission, didn't bear thinking about.

A knot of journalists came into view, huddled beside the cordon, as they passed the top of Swan Street.

Pemberton continued along the road and slowed for a red light. 'What are you thinking?' he asked.

'Truth?' She stared up at the fluffy grey clouds conjoining in the sky. Today, even the weather looked gloomy. 'That Kendrick was bluffing because he has nothing. There is something I still can't fathom, though.'

'What?'

'Why carry out an attack there? At that time? If it's for maximum impact, surely you'd arrange it in the shopping centre on a Saturday afternoon, in the cinema when they had a popular film showing, or the football ground during a home game. This was staged to take place after the theatre-goers had left. As if it was aimed at a particular audience.'

The lights changed, and Pemberton moved off. 'You think it's directed at O'Malley's specifically?'

'At them, or at somebody there. Either way, the location was specially chosen. The question is, why?'

* * *

Helen pressed the keypad beside the entrance to Hampton Mortuary and waited for Charles, the pathologist, to let them in. First thing this morning, as soon as she'd heard the bodies had been transported to the morgue, she'd telephoned him and left a voicemail announcing their intention to attend the autopsies. A close inspection of a body, internally and externally, discovered clues that often went unnoticed at first glance, like scars and tattoos, or whether the subject had a drink or drug problem. In short, an autopsy told a story of a victim's life which often threw up fresh leads, and Helen was keen to hear Charles's take on the dead.

She waited a few seconds for him to answer, examining her reflection in the glass, adjusting her trouser suit jacket and smoothing strands of dark hair that had loosened themselves from her messy half-ponytail.

Pemberton looked across the empty car park. 'No sign of Charles's Range Rover,' he said. 'Are you sure he got your message?'

Helen didn't answer. She hadn't received a reply, but Charles often didn't respond. He wasn't a great one to chat over text. She was about to buzz again when a voice with a rich Irish accent answered, 'Can I help you?'

Assuming it was an assistant she hadn't met, that Charles was knee-deep in an examination – there were five bodies to scrutinise, after all – she introduced them both.

A slight pause. 'Do you have an appointment?'

Helen traded a glance with Pemberton who frowned back at her. 'I said we'd be here around 1 pm.' She glanced at her watch – it was 12.48.

The door clicked open. They entered, their boots tapping the shiny white floor tiles as they made their way up to the labs. A tall man with sky-blue eyes and a strong, square jaw met them in the gowning room. Dressed in blue coveralls, he could only have been in his early thirties. The voice on the intercom, Helen guessed.

'Brandon Eriksen,' he said, pulling back his hood to reveal a head of rich, tousled brown hair, and extending an ungloved hand, which Helen and then Pemberton shook. 'I'm sorry, I think there might have been a misunderstanding.'

Helen looked through the window into the lab, expecting a gurney, a body to be laid out. Perhaps a CSI photographing it from different angles. When she had texted this morning, she had said she'd join them mid-examination, after her meeting with Jenkins. But the mortuary looked clear, the empty stainless-steel surfaces gleaming under the bright lighting.

'We're here for the autopsies from the shooting,' she said. Surely, they hadn't waited for her to arrive before they began. They'd be there all afternoon. 'Where's Charles?'

Brandon stared at her a second. 'Sorry,' he said, blinking, as if he'd forgotten himself. 'I've just moved to Hamptonshire to join the team here. Charles had a family event, couldn't make it today. He called me first thing, asked me to stand in.'

Frustration simmered in Helen's chest. Clearly, her voicemail had got lost somewhere along the way.

'I'm so sorry,' Brandon said again. 'I've just this minute finished. They were relatively straightforward, young adults all in reasonable health. If I'd known you were coming...' He shook his head, hooked her gaze. For a second, it felt as though only the two of them were present in the room. There was something vaguely familiar about him, something Helen couldn't place. She was pretty sure they hadn't met before.

Pemberton cleared his throat.

'Okay,' Helen said. 'Is there anything we should know about the victims?'

'I'm just about to write up my reports. Yes, there is one thing that might be of interest.' He rubbed his chin. 'There was a bullet lodged in the femur of Victim Two, Cass Greenwell. I've bagged it up.'

'Thanks.' They'd been told the magazines of an AK-47 were manually loaded, which meant any one of the bullets could hold a latent fingerprint. Although the chances of finding one on metal that had passed through bodily fluids were slim, it had to be worth a try. 'We'll get it couriered to ballistics.'

Pemberton's phone rang. He excused himself.

'Several other victims had tattoos, birthmarks,' Brandon continued after Pemberton had moved outside. 'I've photographed them, will note them all in the report.'

'What sort of tattoos?' Helen asked. If these individuals were targeted for a reason, it was always possible they had evidence of an affiliation to a group, or a specific symbol, displayed on their bodies.

'A star on one of the girls, a butterfly on another. A lion's head and a coiled snake on one of the guys. Nothing that stands out,' he said, guessing her thoughts. 'One of the guys had broken his collar bone several times.' Brandon rambled on about running routine toxicology tests and promised to get a report across to her within the next few days.

At least he was being thorough. Helen thanked him and made her way down the mortuary stairs to find Pemberton leaning against the brick wall beside the door, watching something on his phone.

He paused the footage as she stepped out of the building and turned to Helen, a teasing smile on his lips. 'He seems keen,' he said, angling his head to the mortuary door.

'Yeah. So keen, he completed the examinations early.'

'That's not what I meant. Looks like you've got yourself a new admirer.'

'Oh, please!' Helen snorted. She couldn't deny, Brandon Eriksen was a man some women might refer to as 'a catch'. Not dissimilar to the actor Gerard Butler, from a distance. Perhaps that was why he seemed familiar. But the charms of a new pathologist were the last thing she needed. 'I'm sure he's like that with everyone.'

'Wasn't with me.'

Helen couldn't help laughing. 'What are you watching?' she asked, changing the subject.

'Looks like the PM's arrived.' He rewound the footage, held out his phone.

Prime Minister Rawley stood beside Chief Constable Adams and the town mayor, both in full regalia, the pitted frontage of O'Malley's behind him, as he straightened his navy suit jacket and talked about how horrific the incident was, how his heart went out to the bereaved families. 'This was a brutal attack on the innocent people of Hampton,' he said, strands of his dark hair lifting in the light wind. He went on to say the police investigation would leave no stone unturned. His words strong, sombre, heartfelt. He added that unlimited resources would be available to bring those responsible to justice. 'This was a ruthless slaying of innocent people. The killer will be caught. We will make our streets safe again.'

'Impressive,' Helen said as the footage ended.

'Yeah. Must be difficult to cancel engagements and hop on a helicopter when you're on the campaign trail.' Pemberton didn't attempt to hide the cynicism in his voice, and it was easy to see why. The general election was less than two months away. The PM's support was waning. He was down in the polls and looking for any opportunity to restore faith, reassure the public he was their man.

'Any news from the office?' she asked as they made their way across the car park.

'The preliminary forensic report is in. Nothing of any value so far. We're working our way through local gun clubs. If anyone has seen anything like an AK-47, they're not talking. Not surprising, really. I mean, it'd stick out, wouldn't it?'

Helen sighed. 'Check with other forces, will you? See if they are aware of any recent illegal importation of this sort of rifle, have seized any, or come across anybody using one.'

'Isn't that Kendrick's remit?'

Pemberton was right; she was stepping on toes. Kendrick was covering intelligence on national issues, but she wasn't about to leave anything to chance, not while she was co-running things. 'I'll deal with that when it arises.'

They were almost at the car when her phone trilled.

'See,' Pemberton said looking back towards the mortuary and nodding. 'Told you he was keen.'

She ignored him, chuckling away to himself, and reached into her pocket for her phone. It was Spencer.

'Where are you, ma'am?' He sounded rushed.

'Just leaving the mortuary. Everything okay?'

'A witness has called in with some dashcam footage. There's something you need to see.'

CHAPTER 12

An excited Spencer met Helen and Pemberton at the incident room door and beckoned them both to his desk. 'The witness was travelling along Markham Street at 10.51 last night. His camera caught something near the car park.'

Spencer clicked a key on his computer. A dark terraced road came into view. Parked cars lined the kerb, nose to tail. Intermittent streetlamps flashed up as the driver cruised along.

'That isn't Markham Street,' Helen said.

'It's Seville Avenue, one of the terraced roads that lead onto Markham Street,' Spencer said. 'Wait.'

Seconds past. The car braked at the junction and turned into Markham Street. It picked up speed as it headed towards Victoria Car Park. It was almost at the turn to Swan Street when a figure appeared at the side of the road, then disappeared. If Helen had blinked, she'd have missed it.

'I'll play it again,' Spencer said. 'This time on slow speed.'

The room quietened. More bodies gathered around Spencer's desk to watch the car turn onto Markham Street and taxi along. Just before it reached the turn-off for the car park, a figure stepped out of the shadows. They were wearing a black top, with the hood pulled down over their face, dark skinny jeans, and carrying a holdall. They slipped into the entrance of the car park.

'That was quick,' Pemberton said.

'It must have been a split second in the driver's peripheral vision,' Spencer said. 'The pavement is wide down there. Somebody slinking along, sticking to the shadows like that, doesn't want to be seen.'

Helen felt a rush of adrenalin. A holdall was the perfect guise to conceal a rifle. 'Have you spoken with the witness?' she asked.

Spencer nodded. 'He was on his way to collect his teenage daughter from the cinema up the road. Didn't think anything of it until he saw the appeal on the news.' He ran it through again, pausing at the salient moment to zoom in. The face was turned away from the camera, but the lens had caught the suspect in a line of light from a nearby streetlamp and the image was surprisingly clear.

'Are there any other cameras nearby?' Helen asked.

'We're checking, though I think Kendrick's team would have already examined them. This is the best still we can pull from this footage.' He brought up an image of a figure in fitted jeans and a hoody that was loose on their slender frame. Against the backdrop of the doorframe, the individual looked to be of medium height.

The mood of the room instantly lightened. Even if it wasn't much to go on: no obvious distinguishing feature, no shot of the face – they couldn't even determine from the still whether it was a man or a woman – this was the first piece of positive news they'd received, and it felt good.

'Is that a sports bag?' Helen asked. If they could find any labels or logos, there was an outside chance they could source the retailer and possibly even the sale if it was rare.

'I'm not sure.' Spencer peered closer at the image. 'I'll see if the techies can enhance it.'

'Okay, let's share this with Kendrick's team and get it circulated within the force,' Helen said. 'I'll ask Vicki in the press office to put out an appeal on all the news sites for other sightings of this person, or anyone else passing through Markham Street who might have seen them. We'll have it uploaded onto our social media too.' She placed a hand on

Spencer's shoulder and gave a gentle squeeze. 'Well done, Steve. Great work!'

* * *

Back in her office, Helen made her calls. It was only a matter of time before the image of their suspect would grace all the major news sites. Surely this would concentrate minds, jog someone's memory.

When everything was in place, she relaxed back in her chair. It was almost 4 pm. She should check in with her family. She grabbed her phone, was selecting the number for home, when the Dad's Army theme tune filled her office. Her mother had beaten her to it.

'Hey,' Helen answered. 'How are things there?'

'Fine,' her mother said. 'Any news? I'm guessing you're working on the shooting. They're covering it on all the major channels.'

'I'm assisting counter-terror,' Helen said. She wasn't assisting, she was working alongside, but she didn't want to give her mother cause to worry. 'We're working on a number of leads.'

'Those poor families.'

'Yeah. How are the boys?' Helen asked, keen to change the subject.

'Matthew is at Luke's and Robert is sleeping over at Zac's.'

Helen's shoulders slackened. At least the boys were at friends' houses. Inside. 'Listen, do me a favour, will you? Keep an eye on them. I don't want them out wandering the streets at the moment.'

'You're worried it'll happen again?' Her mother's voice cracked with concern.

'No. Not at all.' Helen tried to sound reassuring while fully aware she had no basis upon which to do so. 'It just makes sense to be cautious until we apprehend those responsible.'

'Do you want me to keep them at home?'

'No.' The word spilled out of her mouth quicker than her thoughts. She did. She'd certainly feel better if they were imprisoned at home, safe. But it was the school summer holidays. They were sixteen and fourteen. They'd go insane. Plus, the shooting occurred in the town centre, in the middle of a street, late at night. 'Just keep them away from public places for the next few days. If they go out, encourage them to go to a friend's house and arrange drop-off and pick-up.' These were words she never thought she'd utter and not something she was proud of – she'd always encouraged her boys to be strong, resilient – though she couldn't help herself. Right now, she'd advise any member of the public to do the same.

'All right, will do.' A breathless pause. 'You're okay though, aren't you?'

'I'm fine, Mum. Really. Look, I need to go. We're hoping for a development, so I'll probably sleep over at the station tonight. Don't worry, I'm sure this will all be over soon.'

Helen ended the call, placed her phone on the table and rubbed the heels of her hands into her eyes.

Things hadn't always been this tricky. When she'd joined the police after losing her husband, John, in a tragic helicopter accident a little over ten years ago, her mother had been an encouraging driving force. She'd moved in with Helen, eventually taking over the adjoining granny flat, to assist with childcare. Having been married to Helen's late father, a murder detective himself, for most of her adult life, Jane Lavery was accustomed to the unsociable hours the job demanded and happy to help with the boys, relishing the extra time with her grandchildren.

But… Helen switched her mind back. Visiting her bruised and battered daughter in hospital after Helen had apprehended Chilli Franks a few months earlier had caused Jane to re-evaluate.

When Helen returned to homicide, her mother had expressed concern about the dangerous nature of her daughter's job and the possible effects on their family. Problem was, ever since she'd been a little girl, all Helen had ever wanted was to be a homicide detective, just like her father. She couldn't contemplate doing anything else. Which is why she now found herself playing down her role, reassuring her mother that she wasn't in danger.

Helen rubbed her eyes again. She willed Chilli's day in court to be over. Surely, once he was convicted, her mother's concern would ease. She desperately hoped so. Though chasing a rogue gunman around town, weeks before the trial was set to begin, certainly wouldn't do anything to assist her cause.

CHAPTER 13

The click of a lock caused Helen to stir. She was curled up asleep in her office chair, her jacket covering her like a blanket. She blinked twice as a shadow entered.

'Sorry to bother you, ma'am.' It was James, one of the overnight staff.

Helen slipped her feet to the floor and straightened, rubbing the back of her neck as she welcomed him in. She'd stayed alert until midnight and, when all remained quiet, finally closed her blinds, turned off her office light, and gave herself a chance to rest her weary limbs. She blinked again, her eyes taking a while to adjust to the brightness of the incident room now streaming in. 'What time is it? she asked.

'Four thirty-five. We have the custody sergeant at Cross Keys on the line. He says he's got someone in claiming to be the shooter.'

'Thanks. Put him through.'

Her jacket slipped to the floor as he retreated. She answered the phone on the first ring. 'Chief Inspector Lavery.'

'Ma'am, it's PS Tim Baron here. One of our young officers on the night shift picked up a guy sitting on the kerb outside the station twenty minutes ago. The man claims he's responsible for the shooting on Friday evening.'

'What's his name?'

The crackle of paper winged down the line as he checked his notes. 'William Nobleman of Barton's Walk, Worthington. No previous convictions.'

Helen sat forward. Worthington was a small suburb on the county's southern periphery. 'Where is he now?'

'We've arrested him and placed him in a cell here. I thought it best to call your office before anyone questions him.'

'You did the right thing. Call DCI Kendrick from counter-terror, will you? Have him meet me there. I'll be with you in twenty minutes.'

* * *

Cross Keys custody block was quiet for a Saturday evening, a legacy of townspeople staying home. Helen walked in and introduced herself, immediately noting PS Baron's name badge behind the desk. 'Tim, I don't believe we've met,' she said.

'No. I've only been here a couple of weeks. Moved across from Peterborough.' He was a short man with ginger hair and a pale complexion. The black police-issue polo shirt he wore stretched over his wide girth.

'Ah. Where's the officer who brought the suspect in?'

'She's on her tea break. One of our probationers, first time single-crewed. Imagine coping with something like this!' He grinned, exposing a wide gap between his front teeth. 'Anyway, your guy's pretty smelly. Looks like he's been hiding out, sleeping rough. I've had a medic look him over.'

'Thanks.'

'You're welcome. He's good to go when you are. Doesn't want a brief.'

Helen frowned. 'Really?'

'Yup. Refused point blank.'

'Hm.' She couldn't envisage anyone confessing to multiple murders would refuse legal representation. William Nobleman… Something about the name sounded familiar. 'Do you have his cell on camera?' she asked.

The custody sergeant nodded. He motioned for her to join him at the other side of the desk and pressed a few buttons on his computer. A grainy image of the inside of a cell filled the screen, a man sitting on the edge of the bed, his head dipped. His fair hair was close-cropped, and he was dressed in a dark hoody and jeans. Helen was staring at him, willing him to look up, when a bang filled the area. Closely followed by another.

The man on the screen placed his hands over his ears.

'Excuse me,' Tim said. 'Sounds like MacArdle in cell three is trying to knock the door down again.' He moved off towards the cells. Helen heard two more bangs followed by raised voices – though she couldn't make out the words – then silence.

Tim re-emerged, looking flustered. 'All sorted. I hope.'

Helen gave a sympathetic smile. She'd done a short spell as custody sergeant in her early years, and it had been a thankless task. Many of the same suspects passing through the doors. Never seeing a case through from beginning to end. She glanced back at the figure on the screen just as the man looked up at the camera.

Her eyes narrowed. 'Did you take prints?' she asked Tim.

'Not yet. We're short-staffed.'

'Right. Can you let me into William Nobleman's cell? I'd like a word.'

'Why don't I get an interview room ready for you? I'm sure I can find you a scribe—'

'Just a word, Sergeant, thanks. Off the record.'

Tim fiddled with his keys, uncertainty spreading like a stain across his face. Allowing her to question a prisoner in their cell, off the record, didn't adhere to the regulations in the Police and Criminal Evidence Act, the legislation established to safeguard both the police and suspects, which meant he was breaking the rules. If there was a complaint, or if something happened, he could be subjected to a disciplinary hearing.

'Don't worry,' she said. 'I'll take the rap, say I gave you a direct order, if it blows up.'

Tim still looked uneasy as he guided her down to the cells, a series of rooms facing each other, down a narrow corridor. Metal doors with slide hatches gleamed under the strip lighting. Outside room four, he paused. 'Are you sure you don't want to wait for counter-terror? DCI Kendrick is on his way.'

'I'll just be a few minutes,' Helen said with a smile. 'Don't worry.'

Tim unlocked the door and pushed it open.

The suspect's head immediately shot up. As soon as he saw Helen, alarm flitted across his face.

'Hello, Billy,' Helen said, closing the door behind her. 'When did you get out?'

Billy Noble was a thirty-three-year-old serial offender who'd spent most of his adult life in prison. The last Helen heard, he'd been sentenced to four years for burglary, but she couldn't remember exactly how long ago that was.

Billy fidgeted uncomfortably. 'A few weeks ago.'

'A few weeks. Really?'

He nodded, then moved aside for her to perch on the edge of the bed beside him.

Helen did her best not to baulk at the musty stench, not dissimilar to potato peelings, wafting over.

'So, what is it you've done this time?'

'I told the officer. I shot those people on Friday night.'

'Right,' Helen said, elongating the word. 'And what did you do with the weapon afterwards?'

'Disposed of it. I'm not gonna keep it, am I?'

'Where did you dispose of it?'

He shrugged. 'Can't remember exactly.'

'I see.' She inhaled a long audible breath. 'Billy, why don't you talk me through your Friday evening.'

He looked at her, then stared at the floor, uneasy eyes flashing from side to side. 'We're supposed to do this in an interview room,' he said. 'On tape. I've got rights.'

She resisted the temptation to say they didn't use tapes

anymore. All interviews were recorded digitally these days, saved on the cloud. Surely, he hadn't been away that long? 'And we will,' she said. 'I'm just looking for a first account. You've heard of those, haven't you?'

He rolled his shoulders.

'So...'

'So, I went to the car park with a rifle—'

'What type of rifle?'

He cleared his throat. 'I'm not prepared to say.'

'Where did you get it?'

'Sorry?'

'The rifle. Where did you get it?'

'Can't tell you.' He shook his head, looked away.

'Okay, what time did you arrive at the car park?'

'About half ten, after the theatre spilled out.'

The timings certainly concurred. Though he could have read those details in any press article. 'How did you get there?'

'What?'

'You've given your address as Barton's Walk, Worthington. How did you get into town from there?'

'A friend gave me a lift.'

'What friend?'

He dug his hands into his lap, said nothing.

The sound of the custody sergeant's feet shuffling about outside seeped into the room. Helen ignored them. 'What happened when you arrived?'

'I went into the car park—'

'How?'

'What?' A muscle flexed in his jaw, irritation at the constant interruptions.

'How did you access the car park?'

'At the main entrance, on Swan Street.'

'On Swan Street? You are sure of that?'

'Yeah.'

Helen stood and banged on the cell door. 'Thanks, Billy. You've been really helpful. We won't keep you much longer.'

As soon as she was out of earshot, Helen turned to the sergeant. 'Have a member of the Mental Health Crisis Team speak with him, will you? Then, if they're happy to clear him, take him home. He's no more the shooter than I am.'

'What?' Tim looked gobsmacked.

'His name is William Noble, not Nobleman,' Helen said. 'That'll be why there was nothing on the computer. He looks like he hasn't showered in days because he probably hasn't. He's a serial offender. Can't wait to get back inside. Inside, he has somewhere to stay, meals cooked for him, and company.' She blew out a long sigh. So much of police work these days was dealing with the sad and lonely of society.

'How can you be sure?'

'Because he's not aware of the specific weapon used, and he claims to have accessed the car park via the Swan Street entrance. We know the killer entered on Markham Street. We have them on camera – the still we shared with the press.'

Tim looked crestfallen. 'Has he falsely confessed to stuff before?'

'Often. I'll never forget the time he told us he was responsible for a commercial arson at the Talbot Hotel in town.' She snorted. 'He said he'd started the fire in the gym. Fire investigators traced the source to a guest smoking in a room in a completely different part of the hotel.'

Tim ran a hand down the side of his face and with good cause. He'd been duped. This could only happen with a sergeant new to the area, a rookie probationer and a career criminal who'd given a false name for a warm night in a cell and the prospect of returning to jail. You couldn't have made it up.

'Don't worry,' Helen said. 'You'll soon get a handle on the regulars.' She decided not to remind him he should have taken prints immediately; he'd learned his lesson already. Instead, she reached into her bag, pulled out a ten-pound note and handed it over. 'Make sure whoever gives Billy a lift home stops at McDonald's on the way, will you? I doubt he's eaten in days.'

At that moment, the door flapped open, and Kendrick rushed in. He looked ghostly pale, and his jacket was creased as if he'd slept in it. 'What have we got?' he asked, looking from one to another.

'Nothing,' Helen said. 'It's a false alarm.'

CHAPTER 14

Ashleigh sat in the back of the car and stared out of the window as they drove through Hampton. It was Sunday morning, 11 am. Finally, the doctor, in dire need of her bed, had approved her discharge and she was on her way home, a balloon bandage around her arm and a swollen bruise the size of an egg on her forehead, the only physical signs of the horror she'd faced less than forty-eight hours earlier.

A traffic light ahead turned red, causing Noah to brake suddenly. He apologised and cast her a concerned sideways look.

The same look her parents had given when they'd FaceTimed from their home in France this morning. It had taken all her powers of persuasion to deter them from coming over. This was their busiest time of year in the Dordogne, the gites they rented out fully occupied. And she was fine, wasn't she? Her injuries superficial. They'd only acquiesced when Noah said he'd take the week off work to look after her.

'Almost there,' Noah said. 'Not long now.'

Ashleigh attempted a smile, then turned back to the window. Noah was uttering gibberish. He did this when he didn't know what to do, what to say. She could feel him glance at her again, his eyes soft and sad. And her heart hardened. She didn't want his sympathy. She didn't want him to smother her. Whenever she closed her eyes, she could still feel the heat of Nia's warm body propped up against hers, see Cass reach over in her silver dress. She didn't know the other victims or those injured, but five people had perished. She thought of Nia's mother, of Cass's parents. The shock, the grief, the despair. If anyone needed sympathy, it was them.

A van engine revved as it passed. Ashleigh wound the window down an inch and sucked in the warm air. It was a bright summer day outside: a man sat on the bench in High Street puffing at a cigarette, a couple wandered by swinging their arms. A woman hurried down the path, holding the hands of her little ones. Fewer people than she'd normally expect to see out on a balmy Sunday morning. Still… She wanted to shout at them to go home, to clear the streets. Hadn't they heard the news? The shooter hadn't been apprehended. They were still out there, running loose.

The pain in her head soared. Mild concussion, the doctor had said before he discharged her. A few days rest and you'll be fine. But she wasn't fine. She'd never be fine again. Her best friends were gone, yet she'd lived.

She tore her gaze away, focused on the dashboard. Concentrated on breathing. In and out. She was on her way home. Where she and Cass and Nia got ready on Friday evening. Cass dancing around her front room as they knocked back their beloved Cherry Sourz. Revelling in the heady excitement of being together again. It was almost like peeling back the years.

A merry Ed Sheeran song played low on the car radio. But Ashleigh couldn't listen, couldn't focus.

Hampton was a sleepy provincial town. She was always harping on about community spirit and how they should all pull together in the column she wrote for *The Hampton Herald*. She'd felt safe growing up here. Didn't feel the need to leave to attend university – there was a perfectly good one locally – and, anyway, Noah's job as a diesel mechanic was based here. She knew her town.

Or she thought she did.

Her mouth was dry now, her pulse accelerating. Why here, why now, why us? Those three questions persistently picked at her brain. Was the killer aiming at someone, and they were caught in the crossfire? Was it a random terror attack, as the news sites hinted at, or something else? Whatever the explanation, the police still hadn't made an arrest, and the very notion of a gunman still walking the streets left her petrified.

Noah steered into Portland Grove, a dusty side road that housed a row of Victorian stucco-fronted terraces facing the western railings of Oakwall, Hampton's largest park.

'Here we are.' He drove the car down to the dead end at the bottom, turned it around, then parked outside a double-fronted terrace with three stone steps leading to a black front door.

Ashleigh felt her hand tremble as she shaded her eyes from the dazzling sunshine and looked up at the first-floor flat she and Noah called home. She then glanced across the road at the former chapel, now a café named Hives, adjacent to the park. Eddie's, the old newsagent on the corner. A motorbike whizzed past on the busy street at the top.

The scent of a wild rose, climbing the railings of the park, filled her nose as Ashleigh climbed out of the car. She was just waiting for Noah to join her when the front door opened and Sadhika, their neighbour, came bustling down the steps. She was lifting a multi-coloured maxi dress so she didn't trip, a dark braid dancing over one shoulder. The building was divided into four flats, two up, two down, and Sadhika occupied the first-floor flat opposite Ashleigh's. They often passed the time of day, coming and going about their business.

'Hey, Ash!' she said, letting go of her dress and nudging her bag further up her shoulder. The bangles on her wrist clattered together. She noticed the bruise on Ashleigh's forehead, stopped abruptly. 'Oh my God, what happened to you?'

Ashleigh opened her mouth, about to answer, when a crack sounded. She immediately ducked to the pavement, covering her head with her hands. She didn't even hear the scream emitting from her mouth until it stopped.

A whirl of movement around her.

'Hey.' Noah's soothing voice, a hand stroking her hair.

'Hey, Ash, it's okay. It was only a car door slamming up the road.'

Ashleigh raised her head to find Noah crouched beside her. Sadhika, standing next to them, shock etched on her face. 'Is everything okay?'

She could hear Noah saying she'd be all right, though her legs felt like they belonged to someone else, and she wobbled as he hauled her up.

'Let's get you inside,' he said.

CHAPTER 15

A low wind whistled down the side of Ben Windsor's bereaved fiancée's house. Sitting in the front room, Helen resisted the temptation to tug at her shirt collar. She'd showered in the gym earlier and changed into the spare set of clothes she kept in her locker, but the wool jacket was made for winter months, and the heat in the room was oppressive.

'I'm so sorry,' she said again.

Libby, Ben Windsor's fiancée, pressed a damp tissue to her eye. She was a small woman with a pale face, wide blue eyes and sandy hair cut to shoulder length. The long jersey dress she wore accentuated a pronounced baby bump.

Helen took a sip of her tea and gave the woman a moment. Instead, scanning the bereavement cards lining the mantel, the window ledge, the dresser at the far end of the room. When she switched back to Libby, the woman was staring into space, twisting her engagement ring round and round on her finger. She must have been at least six months pregnant. And so young…

'Are you sure there isn't anything I can get you?' Helen asked.

Libby shook her head. Short, sharp shakes.

Even with the extra loaned staff, her unit was stretched to the limit, and Helen had resolved to visit each of the deceased's next of kin herself to update them on the investigation and reassure them that she'd do everything in her power to ensure justice prevailed. This was one of the most gruesome incidents in Hampton's history; families deserved the right level of support, despite the number of people affected.

She'd already spent an hour with Nia Okeke's shell-shocked mother. Another with the partner of Dominic Yardley, immersed in insufferable grief. And now Ben Windsor's poor fiancée. It was harrowing, yet there was a yearning inside Helen, a gravitational pull to meet these people, show her support, and get to know them. The relatives had already given statements, but shock had a habit of casting shadows, blind spots in people's memories, and she couldn't shake the belief that if these individuals were, indeed, targeted for a reason, the more she could find out about them, the better chance she had of discovering a motive.

'Is there anything else you can remember from Ben on Friday night?' Helen asked. 'Maybe something you missed from your statement. Every little detail helps.'

Libby looked across at her with red-rimmed eyes. 'I don't think so. He went out around seven-thirty. I told the officer about Tom and Dan, the friends he was meeting.'

Helen made a mental note to check up on Tom and Dan. With the sheer number of survivors to interview, it was proving difficult to keep track of everyone. 'Did they often go out on a Friday evening together?'

Libby's eyes filled afresh at the 'did'. Past tense. She swallowed before she answered. 'Yes. They all worked together at Winter and Bourne, the accountants in town. They normally went to the Royal Oak for a couple. "To finish off the working week," Ben used to say. He was usually home around nine.'

'The Royal Oak,' Helen confirmed. 'Not O'Malley's?'

'No, it was always the Royal Oak. They have a double happy hour on a Friday night.'

'So, what took him to O'Malley's last Friday?'

Libby's face folded. 'He phoned me, um… about half eight. Said Tom and Dan had gone home, and he'd met an old school friend.' She rubbed her baby bump. 'They were going to O'Malley's to meet up with another old friend, he told me he'd be late.' Her eyes watered again. 'He sounded excited. Said he hadn't seen them in years.'

Helen sat forward. A meet up of old school friends would draw people together. 'Did he give their names?'

'No. I wouldn't have known them anyway. Ben and I have only been together two years. I've never met any of his school friends, he lost contact with them when he went to university.'

'Did he ever mention any of the victims' names?'

She shook her head.

'Go on.'

'He messaged me at nine-thirty, told me not to wait up. That was the last time I heard from him. I went to bed. It wasn't until I received the knock on the door in the early hours that…' She broke off, stifling a sob with her tissue.

Helen took her time to let this new information percolate. A meeting of old school friends hadn't been flagged up in other survivor statements. Though these were young adults out on the town on a Friday night. If the meeting had been chance, the invitation flimsy, it might not have crossed their minds. But it did provide a commonality amongst those in the pub that night. She was aware that two of the dead knew each other – Cass Greenwell and Nia Okeke. They were out with another girl who had survived. Was it possible there was a get-together at O'Malley's they didn't know about?

CHAPTER 16

'Right,' Jenkins said. 'We've just been advised the two victims that were critical have been moved to a ward. They are out of danger.'

The tense muscles in Helen's neck eased a notch. Thank goodness. There had already been enough bloodshed.

Jenkins steepled his fingers and stared across the desk at Helen and Kendrick, his face lit by the afternoon sun streaming into his office. 'So, where are we?' he asked. 'The chief wants an update.'

She gave him the rundown on the survivors they'd spoken to so far – fifty-eight altogether – grateful she'd taken the time to check the status with the incident room before she'd joined the meeting. 'Nothing of any interest yet and no positive IDs from the public appeal either.' She went on to talk him through her visit to Ben Windsor's fiancée and the mention of Ben venturing to O'Malley's to meet an old school friend. 'I'm not sure how relevant it is. I've asked Dark to trawl through the statements we've taken, see if anyone else mentions anything.'

'Okay.' Jenkins exhaled long and hard, clearly hoping for something stronger, and looked across at Kendrick.

'Still no group accepting responsibility,' Kendrick said. 'Which leads me to believe this is either a small organisation or a lone individual.'

It was the second day after the incident and, with no firm suspect, the idea of a single shooter, loose in the town, did nothing to ease the tension in the room.

'We've been looking at a faction in Nottingham, a break-off neo-Nazi organisation calling themselves Order 149,' Kendrick continued. 'Like Combat 18 used the alphabetical positions of the initials of A and H in Adolf Hitler for their name, Order 149 use the N, being the fourteenth letter of the alphabet, and I, being the ninth, from Nazi, to make up theirs,' he explained. 'Anyway, we've had someone on the inside there, an undercover officer, for the last twelve months. In June, he helped us infiltrate an attack one of their cells had planned on a gay bar in Nottingham.' Jenkins' frown echoed Helen's thoughts. They hadn't heard about this, but then, thwarted terror attacks were rarely reported within the force, let alone in the news. 'We charged two men at the time,' Kendrick said. 'Our undercover guy has been monitoring phone calls and messages since, and it seems there are a number of other Order 149 cells in the Midlands, including at least one in Hampton. We think there's a strong chance they might be involved in our shooting.'

Helen stiffened. 'What do we know about the local cell?'

'I can't share too much yet.'

'Have they mentioned Friday's attack?' Jenkins said. 'Or anything related to it?'

'Not to admit involvement, but Order 149, as an underground movement, have condoned it. It supports their cause.'

Helen's brain cells took a moment to work this through. 'Are you saying you think this might be a homophobic attack?' she said to Kendrick.

'O'Malley's is owned by a gay couple. I understand they're notable figures in the town, campaigners for gay rights.'

'They're on the committee for the local Mardi Gras,' Helen said. 'I'd hardly call them activists.' Though she couldn't deny O'Malley's had to have been selected for a reason.

'Doesn't matter. For those with homophobic views, they've drawn attention to themselves. The group we infiltrated in Nottingham was planning a bombing – we found detonators, hydrogen peroxide and electric circuits at the suspects' property. It's possible the Hampton cell are adopting different tactics.'

'What can we do to help?' Jenkins asked.

'We could do with finding out more about the source of the firearm. The gang you brought down trafficking weapons into the county earlier this year,' he said. 'The perpetrator, Chilli Franks, does he still have links in the criminal community outside?'

Out of the corner of her eye, Helen noticed Jenkins close his eyes, squeeze them together and look away. 'Franks's support was diminishing even before he was arrested,' she replied. 'Local intelligence suggests a marked power shift to the East Side Boys, a rival gang, headed by Paul Gladstone. We've received no word to suggest either Gladstone or the East Side Boys are using or importing firearms on this level, though.'

'Okay,' Jenkins said to Kendrick. 'When will you know more?'

'It's a delicate situation. A couple of days to trace the addresses of cells nearby, maybe longer.'

'I'd like us to work together on this,' Helen said.

Kendrick's eyes narrowed to tiny holes. 'It's sensitive. Let me review what we have and come back to you. Meantime, keep this to yourselves. Our officer on the inside is already in a precarious position. I can't risk exposing his cover.'

Helen's throat tightened. She didn't want to be cut out, but she certainly didn't want to put an officer at risk. Before she could speak, Jenkins closed his eyes again, pinched the bridge of his nose and interjected, 'I'm sure I don't need to tell you that we don't have a couple of days. The chief has demanded a call as soon as anything breaks. The world's media are on our back, we need to give them something.'

He wasn't wrong there. Reporters and news vans – BBC, CNN – were camped outside headquarters. Helen had needed to call security to move them to the end of the drive and clear a space for cars to pass through that morning.

'Any significant news, I want to hear about it,' Jenkins said. He lifted his mobile and waved it at them both. 'My phone is on 24/7.'

Chairs squeaked against the floor as everyone rose. Helen quickly gathered her notes. She was planning to catch Kendrick in the corridor – keen to have a quiet word, colleague to colleague, to find out more about what they had on this terror group – when Jenkins called her back.

He indicated for Kendrick to close the door behind him, eased back in his chair and crossed one leg over the other before he spoke. 'Are we sure about Franks?' he asked.

'I beg your pardon, sir?'

'We know Chilli Franks was at the centre of illegal weapon importation.'

Helen felt her jaw drop. 'Oh, come on, sir, you're not suggesting he's involved in this? He's behind bars.'

'Yes, after we seized a haul of illegal firearms from his warehouse. Bit of a coincidence this happens just before his trial is due to begin, don't you think?'

'We seized Baikals, Glocks. Handguns imported from Eastern Europe. Weapons he was planning to use to wage his war with rival drug gangs. Weapons his hitmen could easily dispose of down drains or sell on after they'd used them. Not a bloody AK-47. Anyway, you heard Kendrick. He's pointing the finger at a neo-Nazi cell.'

'It's a theory,' Jenkins said dismissively. 'Chilli didn't make bail. Nothing short of a miracle is keeping him from seeing out his days in prison. Perhaps he wanted to make a point. One last show of power.'

Helen pictured Chilli's hard stare, the edgy twitch beneath his eye. He was undoubtedly the most dangerous and unpredictable criminal she'd ever faced, especially with the added pressure of their family history. But, no... This was more about Jenkins than Chilli. Ever since they'd charged him,

Jenkins had been convinced Chilli would execute revenge on Helen and the people who'd put him away. 'I don't buy it, sir. I really can't see what he'd have to gain.'

Jenkins huffed. 'I only hope you're right.'

CHAPTER 17

The following morning, Helen was woken from her deep slumber by the trill of her mobile. She reached out, patted her bedside table until she located her phone, and squinted at the blindingly bright screen in the half-light of her bedroom. It was 6.33 am.

'Sorry to bother you so early.' It was Kendrick.

'Has something happened?' She hauled herself forward, straining to see as her eyes adjusted.

'There's been a development on the case.'

'Go on.'

'We've just carried out a dawn raid on a property housing a potential neo-Nazi cell in the Hampton suburb of Weston and arrested three people in connection with the shooting.'

'What?' This was not what Helen was expecting. She pulled back the duvet, grabbed her robe off the back of the door and hurried onto the landing. 'Where are the suspects now?' she asked, keeping her voice low to avoid disturbing her sleeping boys.

'They have been taken to an undisclosed location for questioning.'

Of course. The Terrorism Act allowed for terror suspects to be treated differently, detained in separate high-security units, away from police station custody suites. Even the general police force wasn't party to the site addresses.

'What prompted this?' she asked, her mind in overdrive.

She was downstairs now, the kitchen tiles icy cold on her bare feet.

'We had a breakthrough in the early hours. Some intelligence about the Order 149 cell in Hampton.'

'What intelligence?'

'I can't go into specifics. We're searching the house, seizing devices. Just wanted to give you the heads up.' Voices in the background. Shouting. It sounded like a fracas. 'Look, I need to go. I'll let you know when I have more.' He ended the call.

Helen leaned up against the kitchen surface and stared at the fading screen on her phone. A blackbird was singing its heart out on the apple tree outside, the mellifluous sound of its voice seeping into the kitchen, but she barely heard it. Weston was located on the edge of Hampton town centre, walking distance from Victoria Car Park and the cultural quarter. What had Kendrick uncovered to prompt this arrest?

* * *

Twenty minutes later, Helen pulled into headquarters' car park. The drive to work had been fractious: she'd yelled at a car that had pulled out on her, and then a lorry had cut her up on Cross Keys roundabout, almost pushing her into the central island. All serving to top up the frustration hardening to a stone in her chest. Kendrick's elusiveness, and the way he held back information, even at her level, had been niggling her since their first meeting in the early hours of Saturday morning. He'd already left the office when she'd finished her meeting with Jenkins yesterday afternoon and, despite leaving a voicemail on his mobile asking for a quick meeting in the evening to discuss the terror cell in more detail, he hadn't responded. And now, an unexplained arrest.

Why hadn't he contacted her last night when he'd received the information? She understood the need to keep details close to avoid any potential leaks – the last thing they needed was for word to get back to the terror cell, or worse, put his officer at risk – but they were supposed to be managing this investigation together. What was she supposed to say to her staff this morning, let alone the press? She didn't even have an address.

She was on the back stairs, checking her phone again – still no response from Kendrick – when she turned the corner and almost collided with Jenkins.

'Whoa!' he said, catching her before she fell backwards. 'You're in early.'

She decided not to mention that she probably would have been in earlier if she hadn't already missed the best part of two nights' sleep. 'There's been an arrest,' she said.

'Ah, yes—'

He already knows.

Jenkins stepped back. 'Let's find somewhere to talk.' He motioned for her to follow him through a set of double doors and onto the first floor, the floor that housed the rooms counter-terror had been using. Rooms that were quiet this morning.

Jenkins halted beside another door, input a code into the pad beside it – the privacy lock counter-terror had requested – and the door swung open.

They entered a large room that mirrored the layout of the incident room above. Helen immediately spotted a map on the noticeboard of the layout of a semi-detached house in Weston, the address written in black print above: 42 Acorn Walk. Entrances and exits were marked. On another map, access routes to the property were highlighted on the surrounding roads. Kendrick's team must have been up all night.

'Would someone like to fill me in?' she said to Jenkins, anger simmering in her chest. She couldn't have been more in the dark if she'd tried.

He looked taken aback. 'You've not heard?'

'I received a call from Kendrick, twenty minutes or so ago.' She passed on the scant details he'd imparted. 'That's it.'

They were standing beside a bank of desks covered with reams of paperwork containing some sort of code. 'When did you hear about the raid?' she asked.

'He phoned the chief forty minutes ago. Adams then phoned me.'

So, she was the last to hear…

'As you know, Kendrick's team was working on a theory about a homophobic attack at O'Malley's,' Jenkins said. 'Last night, they received cogent word from their undercover officer about a local group, a break-off neo-Nazi cell operating out of an address in Weston on the north of the county. They believe this group is linked to those responsible for the attack they intercepted last month in Nottingham, and their intelligence suggests they've been planning something prominent here.'

'The people calling themselves Order 149,' Helen said. 'Yes, I've gleaned that much.'

'He's arrested one woman, two men. None have a previous record.'

'What did he find in the house search?' Helen asked. She was expecting a weapon, clothing, perhaps someone matching the description of the image in their public appeal.

'It's too early to say. The house is locked down. The search ongoing.'

'Okay.' Kendrick would undoubtedly crow about any findings, which meant the immediate search had revealed nothing. 'What was the nature of their intelligence?'

'Pardon?'

'What did their man on the inside say? They must have had something particular to get a warrant for a house search?'

'They're keeping their cards close to their chest. Apparently, it's all very sensitive. They've seized devices at the property – laptops, iPads, phones – which they believe could prove crucial. The point is, the chief sees this as a critical step forward. He's arranging an urgent press conference this morning to share the news.'

Helen was flabbergasted. 'Why wasn't I told earlier?'

'I doubt there was time. From my understanding, it all happened quickly – Kendrick had to gather his team and carry out a raid at 6 am. I'm sure he'll bring you up to speed in due course.' Jenkins let out an audible sigh. 'Look, I know you're disappointed—'

'Disappointed?' She was spitting feathers, cast-iron anger erupting inside at being excluded from her own case, but she wasn't about to let Jenkins see that. 'On the contrary, I'm pleased we have a result, if indeed that's what it is. We all want to see those responsible behind bars. I'm just wondering what the next steps are for my team.'

CHAPTER 18

Later that morning, Helen stood at the front of the incident room and surveyed the relieved faces before her. She'd just told her team about the morning's arrest, and they looked brighter, fresher. One small mercy to be thankful for.

'Where does that leave us?' Pemberton asked, echoing the thoughts of the room.

'Jenkins wants us to continue as we are, for now, obtaining first accounts and supporting counter-terror.' She stopped short. She had nothing else to offer, and it galled her to feel so impotent. 'Hopefully, Kendrick's team will uncover some evidence and free us up soon. But...' She looked around the room, catching everyone's eye. 'I want you all to leave at a reasonable hour this evening. Have dinner with your partners, spend time with your families, take the evening off. God knows, we all deserve it after this weekend.'

Helen wrapped up the meeting, moved back into her office in the corner of the incident room, and sunk into her chair. She should be relieved, elated. The streets of her town were safe again. It had been a tense few days, difficult too, sharing the reins of an investigation with another department. In many ways, the theory surrounding the arrest made sense. She, herself, was convinced the pub had been chosen for a reason.

She shifted the papers on her desk, pulled out a bunch of statements held together in the corner with a paper clip. The statements of Paul Stilson and David Camberra: the owners of O'Malley's. Most statements were kept online these days and fed into the HOLMES computer system to be cross-referenced. In view of the interest in the pub, she'd requested paper copies of these to keep close, something tangible she could refer to. She scanned the statements again. The owners had been in London on the night of the shooting, celebrating a birthday. The staff present reported business as usual. Nothing untoward. She combed her fingers through her hair and looked out into the incident room. Detectives and support staff were answering phones, tapping into computers, going about their business. She barely noticed them as her mind replayed her conversations with Kendrick. A homophobic attack. Whichever way she looked at it, it didn't make sense. Unlike Rainbows in the town centre, O'Malley's wasn't run as a gay bar, and organising a Mardi Gras didn't seem like a convincing motive for mass murder. Plus, none of the victims had openly identified as gay or demonstrated LGBTQ connections. If the group was targeting the gay community, they could have located a much more appropriate venue.

She'd asked Spencer to do some digging, and he hadn't found anything in the owners' backgrounds to provoke an unwarranted attack. No recent feuds, no disagreements, nothing to draw attention to themselves or their bar. Also, Kendrick seemed to be relying on devices: password-protected laptops, iPads and phones, which were incredibly difficult to break into, even by experienced technicians, especially if they were encrypted, which these would undoubtedly be. What exactly did Kendrick have, and why hadn't he shared it?

She opened her laptop, cursing Kendrick again for leaving her in the dark, just as a new email flashed up. It was from the Crown Prosecution Service, confirming her attendance to give evidence at the trial of Stephen (Chilli) Franks the week after next. Helen's heart sank. It didn't seem to matter how many times she pushed Chilli out of her head, he always seemed to wriggle back in.

She exhaled heavily as she thought about the years she'd

spent trying to protect her children, keeping Chilli's threats away from them. She had hoped they might avoid a trial here. Harbouring the vague hope that Chilli might see sense, plead guilty in the hope of a reduced sentence for cooperating. But, with the court date around the corner, that wasn't looking likely now, which meant she couldn't keep this from her boys any longer. She needed to tackle her youngest son's friendship with Chilli's nephew, speak with Robert, prepare him. Another task on her to-do list she didn't relish.

Helen swivelled in her chair and looked out of the window. It was a grey day, patchy clouds darkening. Her mind switched back to Operation Spruce, as the shooting had now been named. Pemberton was right: Kendrick was arrogant. She could see past that though, the police were full of strong personalities, especially in the senior ranks. It was the secrecy here that was galling. She turned back and tried Kendrick's mobile again, tapping her foot with each ring, cursing again as it went to voicemail. Counter-terror might march to the beat of a different drum but, whichever way she looked at it, something about this arrest didn't sit comfortably and she wouldn't rest easy until she was convinced the right people were in custody. And with that thought, she jumped up, grabbed her jacket off the back of the chair, and left the office.

CHAPTER 19

Ashleigh stared at a spider crawling across the ceiling. Usually, she'd leap out of bed at the sight of the creature, heart racing as she searched for her trap. Ever since she could remember, she'd been petrified of any kind of beetle, bug, or spider.

Today, she stared at it, numb.

She'd spent the night counting the passing hours, watching the room fade from black to grey as night folded into day. Listening to the ebb and flow of Noah's breaths while he slept beside her. Feigning sleep when he woke and crept out of the room this morning to avoid disturbing her.

Now her eyes were tired, itchy, and her head ached, but sleep still evaded her. She turned onto her side. From this position, she could see her reflection in the full-length mirror in the corner. Dark eyes set into a pasty face, her poorly arm resting above the duvet. No blood, no debris. Just a bandaged arm and a bruised head. Soon, the bruises and the bandages would disappear, and there would be nothing to tell the tale of Friday's horror. Yet her friends, her dear best friends, were gone forever. Dead.

The distant babble of the television filtered in. A muffled cough from the kitchen as Noah cooked his breakfast. It was usually Ashleigh in the kitchen. Trying out a new recipe for her food blog, putting together ideas for her weekly Instagram Live events. She'd started a food blog at uni, persuaded by her housemates to share her beloved recipes online, and no one had been more surprised than she when it had taken off. Especially when Cass had stepped in and shown her how to advertise so that it supplied a decent income. These days, Ashleigh spent most of her time in the kitchen or the supermarket or online, pairing different ingredients. Though she couldn't think of anything worse than being in the kitchen this morning. Even the smell of Noah's toast and coffee made her nauseous.

The reality of Friday evening was resurfacing and stronger now that she was in familiar surroundings. The terror raw as she finally allowed herself to reflect, to relive those final moments, leaving O'Malley's on Friday evening. Nia's drunken body leaning on hers. Cass's voice, stopping them as she held up Nia's bag. Cracks piercing the air…

The amber figures on her bedside clock switched to 7.54 am. She reached across, grabbed her mobile and stared at the notifications – over two hundred of them – filling her screen. They'd started coming in on Saturday morning when the people of Hampton woke to the monstrous news, bolstered by the photos of the three of them Nia had shared, alerting all Ashleigh's 1,200 Facebook friends that she'd been at O'Malley's on Friday evening. Sweet, heartfelt messages about her loss. Posts and private messages asking how she was feeling, how she was doing, was there anything she needed? She'd marked herself as safe but couldn't find it in herself to engage.

Ashleigh clicked on Hampton news, scanned a BBC headline – *Three arrested in suspected terror attack* – and jerked forward, flinching as she caught her arm. She opened the article, hungry eyes devouring every word. A police raid. A house in Weston. Her hand shot to her mouth. She finished the article, then reread it. No motive was mentioned, no association with a terror group. The police didn't carry out dawn raids for nothing, they must be pretty sure they'd apprehended the killers. Which meant they weren't running free; the streets were safe again. But, to Ashleigh's surprise, she still felt nothing. No relief, no loosening of the tightly bound knot in her chest.

She moved to place the phone back on the bedside cabinet when it rang in her hand. It was Jason, her editor at *The Hampton Herald*. She'd been expecting this. The short message she'd sent from her hospital bed on Saturday evening, telling him she wouldn't be submitting her column this week, that she needed some time away, had sparked a series of calls and messages. All of which she'd ignored. But she couldn't avoid him forever.

'Hey,' she answered. She needed to put Jason off. She didn't have the capacity to think about work today.

'Ash! Finally! Are you okay?'

Ashleigh swallowed. She had no idea how to answer that.

'I'm sorry. Stupid question. I was sad to hear about your friends. It's bloody awful. We're all thinking of you. Do you need anything?'

'No. Noah's here.'

'Good. That's good.' An awkward silence. For once, the garrulous Jason was lost for words. 'Look, take as much time as you want. Don't worry about your column. I'll get Evan in features to cover.'

Her column – 'The Insider' – a humorous pop at the highs and lows of Hampton life was the last thing on her mind.

'Thanks.' She needed to end the call, to cut him off, before he put on his reporting head and started digging.

'Look. We're obviously reporting on the shooting. You know that, right?'

Here it comes. Ashleigh's chest tightened. 'Sure.'

'And, no pressure, but if you feel like writing anything, perhaps even a feature, a personal piece…'

Ashleigh rolled her eyes. This was one of the reasons why she'd decided against a full-time job at the newspaper when she left university, no matter how persuasive Jason had been. She didn't want to talk about the incident, and she certainly didn't want to write about it. 'I've just lost my two best friends.'

'I know. It's dreadful, and like I said, we are here for you. Anything you need. I'm just saying, you're a great wordsmith.

Capturing the heart of a situation, it's what you do. You might find it cathartic to share the experience. Help others feeling the same the way. Think about it. No pressure. Most of all, take care.'

Ashleigh lowered her phone as the call ended. Bloody Jason. Always sniffing out a fresh angle. How could he possibly suggest a personal piece in the same breath as extending his condolences? How could he expect her to share the effects of a terrifying experience while she was grieving? Did he have no humanity? She wasn't a reporter, she was a columnist, for Christ's sake, and an accidental one at that. She'd only started writing the column at uni to fill in for a friend. When she wrote her light-hearted piece about potholes on the county's road, suggesting the local authority was using them as traffic calming, she wasn't to know it would strike such a chord with readers, resulting in a thousand tweets and messages, seventy per cent more than usual. The paper had offered her a regular slot and, she had to admit, the work had helped to fund her final student year. It was only ever meant to be temporary though, to support her blogging platform. If she was to write for anyone, long-term, it would be for a food magazine.

Urgh! Anger rose within her. But it wasn't just anger. Fear too. She closed her eyes, watched the blood trickling through the cobbles, and forced them open again. They were coming more often now. Flashbacks of the evening, little snapshots lingering in the corners of her brain, haunting her: the crack of the bullets, the sway of the crowd, the discordant din as people struggled to disperse.

Ashleigh shuddered. Who would do something like this?

CHAPTER 20

The roads were noticeably busier that morning as Helen navigated the streets back to headquarters, the earlier news about the arrests quick to restore public confidence. She switched on the local radio and listened to an old Elton John track play out. She'd spent another harrowing few hours, visiting the last two of the victim's next of kin, inconsolable in their grief. Cass Greenwell's mother was still sedated and refusing to leave her daughter's bedroom, her father sick with worry. It was heart-wrenching, but at least with the relatives she could grip the investigation, show support, make a difference.

Though the meetings hadn't uncovered anything new and the persistent questions about the arrest did nothing to bolster Helen's reserve. She found herself squirming in her seat as she batted off queries about the suspects and the operation earlier that morning. Saying that counter-terror colleagues were handling it and imparting any information at this stage might compromise their enquiries. It wasn't in Helen's nature to bluff, and she felt distinctly uncomfortable, especially as the names of the suspects hadn't been released and she'd heard nothing further from Kendrick's team.

Helen slowed to allow the knot of reporters to move aside for her to turn into headquarters. Ignoring the microphones being thrust towards the car, questions shouted from the huddle. The song on the radio faded. The DJ introduced the news. She navigated the drive, reversed into a car park space, cut the engine, and waited in the car to listen. It would be interesting to hear how the press was reporting this morning's events.

As expected, the newsreader headlined with the house raid, reporting pretty much what she knew already. A soundbite from Chief Constable Adams's press conference followed. 'These arrests represent a very significant move forward,' the chief said. 'My gratitude goes out to all the officers from Hamptonshire and neighbouring forces who have given up their time to support us over the past few days.' No mention of the motive – Kendrick's team had decided not to release that detail to the public yet, presumably until he had an admission or evidence to substantiate one.

Helen switched off the radio. *A very significant move forward.* That suggested strong evidence, though, as far as she was aware, what they had was flimsy at best.

The air was fresh and sharp as she climbed out of the car and crossed the car park. She spotted Pemberton standing outside the staff entrance, puffing on a cigarette. He greeted her with a backwards nod.

'Don't suppose you've got a spare?' she asked. Helen didn't smoke, not anymore, but if ever there was a time she needed a cigarette, it was now.

He held out a packet of Lambert and Butler, waited while she took one, and passed over his lighter. 'Any news on the arrests?' he asked.

Helen shook her head and repeated what she knew. Her throat tight as she took care not to mention the undercover officer, instead referring to 'counter-terror intelligence', and keeping it vague. She hated keeping information from Pemberton. He was her second-in-command, her confidante. Earlier this year, he'd proved his unremitting loyalty by going under the radar on another case to save her life. But she had to respect the confidentiality of an undercover operation here, the decision was out of her hands. Just like the case, or that's how it felt.

'Sounds like they don't have much,' Pemberton said.

Helen drew in a long drag. 'That's the problem, we don't know exactly what they do have. The three suspects will have been arrested on "reasonable grounds to suspect their involvement", while counter-terror question them, search the house and their devices. The bigwigs have heralded it as a result anyway.' She looked up at the building beside her. 'I can only imagine the relief on the top floor.'

'Let's hope Kendrick is right then,' Pemberton said, 'for all our sakes.'

They hushed as a figure appeared around the side of the building carrying a buff file. Helen jumped when she noticed it was Brandon Eriksen.

'Sorry, I didn't mean to startle you,' the pathologist said. 'I was just passing by and thought I'd drop this in myself.' He pushed a tousled lock from his face, held out the file.

Helen looked at it and then at Brandon quizzically. He looked bright and breezy in an open-necked white linen shirt hanging loose over black slacks.

'My autopsy reports,' he said. 'I've emailed them across, but I always think a paper copy is so much more helpful, don't you? Especially when there are numerous victims.'

'If you say so,' Pemberton said.

Helen took the file with her free hand and thanked him. If she was honest, she preferred paper files too. So much easier to flick back and forward, and mark pages for reference. For a second, their fingers touched, before she pulled away. 'Is there anything in particular we need to know?' she asked.

'I think we covered the salient points the other day,' Brandon said. 'I've put a summary at the front, just in case. He hovered as Helen stubbed out her cigarette. 'You must be pleased with the result this morning.'

'Yes, we are.'

The ensuing silence was awkward, loaded. 'I'll get off then,' Brandon said. 'Call me if you have any queries.'

'Call me if you have any queries,' Pemberton mimicked

as they left Brandon to walk back to his car and climbed the back stairs up to the incident room.

Helen laughed. 'He's just being helpful. Trying to make an impression.'

'He's certainly doing that.'

CHAPTER 21

Later that afternoon, Helen was leaning down behind her desk, plugging in her mobile phone charger, when DC Rosa Dark knocked on the door and entered.

'I've been looking into Ben Windsor's meeting with school friends on the night of the incident,' she said. 'Have you got a minute?'

Helen indicated for her to take a seat opposite. 'What is it?'

'I spoke with the friends Ben was out with, Tom and Dan,' Dark said. 'They only saw Ben's old school friend fleetingly as they were leaving the pub. They couldn't help much, apart from a brief description. So, I cross-referenced the survivor statements we have so far, one hundred and eighty-five of them now, and several – six in total, including one of those who is still receiving treatment in hospital – did mention a meet-up of old friends. I contacted a couple of them and, apparently, the reunion was from St Mary's School.'

'Well done,' Helen said. St Mary's was a secondary school on the other side of the county.

'One of their Year 9 tutor groups holds annual reunions,' Dark continued. 'A former pupil' – she glanced down at her notes – 'by the name of Eleanor Forster, organises them through her Facebook page. Eleanor's staying with parents on the outskirts of Cambridge, she went up there for a break after the shooting. I'm wondering if it's worth taking a trip over to interview her, if you think it might be relevant?'

'Nothing on her social media?'

Dark shook her head. 'She only has Facebook by the looks of it, and her privacy levels are high, I couldn't view much of it.'

'Hm. It's certainly worth making discreet enquiries to find out more about the reunion: who was invited, who was present, who wasn't. A list of class names if you can get it and whether there was any animosity amongst former pupils. If nothing else, it might highlight survivors who haven't come forward. Arrange to go up there in the morning, see what you can find out.' She paused as another thought tripped into her mind. 'Were any of the victims from the reunion?'

'Yes. Cass Greenwell and Nia Okeke. Their friend, Ashleigh Urquhart, survived.'

Helen baulked. '*The* Ashleigh Urquhart?'

Dark pulled a knowing face and nodded.

Ashleigh Urquhart hadn't crowned herself in glory with the police recently when she'd jumped on a reader's letter to *The Hampton Herald*, moaning about police response time to a night call about a suspected burglar. In her weekly column, the writer had joked that perhaps residents seeking urgent assistance would be better off calling their local takeaway than phoning 999 because they'd probably get quicker attendance from Uber Eats.

'Right,' Helen said. 'I'll take that one.' She wasn't about to place any of her team in the path of a tricky columnist. 'See if you can get me an appointment with her…' She glanced at the time on her computer screen. It was almost five. No point in going at this time of day. She didn't want to prick the young woman's curiosity by making her think these enquiries were urgent. 'Tomorrow morning, at say, 11 am?'

'Sure.' Dark jotted a note and closed her book. 'Do you want me to share this line of enquiry with counter-terror?'

Helen considered this. If Kendrick was right and they already had the guilty parties in custody, it wouldn't be relevant. Though it was still worth probing, just in case… 'No, we'll keep this to ourselves for now.'

The ring of her mobile interrupted them. As if on cue, it

was Kendrick. Helen thanked the young detective and waited for her to leave the room before she answered the call.

'Helen, Hi! Sorry I didn't phone earlier, it's been a manic day.' He sounded rushed.

Manic. You can say that again, Helen thought. 'So, what do you have?' she asked. Maybe, now, they could finally get to the bottom of this.

'The suspects are denying involvement.'

'What?'

'It's as expected. They're a small faction. The reality of what they've done, of what sentences they'll likely get, are starting to kick in. We've got experts working on their laptops, iPads, and phones as we speak.'

'What about the weapon, clothing?'

'I've got forensics in, sweeping the house for any gun residue on clothing etc. As soon as they finish, we'll go deeper. Pull up floorboards, search the drainage system.'

So, they still hadn't found anything.

'We're continuing our intelligence on the ground. I'm pretty confident we'll find something soon.'

… confident we'll find something soon. This wasn't flimsy, this was paper thin. And it was starting to make her nervous. 'What does your undercover guy say?' Helen asked.

'I can't get into that right now.'

'What?' She scoffed. This was getting ridiculous. How was she supposed to co-manage an investigation without all the information?

A voice in the background. 'Excuse me a minute,' Kendrick said.

Seconds passed. Voices muffled, as if someone had placed a hand over the receiver. Helen stared at her phone.

'Helen,' Kendrick said eventually. 'I need to go. Look, I could really do with tracing whoever uploaded that footage of the shooting to YouTube. Can you double-check with any of the survivors? See if they can identify them.'

He rang off, leaving Helen aghast. It was 5.50 pm. The

suspects had been in custody for almost twelve hours and the clock was ticking. But… the rules were different for terror suspects. They could be detained for longer, up to twenty-eight days with a high court judge's authority. Pulling a house to pieces took days, sometimes weeks. And the country was in shock. Who wouldn't support an extension in a high-profile case such as this, especially if Kendrick's team had grounds to suspect those arrested? She tapped her pen irritably on the edge of her desk. He must have had some reasonable grounds to obtain a warrant.

I could really do with tracing whoever uploaded that footage to YouTube. They'd been trying to trace the individual who filmed the shooting since Saturday morning, to no avail.

She clenched her teeth, switched to her laptop and googled Hampton shooting. A stream of articles filled the screen. She clicked on a piece from the BBC covering the morning's raid. A white-washed semi in Acorn Walk, Weston, graced the screen, blue and white police tape stretched around the front hedge. The number 42 painted white on a piece of bark beside the front door. An officer in a yellow fluorescent jacket guarding the gate. She was beginning to think she knew no more about the inquiry than the press.

CHAPTER 22

Ashleigh was sitting in the window seat of her front room, watching a group of boys kicking a football around in the park opposite, using clothing as makeshift goalposts, when the doorbell rang.

'I'll get it,' Noah said, jumping up from the sofa.

He'd taken the promise to her mother seriously and barely left her side since she'd been discharged from hospital, but he already had ants in his pants. Kept switching over the television, offering to make drinks, flicking through magazines. He missed his colleagues, the camaraderie at the workshop. Lord knows what he'll be like by Friday, she thought, rolling her eyes. She should be easier on him, she knew that. He'd known Cass and Nia as long as he'd known her and was grieving too. But the truth was, she was brimming, and at this moment, she simply didn't have the capacity to support anyone else.

She waited for him to go, then turned back to the window. Just in time to see one of the boys score a goal and run around waving his arms in the air victoriously. Ashleigh loved this vista across the park. The grass stretching into the distance beyond the railings, the path running alongside, the wooden bench in the corner, the old bandstand. It was like her own little window into Hampton life.

'Oh my God!' The crisp sound of Sadhika's Essex accent dragged her back to the room. Noah and Sadhika were standing at her front door, talking in low voices, but the flat was small, and Ashleigh could hear every word. Sadhika had only discovered that Ashleigh was involved in the shooting that morning. *If there's anything she needs, anything I can do...* Ashleigh could almost see them in the doorway. The glimmer of excitement in Sadhika's eyes, the light bouncing off her acrylic nails as she pressed a hand to her chest. Sadhika was Portland Grove's very own town crier. She'd be loitering in the shared entrance later, announcing the news to the others.

It was easy to forget they shared the house with tenants of three other flats. Sadhika, a restaurant manager at Wagamama's, was the oldest tenant, a fact she liked to remind people of on a regular basis. Filip, who commuted to London for work and left at the crack of dawn, suited and booted, on the ground floor. Lazy Johnny, who rarely bothered to open his curtains, in the flat below her. Five people, practically strangers apart from her and Noah, living in separate units of the same house. She wouldn't even have known their names if the landlord hadn't set up a Portland Grove group chat when they'd had a water leak in the entrance hall last year. Occasionally, she heard them vacuuming, playing music, or moving around their flats, as neighbours do, and Ashleigh took comfort from their presence nearby, especially when she was alone.

The front door snapped shut. Noah walked in with a bunch of pink carnations. 'Sadhika said—'

'I know. I heard.'

He smiled. 'Thought you might. She brought you these,' he said, holding up the flowers. 'I'll put them in a vase, then I'll pop to the shop. We're out of milk.' He tilted his head invitingly. 'Why don't you come with me, get a bit of fresh air?'

Ashleigh looked out into the sunshine. A red kite circled overhead, gliding gracefully against the cornflower blue sky. It really was a beautiful evening. But... A tingling swept down the back of her neck. Embarrassment at her performance when the car door slammed on Sunday. How could she be sure it wouldn't happen again? Every little unexpected or unusual sound – every shout, bark, crash – made her twitch. She'd wandered through the flat yesterday, closing all the windows, despite the rising temperatures. 'I'd rather stay here, thanks.'

His smile wavered. 'Will you be all right on your own?'

'I'll be fine.'

'Okay, you'll need to let me in. My keyring has broken again, the house key's fallen off.' He held up a car key, a mangled ring.

For someone so coordinated at sports, Noah excelled at breaking and losing stuff. 'Do we need to change the locks?'

'No, it's somewhere in the flat,' he said dismissively. 'I had it when we came back on Sunday.'

He disappeared into the kitchen, clattering about putting the flowers in water. A minute later, he shouted, 'Back in a minute,' and the front door banged shut. Seconds later, Ashleigh watched him lift a willowy arm and push his fringe out of his eyes as he crossed the road and walked up to the shop on the corner.

A bee buzzed past the window; it really was lovely outside. She should have gone with Noah, but while news of the arrests had presented some relief, a trickle through her bones, she still couldn't loosen the knot of panic inside.

A television presenter prattled on in the background – one of Noah's shows. An array of cyclists in different coloured outfits whizzed past on the screen. She grabbed the remote and switched to the news channel. The presenter was talking about a televised debate for the upcoming election. Nothing about the shooting.

All day she'd been doing this. Switching over to the news, waiting for updates on the arrest, and there had been nothing fresh since this morning. They just kept regurgitating the same old stuff: the footage of the house in Weston, the officer guarding the entrance, the police tape fluttering in the breeze. The police chief reassuring the public that three people had been arrested, thanking his staff for working around the clock. Nothing about who they were and no explanation as to why.

That was the part she struggled with. The explanation.

There had to be an explanation, didn't there? A motive. People didn't unleash an attack on a group of unknowing, defenceless individuals without reason. Ashleigh knew Cass and Nia inside out. Their parents, their extended families, their associations. They'd talked incessantly, FaceTimed when Cass was away. There was nothing she could put her finger on to indicate why they'd been targeted.

She looked back over to the park. Johnny, from the flat below, was marching across the grass. And... she squinted. What was that he was carrying? A guitar case. Oh, she hoped he hadn't taken up playing. She could only imagine what Noah would make of that. They struggled to put up with the eclectic brand of folk music he listened to; the discordant sound of guitar strums seeping through the floorboards was all they needed.

Her gaze wandered to a couple sitting on the lip of the bandstand, holding hands. A man throwing a stick for a Spaniel who retrieved it obediently. The young lads still playing football. The people of Hampton, making the most of a warm summer's evening while her friends' bodies lay frozen in the morgue.

She'd expected the world to slow, the roads to empty, the park to quieten, at least for a while. Instead, the arrests had kick-started life straight back into action and the more Ashleigh thought about it, the more it niggled her that there was no explanation. Why had they been singled out? Why that group at that location on that evening? She owed it to Cass and Nia to find out more. They couldn't have died for nothing.

CHAPTER 23

There was something disconcerting about living within walking distance of a dangerous criminal's closest family. Helen knocked on the door of Davy Boyd's semi and waited. It was almost 7 pm, the evening bright and balmy. But the pleasant weather and the summer-infused aromas of honeysuckle and phlox did nothing to stall the trepidation building in her head.

Ever since they'd become aware of the friendship between their respective sons, Helen and Davy had tiptoed around each other. With the court case looming, it didn't feel appropriate for Helen to become too friendly, and she'd had no cause to speak with Chilli Franks's half-brother. Not until she received the email from the court this morning.

Helen knocked again, then checked the driveway and the road outside for Davy's BMW. She hoped he wasn't out. She really wanted to get this over with.

She was just contemplating whether to come back another time when she heard footsteps thumping downstairs. The door snapped open. Helen whizzed round, only to come face to face with Davy. He was dressed in grey jogging bottoms and a black T-shirt that showed off his defined biceps. Beady eyes, hair razored to number one, an ice-cold gaze. Davy looked so like his half-brother she could just as easily have been staring at the man himself and, despite her best efforts, Helen's stomach churned.

'Is Zac okay?' he asked, frowning. His eyes scanning

the driveway. But apart from his appearance, intelligence suggested Davy was nothing like his brother. He had no police record, kept his nose clean, and was supposedly focused on raising his family. Though he was, by his own admission, here managing Chilli's businesses, and something about the arrangement, and him living so close by, put her on edge.

Helen swallowed back her uneasiness and stood tall. It wasn't only Robert who knew nothing of her professional involvement with his friend, Zac's, family. If Davy Boyd was to be believed, Zac didn't either, and since a trial of this magnitude would be widely publicised in the press, it was time they both rectified that. 'Yes, I believe he's at cricket practice. I'm picking the boys up in a bit.' She looked past him, half hoping for his wife to appear, to soften the atmosphere, but he appeared to be alone. 'It's actually you I wanted to speak with.'

Davy's eyes narrowed to tiny slits.

'May I come in?'

Unspeaking, he moved aside for her to enter. She followed him, down a hallway, past pencil portraits of a younger Zac and a little girl she guessed was Zac's sister, into a bright and airy living room that ran the length of the house. An array of red cushions squished into an oversized black leather sofa, a gaming console laid out in front of the television, a women's magazine left open on an armchair, it screamed of a family home, lived in. Nothing like the stark, minimalist pad Chilli used to keep.

Davy indicated for her to take a seat on the sofa, moved the magazine aside and perched on the edge of the armchair. No refreshments were offered. Clearly, he was as uneasy about the visit as she was.

Helen cleared her throat. 'I've been called to give evidence at Chilli's trial.'

He stared at her, deadpan. 'I haven't spoken to my brother in months. I won't be attending the trial.'

'Right. The thing is, I tend to keep my work away from

my family,' Helen said, 'which is why Robert has no notion of my involvement in Chilli's case. I was hoping to continue that, but the upcoming court case is likely to be high-profile.'

He waved his hand in the air dismissively. 'I wouldn't worry. Teenagers aren't interested in the news. It's all TikTok and YouTube these days.'

'That's as may be, but if I'm going to appear in court, I'm afraid I'm going to have to speak with Robert, let him know.'

Davy stiffened. 'I don't want Zac involved. He's a young lad at an impressionable age.'

This was awkward. 'Can I ask what you have told Zac about his uncle?'

'He's aware Chilli's in prison. We told him it was an issue at work and left it at that. Look, Zac barely knows his uncle; he's only met him a couple of times. No sense in complicating the matter.' He sat back, surveyed her with another hard stare. 'I'd like to keep it that way and I'd appreciate your support in doing so. Chilli and I had different fathers. We have different surnames. Hopefully, when the case is reported, people won't make the connection.'

Helen baulked inwardly. She assumed he meant the parents at school, the teachers. True, some of them might not make the link, especially with their different names. Though the fact that Davy was managing his half-brother's hairdressing salon and nail bars gave the game away somewhat. But that wasn't what was really bothering her. What was eating away at Helen was the blasé way in which he'd dismissed Chilli's crimes to his kids as 'an issue at work'. Chilli had been charged with kidnapping a police officer, illegal importation of firearms, and possession with intent to supply cocaine. He was a gangland boss, for Christ's sake! How were they supposed to keep that from their kids when his trial started? She bit back her frustration. 'I realise your predicament and I sympathise with you. But I can't see a way of keeping this from Robert. If my name appears in the news, as an officer on the case, and he hears the details, well... I'd rather it came from me first.' A flashback. Sitting on the floor in the damp cellar, knees and ankles grazed. Chilli looming over her. Thinking she'd never escape alive. Helen blinked the images away.

Davy folded his hands together. 'Court's a part of your working life, right? Surely there's no need to make more of this than necessary.'

'But—'

'Look,' Davy interrupted. His face loosened slightly and when it did, his eyes were softer. 'My daughter struggled with the move from Spain. She's just started to settle, had her first friend over at the weekend. We don't need the stigma of being attached to the criminal fraternity, putting off parents from letting their kids come round. So, if you can find it in yourself to avoid going through the details with your boy, I'd be grateful. We're hoping the trial will pass quickly.' He looked away, shook his head disapprovingly. 'It's a formality anyway. I can't see Chilli wriggling his way out of this one.'

Helen was torn. She felt for Davy, she really did. It couldn't have been easy to come back from Spain, move his kids over here at such a vulnerable age. But as she pondered this, a warning voice called from deep inside – Davy was Chilli Franks's blood. Whichever way she looked at it, his presence here instilled disquiet. 'I'll give it some thought,' she said, 'but my instinct tells me that honesty would be best here. For all of us.'

Davy's nostrils flared. He rose, indicating an end to the conversation.

He was just guiding her out when the front door burst open and his wife, Sofia, entered with a little girl Helen recognised from the photos as Zac's sister. The youngster smiled shyly and pushed a wave of the dark curls she'd clearly inherited from her mother out of her face.

'Hello!' Sofia said, raising her brows. 'It's nice to finally meet you!' Her face broke into a wide, welcoming smile as she extended a hand which Helen shook. Rich shiny eyes. An attractive face. A Spanish accent coating her words. This was where Zac's warmth came from. 'Is Zac okay?'

'Yes, I'm just going to collect him from cricket practice,' Helen said. She didn't want to make idle chat, especially after her conversation with Davy, but Sofia was standing in front of the door and there was nowhere for her to go without appearing rude.

'Ah.' The air thickened in the hallway. Sofia looked at her husband quizzically, then back at Helen. No one spoke. 'Well,' Sofia continued. 'I wanted to say thank you. I'm so grateful Robert encouraged Zac to play cricket. He's been such a great friend to him since we moved here.'

The words tugged at Helen's heartstrings. Out of her two boys, Robert had always been the sociable one, known for his generous nature. Who would have thought that such kind openness would lead him to unknowingly strike up a friendship with her arch-enemy's family? She forced a smile. 'Thank you. He's a good lad. Most of the time.'

Sofia laughed. 'I'm sure.' She took off her jacket, still standing in front of the door. 'The traffic was crazy coming home. The world is out and about now that the police have caught those terrorists.' She turned to Helen. 'You're doing a grand job.'

Helen cringed. The statement reminding her what little she knew about the arrests. 'We have a good team,' she said. 'It's been terrible for the people involved.'

'Oh, I know.' Sofia pressed a hand to her chest and when she spoke again, her accent was stronger, measuring the passion in her voice. 'Those poor families. I can't begin to imagine what it must be like.' She looked at her husband. 'Your friend, Trent, he was there when it happened, wasn't he? Frightened to death, he was…' She caught Davy's eye, and then stopped mid-sentence. 'Well, I'm sure you don't want to hear this.'

Helen forced another smile. 'It was a dreadful incident and

one that's shaken everyone,' she said. 'Listen, I'd better get going. Don't want to be late for the boys.'

She excused herself, sidestepped Sofia, and wandered down the driveway, Sofia's words ringing in her ear. Trent... Quite a distinctive name. She didn't recall anyone named Trent on the survivors' list.

CHAPTER 24

Helen pressed her fist to her mouth and watched the YouTube footage of the shooting play out for the umpteenth time. It was almost 7.30 am. Day five. The arrests had been made over twenty-four hours ago; forensics continued to tear up floorboards and search drainage pipes at 42, Acorn Walk. If they had uncovered anything, Kendrick clearly wasn't about to share it and, once again, he hadn't returned her call, despite her leaving a voicemail first thing, requesting an update. The doubt in the pit of her stomach was growing by the minute. Kendrick needed to make an announcement, to appease the media still camped out at the end of the driveway, if nothing else, and soon.

It didn't help that Sofia Boyd's words had hounded Helen all night. She still couldn't decide what to do about Robert, but it was only in the early hours, when her bedroom began to brighten at sunrise, that she realised why the exchange needled her. The only Trent Helen knew of was Trent Bradshaw, owner of the boxing gym, Connect 12, on Argyle Street in town. Just around the corner from Swan Street.

She recalled a raid she'd done on Bradshaw's gym in her younger years, when the gym had been owned by Trent's father, now retired. Pulling the place apart, searching for a stash of cocaine they'd been tipped off was being stored there. A stash they didn't find. Many similar allegations followed. Trent himself had served twelve months for possession with intent to supply cannabis in his early twenties and, later, after he took over the business, intelligence linked him with key players in Hampton's drugs ring, including Paul Gladstone, Chilli's rival. Some informants even suggested he was money laundering for the East Side Boys, although the organised crime team had never been able to pin anything new on him.

Helen watched the crowd on the screen duck as more bullets filled the air, then froze the frame. Again, and again. Slowing down the images. Working through them gradually. If there was something there, she was determined not to miss it.

She was about to give up when a movement at the corner of the screen caught her eye. She zoomed in on a bald figure, close to the door of O'Malley's, dressed in a dark suit, an open-necked white shirt. Trent Bradshaw had smartened himself up since she'd last seen him, but he still shaved his head and... what was that? The pixels blurred as she tried to enlarge the image. If she wasn't mistaken, there was the top of his hallmark eagle tattoo peeping above his shirt collar.

Helen double-checked their survivor spreadsheet – three hundred and twenty-two at last count, names listed in alphabetical order. All potential witnesses. All people her team needed to reach out to, interview, examine their background and connections. Yet Trent didn't feature there. Why hadn't he come forward? Especially since his gym was only a couple of streets away from the crime scene.

And there was something else...

'Your friend, Trent...' Sofia had said. If Davy was only managing Chilli's legitimate businesses, if he was as clean as he presented, why was he associating with someone like Trent? And what was Trent doing there?

The door to the incident room swung open to reveal Pemberton holding two steaming mugs.

'You're in early,' he said. He placed them down on her desk, catching the freeze frame on her laptop. 'What's Bradshaw doing there?'

Helen thanked him for the coffee and looked past him into the incident room. Detectives and support staff were arriving to start their day. Turning on computers, sliding into chairs. The aroma of coffee and toast hung in the air. 'Close the door, will you?'

She waited for him to do so, then talked him through her visit with Davy Boyd yesterday evening.

'You're concerned about Robert,' he said as she finished up.

'Partly.' She couldn't deny she hadn't been thrilled to discover Robert's new best friend was Franks's nephew, but Zac had seemed like a good kid, and she'd always been careful not to pressure her boys to pick and choose their friends based on associations with her job. Not without good cause, she didn't want to be 'that cop'. So, since the intelligence on Davy had been positive, she'd made no attempts to discourage their friendship. Though now she was beginning to wonder if she should have stepped in sooner. 'If Davy Boyd is associating with the likes of Bradshaw, then maybe he isn't as clean as he makes out. And that's not all.' Pemberton looked taken aback as she passed on Jenkins's concerns about Chilli Franks's possible involvement in organising the shooting.

'I can't see it,' he said, sinking his hands into his pockets.

'That was my initial response. But why would Davy associate with someone who mixes with his half-brother's competitor? He made it quite clear he disapproved of Chilli's actions.'

'Hm.' Pemberton stared into space. 'Disapproved of, or distanced himself from?'

'What do you mean?'

'Trent and Gladstone's association wouldn't be popular with Chilli. Trent's father was one of Chilli's closest supporters. And with Davy now in the mix as well… It might explain why the brothers aren't speaking.'

Helen thought again about the shooting. The radio silence from Kendrick's crew. The meticulous planning. The offender who seemingly disappeared into thin air. Almost as if they'd been hired… 'Surely a connection between Davy Boyd and his rival gang wouldn't be enough to prompt Chilli to pay someone to do this?' The idea, spoken aloud, sounded preposterous. And yet...

Pemberton rubbed his chin. 'A year ago, I'd say Chilli would never make a public display like this. By the time we charged him, he was losing support and paranoid about others trying to overthrow him. There are suggestions he's still running his racket from the inside, but his support in the field has dramatically reduced. If perhaps he now feels he's lost control, that even his half-brother, his closest relative, has turned to his adversaries, something like this would send a strong message. Perhaps scare some of his old team into remaining loyal. It's all about manpower in his game.'

Helen shook her head in disbelief. 'If that was the case, surely we'd have heard word from the street? Someone would know. What's the point of a message if it doesn't get across?'

Pemberton shrugged. 'Maybe nobody dared speak up. Gladstone's East Side Boys certainly wouldn't welcome the attention, it's bad for business. If nothing else, they'd be pleased to hear the incident being put down to terrorism. The point would be made, though.'

Helen wasn't sure what to think. A part of her couldn't believe that the shooting could be attributed to Franks, that it could be part of a gang war, but she couldn't afford to ignore the possibility either. 'Make some enquiries with the remand wing at Wakefield Prison, will you?' she said. 'See who Chilli's associating with, whether he's had any visitors, who he's phoned, and be discreet. I don't want him to know we're asking questions.' She thought for a second, then checked the time on her laptop. Her appointment with Ashleigh Urquhart was at eleven. She clicked on google search and typed in 'Connect 12, Hampton'. It opened at 8 am. 'Meantime, let's pay Trent a visit. See what he's got to say.'

CHAPTER 25

Helen and Pemberton stepped into a lively Connect 12, despite the early hour. A couple of men were sparring in the ring. A young woman was punching a bag hanging from the ceiling – the thump, thump, thump of her blows reverberating around the room, mingling with the rhythmic whip of rope from another woman skipping in the corner.

Helen blocked out the smell of musty old leather and approached a grey-haired man in a tracksuit at the side of the ring, shouting words of encouragement to the sparring pair. She flashed her badge, introduced them both. 'We're looking for Trent Bradshaw,' she said.

The man, in his fifties she guessed, gazed down at her beneath hooded brows. 'What's it about?'

'And you are?'

'Darren Gregory. I'm one of his trainers.'

'Well, Darren, it's Trent we really need to speak to,' Helen said. 'Is he here?'

'I'll have to check.' He rolled his eyes, signalled to the men in the ring to take a break, instructed Helen and Pemberton to wait there, and then disappeared through a painted black door in the corner marked Private – Staff Only.

Helen glanced around as the men climbed out of the ring and pulled off their headguards, catching their breath. She took in the red walls, the crash mats in front of the mirror, the racks of free weights at the far end. She caught herself in the floor to ceiling mirror and flinched at her pasty face, her trouser suit that could do with a good press. Even her dark hair, tied back into a messy half-ponytail, looked limp and tired this morning.

A pair of lads jostled shoulders as they emerged from the changing rooms, inadvertently knocking into Pemberton.

'Sorry, Grandad,' one of them uttered.

Pemberton's jaw dropped as he met Helen's gaze. 'Grandad! I could take on those two together.' He stared at the lads who, oblivious to his indignation, had moved over to the free weights and started curling dumbbells in the corner.

Helen couldn't help laughing. 'Yeah, maybe twenty years ago.' She glanced towards the door at the rear of the gym. 'What's taking so long?'

'Probably disposing of their stash,' Pemberton said cynically.

Almost on cue, the door opened, and Darren reappeared. He gave them a backwards nod to join him. 'Mr Bradshaw is in the back office,' he said. 'I'll take you through.'

Mr Bradshaw. At thirty, Trent must be almost half his age, Helen thought.

They were led down a dingy, narrow corridor, the cream walls littered with years of scuffs and scratches, the only light a dull, fluorescent strip above. They passed a door on the right marked Private, then an iron staircase to the left, which Helen guessed led to the flat above, and paused outside the next door. Darren knocked once and entered.

Trent Bradshaw was sitting in a black leather chair behind a laminated desk. He wasn't a tall man, only about 5ft 8, and lean, the definition of his pectoral muscles accentuated by the tight white T-shirt he wore. Morning sunshine streamed into the room, courtesy of a long window facing a concrete yard behind, stacked with overflowing wheelie bins. Not the most pleasing aspect.

'Detective Lavery,' Trent said, slouching back in his chair. He tapped his knuckles together twice, the gold signet rings he wore clanging as they touched, and then indicated for them to sit on the plastic chairs opposite.

'Hello, Trent,' Helen said. 'You remember Sergeant Pemberton?'

'How could I forget?' His smile revealed a gold upper tooth at the side of his mouth. 'How you doin', man?'

Pemberton didn't answer. His face filled with disdain at being addressed as 'man'. He squeezed himself into a chair.

'So, what can I do for you at this early hour?' Trent said.

Helen hesitated. She desperately wanted to find out about his relationship with Davy Boyd, but that was a personal issue. Better to stick to the case in hand, for now. 'I was wondering if you can help us with our enquiries,' she said, watching Trent puffing out his chest. 'We're investigating the shooting last Friday evening in Swan Street. Looking to trace the weapon used.' She took care not to mention details. They hadn't released the specifics of the firearm to the press, there was no sense in panicking the public further by talking about an illegal assault rifle, and she wasn't about to let it slip here. 'I thought, someone like you, with your ear to the ground... that maybe you might have heard something. On the street, maybe?'

He squinted at her warily. 'I thought you guys had made an arrest.'

'Oh, we have. But we could do with finding the weapon. We need to make the case water-tight for the CPS. You know what it's like, Trent,' she said engagingly. 'The more we have, the better chance we've got.'

Trent did know what it was like. Following his prison term, he'd wriggled out of plenty of other charges due to lack of evidence or savvy solicitors. Trent certainly knew about the legal system.

Trent ran his tongue across his teeth as he appeared to consider his options. 'I think you have me wrong, detective,' he said eventually. 'I've been straight since I took over the gym, five years ago.' He held out his hands wide. 'I don't move in those circles anymore.'

Yeah, right. 'I'm sure you've still got your contacts.'

He surveyed her a second, as if he was trying to read her. 'You're asking the wrong man this time.'

'Well, you must get an awful lot of people pass through this gym,' Helen said, glancing at the door. 'If you happen to hear anything…' She let her words trail, reached into her pocket, and held out her card. 'Give me a call.' He looked at the card and then at her, making no effort to take it, so she placed it on the edge of the desk and rose, as if she was about to leave.

She was almost at the door, Pemberton on her tail, when she turned. 'Oh, what were you doing at O'Malley's last Friday night?'

If he was surprised by her question, he didn't show it. 'Why're you asking?'

She needed to be careful here. The situation with Zac's parents and her son was delicate enough as it was. She didn't want to upset matters further by letting it slip she'd discovered his presence from them. 'Someone caught the incident on film and put it on YouTube. We've been examining the footage to identify who was present and hasn't come forward. Maybe you didn't see the public appeal.'

'I wasn't hurt, so there was no need to come forward.'

'Did you notice anyone filming?'

'No.' He held her gaze.

'Right. Can I ask who you were with at O'Malley's?'

'A mate.' He stared at her, clearly not about to expand.

'Were you there all evening?'

He gave a single nod. 'My mate likes their DJ evenings. Not really my taste, I'm more of a Tinie Tempah fan.'

'So, you'd planned to go there?'

'Yeah, but I don't see what—'

'Like I said, we're tracing everyone present. Interviewing them to see if they saw anything. Putting together a list for the local authorities who will be offering counselling,' she added, grateful for the recent press announcement from the Community Health Team confirming that they would be offering counselling to all survivors. 'You've been through a traumatic experience.'

He held her gaze a second longer. 'Look, we didn't see anything, not apart from a lot of people running around and screaming. And we don't need no counselling.'

'Perhaps your friend might appreciate some support.'

'They don't.'

Helen desperately wanted to probe Trent further about who had accompanied him, his wider connections. If this was a gangland attack, if Chilli had targeted the pub because of who was present, to send a message, she needed to find out more. But the chief had heralded the arrests as a result, and she couldn't afford to alert Trent to her doubts. 'Okay, well... Perhaps you could pass on my details to your friend in case they change their mind. You know where to find me.' And with that, she made her way out.

* * *

'What do you think?' Pemberton asked as they climbed into the car outside the gym.

'I'm not sure,' Helen said. 'His presence at the shooting makes me uncomfortable.' She clicked her seatbelt into the catch, thought for a moment. 'Did I hear Dickie Wright has just joined organised crime?' she asked.

'Yeah. Last month.'

Helen didn't want to take this to the organised crime inspector, not at this stage, especially with her personal interest in Davy Boyd's involvement, but Dickie was an old friend. 'I think I might pull him aside, have a quiet word,' she said. 'Organised crime have been keeping a close eye on Gladstone and his associations since Chilli went away. If Trent is active, and if Davy and him are associated, they'll have noticed. At least then, we'll know whether we need to take things further.'

She glanced at the clock on the dash. 'Come on. We've got a columnist to question next.'

CHAPTER 26

Helen and Pemberton were met at the door of Ashleigh Urquhart's first-floor flat on Portland Grove by an attractive man in his early twenties who introduced himself as Ashleigh's fiancé, Noah. He showed them into a compact living room that was surprisingly light and airy.

Ashleigh, who was sitting in an armchair beside the window, stood as they entered. Dressed in jeans and a loose black T-shirt, her chocolate brown hair was tied at the nape of her neck, and her face, devoid of make-up, looked ashen. A far cry from the glamorous photo that accompanied her column at *The Herald*.

'Thank you for seeing us this morning,' Helen said. 'I realise this can't be easy for you.'

Noah checked their drink preferences and disappeared into the kitchen. Helen and Pemberton settled themselves on a long sofa that faced an ornate Victorian fireplace. 'I was very sorry to hear about your friends,' Helen said.

Ashleigh gave a single nod. 'Are you here to tell me more about the arrest? The detective was vague when she called to arrange the visit yesterday.'

'I'm afraid not. Colleagues in counter-terror will be releasing more information as soon as they are able.'

'What exactly does that mean?'

'It means I can't tell you anything more at present. I'm sorry.'

She watched the young woman purse her lips and look

away. The dearth of information from counter-terror was exasperating, but that wasn't the only thing bothering Helen. She needed to find a way to question Ashleigh without prompting suspicion; she couldn't afford for the columnist to express concern to colleagues at the newspaper. 'We're following up on enquiries from the shooting,' Helen said gently. 'Are you comfortable answering some more questions about the evening?'

'I gave a statement at the hospital.'

'Yes, and that was helpful. We're just going through individual accounts, firming up some of the details, like who else was in the pub, that sort of thing. Often people remember little details afterwards that escaped them at the time.'

'I thought you'd made an arrest.'

Helen forced a disarming smile. 'The suspects are still being questioned. As I say, hopefully, we'll have more news on that soon. We still need to draw up a list of everyone present though, make sure they are getting the right support. Confirm everything ties together.' She looked down at her notes. 'I understand there was a school reunion going on for your Year 9 class that night.'

'Yes.'

'How did you hear about it?'

'There's a Facebook page run by Eleanor Forster, an old school friend. She organises the reunion every year.'

'That's interesting.' By Helen's estimate, Ashleigh must have been out of secondary school at least six years now. She couldn't think of one school friend she herself had carried into her early twenties, especially from Year 9. 'What brings you all together?'

The young woman's face contorted. 'Is this relevant?'

'As I say, we're building up a picture of the evening, confirming who was present. It's quite routine.' Helen let the silence hang in the air. 'The local authority is arranging to offer trauma counselling,' she added. 'They'll need details of survivors present.'

A couple of seconds ticked past. 'It's complicated.'

'Take your time.'

Ashleigh drew a long breath. 'Our tutor group lost a classmate, Heather Osborne, at the end of Year 9.'

'That must have been tough. Can you tell me more about it?'

Ashleigh stared at her. For a second, Helen thought she was going to refuse and ask about the pertinence of the questioning. But the woman's face simply creased as if she recalled a distant memory. 'Heather was diagnosed with stomach cancer when we were in Year 9. It was a shock to everyone at the time.' She looked wistful. 'The prognosis was promising at first. Our form tutor, Mr Hacknell, helped us organise fundraising for her when she was having chemotherapy: fun runs, sponsored silences, that sort of thing. He united the class. Made us feel like we were doing something to help. Anyway, Heather finished her treatment. We were all looking forward to her returning to school, when...' She paused. 'There were complications. She contracted sepsis. Died within three days.'

'I'm so sorry.'

'It was a long time ago. Eleanor was Heather's best friend. She vowed to have a party every year to celebrate Heather's birthday. After we left school, it became a reunion.'

'And you all continued to attend?'

'Sort of. We were at a tricky age when we lost Heather. It bonded us, I think. Reunion numbers have dwindled over the years. People moved away, went travelling, some lost interest. I've missed the last couple of years myself.'

'What made you go this year?'

'What?'

'You said, you hadn't been to the last couple.'

'Oh, our form tutor, Mr Hacknell, died of a heart attack in March. He was only fifty-two.' Her nose scrunched. 'He attended every reunion without fail. Eleanor wanted to get as many people together as possible this year, as a tribute to him.'

'So, that encouraged you to attend.'

'Yes. Well... Sort of. We, that is Cass, Nia and I, were out celebrating Cass's return from travelling in Asia.' Her face twisted again as memories of the evening resurfaced. 'It happened to coincide with the reunion. When we received the invitation, we decided to have our night out at O'Malley's, combine the two.' She turned to look out of the window as a tear slipped out and rolled down her cheek.

'Were the reunions always held at O'Malley's?'

'Not always.' She looked back at Helen, brushed the tear away. 'Why do you need to know all this?'

'As I say, it's all part of routine enquiries. How many from your class attended?'

'I'm not sure exactly. Eleanor would be able to tell you more. There was me, Nia, Cass...' She listed other names.

Pemberton's ballpoint pen scratched the paper as he noted them down. Fifteen altogether.

Helen glanced towards the kitchen. 'What about your fiancé?'

'Noah? No. He didn't join our school until after Heather had passed away, and he was in a different class. It was mainly for our tutor group.'

Noah brought in mugs of coffee on a tray. They sipped their drinks quietly. Helen was tempted to ask the young woman to run through the events of the evening again, to confirm her account, but she already looked wary. She asked whether Ashleigh had seen anyone filming the shooting, and the young woman shook her head.

'Is there anything you'd like to add to your earlier account?' Helen asked. 'Perhaps something you later remembered, and didn't mention to officers at the time?'

Noah moved to Ashleigh's side and placed a protective hand on her shoulder. 'Is this really necessary?' he said. 'She's already told you everything.'

* * *

Helen and Pemberton were on their way back to their car, musing about their discussion with Ashleigh Urquhart when Helen's mobile rang. It was Jenkins. 'Kendrick has called a meeting for tomorrow morning at 9.30 am with you, me, and Adams. There's been a development.'

Helen stopped in her tracks. It was Tuesday lunchtime. Kendrick still hadn't returned her call from this morning, and his clandestine approach was really grating now. He should be calling *her* about any developments, not her superiors. 'What has happened?'

'Apparently, it's sensitive. He wants to speak with us face to face. He'll fill us in in the morning.'

CHAPTER 27

Ashleigh was viewing a newsreader interview an expert marksman about the shooting, listening as they speculated on the make of the rifle used – something high calibre, semi-automatic – when her mobile rang. It was Jason.

'How are you doing, Ash? Just checking in.'

'Same as I was yesterday. No change.' She glanced out of the window. A man in a baseball cap was sitting on the bench at the corner of the park, vaping.

'I just wondered if you'd given that article any thought? I know our readers would appreciate hearing your take.'

'The answer's still no.' Undeterred, Jason rambled on in his usual thick-skinned way about how much they'd missed her quirky column and how he hoped she'd be well enough to pen a piece for next week. Ashleigh zoned out. She was watching the man on the bench finish his vape and place it in his pocket when suddenly he looked up at her. Almost as if he felt the heat of her eyes on him. Ashleigh turned away abruptly. 'Have you heard any more from the police about the suspects?' she asked Jason. 'It's been over twenty-four hours since the arrest, surely there must be some news.'

His voice dropped an octave. 'Even if we had, we couldn't print it.'

'What do you mean?'

'The police have requested a blanket moratorium on reports about those arrested. Something to do with it compromising the case.'

'What?'

'I know. It's a crock of shit. Anyway, I gotta go. Give that article some thought, eh? My phone is always on.'

The line went dead. Ashleigh lowered her phone and stared back at the television, aghast. No wonder the shooting wasn't making the headlines today.

She was still churning this over as Noah entered the room. 'You really need to stop watching that,' he said, looking at the television.

'I thought you were listening to your music in the bedroom.' The words came out icier than intended.

'I was and now I've finished,' he retorted. 'It's not good for you, you know. To keep following this stuff.'

She'd almost forgotten about the interview. Back on the screen, the marksman was holding up a rifle, pointing out the sights. 'I was just checking,' she said. *What did he know about what was good for her?*

'Checking what?'

'I don't know, to see what they have. Did you find your key?'

'Yeah, it's on the side,' he said, refusing to change the subject. 'Why don't you turn the TV over?'

Ashleigh scratched the back of her neck, desperately trying to crush the barbs in her voice. She didn't want to fight with Noah, he was only trying to help. 'The police visit this morning. It made me uncomfortable.' She decided against mentioning her phone call with the editor, he wouldn't appreciate Jason badgering her about an article when she was taking time out. 'Why do you think they asked so much about the reunion?'

'You heard the detective, they're just establishing who was there, putting a case together. It's what they do. Listen, why don't we go for a walk? Take your mind off things.'

'I'm not sure.'

'Come on. It'll be good for you, a change of scenery.'

He wasn't wrong. It was Tuesday afternoon. She hadn't stepped out of the flat since returning from hospital on Sunday morning and all this sitting in the window, watching the world go by… It wasn't healthy. Even her mother was concerned. As much as Ashleigh tried to stay upbeat on their daily calls, she'd picked up on her tension and anxiety and decided to book a flight to come over at the weekend.

But Ashleigh was still fearful, jumpy. Haunted by every clatter, every bump, every sudden noise. 'Maybe tomorrow, eh? Why don't you go for a run today? You haven't been all week. You'll be losing your Olympic prowess.'

His face slackened at her attempt at a joke. Noah was super fit and ran a lot but quaffed far too much beer to make county standard, let alone Olympic. 'Okay, if you're sure?'

She nodded.

'All right. I'll just get changed.'

Ashleigh's shoulders relaxed as he moved out to the bedroom, her mind turning back to Jason's words. A moratorium on the press. What did that mean?

'All done!' Noah reappeared in the doorway wearing a pair of blue shorts and a black T-shirt, already looking brighter. A run was just what he needed. 'Is there anything I can get for you before I go?'

She shook her head, pecked his offered cheek, and turned back to the window. The man had gone, the bench was empty now. She watched Noah jog across the road and disappear round the back of the bandstand.

Ashleigh tore herself away from the scene outside and moved into the kitchen, idly running her finger across the worktop. She couldn't think straight. Maybe she should throw herself into her work. Before the shooting, she'd been constructing new recipes for coeliacs, only four ingredients, all gluten-free. She opened the fridge, pulled out a bunch of asparagus, a pot of parmesan, some crème fraiche, and garlic. Ashleigh loved the science of food, the pairing of ingredients. How some recipes worked, and others fell foul. The kitchen was her happy place, her space to lose herself, create, indulge. Though… she stared at the sparse ingredients laid out on the shiny surface. Right now, she couldn't muster the energy, let alone the enthusiasm, especially after her conversation with Jason. Why didn't the police want the press to talk about the arrests?

The public was grieving. They needed answers.

Jason's request for a personal piece skipped into her mind. She didn't want to share her experience, she couldn't think of anything worse, but... it could be a tactical way of keeping the story alive.

She twisted her engagement ring around her finger. Survivors. The word had wriggled around her head like a hungry maggot since the detective's visit yesterday. Other people like her. People that shared her fears, her isolation. People who were grief-stricken, terrified. If she did write a piece, she could insist on including an invitation for survivors to form an informal online group to support each other. Her way of bringing people together positively. Cass and Nia would approve of that. At the same time, once she gained their confidence, she could gently probe them. People tended to open up more in casual situations, didn't they? Perhaps mention something they wouldn't to a police officer.

She grabbed her phone and selected her editor's number. Perhaps Jason was right. Maybe it was time to share her experience with the world.

CHAPTER 28

Back at headquarters, Spencer leaned against the radiator at the side of Helen's office and tapped his pen on his chin. 'No one from our current survivors' list can identify the person who filmed the shooting.'

Helen let out a long sigh. Tracing the person who filmed the YouTube footage was becoming an irritating itch she couldn't scratch. The techies had drawn a blank: those responsible had set up a channel for this one video, uploading it and tagging #hamptonshooting to ensure visibility, while using an untraceable email address. Their best chance of tracking them down was a public appeal, yet no one had come forward, and she couldn't help wondering what they had to hide.

She relayed the details of her visit with the newspaper columnist. Pemberton passed the names to Spencer to cross-reference with their list of survivors, then Helen asked Dark how she'd got on with the reunion organiser.

Dark perched on the side of the desk and flipped open her notebook. 'Eleanor Forster. Works for Reynards, the accountants, in town. It took a while to coax her to speak, she's still struggling with anxiety about the attack.' Dark went on to describe how Eleanor organised these events annually, how this was a special night, after their tutor's sudden death. 'The turnout was the best they'd had in years – fifteen out of the twenty-eight class members.'

That concurred with Ashleigh Urquhart's account.

'She also gave me a detailed list of the original class

members,' Dark said. 'She's continued to follow most of them on social media, so we should be able to identify those who weren't present.'

'Right,' Helen said. They'd check the names against the survivors' list, but it was all beginning to feel like a formality, an administration exercise. 'Anything noteworthy?'

'Actually, there is.' Dark glanced back at her notes, and when she looked up, her eyes gleamed. 'There's been a bit of animosity between two of the class members. And that's where it gets interesting.' She flipped another page. 'Two men from the class had an altercation, four years ago, in a road rage incident. Ivan Shaw and Eugene Grant. Shaw was sent to prison. I looked the case up when I got back. Shaw was convicted of possession of an imitation firearm with intent to cause fear when he tailed the car Eugene Grant was driving on the outskirts of Hampton. Apparently, Ivan forced Eugene to pull over then brandished a weapon before he drove off. Eugene reported the incident to the police afterwards. When questioned, Ivan claimed he was just teasing him – the weapon was actually a ball bearing gun – but the incident was caught on CCTV. He served two years in prison.

'Strange. Ashleigh Urquhart didn't mention anything. Were either of them present last Friday?'

'No, sadly. Eleanor hasn't seen them in years. She heard on the grapevine that Eugene Grant emigrated to New Zealand. Ivan Shaw moved away from the Midlands when he was released from prison, but she doesn't know where he went.'

'So, that's it then,' Spencer said.

'Not quite,' Helen replied. 'Something must have prompted the road rage incident. Do we know why they had a falling out, or whether it was a long-running feud?'

'Eleanor couldn't recall anything. According to her, they were very different characters and didn't have a lot to do with each other at school. In his statement at the time, Eugene claimed to have no idea what prompted the incident; they hadn't seen each other for some time. During the interview,

Shaw went no comment, but he did eventually plead guilty. In mitigation, Shaw's barrister said his client claimed to have been teased and bullied by Eugene and other students at school. When he spotted Eugene again, years later, he sought to frighten him, teach him a lesson.'

'Interesting.' A traumatised ex-pupil could certainly provide a motive. But enough to carry out a mass shooting when his target wasn't even present? It seemed unlikely. Unless, of course, there was more to it. 'Were there any others involved?'

'No one else was mentioned in the case. I could instigate traces for Eugene Grant and Ivan Shaw if you like?' Dark said. 'See what they've got to say.'

Helen's instincts told her to go ahead – she was intrigued, and she couldn't help thinking the class reunion, the location, was significant. But... Damn, Kendrick. He still hadn't bothered to return her call, and his 'new development' was a thorn in her side. If he'd found something substantial, some hard evidence against the terror suspects, all this work, all their supposition, would be wasted.

'No. Hang fire for the moment. Let's see what counter-terror have, then review. Thanks, Rosa. You've done good work here.'

CHAPTER 29

Early evening sunshine reached into the canteen, casting frail shards of light across the room as Helen placed down a couple of coffees and slid into a chair opposite DC Dickie Wright from organised crime. She'd worked with him on an operation to reduce Hampton's auto-crime some years ago, her first operation as a newly promoted sergeant, and he'd been so supportive at the time, she'd secretly questioned who was managing who.

He beamed now, ruddy cheeks shining, as she settled herself down. 'It's good to see you again, Helen,' he said. A bull of a man, in height and width, Helen couldn't help thinking how the threads of grey in his dark hair and deep crinkles around his eyes suited him. 'It was good of you to call. It must be...' He looked down at the table. 'Four years or so since I've seen you.'

Helen returned his smile. The depth of his Scottish accent was warm and comforting. 'Yes. You went back into uniform, moved out to rural, if I remember.'

'Sure did, and it was lovely.' A faraway look flickered across his face. 'Horses escaping from fields, the odd burglary. Was hoping to see out my time there until some bigwig decided to pull trained detectives back to headquarters to block a shortage. I'm sure they could have schooled some of the new guys – there're so many bloody new recruits coming through these days.'

'You're looking well, anyway.' She resisted the temptation

to gaze at his burgeoning paunch. 'Only a year off retirement too, I hear. Bet you can't wait!'

They shared pleasantries: Dickie asked about her family and told her he'd taken up canoeing, something he wanted to indulge in during his retirement. They reminisced about the old days, gossiped about friends that had come and gone. Lovely, indulgent, light-hearted conversation with an old colleague. Time passed easily, and for the first time in days, Helen felt an ounce of the tension trickle from her shoulders.

She was finishing the last mouthful of her coffee when he said, 'Well, it's lovely to catch up and all that, but I'm guessing you haven't just asked me here on a nostalgia trip?'

Astute, as ever. 'No, you're quite right. I'm looking to pick your brains.' She hesitated a second. 'It's a tricky matter.'

Dickie raised a bushy brow. 'I'm intrigued.'

She lowered her voice. 'Can I speak in confidence?'

He nodded, leaned in closer.

Helen took her time to formulate the words. She needed to tread cautiously. News travelled fast in the police, and everyone in the station, it seemed, was aware of her son's close friendship with Davy Boyd's son. Any whiff of compromise, or hint that she was exploiting intelligence for personal reasons, and she'd be dragged straight off the case, not to mention facing the possibility of an internal inquiry. 'I hear you've moved to organised crime?'

'You heard right.'

She paused as a couple of uniformed coppers at a nearby table rose and moved out, leaving the canteen comfortably empty. 'What do you know of Chilli Franks's old operation?' she asked.

Dickie sat back, arching his eyebrows. 'Are you asking me about what he's doing from the inside? Because, if you are, from what I can gather, not a lot. He doesn't seem to wield much power locally these days. Our focus is presently on that young laddie, Gladstone.'

'Right.' That concurred with what Pemberton had gleaned.

When he'd phoned the prison liaison officer at Wakefield earlier, they'd said Chilli was keeping himself to himself. He'd had no visitors and made few phone calls – the model prisoner, by all accounts. Though she couldn't rule out Chilli having an illegal phone or cajoling one of the other inmates on the wing into making his calls.

She shared her visit to Davy Boyd with him, his association with Trent Bradshaw and Trent's presence at the shooting. When she touched on her discussion with Pemberton about Chilli's possible involvement in the shooting, Dickie's eyes bulged.

'I thought you were asking because of your son's friendship with Chilli's nephew,' he said. 'Are you telling me you think Franks might be behind the shooting? I thought it was terror-related.'

'The current theory is that it still is. Counter-terror are working on their suspects.'

'And you don't believe them.'

'Let's just say, I'm bottoming out all other possible scenarios. Which is why I need you to be particularly discreet.'

His cheeks puffed as he pushed out a long breath. 'Bloody hell.'

'What do you know about Davy Boyd?'

'We all know Davy's back, all right, but as far as I'm aware, he's not a person of interest.'

'What about Bradshaw's links with Gladstone?'

'I've not heard Trent Bradshaw's name come up in a while. I can certainly do some quiet digging. See what intel I can uncover.'

'Thanks, I'd appreciate it. Oh, and…'

'I know. Keep it to myself. Gotcha.' He placed down his mug and stood. 'Be careful, Helen. This isn't a scenario anyone will want to entertain.'

CHAPTER 30

Wednesday morning loomed grey and gloomy. Helen's head began to ache as she took her chair in the conference room beside Jenkins. Chief Constable Adams sat sombrely at the head of the table. Kendrick, sitting opposite, an A4 file arranged neatly in front of him, rolled his pen through his fingers.

'Right,' Adams said to Kendrick. 'What have you got for us?'

Kendrick placed the pen down. 'As you know, we arrested two men and one woman on Monday with conspiracy to commit acts of terrorism. What I'm going to show you now is to stay in this room.' He passed around the suspects' photos and introduced each of them individually. 'They come from different parts of the country – Manchester, Nottingham, Liverpool. They've each been living and working in Hampton for about eighteen months, two in the care industry, one as a chef in a small café on Cross Keys Trading Estate. They all moved into 42 Acorn Place, a rental property, within the last six months.'

'What do you have on them?' the chief asked.

'Connections to the neo-Nazi organisation, Order 149, and intelligence from our inside source suggesting they were planning something locally. The deeper house search uncovered several handguns and some bomb-making equipment beneath the floorboards in the bedroom. In a gap above the ceiling in the converted garage, we found pamphlets inciting violence against the gay community.'

'Handguns,' Helen repeated. 'Not an AK-47?'

'That's right. We haven't recovered the murder weapon. We're working on the basis that whoever committed the crime disposed of it soon after the event, along with their clothes.'

So, no residues of gunpowder either, Helen thought. 'Can we put them in the vicinity of Swan Street on the night in question?'

'Their phones site them in Weston, and they are all giving each other alibis for last Friday. As I'm sure you know, Weston is within walking distance of Swan Street.' He tapped one of the pictures – a tall slim woman with cropped dark hair. 'As you can see, any one of them could match the profile picture caught on the dashcam entering Victoria Car Park.'

'But nothing to actually put them at the crime scene?' Adams checked.

'Sadly, the labs found no prints on the bullets. We believe the suspects left their phones at home for fear of being tracked. These people are clever, organised.'

'And I presume they are not admitting complicity?' Jenkins said.

'No. That's quite common in these circumstances. Unless the wider group claim responsibility, and even sometimes when they do, suspects often refuse to plead guilty. Some prefer to have their day in court. Others hold back for fear of compromising future planned incidents. And this is what I really wanted to talk to you about. We believe they were put together to carry out terror attacks and, if our intelligence is correct, we understand this to be part of a larger coordinated operation.'

The chief's face clouded. 'What does that mean?'

'Rather than a small break-off faction, we now believe this cell is not only linked to the one we infiltrated in Nottingham, but also connected to several others in the Midlands and the Southeast. We further believe that there is a program of terror incidents planned, to run alongside the election campaign.'

A loose window rattled in the breeze as they each computed what this meant. 'What exactly does your person on the inside say about this "program of incidents"?' Helen asked.

'It's complicated. It's common for terror cells to align with a major cause but isolate themselves, in case they are discovered. We believe Order 149 is part of something much larger, and possibly linked to the wider neo-Nazi community. It's now our job to locate these other cells and stop them before they act.'

'The chief sat back in his chair. 'Are you telling us there are more planned shootings?'

'Again, we don't have all the details, we're still building an intelligence picture. Tracing contacts, linking cells. I can't say much more, even in present company. We're struggling to get into the suspect's devices in this case, but we did manage to break into one of the phones and identify messages with another contact, scoping out areas for potential attacks in the southeast. It seems the immediate threat here has passed.' The sound of a low-flying aeroplane filled the room. Kendrick waited for it to pass before he continued, 'We're expecting to pinpoint and shutdown more cells and make a number of arrests over the next few days,' he said. 'So, I'm asking for patience. We are on the right lines. We just need to keep the press at bay, for now.'

Helen rubbed a hand across her forehead. She appreciated the difficulties with the wider issue, but the lack of firm evidence to charge for the attack at O'Malley's was like a stone in her shoe. She was reminded of Pemberton's enquiries on the presence of AK-47s. None of his digging had uncovered any outside Hampton either. 'Do any of your suspects on Operation Spruce have military training, or experience with firearms?' she asked. 'I expect an AK-47 will take some work, learning how to load it and use it competently.'

Kendrick threw her a look. 'Not that we've established. Often terror cells do their own training, organise holidays in rural areas, sometimes abroad, to avoid attracting suspicion.

Look, I'm pretty sure we have the right people. This is a counter-terror investigation now and part of a bigger operation. Diffusing incidents, infiltrating cells, this is what we are familiar with. We deal with it all the time.'

'So, you're asking us to scale back,' Adams confirmed.

'A small team to continue identifying everyone present on Friday night would be useful, if you can manage the resources. Each one of them are potential witnesses. And we are still interested in who filmed the YouTube footage. I take it there have been no developments there?'

Helen shook her head.

'Then, yes. I'm asking you to leave it to us. We'll put out a statement saying we are confident we have those responsible. We won't be releasing identities yet, and I'd like to keep the press at bay, at least for another week or so. Until we know where we are with other arrests.'

* * *

The air felt lighter as Kendrick left the conference room, the relief palpable. They'd been told the immediate risk, for Hamptonshire at least, had diminished. Perhaps Kendrick's team were onto the right people, there certainly seemed to be information he wasn't going to share. But something about it felt wrong, askew, to Helen.

She listened to the chief and Jenkins talk eagerly about cutting the team, reallocating resources, stepping back from the press, passing the operation over. But she didn't share their excitement, and her fragile pleas to reconsider, at least until Kendrick's team had enough evidence to move forward on a murder charge, fell upon deaf ears. They didn't want to hear her suppositions about Chilli Franks – Jenkins had rather conveniently forgotten about his theory the other day – or the school reunion. As far as they were concerned, it wasn't relevant now. Though, as much as Helen tried to reconcile the claims, Kendrick's assurances about arresting the right people didn't reassure her. There was no weapon, no prints, no gunpowder residue, and no evidence to place the suspects at the scene. In fact, no actual evidence that any of the three suspects committed the attack at O'Malley's.

Once the meeting was over, she traipsed back to the incident room in a zombie-like state, her thoughts turning to her father. She'd lost count of the number of times he'd told her that a detective should trust their judgement, stick to their guns. It wasn't a gut feeling, or the hunch they talked about on television dramas, more a state of mind, based on evidence. And the more she thought about it, the more adamant she became. She couldn't leave it. Not now and not based on Kendrick's information. No. She wouldn't be doing her duty if she didn't make it her mission to exhaust all available leads before she cut ties with the investigation.

CHAPTER 31

'There you go,' Noah said, passing the newspaper across to Ashleigh. 'You made front page.'

He avoided her eyeline, his gaze flitting around the room as he passed her the paper. Worry etched into his face. The same worry, the same concern he'd voiced when he'd arrived back from his run yesterday to find she'd already written and submitted the piece to the newspaper. He'd been angry with her then. Angry she hadn't discussed it with him, hadn't considered the ramifications of her actions. What about the bereaved families? What about Cass and Nia's parents? But Ashleigh had thought it through. She'd thought about nothing else, and she'd immediately struck back, causing an atmosphere that continued to stilt their conversation. Ultimately, he was thinking of her and she knew that. But Ashleigh didn't need the overprotective partner act. She was doing the right thing here, keeping the story alive for Cass and for Nia, and she wasn't about to let anything stand in her way.

Jason, on the other hand, had been elated when she'd emailed her piece across, titled *Being a Target – The inside story of a survivor of Hampton's most gruesome crime.* Within minutes responding, *Great copy!* Another email then followed. *Just in time to catch the print run too. Well done, Ash!* She imagined him rushing around the office, his step lighter, eyes hungry, as they always were when he was working on something new. Thrilled that, with the restrictions around reporting the incident, they had an exclusive piece to offer, something different to the nationals.

Noah squeezed in beside her on the sofa, reading the article quietly over her shoulder.

When I was getting ready to go out on the town with my best friends on Friday evening, I had no idea that, by the end of the evening, two of us would be dead. My dear friends, gunned down by a ruthless killer in an act of murderous terror.

Ashleigh felt heat rise to her face. There was no fun to poke here, none of her usual humour. The article was sombre, going on to talk about her and Nia meeting Cass at the airport, getting ready at her flat, taking snapshots as they arrived at O'Malley's. A normal evening that became the subject of nightmares. She'd deliberately not talked about the arrests, the lack of information released by the police. This was a personal article to relay her experience, one which she hoped other survivors would relate to. And one which had simultaneously drained every ounce of emotion from her.

Nia Okeke and Cass Greenwell were two of the victims of the O'Malley's shooting on Friday that saw five people killed and six injured. I was one of the survivors, one of the so-called lucky ones, though I'm currently trying to work out how I'm lucky. I don't feel lucky. If I was lucky, I wouldn't have chosen that venue. If I was lucky, me and my friends wouldn't have been there at all.

Her eyes watered as she read her own words detailing the experience as they left the pub, those crucial final moments. By the time she reached the end and the part about inviting other survivors to join a support group, tears tracked her cheeks.

Jason hadn't edited any of it, not a single word. Just included a paragraph at the end about the police investigation, adding another plea for information, along with the incident room number for people to call. 'Just an extra line to keep the police on side,' he'd said when he'd messaged her yesterday evening. 'We need to make sure we're first choice when they're ready to release something fresh.' It was always a tricky relationship with the police. What to print, what not to print. The newspaper couldn't afford to alienate them, and he'd struck just the right balance.

Ashleigh was aware of Noah, rigid beside her. The argument from yesterday still lingering in the air. She sat with bated breath, waiting for his reaction. But she needn't have worried. As soon as he finished reading, he pulled her close, kissed the top of her head, then nuzzled the side of her face gently.

'You're not angry?'

'You know my feelings on the matter.' He nudged her teasingly. 'Not that you ever listen to them. No. I'm not angry. It's a beautiful piece. Heartfelt.' His voice croaked into her hair. 'Makes for difficult reading when it's someone you care about.'

'Sorry.' She snaked an arm around his back, leaned her head against his. Time ticked by. Eventually, she released herself, grabbed a couple of tissues and passed one over to him. 'I hate to agree with Jason, but it did make me feel better to get it all out.'

'I'm glad. It's good to see you looking brighter.'

'Thanks. I really feel like I can make a difference with this support group, you know? Do something useful.' She didn't mention that it also gave her the opportunity to question other survivors, dig deeper into the reasons behind the shooting. There was no sense in upsetting Noah any more than necessary.

CHAPTER 32

Helen re-entered the incident room to find Pemberton gathered around Dark's computer screen with a hoard of other colleagues.

'What is it?' she asked.

Pemberton spun round to face her. 'Ashleigh Urquhart has written a piece about the shooting for *The Herald*.' He followed her into her office. 'How did it go upstairs?'

Helen waited for him to close the door and passed on the details about their side of the inquiry winding down.

'About time if you ask me.'

'Maybe. We'll need to get everyone together, let them know.' She kick-started her laptop and input her password. 'What does the article in *The Herald* say?'

'It's an experience piece, pretty soft.' He walked behind her desk, clicked a few keys on her computer and brought it up.

Helen took her time to read it through, raising an impressed brow at the invitation to form a support group at the bottom, the reiteration of the appeal for witnesses. 'It's a good piece,' she said. 'It'll help to keep the story alive.'

Pemberton looked baffled. 'I thought the idea was that it went quiet. At least for a few days, until Kendrick's operation is out of the way.'

'He doesn't want any fresh details released, that's all.'

Pemberton stepped back and frowned. 'You don't sound happy about the situation.'

'Are you?'

His frown deepened as he slid into the chair opposite. 'That depends on what you are about to tell me.'

'I won't be convinced until counter-terror come up with some hard evidence linking the suspects with the crime. Meanwhile, I reckon we should quietly work through those leads we have outstanding. Including tracing the attendees from the school reunion, connecting them together. You up for that?' The edge of a smile played on Pemberton's lips as he gave a single nod. Good old Pemberton. He could always be relied on to make a few furtive enquiries, especially when he wanted to prove a point. Her phone rang as he retreated. It was Dickie Wright from organised crime.

'Hey,' she said. 'Any news?'

'Can you meet me beneath the old oak tree in the car park in ten minutes?' Dickie said. He was talking in a low voice, to avoid being overheard. 'There's something I want to run by you.'

'Of course. I'll see you there.'

* * *

Helen was leaning against the tree trunk, scrolling through her phone when Dickie arrived, almost twenty minutes later.

'Sorry,' he said, scuttling over. 'The DI called a last-minute meeting about reductions in the surveillance budget.' He rolled his eyes. 'Couldn't get away without drawing attention to myself.' He checked behind him as he spoke.

'Nice choice of venue.'

'It's almost lunchtime. Couldn't risk being overheard in a busy canteen.' He leaned in closer. 'We don't have much on Chilli. According to our sources, he's gone quiet.'

Helen let this sink in. Perhaps she was overthinking his involvement. Allowing a little of Jenkins's earlier paranoia to rub off. 'What about Boyd?'

'His name hasn't been flagged as a person of interest. Trent Bradshaw, on the other hand, he's a different kettle of fish.

We've had new intelligence in this week, suggesting he's moving stuff for Gladstone through his gym.'

'Supplying?'

'That's what we are being told. The boss is talking about putting a lump on his car.'

A lump – police slang for a tracker. They needed high-level clearance to put a tracker on someone's car. Considered a potential invasion of human rights, they had to have real reason to suspect he was involved in illegal activities to even contemplate the proposition. And Sofia had referred to Trent as Davy's friend...

Dickie's phone buzzed. 'I gotta go, I hope that helps a bit.' He gave her a wink. 'You didn't hear any of that from me.'

Helen stood in the car park for several minutes after Dickie left, turning over the details. While she still had her doubts about Kendrick's arrest, it was looking less likely Chilli could be involved now, and the notion was reassuring. But any relief she enjoyed was short-lived because organised crime had marked Trent Bradshaw as a major player in Hampton's gangland scene, and while the father of her son's best friend wasn't a person of interest, he was certainly associating with those who were.

She thought about how Davy had mellowed the other evening when he talked about his daughter and the difficulties she'd faced with the move. How he'd tried to dissuade Helen from talking to Robert. She didn't want to make things tough for the children, but Davy associating with an ex-con with continued criminal links cast doubt over his good intentions. She needed to put Robert right, apprise him of her involvement with Zac's uncle and what he'd been charged with. And she needed to do it soon.

CHAPTER 33

'Ivan Shaw is dead,' Dark said.

Helen lurched forward, correcting herself just in time to save spilling coffee from the mug in her hand. 'What?' She, Pemberton, Spencer, and Dark were squeezed around the desk in her small office, talking about the reunion at O'Malley's.

'I checked with DWP. He moved to Sunderland after he was released from prison, died two years later.'

'How did we not know that?' Pemberton asked.

'It wasn't on the national computer. I've spoken to Northumbria Police, it was a local issue. Apparently, Shaw worked as a warehouseman after leaving prison. He incurred a back injury there, was on sick leave when he overdosed on a mixture of tramadol and a bottle of vodka. He choked on his vomit.'

'Wait,' Helen said. 'Are you saying he committed suicide?'

'Well, that's where it gets interesting.' Dark's eyes widened. 'Northumbria Police weren't sure at first. Shaw had separated from his girlfriend a couple of months earlier, but he left no note, and he wasn't being treated for depression. The local force carried out all the usual enquiries and seized his devices to see if he'd been scouring suicide sites etc., and, get this, on his iPad they found hostile, aggressive porn, and material relating to the incel movement.'

Helen and Pemberton exchanged a loaded glance. Also known as involuntary celibates, incels were a group of predominately young, aggrieved men who believed they were entitled to a loving, sexual relationship with an attractive female but were denied this right by the behaviour of society. Mostly because too much emphasis was placed on looks and material success. In the eyes of incel supporters, all women aspired to attract the best-looking, most successful men – the alpha males – leaving those who didn't fall into this category unable to form meaningful relationships. Helen was aware the incel movement was gaining greater support within the UK, but what bothered her here, was that incel had been voiced as the motive for several mass shootings in Europe, North America, and Canada, in recent years. 'What kind of material?' she asked.

'A history of visiting incel sites. Reading incel-related news articles. He'd even downloaded Elliot Rodger's manifesto.'

They all knew the case well. In California in May 2014, Elliot Rodger placed a video on YouTube saying he wanted to punish women for rejecting him, and sexually active men because he envied them. He went on to kill six people and injure fourteen, before turning his gun on himself, and not before he'd written a 141-page document expressing his frustrations with humanity. His actions had made him an icon within the incel community.

'I presume the verdict was eventually suicide,' said Spencer.

'Yes.'

'I don't see the relevance here, then. Shaw's dead.'

'There's more.' Dark cleared her voice before she continued. 'They found several email exchanges on Shaw's iPad with a contact calling himself TopBoy. Mostly Shaw complaining his life had gone to shit, he couldn't deal with things anymore, and the one woman he trusted took him to the cleaners – a reference, I presume, to the failed relationship. In one of the emails, he said the Chads and the Staceys of this world were taking over.'

Helen stared at the young detective. Incel supporters directed their anger at successful males they referred to in online forums as Chads, and attractive women they called

Staceys. Young, successful men and women. Just the sort of people attacked at O'Malley's…

'In the emails, Shaw harked back to his school years,' Dark continued. 'He talked about how badly he was treated. Said he should have pulled a Columbine when he had the chance.'

Pemberton wiped a hand down the front of his face. In 1999, two teenage boys murdered twelve students and one teacher at Columbine High School in a mass shooting. Right here was a crystal-clear motive, and a threat, with direct links to those targeted.

'Did Northumbria ever identify this TopBoy?' Helen asked.

Dark shook her head. 'They tried, but the contact was untraceable. Shaw was dead. The file was referred to a coroner who recorded a verdict of suicide. Case closed.'

'An interest in the incel movement isn't a crime as such,' Spencer said. 'Even if, in his warped mind, Shaw did feel his treatment at school or college gave him a motive for the attack, he's dead anyway. It couldn't have been him.'

Pemberton held his gaze. 'Maybe someone else carried out his wishes.'

'He'd need to have formed a cast-iron bond with someone for them to go to these lengths on his behalf,' Spencer added, almost to himself.

Incel forums were notoriously secretive, often accessed through the encrypted dark web. Identifying Shaw's online peers wouldn't be easy. 'Right,' Helen said. 'We need to find out as much about the late Ivan Shaw's associations as possible. We can't rule out friends, family, or work colleagues he might have been close to.' She looked across at Dark and Spencer. 'I'd like you two to take a trip up to Northumbria. Speak to the officer on the case, see how far they went to track down this TopBoy. Also, speak with Shaw's former work colleagues, friends, neighbours, and his ex-girlfriend. See what you can find out. Grab a hotel if you need to, I'll cover expenses.'

'I'm happy to leave tonight,' Dark said.

Spencer gave a half-hearted nod. 'Might as well hit the ground running in the morning.'

'Great, thanks.' She turned to Pemberton. 'Find out what family Shaw has and where they are based, will you? And which prison he served at, what his record was like and whether any of his cellmates are still there. If this is someone who was close to Shaw, we need to find them.' She paused a second. 'What do we know about the ex-school student he took a pop at?' she said to Dark.

'I went through Eugene Grant's social media,' Dark said, 'and traced him to a company called Chalks in Wellington, New Zealand. It's a bar and night club. Eugene was on his day off, but they gave me his number. He was sleeping when I called. He's agreed to do a Skype interview with us tomorrow morning at 7 am our time. He'll just be finishing his shift then.'

'Okay. The sergeant and I will take that interview,' Helen said. Then she leaned forward, cautiously adding, 'In view of the changes in the investigation, we'll keep this to ourselves for now. Everyone reports to me and me only. I don't want this going wider until we have something definitive to share.'

CHAPTER 34

The babble of the television filtered through to the hall as Helen arrived home that evening. She elbowed the door closed and called out, 'Hello!', dropping her bags at her feet. No one answered. Not surprising really, her boys were usually engrossed in a film, diverted by a game on their console, or had their headphones in, listening to music. She often wondered if they'd notice if she walked through the house naked these days.

She kicked off her shoes, shed her jacket and wandered into the front room. Matthew was laid out on the sofa, rewatching a *Lord of the Rings* battle scene on the television. He looked so young lying there, yet he was only a handful of years away from the victims in Operation Spruce. Helen's chest tightened at the thought.

'Hey,' she said. 'Didn't you hear me come in?'

He jerked away as she leaned down and tried to ruffle his hair. After shaving his head last year, a gesture to state his independence, it was good to see the edges of thick curls now growing back. Not that she'd tell him that.

'What? No, sorry.' He turned back to the screen.

'Where's your gran?' Helen asked.

'She's gone to Sheila's to see reruns of Downton Abbey.'

'Ah.' It was good to see her mother getting out and about more now the boys were older. 'So,' Helen said, leaning against the doorframe, 'GCSE results next week.'

Matthew flicked her a glance, nodded, and turned back to

the screen. GCSEs. It didn't seem five minutes ago that he'd told her he wanted to follow in his father's footsteps, join the Air Force and fly planes for a living. After losing her husband, John, in a helicopter crash, the very thought of her eldest son in the sky sucked the air from her lungs. Which is why she was thankful he would be staying on at school, taking his A levels first – anything to delay the inevitable.

'Excited?' she asked. 'Nervous?'

He glanced up at her. 'Not thought about it.' His usual cool response. Matthew took after his father and sailed through exams, without stress.

At the bottom of the stairs, she stole herself a second. Gripping the wooden banister hard, before continuing up to her youngest's room. She wasn't looking forward to the next conversation at all.

Robert was lying on his side on his bed, absorbed in his phone screen when she entered his bedroom. 'Hello, son.'

He looked up, passed her a greeting. Curling back his legs to make space for her to perch on the end. 'Everything all right?' he said, pressing pause on his phone.

'Fine. Good day?'

He lifted a single shoulder, let it drop. 'Okay. Bowled three out in cricket practice.'

A warm rush of pride. Unlike Matthew, Robert struggled academically but was a whizz at sports. He'd only taken up cricket in the last year and had already been selected to play for the school. 'That's great news!' Helen said. 'Your bowling's really coming on.' She elbowed his knees. 'Ian Botham, eat your heart out.'

'Who's that?'

Helen laughed to herself. Feeling her age as she told him about her father's favourite cricketer from the 1980s. 'Listen, there is something I need to talk to you about,' she said.

The way he looked up at her with expectant eyes plucked a heartstring. Suddenly, he was five again and waiting for her to tell him about a forthcoming holiday, a picnic, or a trip to the beach. Though this was nowhere near as pleasant. She swallowed her disappointment. 'I've been called to give evidence in court next month,' she said. Robert stared back at her, impassive. 'I'll be giving evidence at the trial of Stephen Franks, or Chilli as he's better known. Zac's uncle.' Recognition spread like a stain across Robert's face. 'I'm just telling you because you might hear it mentioned in the news, at school, or maybe at Zac's. I wanted you to hear it from me first.'

'What did he do?'

This was it. The moment when she should tell him everything. But... How could she? Zac was Robert's best buddy. She'd never seen him so close with anyone and, at fourteen, friends were not only important, they were revered. How could she possibly taint their friendship by telling her son that Zac's uncle was responsible for the injuries she'd sustained months earlier? That he'd threatened her father before her, his grandfather, and held a vendetta against their family for years? She'd worked hard to protect her boys, to keep this from them, adamant they shouldn't grow up in the shadow of Chilli's threats. Plus, it was impossible to share a lifetime of information in one conversation. She also had the prospect of Davy and his criminal associations pressing down on her, though she would be breaking every rule in the book, not to mention hanging a colleague out to dry if she shared that. No. Maybe she should keep it light, for now. Give the boy time. They could always discuss the particulars later when he'd let it sink in. 'There are a number of criminal charges,' she said. 'Illegal importation of firearms, possession with intent to supply cocaine. We found guns, drugs in his warehouse.'

Robert gave a backwards nod, his eyes still wide. It was difficult to read him.

'I was the officer in the case,' she said. She gave him a moment to digest. 'Is there anything you'd like to ask me?'

He shook his head.

'Okay. I just wanted you to know. We can talk more about it later.' She leaned over, gave him a hug. 'Oh, I wouldn't mention this to Zac, if I was you,' she said as she released him.

'Why?'

'He might feel uncomfortable. Chilli is his uncle, after all.'

As soon as Helen closed the door behind her, she leaned against it, pressing the back of her head against the wood, replaying the conversation in her mind. That had gone far better than she'd anticipated. Hadn't it?

CHAPTER 35

'This is nice,' Noah said.

Ashleigh looked across the table at him and gave a half-smile. The first anniversary of their engagement. It was hard to believe a year had passed since Noah had knelt on one knee in the middle of a packed Bamboo Garden, the Chinese restaurant at the top of Hampton High Street. She'd just finished her sesame prawn toast, was waiting for the waiter to clear their plates in readiness for the main course, when Noah had surprised her by brandishing his late grandmother's diamond solitaire ring.

She spooned the last mouthful of lemon tart into her mouth and sat back, her ring glistening in the low lighting as she rubbed her stomach. 'I'm beat,' she said. 'That dessert was lovely, thank you.'

Noah laughed. 'Sainsbury's own. Not like your Carbonara with a difference. What was that you grated on the top?'

'Nutmeg. I pinched the idea from Nigella.' She looked across the table, past the tea light burning in the saucer, and into the eyes of her easy-going fiancé as he laughed. When he'd asked this morning what she wanted to do to mark the occasion, she'd said, 'Why don't I cook something nice for us? Make a change.' Only it wasn't a change. They'd stayed in since she'd arrived home from hospital on Sunday, sitting with plates on their laps, watching the latest Netflix movies, interspersed with sports and news. Celebrating was the last thing she felt like doing right now, but she didn't want to disappoint Noah. And it was okay. She'd unfolded the table in the corner of their living room this evening and made it special, hadn't she?

'To us,' Noah said, raising his glass.

Ashleigh chinked her glass against his and smiled again.

'So, what does the weekend hold?' he asked.

'Mum's arriving on Saturday morning,' she said, placing down her glass and smoothing a crease in her skirt. 'And I've got the support group to organise.' The emails had been pouring in since her article had gone live that morning – twenty-four at last count. Twenty-four survivors keen to join her group. It warmed her heart to be doing something useful.

'I'm proud of you,' Noah said. 'How you're handling all of this. It can't be easy.' His phone buzzed. He checked the message, clicked it off. 'All Saints Church are organising a candlelit vigil outside O'Malley's to remember the victims this Friday evening. Maybe we should go along?'

Ashleigh gulped her drink. The wine was tangy, acidic on her tongue. 'We'll see.' A part of her wanted to go. She should pay her respects. She owed it to her friends, to all the victims. Though the notion of being there again, outside the pub, stuck in a crowd, unable to get away, induced a fresh wave of nausea.

'You have to go out sometime, Ash.'

The fact that her thoughts were so transparent made her reel. 'I know, and I will.' Noah's phone buzzed again, and she watched him read the message, then fidget awkwardly in his chair.

'Sorry, it's only Ellis,' he said. 'He's texting me about the Tyson Fury fight.'

'Oh, is that tonight?'

'Yeah. It's okay. I can always catch up another time.'

'You should have said.' Noah's family were big fans of Fury. Noah's father and brother, Ellis, stayed up until all hours watching the fights together, and he usually joined them.

'It's our anniversary.'

'We've been together all week. We can celebrate more tomorrow. You don't want to miss it.'

He scratched his ear. 'It's all right, really.'

'No, Noah. It's not fair. Listen, you've been great taking time off work this week, but I am okay. I don't want you to miss the fight. It's not the same on catch up, someone's bound to tell you the result.'

'Honestly, Ash. I don't mind missing it.'

Ashleigh leaned forward and collected the bowls. 'Yes, you do. Come on. You're going, I insist.' She placed the bowls down and stood. 'Then you can tell me all about it tomorrow.' Ashleigh wasn't the faintest bit interested in boxing, but at least they'd have something different to talk about. 'Please,' she implored.

Noah looked uncertain. 'Are you sure you'll be all right?'

'Of course. It'll give me a chance to have a bath, get an early night, catch up on some sleep.'

His face brightened. 'Okay. If you're certain?'

'Go on. Go now, before you change your mind.' She herded him out of the room, collected the crockery and took it into the kitchen. She was packing the dishwasher when he reappeared with a rucksack over his shoulder.

'Are you positive about this?' he asked.

Ashleigh pulled him close and kissed him long and hard.

'If you put it like that, I think I'll stay.'

She chuckled. 'Go. I'll see you in the morning.' She followed him out to the hall, kissed him again then waited for him to leave and bolted the door after him.

Ashleigh took her time to wipe down the table and refold it in the corner, then ran herself a hot bath. Closing her eyes, relishing the soak, enjoying the peace of having the flat back to herself. By the time she crashed on the sofa in her pyjamas with a mug of hot chocolate, it was almost 10 pm. Soft footfalls sounded as Sadhika moved around next door. The dull beat of Johnny's music rose from below. The familiar, comforting sounds of her neighbours. A reminder she was only a wall or a floor away from the presence of others.

She reached down, lifted her laptop from the floor beside the sofa where it was plugged in, charging. The response to the article had far outweighed her expectations. Heart-warming, upbeat messages, thanking her for her generous invitation. She needed to decide how to set up an online support group for everyone. Facebook or WhatsApp, or something else? Initially, she'd started by arranging a Zoom meeting tomorrow evening, to give people the choice.

She pulled out the charging lead and switched on her laptop, waiting for the screen to light. Since the initial kernel of an idea yesterday, the concept of talking to survivors, like her, had grown and blossomed in her mind. Lifting her spirits, strengthening her heart with each Zoom invitation she sent. These were the first steps to possibly discovering more about the shooting, the first steps to getting her life back on course.

She logged into her email. Five new ones had arrived while she was having dinner. She worked her way through the first two, posting a 'welcome' reply, and including the invitation for the online meeting. She opened the third, titled Important – Support Needed, and froze.

WARNING – DO NOT FORWARD THIS EMAIL TO ANYONE, OR SHARE IT WITH THE POLICE. I WILL KNOW IF YOU DO!!!

Dear Ashleigh,

I'm not sure how to open this email, I'm not as good with words as you are, so I'll just be blunt and say it. I murdered those people last Friday evening. I was the shooter, the marksman, who fired thirty rounds at O'Malley's.

Please don't delete this email. I'm telling the truth, and I'm reaching out to you for a reason. You see, you and I can help each other. I've been following your column, The Insider, for some time. Like me, you aim to highlight important issues. Issues that affect people in our society, the way we live.

I can shine a light on the most serious issue you've ever reported – the shooting. If you become my voice and share it in your newspaper, I'll tell you why I killed those people. You see, the police have got it all wrong. It's time to put the record straight.

The question is, are you willing to help?

I repeat, do not pass this email to the police. If you do, you will regret it and more will die.

No sign-off. No signature. The Hotmail address an unrecognisable mismatch of letters and numbers. Ashleigh snapped her laptop closed and pushed it away. Scooting back to the other end of the sofa, away from it, as if it were about to explode. All she could hear was the sound of her blood rushing through her ears and her heart pounding in her chest. If the police had the killers in custody, then who the hell was this?

CHAPTER 36

The sound of the door buzzer rang through Ashleigh's flat.

The email had sent her into a tailspin – she couldn't think of what to do, who to speak with first. But of one thing, she was sure – she didn't want to be alone. She'd called Noah, told him about the message, and immediately, his voice had turned grave. He'd told her to stay in the flat, not to answer the door until he got there. But… A glance at the clock. That was only ten minutes ago. His parents lived on the other side of town; he couldn't possibly have got there yet. Her mind whirled. She'd been spooked, and now she felt on edge. Vulnerable. Was it possible the email sender knew where she lived?

The buzzer sounded again. Ashleigh approached the intercom gingerly, her head pounding.

Her mobile trilled. She answered on the first ring. Noah.

'Ash, I'm downstairs. Let me in.'

She couldn't respond. Instead, she pressed the button to release the lock on the main entrance and stood by her front door. Listening to footsteps rush up the stairs.

A single knock. 'It's me.'

Ashleigh opened the door, waited for Noah to come in, then locked the door behind him, her hand trembling as she drew the bolt across. 'Where's your house key?'

'I didn't take it, I need to get another keyring.' She vaguely recalled his comments about the broken keyring the other day. She turned, looked into his eyes. And that's when the tears started, and she crumpled into his embrace.

God, she hated this. The vulnerable woman falling into the man's arms. There was a time when she'd regarded herself as staunchly independent. When her parents left, she prided herself in finding them both a flat, arranging the move. She advocated for equality in her column whenever the opportunity arose, was known for celebrating the achievements of local women. In the past, if a situation like this had arisen, she'd have called Nia. Cass too, if she'd been nearby.

Though this was different from anything she'd ever faced before.

'Oh, Ash.'

His hold was warm, comforting. She wasn't sure how long they stood there. Her head buried in Noah's bony shoulder, dampening his shirt with her tears. Him stroking her back, telling her she was safe.

Slowly, as her breaths started to even, she pulled back. Blowing her nose on the tissue he handed her, wiping her eyes. 'How did you get here so quickly?' she asked.

'There was a hold-up, an accident on the ring road. I'd only just started moving again when you called.'

She'd usually ask him about it, check everyone was okay, or maybe even google the news, but she didn't have the capacity to think about a road traffic accident now. She led him into the front room, to her laptop on the sofa.

Noah slid onto the sofa beside her, waited patiently for her to reopen her emails and devoured the words. The enormity of it filled the room, suffocating her as she watched the expression on his face tighten. 'You need to call the police,' he said.

'Yes.' She was staring into space. Of course she did.

He glanced at her askance. 'What's stopping you?'

'I don't know. You are right. It's just… the police aren't releasing any information. The media aren't even allowed to print anything about the suspects they have in custody. Then I get this. Don't you think it's odd?'

'It's probably some weirdo, trying to scare you.'

'What if it isn't? What if the police have arrested the wrong people?'

'Oh, Ash. I don't know what to think. But you can't possibly sit on this, and you can't ignore it either.' He stared at her, concern growing behind his eyes. 'You're not thinking of responding…'

'No!'

'Or sharing it in the newspaper.'

Ashleigh couldn't deny the thought had occurred to her. Frustration with the investigation was eating away at her in bite-sized chunks. It would certainly grab readers' attention. Make them think. Possibly even bring in new information. But she had to be practical. 'If this is genuine, I really should show it to the police first,' she said, as much as it galled her.

'Then call them.'

'It says, "Do not call the police." It's like a warning. Do you think I'm in danger?'

'I don't know, Ash. It's an email asking for help.'

'And if I refuse?'

'Hey, listen.' He stretched an arm around her shoulder, pulled her close. 'It's probably just some idiot messing around. The detective who was here the other day. Do you still have her card?'

Ash gave a juddered nod.

'Right. I'll call her now.'

CHAPTER 37

Half an hour later, Helen was sitting in Ashleigh's living room, the streetlight from outside bleeding through the curtains as she read the email.

She'd been having a final cup of tea, getting ready for an early night when Noah called and, as soon as he told her about the email, her senses had switched to hyper-alert. The suspects were still in custody; the press had gone quiet after Kendrick's statement reassuring the public yesterday. Apart from Ashleigh's personal piece, the media were adhering to the enforced silence, yet someone wanted to keep the shooting firmly at the forefront of the news.

She finished the message, read it through again, then looked up at the two pairs of eyes boring into her from the sofa. Aside from the obvious, something about the message bothered her but she couldn't put her finger on what it was. 'I take it this is the only message you've received?' she asked Ashleigh. 'There's been nothing else via your phone or social media?'

Ashleigh shook her head. The poor woman looked white with worry.

'I don't think you should worry unduly. It could be someone seeking attention, a harmless crank who read your article and decided to reach out. It's not unusual in a case like this. I'm sure, working for the newspaper, you get your fair share of them.' She tried to reassure Ashleigh, though she couldn't ignore the dull beat in her head. If Kendrick didn't have the right people in custody, then whoever it was needed a voice, and the threat of more killings filled her with disquiet.

'That's what I said,' Noah added.

'What if it isn't?' Ashleigh asked. 'Are you positive you have the correct people in custody?'

Helen wasn't sure how to answer this. 'This is a counter-terror unit investigation, but I've been assured–'

'Am I in danger?'

'There's nothing here to suggest you are,' Helen said, ignoring the interruption. She was desperately trying to work out what it was that was niggling her. 'It's an email seeking attention. It could be a one-off, particularly since you've received nothing through other channels.'

She watched the woman's shoulders drop a notch, looked back at the message, and reread the first few lines. And then she saw it. '… thirty rounds'. A tremor of unease flushed through her. They'd been careful not to share details of the weapon or the number of shots fired, but she was pretty sure the discarded shells indicated thirty casings had been found.

Only the killer and investigation team knew this.

'What happens next?'

Ashleigh's words dragged her back to the present. 'You don't reply, don't engage at all,' she said, careful to keep her face impassive. 'You've done the right thing by calling me. I'll have an expert examine it. We may be able to trace the sender. In the meantime, try not to worry, and I cannot stress this enough, keep this to yourself. It could be something and nothing, we don't want to send your readers into a panic.'

* * *

'It's a hoax, it's got to be,' Kendrick said.

Back at headquarters, Helen stared through the gaps in her blinds into the dark incident room beyond. It was almost midnight. Moonlight crept in through the window behind her, combining with the screen of her laptop to light her office in a soft glow. She'd asked Ashleigh to forward the message to her and, as soon as she'd left, copied in Kendrick and Jenkins who were now on a conference call.

'You can't be sure of that.' Helen rolled her shoulders. The pressure of the investigation, the unanswered questions, bore down heavily on her.

'Incidents like this bring out idiots like moths to a night lamp. It was only a few days ago I was pulled out of bed because a self-confessed shooter had walked into your local station, for Christ's sake!'

He was right, of course. William Noble's Oscar-winning performance at Cross Keys had resulted in him being cautioned about wasting police time and sent on his way. Helen couldn't understand the motives of time wasters who falsely presented themselves as guilty in murder cases, but the fact remained that they were obliged to pursue any reasonable line of enquiry. 'Could this be somebody linked to your suspects, their cell, or terrorist organisation? Maybe they're finally ready to share their message.'

'They wouldn't do it this way,' Kendrick said dismissively. 'They'd upload a video to a social media channel, tag in the newsgroups to instantly reach a wider audience.'

'Whoever wrote this knew exactly how many rounds had been fired,' Helen said. She'd taken her time, done her homework, reread the ballistics report as soon as she'd arrived at headquarters, to double-check. 'The shells indicate thirty bullets were fired. That information hasn't been released.'

'The average AK-47 magazine holds thirty rounds.'

'We haven't released that it was an AK-47.'

'It'll be the same for other semi-automatics. Anyone could look at the number of bullet holes in the front of O'Malley's and speculate the shooter emptied their magazine.' The line quietened a second. 'It's either that or the information about the weapon's been leaked,' Kendrick added quietly.

'What?' Helen could barely believe her ears. 'If it was

leaked, we'd expect it to be announced somewhere. It hasn't been mentioned in the press.'

'It could have been leaked online. The press aren't likely to print it, they're adhering to our request for silence. Anyone else could upload material.'

Helen clenched her teeth. This was the biggest case Hampton Force had worked on during her police career, and in conjunction with an external unit. The more people involved in a case, the higher the risk of something slipping through. She knew that. But... this was getting ridiculous. 'Surely we'd have heard about it?' she said.

'Let's focus on what we have,' Jenkins said. 'How is the young columnist?'

'Shaken,' Helen said. 'Understandably so. I've reassured her for now. Asked her to keep this to herself until we've looked into it. Given her the usual safeguarding advice about not going out alone, keeping her phone with her. I've flagged her phone number with control room, should she have any problems, given her my card and told her to call me if she receives anything further.'

'Good.' The relief in his voice was palpable.

Helen scratched the back of her head. She was tempted to mention her surreptitious enquiries, the revelation about Shaw's connections with the incel network, talk about her detectives in Northumbria. But all she had were suppositions about a dead man. She didn't even have a suspect. She needed firm evidence before she could challenge Kendrick. 'The point is, what are we going to do about it? The email needs to be investigated urgently by a digital media investigator, an expert, to track down the source.'

'Perhaps counter-terror can send us someone?' Jenkins asked.

Hampton had their own DMIs, but clearly, Jenkins wasn't about to let Kendrick off the hook that easily.

The line crackled. 'Of course,' Kendrick said. 'I'll send you Jack Valentine, he lives over your way. He's only been with us eight months and he's already helped us infiltrate the devices for the cell in Nottingham and get into one of the suspect's phones. If anyone can trace the sender, he can. We'll ask him to sweep the social media channels too, see what has been shared online. I'll get him to report to you first thing in the morning.'

'In the morning!' Helen scoffed.

'Yes.' Kendrick's voice was tight. 'I really don't think this is anything to worry about.'

'Okay,' Jenkins said before Helen could object. 'It's your investigation. Your decision. Anything else we need to know? Any updates on the inquiry?'

'Nothing I can share at the moment.'

'Right, that's sorted then,' Jenkins said. 'I'll catch up with you both tomorrow.' The line disconnected.

Helen swivelled in her chair and looked out at the empty car park. It was day six. No one shared her sense of urgency because Kendrick was convinced he had charged those responsible. But, if she was right and the killer was still at large, it made sense for them to resurface to get their message out there. And the email left her with a great sense of foreboding.

CHAPTER 38

The following morning, Ashleigh woke to the sound of distant voices. Blinking at the bright day streaming into her front room, she hauled herself forward. She'd been lying on the sofa wearing only Noah's black Nike T-shirt, and her legs were bone cold.

She reached up, stretched out her back and rubbed her calves, her gaze resting on a creased throw pooled on the floor beside her. It must have slipped off when she was sleeping.

Where was Noah? She was about to look for him when she heard voices again. Louder this time, coming from outside. She put on her glasses.

At the window, she could see a commotion further up the road. People huddled together on the tarmac. Shocked, frightened faces, crowded around something. Ashleigh craned her neck, but the angle was tight, and she could only see the edge of the crowd, not the subject of their attention. A paramedic jogged across the park to join them.

Then she glimpsed it. A blue running jacket lying at the side of the road. Blue with yellow piping. She knew that jacket.

'Noah!' Ashleigh rushed into the bedroom, then checked the bathroom and the kitchen, a feeling of dread crashing through her. He must have woken early, gone for a run. Had he been involved in an accident? No! Not her sweet, kind Noah. She dashed back to the window, tried to prise it open, but however much she tried the catch was stiff and it wouldn't move.

She ran to the bedroom, grabbed a pair of joggers, her fingernails snagging the thin fabric as she pulled them on. In the hallway, she slipped her feet into her trainers, leaving the laces untied.

She was almost at the door, gripping the handle, when a wave of nausea hit her. Blurring her vision. Stopping her in her tracks.

Heat rose to her face. Her feet were unsteady. Noah needed her. She couldn't have a panic attack now.

She forced herself to breathe. Big, deep breaths. She had to beat this. But when she tried to lift a foot, it felt like it was immersed in glue.

Ashleigh wavered. Holding the handle tight. She could see the front door of Sadhika's flat in front of her. She swallowed. Lifted her foot another inch, swayed. Felt the movement of the air as she lunged forward. And again. All happening in slow motion, as if she was underwater. She was almost through the doorway and onto the landing when she lost her balance. And felt herself tumble, down, down, down. Onto the floor with a crash.

'Ash!'

A tugging sensation, like an anchor being dragged from the depths of the ocean. She pulled away from it, then jumped. Opening her eyes to find Noah's face in hers, she jumped again.

Noah jolted back. 'Sorry, I didn't mean to scare you.'

Ashleigh stared at him, then glanced around. She was in their bedroom. Noah beside her. It was a dream. It was only a dream. Her head hurt, her teeth ached, but… relief flooded her bones. He was safe.

She grabbed him, held him tightly. Hot tears burning her eyes.

'Hey!' he said, stroking her hair.

Ashleigh pulled back and tossed her head towards the clock on her bedside table – 10 am. She'd barely slept last night, watching hour after hour pass, listening out for cars passing on the main road nearby. The hoot of an owl, its mate calling back. The email racing around her head like a Formula One racing car. Who sent the message? What if the police couldn't trace them? What did they want? So many questions.

The detective said they would investigate, she'd call her back today with an update, but the presence of it brought back the images with gusto. The blood trickling through the gutter. The slump of the crowd. Losing Nia. And when sleep finally arrived, it had brought the dream in all its vivid richness, leaving her discombobulated. She rubbed her dry eyes.

'Are you okay, Ash? You were crying out.'

'I'm sorry. It was just a bad dream.' She hauled herself up, grabbed the glass of water on her bedside table and took a huge gulp, relishing the cold liquid, alerting her senses.

Noah's face crumpled in concern. 'Do you want to tell me about it?'

She shook her head. She didn't want to talk about it. She wanted it to go away, forever. She checked her phone. More emails had arrived overnight. More Zoom invitations she needed to send. The Zoom meeting! The detective said they should keep the email to themselves for now, alert no one until they'd had a chance to investigate, but how could she?

'Maybe you ought to see your doctor,' Noah said gently, smoothing her hair away from her face. 'Get something to help. You've been through so much.'

'I'll be fine,' she said, still staring at her phone. The emails were from Alannah Joyce, Ruth Bailey, and Harriet Devonport. No hint of the sender claiming to be the shooter. Thank God.

'Do you think you should go ahead with the meeting tonight? I mean, after yesterday evening.'

He had a point. The raison d'être for this group was to voice feelings and emotions with people who'd been through a shared experience, yet she'd have to be guarded. Careful with what she said, how she acted. 'I have to,' she said. 'These people are relying on me. I can't let them down.'

Noah bit his lip. 'Can I do anything to help?'

'A cup of tea. Your mum seems to reckon tea solves everything.' *She bloody wished it did.*

He snorted, pulled back the bedclothes and climbed out of bed. Seconds later, she heard his bare feet slap the kitchen floor. Mugs chinked together as he lifted them from the dishwasher. The dream. She couldn't get to Noah when he needed her. Even now, seven days after the shooting, the very idea of leaving the flat made her dizzy. She was usually so headstrong, so organised. It was always her that booked the table when she and Noah went out to dinner. Her that arranged the flights, the accommodation when they went on holiday. She hated this feeling of being out of control.

Her phone rang. 'Zuri' flashed up on the screen. Zuri, Nia's mother. Ashleigh's chest tightened. Zuri had telephoned on Sunday evening to enquire after Ashleigh, and they'd sobbed down the line together, immersed in their joint grief. Cass's mother had always been highly strung, distant, but Zuri oozed warmth, and with both Cass and Ashleigh's parents working full-time when they were young and Zuri being a stay-at-home mum, the girls had spent most of their formative years at Nia's house. Lounging on her sofas, staying for tea, squeezing into Nia's tiny bedroom for sleepovers. Zuri was easy. She didn't expect the messy pile of shoes beside the front door to be lined neatly, didn't worry that the sound of young voices drowned out the television at full volume. Her front door was always open, her home full of the spices of her beloved Somalian dishes, the deep gurgle of her laugh. Zuri was everyone's mum, and it was comforting that, even in the wake of her own daughter's death, she'd found the strength, the consideration to reach out.

That was before her piece in the newspaper. Ashleigh watched the phone dance across the surface, her palms dampening as Noah's concern about the article resurfaced. Perhaps she should have checked with others before she filed her copy. The last thing she wanted to do was to upset Nia's mother.

A lump gathered in her throat as she reached across and answered.

'Hello, darling.' Zuri's voice, usually deep and smooth like chocolate, was clipped. 'How are you doing?'

'I'm okay.' But she didn't feel okay. The nervous tension was too much, and the lump in her throat dissolved into a choke.

But she needn't have worried. 'Don't cry,' Zuri said. 'I read your article in the newspaper. Nia would have been proud.'

A strangled sob escaped. Ashleigh pressed a hand to her mouth. Despite the relief, she couldn't stall the tears tumbling down her cheeks.

'Is Noah with you?'

'Yes.'

'Good. That's good. Listen, are you up to visitors? I need to come and see you.'

Ashleigh squeezed out another juddered 'yes'.

'Tomorrow morning. Ten o'clock?'

Ashleigh didn't have the strength to ask why. She could barely whimper her agreement as the woman told her to take care of herself. 'I'll leave you now. See you tomorrow, we can discuss things then.'

As soon as Ashleigh put down the phone, questions started dropping into her head. Why did Nia's mother want to see her? Did she also have concerns about the arrest? Relief washed through her. And fear too... Fear of whether the police had the right people in custody. Fear of the email she couldn't tell anyone about.

Everything was winding around, tangling together in her chest like a ball of wool she couldn't find the end of.

The support group was expecting her to lead the Zoom meeting this evening, Nia's mother was visiting in the morning, her own mother was coming over at the weekend, and she felt sick to the pit of her stomach. She desperately hoped there was a new development on the investigation today because, if there wasn't, she couldn't conceive how she was going to face any of them.

CHAPTER 39

'Thanks for joining us,' Helen said. 'I appreciate this isn't easy given the time differences.' She stared at the bronzed face of Eugene Grant on the screen, winging its way over from New Zealand, and sighed. It was 7 am, Thursday. Seven days after the shooting. She tapped her toe silently beneath the desk. She'd barely slept last night, the email to Ashleigh Urquhart crawling around inside her head like an army of ants trying to find a way out. Kendrick's DMI was due to arrive shortly. Her priority was to trace the source of the email, verify who they were. If Kendrick was right and it was a hoax, the immediate danger would be alleviated. But with Ashleigh's part in the reunion and Shaw's obvious motive, she couldn't help wondering if it all linked together.

'How can I help you?' Eugene said. His cheek twitched. With his sky-blue eyes and floppy blond hair, he looked every inch the surfer dude. Before Helen could answer, he launched into, 'Are you investigating the shooting over there? Bloody awful, isn't it? I couldn't believe it when I saw it on the news. In my hometown as well! Some of those people were from my class at school.'

'Terrible,' Helen said, sidestepping the question. 'I realise it must be a distressing time for you.'

'You can say that again. It's been all over the news here. If I was still living in Hampton, it could have been me.'

He continued about how he used to go to O'Malley's regularly before he moved to New Zealand, how he used to park at Victoria Car Park when he went to the cinema, how he was relieved they'd caught the guilty parties. Helen let him talk it out. He was obviously still in shock and needed to get things off his chest.

'Actually,' she said when he finally paused, 'we're looking at a case you were involved in some years ago.' She passed on the details.

Eugene frowned. 'Why're you looking at that? Ivan pleaded guilty. I thought it was done and dusted.'

'We are interested in Mr Shaw about another matter,' she said carefully.

'What other matter?'

He doesn't know Shaw's dead. Helen and Pemberton traded glances. *Interesting.* Clearly, Ashleigh Urquhart didn't either, or Eleanor, the woman who organised the reunions, otherwise they would have mentioned it.

'I'm afraid I can't comment on the details.'

'Well, I can't say I'm surprised. He's a psycho.'

'What makes you say that?'

'He chased me down in my car and held a gun in my face. I'd say that's a pretty good description of a psycho, wouldn't you?'

Helen ignored the question. 'He told his barrister he was bullied, teased at school.'

'Not by me. I mean, I might have made the odd remark, the dude was odd, but I never laid a finger on him. And neither did anyone else. He was a loner, kept himself to himself. Honestly, most of us thought he was a weirdo.'

Helen resisted the temptation to roll her eyes at Eugene's narrow definition of bullying. 'In what way?'

'Well, it's not natural to go out at night with your air rifle, shooting flowers off gravestones.'

Helen felt Pemberton shift beside her. 'He did that?'

'Yup. Me and the guys spotted him one night walking back from town. We'd just finished our A levels.'

'Did you speak with him?'

'Yeah. We called him a freak. Then gave him a very wide berth.' He stretched out the word 'very'.

Helen stilled her foot and edged forward. 'Would you be happy to talk me through your recollection of the night of the road rage incident again?' If Ivan Shaw was behind the preparation for this incident, she needed to slip into his shoes, understand where he was coming from.

'Why? I gave a statement at the time.'

'If you could go through the evening again in detail, it would be most helpful.'

A beat passed. Silence hovered between them. Eventually, Eugene glanced at the ceiling, eyes darting from side to side, trying to retrieve the memory from the vaults of his brain. 'Well, it was a summer's evening,' he said, turning back to the screen. 'I was working behind the bar at Memington Hall, the hotel outside town. I hadn't been feeling well all day. Bit of a hangover, to be honest, but I didn't want to tell my boss that, so I told him I must have caught a bug. He let me off early. About eightish, I think. I drove back to Hampton past Blackwell Wood. The road was empty. I'd just joined the ring road when I saw the Audi behind me. I didn't pay attention at first, thought it was some idiot driving too close. Then I had to break suddenly, there was a bit of cardboard or something in the road, and the driver behind started flashing his lights.' Eugene sat forward. 'I was in my mum's car. I pulled over, thought maybe a brake light had gone. The car behind me stopped too. We both climbed out. And that's when I saw the gun.'

'Did you recognise Ivan?'

'Not at first. His hair was longer, his face thinner. I hadn't seen him in years and, like I said, I didn't pay much attention to him back then.'

'What happened next?'

'He spouted some stuff about me not being the tough guy now. Said I was full of myself, always showing off with a different girl.' He rolled his eyes. 'He said I needed to be taken down a notch.'

'What did you say?'

'Not much. I was shit-scared, to be honest. His eyes were all weird and stuff. I thought it was a real gun. It was only when another vehicle approached that he waved the gun at me one more time, climbed into his car and drove off. Just like that.'

'He didn't say anything else?'

'Oh, some stuff about a girl at Year Eleven prom.'

'What girl?'

'That's just it. I don't remember much about Year Eleven prom. Me and the boys, we'd snuck in our dads' hip flasks. I spent most of the evening bladdered.'

'So, you have no idea who he was talking about?'

'I talked it through with mates afterwards. They reckoned there was some girl he'd taken a shine to at prom. A friend of a friend, from a different school. No one we knew. Apparently, I got off with her.' He gave a conceited shrug. 'Not that I remember much.'

'Did you tell the police about the girl at the time?'

'No, it was nothing. I didn't even know her name.' He shrugged again. 'Anyway, there was no point. He confessed.'

'Did you see Ivan after prom?'

'Yeah, we both went to Hampton College. But, like I said, I didn't have much to do with him. He's not the sort of guy I'd choose to hang around with.'

'Just one last thing,' Helen said. 'Why do you think he waited three years to raise the issue of the girl with you?'

'No idea. I found out after the incident that he'd started working at Memington Hall in the kitchens. The police at the time reckoned he'd spotted me in the bar and followed me when I left, the sick bastard.'

Pemberton looked up from his notes. 'Was there anyone else at school he was friendly with?'

'Ivan didn't have any friends at school. Not that I know of. Like I said, he was an oddball.'

CHAPTER 40

Helen rubbed the back of her neck as Eugene Grant disappeared from the screen. The more she heard about Ivan Shaw, the more uneasy she felt.

'It certainly sounds like he was looking to settle scores,' Pemberton said. He nodded to a printout of the email on her desk. 'If the killer is linked to him, it may explain why they chose Ashleigh Urquhart to voice their message. She was from the same class.'

'Whoever did this didn't just hit fellow pupils, they shot innocent bystanders too.'

'An incel advocate might regard them all as potential targets.'

'Hmm.' Helen didn't like the sound of this. 'Where did we get with tracing Shaw's family?'

'He was raised in Hampton by his mother, Emily Shaw. No siblings. Emily died a couple of years ago. They didn't appear to get along; he refused her visitation requests when he was inside.'

'Okay, speak to the staff at Memington Hall. It's a long shot after all this time, but if he worked there, he might have talked about or met someone there.'

Pemberton nodded.

'What did the prison say about Shaw?'

'Not much. He served most of his sentence at Bedford. He was polite to guards, participated in counselling, expressed remorse for his crime. The only issue they had was at the beginning of his sentence – he had to be moved frequently to different cells. It seems he rubbed other inmates up the wrong way, and I'm not talking about literally. People gave him a wide berth.'

Interesting. Governors didn't routinely move people around because they were unhappy with their cellmate. 'Did anyone document why?'

'You know what these places are like. Nobody made a formal complaint, but the word around the prison was that he was strange. When they finally found someone who would tolerate him, the guards were called to a fight in the middle of the night.'

'Do we know what it was about?'

Pemberton shook his head. 'Shaw was treated for a broken nose, Stanton, his cellmate, a cut eye. Sounds like six of one and half a dozen of the other. When the men were questioned, they said it was a misunderstanding. They went on to share a cell for eleven months until Shaw was released.'

'Interesting. What do we know about Stanton?'

Pemberton gave a sarcastic smile. 'Nice character. Serving eight years for three counts of stealing mobile phones at knifepoint.'

Helen thought hard. Shaw had detached himself from his family since his conviction and then disappeared into thin air after his release. Perhaps his former cellmate could shed some light on his acquaintances. 'Is Stanton still at Bedford?'

'No, he's been moved to the new Five Wells in Wellingborough.'

Even better, HM Prison Five Wells was just over an hour's drive away. 'See if you can wangle me a pass to see Stanton tomorrow,' Helen said to Pemberton. 'And speak to the prison liaison officer at Wellingborough, see what you can find out about Stanton's prison record there.'

Pemberton gave her a blank look. 'Stanton's record. Are you sure?'

'Absolutely.'

The trill of her phone interrupted her.

'Detective Lavery?' It was Gil, the security guy from the front gate.

'Yes.'

'I've got a Jack Valentine here. Says he's joining you from counter-terror this morning.'

Finally, Kendrick's DMI had arrived. 'Thanks,' Helen said. 'Book him in, will you, and give him a pass. I'll be right down.'

* * *

As soon as she approached the gate, Helen immediately recognised the man with the thin head of dark hair waiting for her. 'Jack,' she said, 'I didn't realise it was you! Come for more coffee?'

He hunched his shoulders, gave a small smile, and lifted the flask in his hand. 'Brought my own this time.'

'Don't blame you. All tastes of wood smoke here anyway.' Helen laughed, recalling the image of the waif-like man she'd found wandering the corridors of headquarters six months ago, looking for IT services. He'd been bowled over when she'd got him a coffee, taken him there herself.

'Wasn't sure you'd remember me,' he muttered, following her inside.

'Oh, I never forget a face,' she said, glancing across at his navy checked shirt with iron lines down the sleeves, tucked into dark trousers. 'I didn't realise you lived over our way.'

'Yes, in the town centre.'

'Ah. At least we're handy for you.'

'Yup.' He pushed his hands into his pockets, lowered his eyes to the floor. His months in the police hadn't improved his small talk.

'So, how much do you know about the case?' Helen asked.

'The super forwarded the email and briefed me,' he said without expanding.

'Right.' Helen gave him the rundown on their priorities. In the incident room, she introduced him to Pemberton, who towered over him, and then the others. 'What do you need?' she asked.

'A large desk.' Jack scanned the room, picking one at the far corner, away from the others. 'That'll do.'

A phone rang. Pemberton excused himself to answer it. 'How long before you can tell us anything?'

'A while. I want to do some digging first, see if I can trace the sender. Then we can discuss how you want to take it forward.' He left her standing there, was already halfway across the room by the time he'd finished speaking.

They were interrupted by an excited Pemberton, 'Thanks! We'll be right there.' He dropped the phone handset into the cradle and looked across at Helen. 'Some kids magnet-fishing at the canal have pulled out a black holdall containing an assault rifle. Looks like it's been dumped recently.'

Helen felt a bolt of adrenalin. 'Where?'

'Beside Crawley Bridge.'

Crawley Bridge marked the canal's closest point to the town centre, only a ten-minute walk from Victoria Car Park, faster if you ran. Helen was torn. She desperately wanted to visit the location, but she was also aware of the ticking clock. The email needed action, and soon.

'Jack,' she called across the office. 'I have to pop out. Please ring me as soon as you find anything.'

CHAPTER 41

The first thing Helen noticed when she and Pemberton parked up along the track that led to Crawley Bridge was a gathering of onlookers. A group of teenage boys jostled shoulders, a mother, clasping the hands of her young children, a couple of elderly men who looked like they'd abandoned their morning walk. All gathered at the top of the bank, peering past the uniformed officer blocking the entrance to the bridge and towpath, to see what the fuss was about. It wouldn't be long before the press arrived.

They held out their badges and made their way down the bank, relieved to find this stretch of the canal empty apart from two boats moored opposite. Thick blinds pulled down over their windows, grass snaking around the guy ropes – they hadn't moved in a while.

On the towpath, immediately beside the entrance to the bridge, a man in cargo trousers and a loose T-shirt stood beside two young boys that looked to be around ten or so. The man had his back to them as he spoke to another uniformed officer. The boys stood silently, hands in their pockets, looking bewildered. A heavy-duty magnet attached to a piece of rope beside them glistened in the morning sunlight. Beside the magnet, a black bin liner was laid out on the ground and topped with old coke cans, bits of chain, a rusty old tool.

A memory of Matthew a few years ago came to mind. His fresh face pleading Helen to take them magnet-fishing in the school holidays. 'It's like metal detecting underwater,' he'd said. 'We might find something important!' She'd put him off at the time. She couldn't think of anything worse than retrieving dirty old metal from the base of the canal, but she was aware the craze had grown in popularity, and she could see how people, kids especially, could be drawn to the possibility of finding 'treasure'.

They inched past the men and over to a uniformed officer in gloves, who was bent over, examining the rifle.

'All right, Jimbo,' Pemberton said, a grin stretching from ear to ear as he clapped him on the back. The officer stood and they greeted each other like old friends. 'What are you doing here?'

Jimbo smiled, holding out his gloved hands at an angle as if they smelt rancid. 'Good to see you, mate. I'm with firearms now. I was sent out to secure the weapon.'

Pemberton introduced Helen and she gave a nod of acknowledgement. 'We joined together,' Pemberton said.

'Ah!' Helen was aware of Jimbo enquiring about Pemberton's family, but she wasn't really listening. The zip to the holdall was undone, the bag sitting open to reveal the rifle inside. She crouched, peering in for a closer look. The weapon gleamed back at her. It hadn't been in the water long and looked to be intact, the walnut stock retracted. Whoever had dumped it there hadn't risked losing any time by taking it apart.

'It's an AK all right,' Jimbo said, catching her eye. 'Looks like it's seen a bit of service too from the chips and scratches along the barrel.'

'Service?'

'Military service. Places like the Balkans are full of them, left over from the war. We'll know more when forensics have examined it.'

Helen looked up at the bridge. Imagining the killer leaving the car park, making their way down Markham Street. Perhaps they'd headed straight here, determined to lose the

evidence quickly. If they'd retraced their steps, the
have disappeared into any of the side streets into tow.
other side of the bridge headed out to the suburbs. Both 1
offering easy, quick exits.

'Any CCTV around here?' she asked Jimbo.

'Not that I'm aware of.' He looked this way and th
This stretch of the canal wasn't even overlooked by the ne
modern flats like those the other side of the town centre.

'What about the boats over there? Anyone living there?'

'We'll check, of course, but it's doubtful. This area is often
used as permanent mooring for holidaymakers.'

Helen thanked him and sighed. The killer couldn't
have sought out a more isolated location. 'The magazine
is empty, the safety catch on,' Jimbo said. 'Unless there's
anything else you need to see, we'll get this bagged up and
across to forensics.'

She thanked him, moved off towards the father and
children, still talking to the officer on the bank, and introduced
herself. 'Is this the first time you've fished here?' she asked.

The man eyed her suspiciously and gave a slow nod.
Although it wasn't illegal to magnet-fish on land where the
hobbyists had gained permission, the Canal and River Trust
disapproved of it and had byelaws prohibiting the removal of
materials discovered.

'I'm not interested in why you're here,' she said, to
reassure him, 'that's an issue between you and the trust. I just
wanted to know whether you've fished here before.'

'No. We've tended to go further down, out of town, in the
past. But the boys were bored this morning and we have a
dentist appointment later. I thought a couple of hours here…
We only live up the road.'

Helen smiled. A father, trying to keep his children occupied
during the school holidays. Her eyes landed on a pile of rusty
nails at the edge of the bin bag. They hadn't had much luck
today. Not until they pulled up the holdall.

'Did you touch it or tamper with the bag?' she asked the man.

'Only to see what was inside. As soon as I spotted what it was, I called you guys.'

She thanked him, left the officer to take down his details, they'd need to eliminate his prints and DNA at the very least, then moved along the bank and checked her phone. No new messages. Almost an hour had passed since she'd left the new DMI at the office, and there was no word yet about the email. Hopefully, that didn't mean he was still setting up his equipment. She dialled the incident room and asked for Jack.

'Ma'am.' Jack's voice was quiet, light.

'How's it going?'

'Bad news, I'm afraid. Whoever sent the email has been careful, covered their tracks. Probably used a VPN to encrypt their ISP.'

Helen closed her eyes as he continued with some other technical jargon she didn't understand. She was no techie, but she'd gleaned enough to know that the sender had deliberately taken steps to ensure they couldn't be found.

'There's nothing else we can try?'

'I'm afraid not.'

They seemed to be thwarted at every stage on this case. She hung up and phoned Kendrick. Leaving him a voicemail message about the recovered weapon and asking him to call her back urgently. It would be a while before they could confirm definitively that it was the murder weapon. Both the bag and the rifle needed to undergo a full forensic examination, and then be couriered to ballistics to confirm whether the bullets were discharged by this machine gun. But she had to face facts. It matched the type of assault rifle used, and AK-47s weren't exactly in rich supply. She glanced back at the bridge. What really niggled her was the location. Assuming the killer headed straight here and dumped the bag after the shooting, this track headed out towards Weston – where the suspected terrorist cell lived and, on that basis,

it was looking more and more like Kendrick was right and the correct suspects were in custody. Maybe, despite all the markers with Shaw, they were on a hiding to nothing. So, where did that leave them with the email?

CHAPTER 42

Back at headquarters, Helen parted with Pemberton and took the stairs to the top floor, two at a time, the heels of her boots clicking the laminate. The email was niggling her, and with no chance of tracing the source, she wanted to discuss the next steps with Jenkins urgently. She'd just reached the top floor and was rounding the bend in the corridor when she almost collided with someone coming the other way. It wasn't until she stepped back and brushed herself down, apologising profusely, that she realised it was the chief constable in front of her.

'Sorry, sir,' she said again. 'I was just on my way to see the superintendent.'

Adams gazed down at her. 'That won't be necessary.'

'What?'

'I was actually coming down to see you. I'm afraid Jenkins has been called away. David's had a relapse.'

'Oh no.' The last time Jenkins had spoken about his partner, David, he was doing better, in remission. 'Is he okay?'

'I'm not completely sure. He collapsed at home, they had to call an ambulance. I've told Jenkins to take as much time as he needs, obviously.' He invited her into his office – a bright and breezy room at the end of the corridor with a large, shiny table surrounded by high-backed chairs at one end, and an oak desk in the middle beneath the window. The neat piles of files and abundant space made Helen's office look like a storage room. 'So, we're going to have to pull together here, Helen, do what's needed.' He indicated for her to take a chair. 'At least in the short term.'

The loss of the super amidst a major investigation was like a good hard kick in the gut. Jenkins might only just be getting settled back into the job, but he'd hit the ground running, acquainted himself closely with Operation Spruce. Plus, they'd worked together for almost a year, and Jenkins knew Helen. He was familiar with her occasionally unorthodox approach to policing and, deep in her heart, she felt sure that if she found substantive evidence to cast doubt on Kendrick's arrests, no matter how clandestine her inquiries, he would back her. She had no such rapport with the chief constable.

'Of course.' She swallowed her disappointment and gave the chief a progress update.

When she mentioned the email to Ashleigh Urquhart, the chief cut in. 'Yes, Jenkins forwarded me a copy of the note.' He steepled his fingers, rested back in his chair. 'I believe we're working on the basis that it's a hoax.'

'That has been suggested.' Helen got up and closed the door. 'But we have no proof and, I'm sure you appreciate, we need to put public safety first, examine all avenues. The team and I have been looking at other potential theories for the shooting.' She didn't want to share this now, especially not with the chief, not until she had something substantial. But if this was her one chance to get him on board, she couldn't afford to waste the opportunity.

She took a seat and started talking about the reunion and Shaw and his background. Highlighting the salient points, the connections. The chief seemed to be listening intently, rapt, until she mentioned that Shaw was dead.

His face hardened, he raised a flat hand to silence her. 'I don't want to hear this, Helen,' he said. 'This is a counter-terror investigation, not Hampton Homicide. Any queries you have about the suspects should be addressed to Kendrick.'

'But, sir. Someone close to Shaw, carrying out his wishes,

makes sense with the demographic and ties in with the email sent to Ashleigh Urquhart.'

He stared at her a second as if he was weighing up his options. 'From what you've told me, all you have is a dead man with some questionable interests, who wasn't even present at the reunion,' he said. 'Frankly, I'm disappointed you're wasting valuable time on this. It needs to stop. We're limited in normal circumstances without losing our superintendent at the last minute. You focus on the email. Identify the sender, sort it out. No more additional resources are to be expended on investigating Operation Spruce. And that's an order.'

CHAPTER 43

The chief's words were still ringing in Helen's ears when she stepped back into the incident room. How dare he shut down her enquiries when there were so many links, so many connections? True, the location of the murder weapon pointed towards Kendrick's suspects. But there was something else going on here, she could feel it in every fibre of her body. She couldn't abandon her investigation yet. She wouldn't be doing the bereaved families justice if she didn't at least try to track down Shaw's associates – especially the one calling himself TopBoy.

She spotted Pemberton in her office, sitting at her desk, working on a laptop. Instead of making her way over to see what he was up to, she headed in the opposite direction. To Jack, who was poring over one of two computer screens in the far corner.

'Hey!' she said as she approached, eyeing an enlarged version of the email on one of the screens, as if Jack was analysing every word.

She was less than a metre away when the DMI looked up, startled. Engrossed in his work, he clearly didn't think she was addressing him.

'How are you doing?' Helen asked. 'Any more news?'

'Sadly not. I'm still sweeping the social media channels,' he said. 'There's a lot of discussion about the shooting online, plenty of comments. Nothing yet to indicate who sent the message.'

'Is there really nothing more we can do to trace the email source?'

He pulled down the corners of his mouth, shook his head. 'I've tried everything I can think of. It's not difficult to remain anonymous if you know how. I'm sorry.'

He looked so crestfallen Helen felt guilty. 'Not at all,' she said reassuringly. 'Thanks for all your efforts.' The last thing she wanted was for any of her team, even a temporary member, to feel defeated. She patted his shoulder. 'Anything you find will be welcome. We're grateful you're here.'

Jack fell silent. He squinted at her hand and then at her. Then his face blossomed into a startled smile that made him look almost childlike. 'I'll keep trying.'

Helen thanked him and made her way to her office.

'Not one for chat, is he?' Pemberton said, nodding towards the DMI as Helen entered the office. 'He hasn't uttered a word to anyone all morning, by all accounts. Even brought his own coffee with him.'

Helen followed his gaze. Jack was back at work, focused on his keyboard. His two screens bearing down on him, the black flask at his side. 'I get the impression he doesn't come from a very sociable office,' she said. From his reaction just now, it didn't look like Kendrick was open about expressing gratitude to his team either. She turned back to her sergeant. 'What are you up to anyway?'

'Dark just texted. She's calling at two with an update.' It was almost 1.30 pm. They had half an hour. 'I'm just studying Ashleigh Urquhart's past columns,' he continued. 'Her writing style.'

'Ah.' They'd discussed their approach on the drive back to the station. If they were to have any chance of tracing the source of the email, they'd have to respond, draw the sender in. They needed to take it delicately though. They couldn't afford to put them off until they could assess the threat, which meant the email needed to be written in the columnist's words.

'And I've ordered us a pizza delivery. Should be here any minute.'

'Good idea.' Pemberton could always be relied upon to keep them topped up. She dropped into a chair opposite and relayed her conversation with the chief while she opened her laptop.

'Christ!' Pemberton said. 'Do you want me to pull Dark and Spencer back?'

Helen had been considering this since she'd stepped out of the chief's office, but... 'No.' Kendrick was so dogged about his suspects, if she passed over her information it would undoubtedly become low priority. She couldn't even be sure he'd follow it up. They only needed another day up north to check things out, a couple at most, and it was much easier if she had officers stationed there. 'Let's see how things pan out. I'll take the wrap if anything goes wrong.'

Pemberton's brows shot up. 'Are you sure?'

'Absolutely.'

'As you wish.' He turned back to the screen and scratched the side of his neck. 'Do you really think Ashleigh Urquhart will play ball?' he said, returning to the subject of the email.

For the plan to work, the response had to come from Ashleigh's email address. Hopefully, without the input of her editor, which meant Helen needed to find a way to sell it to the columnist. 'Leave that to me,' she said. 'I'll think of something.'

She opened her laptop, reread the email, then started writing notes to include in their response. 'Ashleigh wouldn't necessarily have picked up on the number of rounds fired in the first email, especially if it is generic for semi-automatic rifles,' she said to herself. 'We need to think like her.' She tapped her pen on the desk, jotted another note.

Time ticked by. They worked in silence, running ideas by each other, penning notes. Demolishing the pizza within minutes of its arrival. 2 pm arrived and, right on cue, Helen's office phone trilled.

'Hey,' Pemberton said. 'The DCI is with me. You're on speaker.' He placed the handset down.

'Hi!' Helen said. 'How are you both doing?'

'All right.' Dark's high-pitched voice winged down the line. 'Found a lovely B&B near the police station.'

'Yeah,' Spencer added. 'Served the mother of all breakfasts. You're missing out there, Sarge.'

Pemberton snorted.

'Anyway…' Dark said. 'More importantly, we spoke to the officer in the case. He couldn't tell us much more than he'd given me on the phone, but he did provide Shaw's ex-girlfriend's details and also his place of work. His girlfriend took a bit of tracking down. She's moved several times since she left Shaw, she's now shacked up with a guy in Gateshead.'

'How was she?'

'Hmm. Safe to say, there's no love lost there. She said Shaw was grieving for his nan when she met him. Seemed nice, polite. But, almost as soon as she moved in with him, he changed. Became possessive. Wanted to know where she was, who she was with, all the time. Started following her, creeping her out. She called it off when she found he'd put a tracker on her phone. After they separated, he kept contacting her, ringing in the middle of the night, arriving on her doorstep unannounced. Hence the number of times she moved. She didn't even go to Shaw's funeral.'

'Could she give you details about his friends, family?'

'A bit. He was raised by his mother, has her last name. Never knew his father. He and his mother didn't get along. A former teacher, she had high expectations. Wanted him to become a lawyer or a banker, was always pushing him at school, getting in private tutors, but he wasn't academic. When he took a chef's course at college, she told him she was disappointed in him, said he could do better. He moved up to Sunderland to be with his nan after he left prison. Apparently, he used to spend his summers up here with her when he was young, called it his happy place. His nan died suddenly six months after he moved, a heart attack, and she left her house to him. His girlfriend worked for the funeral director. That's how she met Shaw.'

'Okay,' Helen said. 'What about other family, friends?'

'No other family, not that she knows of. According to her, apart from a couple of guys at work, he didn't have much in the way of friends either, and he didn't mention them often. She couldn't shed any light on the TopBoy contact.'

It sounded like a dead end. 'Anything else?'

'Shaw's body was identified by his neighbour, an Ellen Granger,' Spencer said. He paused a second, as if he was reading off his notes. 'She was the executor of his will; the police returned all his possessions to her when the case closed, including his computer. If she's still got the computer, it might be worth getting our techies to do a deeper dive, see if they can trace his contacts. She wasn't home when we called. We'll try her again later. We're off to his workplace now, a warehouse on an industrial estate on the edge of town.'

Helen avoided Pemberton's eyeline as she ended the call. Pemberton was a great one for fighting for what he believed in, seeking justice at whatever cost, but even she had to agree, this was all sounding tenuous. Especially when she was disobeying a direct order, not to mention side-lining Kendrick's team. They needed to find something to justify her covert investigation, and soon.

CHAPTER 44

Ashleigh sat on the sofa with Noah, watching out of the window as a pair of crows circled the park. The detective had brought a colleague with her today. A bear of a man with a bulbous chest, who stood beside her at the fireplace, ramrod straight, as they explained that, despite their best efforts, colleagues hadn't been able to track down the sender of the email.

Noah's hand tightened over hers. 'What happens now?' he asked.

'We'll discuss that in a minute,' Helen said. 'Before we do that, I need to tell you that a rifle was discovered in the canal near Crawley Bridge this morning.'

Ashleigh's pulse accelerated. 'Was it the one used on Friday?'

'We can't be completely sure until it has been rigorously tested, but it was certainly dumped recently, and it does match the type of weapon used.' Ashleigh listened as the detective talked her through the proximity of the canal to the car park and the house where the suspects had been arrested.

'What does that mean for Ash?' Noah said. 'Are you saying this email was a time-waster?'

'That's the line counter-terror are taking.'

Ashleigh narrowed her eyes. The detective didn't sound convinced. 'What about you?'

Helen held her gaze. 'I think we should do everything we can to track down the sender. At the very least it's harassment and we need to put a stop to it.'

A door slammed in the corridor outside. Sadhika leaving her flat. Ashleigh turned back to the detective. 'You think it might be genuine.'

'I didn't say that. Colleagues in counter-terror are convinced they have the right suspects in custody. It is important to follow this up though. And I will need your help to do so.'

Ashleigh didn't like the sound of that. She was already far more involved than she wanted to be. 'What do you mean?'

'We've drafted a response we'd like you to send from your email. As you'll see, we've kept it brief.' The detective pulled a folded A4 sheet out of her bag and passed it over.

Thank you for your email, and for reaching out to me. I am interested in speaking with you.

Before we progress, I need to verify you are genuine. This is crucial to convincing my editor to work with your story. Can you please tell me a piece of information, about yourself or the incident at O'Malley's, that hasn't been reported in the press.

I look forward to hearing from you.

By the time she reached the final line, an ache pressed at Ashleigh's temple. 'Is this really necessary? Surely, we can just ignore it if it's a hoax.'

'We can,' Helen said. 'It could be something and nothing. But someone has singled you out. Maybe because of your presence on Friday evening, or your connection with the newspaper. And they've included a threat. I'd be more comfortable if we identified them.'

'Even if they do respond, what makes you think you'll be able to find them? You haven't been able to so far.'

'We're opening the lines of communication, drawing them in. Plus, their reply might include other information that could help.'

'Can't you use a fake address?'

'It doesn't work that way. Whoever sent this is tech-savvy. They'd likely spot a fake email address a mile off.'

'Then perhaps it would be better to share it with my editor,'

Ashleigh said, with far more bravado than she felt. 'Write an open response in the newspaper.' In truth, that was the last thing she wanted. She could only imagine Jason's face if he got his hands on this, the sensational headline…

'I'd ask you not to do that.'

Ashleigh gritted her teeth at the iniquitous situation she'd been placed in. Send. Don't send. Share with the world. None of them sounded palatable but, she couldn't deny the sender needed to be outed, to be dealt with. It wasn't fair to go around frightening people like this, and she certainly needed to do something to dispel the tension before her mother arrived. 'Okay. What if I agree?' Noah's hand tightened further on hers, whitening her fingers.

'I forward a typed version to you. If the sender is one of your readers, they'll be familiar with your style. When you are completely content, you press send. If you receive a reply, you don't respond, you contact me immediately.'

'And if they don't reply?'

'The correspondence ends and we all assume this was a sick game. When adequate time has passed, the subject of cranks or time wasters in criminal cases could prove an interesting discussion for a future column piece. I might even be able to help you with a few other examples. For now, I must ask you to keep this to yourselves. The public are already panicked. We don't want to upset people unnecessarily.'

'What if there is more to it?' Ashleigh croaked.

'Then we will deal with it. I promise.'

CHAPTER 45

'Shaw's got a half-brother,' Dark said.

Back in her office, Helen listened to Dark update her on their afternoon's enquiries in Northumbria.

'They share the same father, different mothers. Shaw didn't know anything about him until a few months before he died. He told a colleague that some guy tracked him down via Facebook.'

Helen gazed at the empty chair in front of her. After spending the best part of the afternoon with the columnist, she'd sent Pemberton home to celebrate his wife's birthday while they played the waiting game. On standby for a reply from the sender claiming to be the shooter. 'Do we have a name?'

'It was never mentioned. He later told the colleague his half-brother visited a few times and they hit it off. Seemed pleased to have met him.'

'No other details?'

'Afraid not. He wasn't a great one for socialising. It seems he confided in this one colleague during fag breaks. Even then, he didn't say much.'

They'd check with Births, Deaths, and Marriages, but with Shaw being given his mother's surname, it was possible his father's name wasn't mentioned on the birth certificate. 'What about the neighbour?'

'We called round again this evening,' Spencer said. 'Still out. We've tried other houses nearby, no one knows where she is.'

They could apply for a copy of the will to determine the beneficiaries, but those requests were nearly always delayed by red tape and what Helen didn't have was time. 'Try again tomorrow, will you? If she executed his will, it sounds like they were close. She'll know who was mentioned. She might also know about friends, or even the half-brother. I'd really like to trace him. I take it nobody mentioned TopBoy?'

'No.'

Helen thanked them both and cut the call. She'd been tempted to question Ashleigh about Shaw this afternoon, the altercation she'd omitted to mention, but... she needed evidence, something substantial before she could widen the enquiry and question survivors.

She viewed her messages again. Nothing new from Ashleigh Urquhart. Three hours had now passed since the young woman had pressed send on the email. She fired off a text. *Everything okay?*

The reply was almost instant. *All good. No response yet.*

It was almost nine. Dusk was starting to fall, the light in her office gently fading. Helen massaged the back of her neck. She was tired, weary. The events of the day catching up with her. Maybe she should call it a night.

She reached for her jacket and wandered out into the incident room, surprised to find Jack still ensconced in the corner, tapping away at his keyboard.

'Working late?' Helen asked. She couldn't fault his dedication.

Jack smiled up at her. 'Still trying to break into the suspect's tablets,' he said. 'It's laborious work, trying so many different combinations.'

'You'll need a holiday when all this is over.'

'Yeah.' He pulled another smile. 'I'm planning a trip out to the States.'

'Nice!' It was good to see him relax, talk about life outside work. 'Whereabouts?'

'My sister married an American. They live in Nevada. Have you ever been?'

A wistful memory of sun hats and blistering sunshine on bare forearms filled Helen with nostalgia. 'Only to take the kids to Disneyland, Florida. Nevada sounds lovely. My boys have always wanted to visit Las Vegas.'

'Ah, Vegas is fab. I love the desert. The heat, the open landscape. There's so much room there, so much to do.'

His enthusiasm was infectious. Perhaps she should book a family trip when Chilli's trial was over. Spend some quality time together while her sons still wanted to holiday with her. Speaking of family time, she really ought to get back and check how Robert was doing. He'd taken the news of her involvement in his friend's uncle's case well yesterday. Perhaps it was now time to delve a bit deeper, share more details. 'Well, I hope you get a break soon,' Helen said, pulling on her jacket and heading towards the door. 'Don't stay too late!'

CHAPTER 46

Ashleigh stared at the tiny boxed faces on the screen in front of her. Forty-six people had tuned into her Zoom meeting. Forty-six survivors of the shooting who were now taking their time to introduce themselves, one by one. Sharing their biggest fears about the aftermath of the incident. Sienna hadn't been able to walk her daughter to school since it happened. Theo was still off work. Louise was haunted by terrifying dreams.

These were people like her, with the same fears, the same worries. Some manifested differently, but it all boiled down to trauma. The trauma of being there that evening, of experiencing the shock and horror of gunfire that came from nowhere. That it could be any one of them lying in the morgue. Of constantly looking over your shoulder, jumping at any sound. As each one spoke, others nodded, comforted they weren't alone. One even thanked Ashleigh for arranging the group, saying they no longer felt isolated. She'd wanted to discuss things, lobby police, try to get answers, yet these people were raw. They sought reassurance, solidarity. As far as they were concerned, the killers were in custody.

As she moved along the line, the guilt inside Ashleigh bred like a germ. Because she was carrying a secret. A secret none of them knew. And, right now, as they were bearing their souls to each other, the guilt about the email was eating her from the inside out. She couldn't tell them. Even if she hadn't promised the detective, sharing the email tonight, here, would be like heaping shedloads of salt into their already weeping wounds of fear and grief.

She looked down at her keyboard. The same keyboard that bore her prints from adjusting the wording of the email earlier, making a few minor changes, before she pressed send and watched it fly off into the ether.

Ashleigh cursed at being placed in this position and checked her inbox again. What if the sender responded? What if the police had the wrong suspects in custody? What if the sniper struck again? What if? What if? What if?

And still, the survivors spoke up on her screen. Chloe now. A young blonde woman combed her fair hair from her face with her hand, said she'd contacted her GP for help.

Noah coughed from the bedroom. He'd been out to the shop earlier to get bread and had a long conversation with Filip in the shared entrance when he returned. Filip, their neighbour, who'd read her article, enquired how she was doing. Even Johnny, the other downstairs neighbour they rarely saw, had noticed Noah and come out to enquire after her. They'd also sent goodwill messages on the Portland Grove group chat, checking if there was anything she needed. Everyone was concerned. Yet she felt like an imposter. She wasn't who these people thought she was.

To top it all, Nia's mother was visiting tomorrow…

Ashleigh gnawed the side of her thumbnail as Eddie from Little Hampstead took the mic and introduced himself, drawing her back to the screen. When she'd written the article, her intention had been to bring people together and root out the reason for her friends' deaths. Not for one minute had she conceived it might bring the killer to her. Because, if that email was genuine, that's exactly what she'd done.

CHAPTER 47

Orla Gallagher unlocked the cubicle door and surveyed herself in the line of mirrors above the sink units. The toilets were empty. It was the last night of Hampton University's summer school, and everyone was at the students' union bar or on the lawn outside, jigging to the tunes the DJ was banging out. She'd only come upstairs to her room to collect a hair tie.

The distant thud of a dance beat was infectious. She couldn't help swaying to the music as she washed her hands and shoved them under the drier. She turned back to the mirror and shuffled the elastic neckline of her top down to expose her shoulders. Oh, if only her hair hadn't gone limp and wispy. It always did that when she was hot from dancing. Never mind. She'd scrape it back, tie it up and forget about it. A cheer rolled around the campus as the tune changed to a rap song. Orla couldn't wait to start university. If this was how they celebrated the end of summer school, she couldn't wait to see what the real thing was like! Her phone buzzed. It was Caitlin. *Where are you? DJ's about to play Avicii.*

It was hard to believe that she and Caitlin hadn't known each other until a few days ago. She remembered the nerves swirling around her insides as she'd waited to register on that first day, surrounded by thirty-plus other would-be students from all over the country. But a few days of staying over in halls, eating together, wandering into each other's rooms, chatting until all hours, cured that. There was no curfew here. No one cared what time you went to bed, or whether you slept at all for that matter, and with Caitlin on one side and Jade on the other, they soon became firm friends. They didn't even bother locking their doors after the first night.

Another roar from outside. She needed to get going, rejoin the others. She didn't want to miss out.

She smoothed down her top, was hurrying out of the bathroom when she heard a pop, pop, pop. Orla halted, momentarily disorientated. Where was that coming from? More followed, then a series of cracks. The music still thudding in the background. It sounded a bit like… fireworks? This university really was going all out. She'd never expected this at a summer school! She dashed down the corridor to her room. Just quickly grab the hair tie, and she'd be down the stairs within a minute.

It wasn't until she turned the corner that she saw the door to her room ajar. She stopped again, checked over her shoulder. Had Jade or Caitlin come up to find her? They hadn't texted to say so. Or maybe someone had come back to trash it. There'd been jokes all week about rooms being trashed at the end of summer school. Perhaps she should have taken them seriously. She was about to call out when it occurred to her that the culprits might still be inside. Cheeky beggars. Well, if they were, she'd give them a shock.

Orla tiptoed towards the door. Then, pushed it back with all her might and shouted, 'Hey!'

The door hit the wall and bounced back against her hand. But it wasn't the door that grabbed her attention. It was the man in her room that jumped back, startled. Dressed in black. Wolf-like eyes peering up at her from beneath the low hood. Orla froze. Her gaze dropped to the rifle in his arms. And then she understood. As clearly as if someone had flicked on a light in her head. It wasn't fireworks she'd heard outside. It was gunfire.

For a split second they both froze, stock still, staring at each other. Orla wanted to speak, to scream, to shout, but her mouth wouldn't work. All she could do was release her head, shake it from side to side, then place up a hand as the figure approached. Slowly, she backed away. He lifted the rifle. Orla trembled, head shaking faster and faster, she tripped, lost her balance, and thudded to the floor. Clambering backwards, clawing her way across the carpet. Before another crack sounded and the room disappeared.

CHAPTER 48

The house was quiet when Helen arrived home that evening. She shrugged off her jacket and checked her phone as she wandered into the kitchen. No new messages from the columnist. The longer the response took, the more it looked like the others were right and the email was sent by a hopeless time-waster.

Surely, she couldn't be wrong. There had to be more to Ivan Shaw's story, didn't there? All those markers, the background, the motive… She desperately hoped so because otherwise she'd be lucky if she didn't face a disciplinary panel for her covert enquiries in Northumbria.

It wasn't until she looked up that she noticed Robert, sitting at the table, staring at the screen of his phone. 'Hey!' she said. 'What're you up to?'

Before he had a chance to answer, footsteps clattered down the stairs to the adjoining flat and her mother appeared in the doorway. Jane Lavery was dressed in baby-blue pyjamas, her usually groomed grey hair hanging loose across her shoulders and she looked tired, drawn.

'You okay?' Helen asked.

'Worn out. Just about to have an early night.' Her mother went on to talk about taking a friend to hospital, then doing a supermarket shop for a neighbour in the next road. 'It's been a long day,' she finished up.

'Know the feeling.' Helen flicked a switch on the kettle. 'Tea?'

Her mother shook her head. 'I won't, thanks.'

Helen looked across at Robert who was now scowling at his phone. 'You're quiet,' she said to her son. 'Have you had a difficult day too?'

'It was all right,' he mumbled sullenly. Eyes glued to his phone.

'Right.' Helen glanced quizzically at her mother whose brow furrowed. Clearly, something had gone on. 'I'm making tea. Are you in?'

'No.' He grimaced.

Helen placed the mug on the side. 'Robert, what is it?'

'You didn't tell me the truth about Zac's uncle,' he muttered.

Helen's heart skipped a beat. 'Pardon?'

'He was set up. How could you let that happen?'

Helen couldn't believe what she was hearing. 'I did not let anything happen,' she said, enunciating every syllable. 'What exactly did Zac tell you?'

'That the weapons in the warehouse weren't his uncle's.'

'Chilli was charged with drug trafficking too.'

'They belonged to someone else. It's not what you think.'

Helen stared at her son, aghast. Davy had fed his kids a line to soften the blow. Something to say to school friends who asked difficult questions, and it couldn't be more untrue.

'Listen, Robert. You've got this wrong. We seized a...' She halted. Giving out specifics could compromise the case in court. '... substantial haul of drugs from his warehouse.'

'It wasn't his fault.'

'Is that what Zac's dad said?'

'No, it's what his mum said.' His voice lifted a decibel. 'And she's nice. She doesn't lie.'

'Neither do I.' Helen recalled Davy's comments the other day. She understood them not wanting to be stigmatised because of their relationship with Chilli but this wasn't the way to go about things. The boys weren't kids anymore, they were teenagers, soon to be adults.

Though she hadn't told her son the full story either... Oh, what a mess!

'I'm sorry, love.' She moved across the room, placed a hand on his shoulder. 'Zac's uncle's culpability is for a court of law to decide. I told you because I'm involved. Maybe I should tell you everything he was charged with, the whole story, and then you can make your own decision.'

'I don't want to know!' He stood and wrestled her hand off his shoulder. 'I don't want to know anything about your work. Not now. Not ever.'

'Hey!' Her response diffused into the air as he dashed out of the room; his feet thud, thud, thudding the stairs. The sound of a bedroom door slamming shut reverberated through the house.

Helen looked at her mother, flabbergasted.

'He's been like this since he came in from school,' Jane said. 'Apparently, Zac got angry and went home at lunchtime.'

Helen closed her eyes a second, pressing her eyelids together hard. When she opened them again, she told her mother about their conversation yesterday. 'I told him not to say anything to Zac.'

'He's fourteen. They're best friends. This was always going to be difficult.'

Helen opened her mouth and closed it, lost for words. She'd tried to do the right thing, to put her son in the picture, but she hadn't bargained on the Boyds deliberately feeding their kids a different story. Urgh! Of all the boys in the school, why did Zac have to choose Robert? Her head told her it was because her son was sociable, friendly. It was one of the reasons why he'd been appointed to 'buddy' the new kids. She tugged at the skin on her neck as a sneaky thought crept in. Just the sort of person Chilli could get close to… 'I'm going after him. He needs to know the truth.'

'Leave him be for now,' her mother said, pressing an understanding hand on her daughter's arm. 'It'll be easier when he's cooled down.'

Helen wasn't so sure about that, especially with what she had to tell him. She bade her mother goodnight, watched her disappear up the stairs to her flat and slumped into a chair, deflated. Staring at the gilt-edged photo on the wall of John, her late husband, his arms wrapped around younger versions of her boys. How she longed to have him back, even just for a few minutes. He'd know exactly what to say now, how to handle Robert.

John was so level, so grounded, she found herself missing him more as the boys aged, and not only for them. It was the little things about relationships. The support, the cute texts when she was having a tough day. Someone to have a glass of wine with; someone to watch a movie with in the evening. All those little remarks, stories, anecdotes that amassed from a life navigated together. She could barely even remember the last time she'd had sex. How sad was that! Though, the way her life was unfolding, she couldn't see that situation changing any time soon. What with work and family, she barely had time for herself, let alone a partner.

The sound of her mobile ringing broke her abstraction. 'Hello?'

'Ma'am, it's Inspector Carrington in the control room. We have an active shooter incident.'

Helen jerked forward. 'What? Where?'

'At the university. At least two casualties. Firearms are just securing the area.'

'And the shooters?'

'Not apprehended.'

'Get uniform to set up urgent roadblocks, and make sure no one leaves the scene,' she said. 'I'm on my way.'

CHAPTER 49

Hampton University, formerly the site of the sixth form college until it moved across town a few years ago, was a mixture of the old and new. The old Georgian stone frontage which ran the length of Tierney Street was impressive, with long sash windows facing the road and a series of stone steps leading up to a portico entrance. The modern extension, invisible from the road, ran behind, consisting of several new red-brick buildings – lecture halls, a library, two cafés, student accommodation blocks – and were arranged around a quadrangle which contained the sports field. Helen remembered the photographs of the grand opening appearing in the local press two years earlier, reporters heralding it as an architectural triumph.

Tonight, it lit up the street like Blackpool illuminations. And for all the wrong reasons.

She was met at her car by PS Dez Eldred, the tactical support team sergeant, his Heckler and Koch rifle still, rather disconcertingly, cradled in his arms.

Eldred's chest strained within his ballistic vest as he waited patiently for her to climb out of her car. A helicopter whirred overhead. 'Ma'am, we've searched and secured the area,' he said. 'The shooter is no longer on the premises.'

No preamble. No greeting. Eldred wasn't known for his social niceties. Colleagues teased him about his tendency to treat every detail: every house search, every chase, every deployment, as a major incident. But – Helen glanced across at a uniformed PC fixing police tape around the bottom of the stone steps leading to the university entrance – it was that intensity that made Eldred focused and thorough, which was exactly what she needed here.

'What do we know about casualties?' she asked after thanking him.

He peered down at her from beneath his baseball cap. 'Two confirmed dead. Three injured – two looked to be trampled in the panic. Another with head injuries.'

'Christ! No sign of those responsible?'

He shook his head.

To be in this position, with a sniper running loose, twice in one week, was unthinkable.

He nodded at another colleague standing at the newly-tied cordon with a log, waited for Helen to flash her badge and sign in, then lifted the tape and guided her up the stone steps towards the entrance.

It was quiet inside. Empty. The reception decorated with cream walls, cornices, glass doors at the rear. Stars peeped down at them through the high atrium ceiling – a late addition to the recent extension. The musty aroma of stale air filled the area.

'Talk me through what we know so far,' she asked.

Eldred motioned for her to follow him to the glass doors and looked out into the night. The peaked rooftops of the library, the lecture theatres, the cafés rose into the indigo sky beyond. The goalposts of the sports field shone eerily white in the centre.

'The university was running a five-day summer school for potential new undergraduates this week,' he said. 'Seventeen and eighteen-year-old boys and girls who'd travelled here from all over the country. They were having a party in the students' union bar this evening, a disco, soft drinks only as most of them were underage, to mark their last night.' He nodded at a lit building to their right. Tables and chairs were scattered haphazardly to the floor, as if a stampede of horses had run through. Helen spotted the silhouettes of people gathered inside through the lit windows. Survivors hunched, waiting to be questioned. Others comforting them. Outside, paramedics hovered over two covered lumps on the ground. It was a pitiful sight.

'The shooter took aim from the top floor of Aaron Hall of Residence,' Eldred continued. He gestured towards a block, diagonally opposite with a clear view across the tables outside the bar. Several rooms were lit inside.

'You're sure that was the correct position?' Helen checked.

Eldred nodded. 'Absolutely.'

Suddenly, something occurred to her. She cocked her head. 'You said shooter. Are you absolutely sure there was only one?'

'We are. They were interrupted.'

'By who?'

'The offender broke into one of the student's rooms. Young woman named Orla Gallagher. Friends say she returned to her room to collect something. Looks like there was a struggle. She was badly beaten, unconscious when we found her.'

'But alive?'

'Yes.'

Thank goodness. 'Where is she now?'

'Paramedics rushed her to hospital. She woke briefly, appears to be floating in and out of consciousness.'

'She wasn't shot?'

Eldred shook his head. 'No gunshot wounds were reported by paramedics.'

It seemed odd that the killer didn't turn the gun on her. 'And the shooter's exit?'

'There are many possibilities,' Eldred said. 'It's an open campus. I've had to put officers on guard at numerous points around the place. But the most likely exit and entrance, I would guess, is the rear of Aaron residence. The door was propped open. The exit there leads onto some waste ground, and then to the canal.'

The canal. Like last time. 'What about the survivors?'

'We've locked down the scene. Officers have moved them back into the bar while they take first accounts.'

Eldred's phone rang. He excused himself, moved away to answer it, and Helen looked out into the clear night, imagining the scene just a couple of hours earlier. Young people in good spirits. Laughing, dancing, spilling out onto the grass, the tables outside the bar. Celebrating the final night of their course. No idea of the horror that was about to begin.

'Helen!' She turned on her heels to find Brandon Eriksen, the pathologist, emerge from behind the reception desk. 'I take it you didn't get my earlier message?'

'What message?' She didn't recall receiving anything.

'I left a note with a member of your team this morning. Can't get the staff these days!' He reddened, as if he'd made a joke that had fallen flat. 'Don't worry. It wasn't important.'

'What was it about?'

'Um, a personal matter. Nothing to worry about.' He shook his head awkwardly.

'Okay…' Helen frowned, but there wasn't time to probe further now. 'I wasn't expecting to find you here tonight.'

'The sergeant called everyone out.'

'Right.' Usual Eldred response but she didn't blame him this time. The handling of this case would be under a media microscope from the outset. Nobody wanted to be accused of missing anything. But she couldn't for the life of her see what a pathologist could add here. There'd be no forensic trace on the bodies apart from bullets, and the cause of death wasn't in question.

'Not a lot I can respectfully do from here,' Brandon said, echoing her thoughts. He reached out, touched her elbow. 'Rest assured, I'll examine the deceased as soon as they are brought to the morgue. Be in touch early tomorrow.'

'I'd appreciate that. The earlier the better, don't wait for us to attend. Call if you pick up on anything. You've got my card.'

'Of course.' His gaze, soft and kind, lingered a second. Then he nodded and headed for the door.

Helen didn't watch him leave. She was waiting for Eldred to finish his call, desperate to examine the scene, when she heard loud voices, a commotion outside. The door crashed open. She rounded, half expecting the pathologist to return, that perhaps he'd forgotten something. Instead, Sergeant Pemberton entered.

'It's all kicking off out there,' Pemberton said without greeting. 'A set of parents have arrived demanding to see their kid. Apparently, they're local. One of the kids must have texted them, they're making a right fuss.'

'Right.' They needed to get on top of this before the floodgates opened. She gave Pemberton a brisk update on what she knew so far. 'Can you speak with the vice-chancellor and get a list of all the students and staff present? Send officers out to notify the parents of the deceased urgently, then set up a team to work through the list and contact next of kin for everyone else to let them know they are safe.'

Pemberton nodded.

She turned to Eldred who'd finished his call and was pocketing his phone. 'How sure are we the killer didn't pass through this entrance?'

'As sure as we can be. It's summertime, the college aren't using the reception. All summer school students booked in at the library. Plus, there's CCTV everywhere here. I'd put my money on the killer restricting their presence to Aaron block in the halls of residence.'

'Okay,' she said to Pemberton. 'Close the curtains over these doors, find a room and invite those people inside. Give them some tea, and an update on their kid. I can't afford to release anyone until they've given their details and a first account, but at least we can give them some news. And get the CCTV footage recovered and sent to the office for urgent analysis, just in case. I'm going to head over and see the witness's room.'

CHAPTER 50

Cool night air swished around Helen as she followed Eldred across the sports field. A couple of hours earlier, this would have been the picture of merriment. Young people, carefree. Spilling out of the students' union bar, dancing, having fun on the grass, enjoying the balmy summer's evening. Exactly what they should be doing at their tender age. Her gaze brushed the two heaps covered with sheets on the edge of the grass, and her heart contracted. Now it was the site of slaughter.

She thought again of the parents at the front entrance. Parents who'd trusted their loved ones into the care of the university. With no idea, no notion, that the week would end in utter carnage: two dead, others injured. As a parent herself, she could barely contemplate the shock, the horror, the gut-wrenching pain of losing a child. Your children weren't meant to die before you – that wasn't the natural order – and to face such a tragic end too. It was torturous.

Helen's Tyvek suit scratched at her skin as they reached the building at the end of the sports field and walked around the side. Orla's room was the one place where they knew the killer had been, the one place where they might find fibres, hairs, particles. She wasn't about to jeopardise a forensic search by failing to suit up.

'Is this the only entrance?' she asked as they arrived at Aaron block, a red-brick, two-storey perfunctory building. The glass door on the side was propped open.

'The main one the students use from what I understand. There's a fire exit at the other end of the building but it's secure and appears undisturbed.'

So, this was the killer's access point. Helen examined the lock. No dents, no breakages, no sign of forced entry.

'The door's been open all evening,' Eldred said, guessing her thoughts. The students are all staying in this block. One of them said it's been on the latch for most of the week.'

Which meant anyone could have entered at any point. They couldn't have made it easier. 'Don't the university have security?'

'In the summer they run on skeleton staff. An officer only calls by twice a night, usually in the early hours.'

They walked into a tiled entrance area, passing a single door which led off to the ground floor rooms. Up the stairs, they crossed a landing into a long corridor, the white walls devoid of chips and scratches, as if they'd been freshly painted over the summer. The fourth door along hung open.

Helen greeted the CSI checking for prints on the window ledge as they entered Orla Gallagher's room. It was small, just enough room for a single bed, a desk, a wardrobe. Helen stepped over a chair on its side, a cushion resting on the floor. Items possibly knocked over in the scuffle between Orla Gallagher and the sniper. 'No bullet casings?' she asked.

The CSI shook their head and moved aside for her to look out of the window. More CSIs were outside, moving one of the dead into a body bag. She turned, scanned the room one last time, then nodded her thanks.

'I take it the room wasn't locked?' she asked Eldred as she moved out.

Eldred shook his head. 'Like I said, the students weren't particularly diligent. The killer probably moved down the corridor until they found one open. Every room on this side of the block has a clear view of the students' bar.'

It made sense. Would save the risk of attracting attention by forcing entry. 'And there's no boundary fencing?'

'Universities aren't governed by the same rules as schools. It's an open campus for young adults.'

With easy access in and out, Helen thought. It all screamed of another planned incident. The killer watching his prey, casing the location, seeking out his opportunity.

The sound of her phone ringing broke her abstraction. It was Pemberton. 'I've just spoken to the officer at the hospital. Orla Gallagher's awake and well enough to be questioned.'

* * *

Orla Gallagher looked like a deer in headlights when Helen and Pemberton entered her room, barely twenty minutes later.

She was a petite girl, with limp dark hair and a ghostly white face that sported a bruise the size of a lemon on her cheek.

'Two minutes and no more,' the nurse said in a strong Glaswegian accent. 'Her parents are due any second.'

Helen waited for the nurse to leave before she introduced herself and Pemberton. 'How are you feeling?' she said.

Orla's eyes filled. 'Is it true that two people died?' she said, ignoring the question.

Helen nodded. 'I'm afraid it is. I'm so sorry.'

'Who were they?'

'I can't give you their names yet, we're still waiting for them to be officially identified. I'm very sorry.'

The poor girl looked distraught. 'What about the gunman?'

'We're still searching.' A tear trickled off the side of the young woman's face and spotted the sheet. 'We're doing everything we can to find them,' Helen said. 'Do you feel up to talking us through what happened? I'm certain it'll help.'

Orla's face pained. 'I'll try.' More tears gathered as she talked about nipping back to her accommodation, coming out of the toilets, tracking back to her room. 'I had no idea what was going on,' she said. 'I thought it was all part of the party.'

'What happened next?'

'I walked in on him. In my room. Literally standing there at the window, a great big gun in his hand.'

'Him.'

'What?'

Helen leaned in closer. 'You said him. Are you sure it was a man?'

'Definitely. I got a good look at him.'

Finally, they had something distinctive. 'Did you recognise him?'

'No. I've never seen him before.'

'Did he have any particular accent?' An accent would certainly help narrow things down.

'He didn't speak, didn't say a word. It was so quick. He whizzed round. For a second, I think he was as shocked as me. Then he lifted the gun. I thought I was a gonna.' She pressed her hand to her chest, moved her head from side to side, more tears spilling down her face. 'But the gun just clicked, it must have been empty. I can't remember much after that.'

CHAPTER 51

An hour later, the headlights of passing cars on Hampton ring road flashed intermittently through the uncovered windows of the conference room as Chief Constable Adams stood with Kendrick and Helen, tugging at his cuffs. 'How could this happen?' he said to Kendrick. 'I thought you said Hampton was no longer a target.'

Kendrick stood tall. 'According to my intelligence, you're not.'

'What the hell does that mean? You said you were convinced you had the right people in custody.' The phones were already ringing off the hook. Helen's team were out visiting families, speaking with parents. Before long, international media would return to resume their position at the end of the drive.

'Everything we found in their house – the homophobic literature, the bomb-making equipment, the site of the recovered weapon – suggests we have the right people.'

'But you don't have any evidence or an admission,' Helen said quietly. While she didn't relish pointing out the obvious, this was an emergency. It required a change of strategy, and fast.

'Not as yet.' Kendrick was steely. 'We're still working on it. We do have intelligence suggesting this cell is part of a group building up to something big though, and a series of incidents impacting the current election campaign—'

'Yes, yes, so you've said,' Adams snapped. 'But what we need here is admissible evidence. What exactly do you know about this second incident?'

Kendrick exhaled heavily. 'I've reached out to our source. He hasn't heard anything.'

'And yet again no group has accepted responsibility?' Kendrick shook his head.

Adams swore under his breath. 'Right, what do we know?' he said to Helen.

'It's pretty much like the last one, sir. Witnesses at the scene describe a series of shots, consistent with a semi-automatic rifle.' She went on to talk about the student room and the attack on the final victim who'd stumbled upon the killer. 'Orla took a blow to the head with a blunt instrument, was knocked unconscious, but she did get a good look at the attacker. She's working with an identification specialist to create a composite image of the suspect. Meantime, she's given us a detailed description – male, white, dark hair, slim, medium height. Estimated age, mid to late twenties.'

'No distinguishing features?' The chief looked desperate.

'Sadly not.'

He stared at Helen a second. 'Does the description match the image from the O'Malley's shooting?'

'What we recovered from the dashcam image near O'Malley's was restricted by the angle, but it certainly shares similarities. Both were slim, medium build, dressed in black jeans and a hoody.'

'For crying out loud.'

'There is always the possibility this is a copycat,' Kendrick piped up, 'someone completely unrelated.'

'For what purpose?' Adams looked appalled at the suggestion. 'Both incidents were shootings carried out on young adults with semi-automatic assault rifles. Rifles that are illegal in this country.'

'This was a riskier plan than the last, not as well executed. With the first incident they left the shells behind, chose an exit route where they could easily discard the weapon. This perpetrator was happened upon while he was finishing up. It all feels... less professional.'

'Nevertheless, the description and the type of weapon remains the same. Were any of the targets in the second shooting connected to the LGBTQ community?'

'It's too early to say,' Helen said. 'But we cannot afford to ignore any potential scenarios. There is something else to consider here.' She could feel their eyes on her, burning hot. 'My team have been digging deeper into the school reunion at O'Malley's last Friday.' She ignored the chief's jaw dropping. Kendrick's sharp gaze. Her nerves on a knife-edge as she raced them through the enquiries so far. She wasn't about to be silenced this time, not until she'd told them everything.

As she spoke, they both remained silent, gaze averted, as if they were absorbing every word, every possible lifeline to pull them out of this melee. When she mentioned the incel connection and Dark and Spencer's visit to Northumbria, Adams's face contorted. 'I thought you said Shaw was dead.'

'He is. We're working on the basis that an associate, possibly from the incel network, has carried out his wishes.'

'Christ, Helen. Why didn't I know about this?'

'With respect, sir, I tried to tell you yesterday.' She omitted to mention his response. This wasn't the time to kick the hornet's nest.

'So, where are we now?'

'My officers are still in Northumbria, talking to Shaw's work colleagues, friends, neighbours as we speak. We also have a pass to visit his cellmate at HMP Five Wells today. Our current priorities,' – she cringed inwardly as she uttered the word priorities; she wasn't just disobeying an order, she was completely ignoring it – 'are to track down the contact, TopBoy, and the half-brother.'

When Helen finished, Kendrick's face was taut. 'You didn't think to mention this to me,' he said.

'It came up as part of our background checks. I wanted to be sure before I approached you.'

'And, I take it, despite your ongoing inquiry, you still have no evidence to link the crime to Shaw,' he said, throwing her own allegations back at her.

Helen avoided his gaze, looking directly at the chief. 'I haven't finished. There's another connection. Ashleigh Urquhart, the columnist who received the email allegedly from the killer, was part of the reunion and in Shaw's class at school. If the killer was associated with Shaw, and they sent the email, it might explain why they chose to approach her.'

'Right.' He turned to Kendrick. 'What do you have on active incel groups in the Midlands?'

'Not much. Couple of names we are aware of, but no one with the capacity or capability to carry out something like this.'

'Okay, we're moving back to a two-pronged approach.' Adams leaned forward, splaying his hands on the desk in front of him. 'I want you both on this day and night. Whatever resources you need, we'll beg, borrow, or steal to make sure you have them. Our priority remains to apprehend this shooter.

'Chase that composite image of the suspect, will you?' he said to Helen. 'I want it circulated nationally throughout the force and included in an urgent statement to the media.

'Meantime, I'll get Vicki to set up a press conference in the Guildhall at 7 am. I want you both there. I've already had the mayor and the crime commissioner on the phone. They're losing confidence in the investigation by the second, talking about sending in senior investigators from Counter Terrorism Command. We need to make an arrest, and quick.'

CHAPTER 52

Helen was woken by something stroking her arm. She stirred, blinked. Looked up and blinked again at Matthew, her eldest son, leaning over her. Then jerked forward. 'What time is it?'

'Twenty to six.'

Helen scanned the room, befuddled. She was at home, on the sofa.

'I made you a cup of tea,' Matthew said.

She thanked him, a faint glow filling her chest as she took the proffered mug – Matthew rarely made anyone tea – and blinked again, forcing her addled brain into action. She'd come home to get a change of clothes for the press conference this morning. Yes, that was it. Arrived back around 4.30 am. She remembered settling into the sofa, taking the load off her feet. A wave of fatigue washing over her. Closing her eyes for a split second. Damn! She must have slipped into a deep slumber. Little wonder, given the night she'd had. She checked her phone. No new messages from the incident room. No news on the shooter. Detectives would be feeding first accounts into the system, forensics combing the scene. All night, she'd marshalled her troops. Organised a thorough forensic search of the university campus, briefed her staff, captured CCTV, helped draw up a press statement, shared the image of the killer. And so far, they had nothing. No firm leads to go on. According to the vice-chancellor, details of the summer school and the end of course party were on their website, available for anyone to see. Now they were forced to wait for the people of Hampton to wake up to the horrific news and hope that someone, somewhere, had spotted the killer and would come forward.

'You're up early,' she said to her son.

'I got up for work.'

Of course. It was Friday. He helped at the local newsagent. The owner, Sterling, was old-fashioned. Liked his newspapers sorted and delivered at the crack of dawn. 'What time are you leaving?'

'I'm not. They just messaged.' He glanced at his phone, as if he was expecting an update. 'The papers are delayed. They're not delivering until later.'

Probably a blessing. She certainly felt easier knowing her kids were at home this morning. Safe.

He sat on the sofa opposite her, a steaming mug in his hand. 'Is it true there's been another shooting at the uni?'

'Where did you hear that?'

'I got a news prompt on my phone this morning. Thought it was a joke at first.'

Helen's pulse quickened. At least the message was getting out there. Filling people's news feeds as they woke. 'Yes, I'm afraid so.' She checked her phone again. She needed to get to the office.

'How many were killed?'

'Two. A man and a woman. Three more injured. Seventeen- and eighteen-year-olds.' Barely adults. She watched his mind compute – only a year or so older than him – and her heart squeezed tight. She wanted to grab him, hug him, never let him go. The very idea of something like this happening to her own children sent her into a tailspin. But Matthew wasn't a fan of hugs and kisses.

'Christ!' His eyes were like saucers.

Silence fell upon them. The enormity of the situation thickening the air.

'And the killer got away again?'

Helen nodded.

'I thought you'd arrested the murderers.'

'Counter-terror do have suspects in custody for the O'Malley's shooting. It's difficult to say whether the incidents are linked.' The sight of his bulging eyes plucked a fresh heartstring. 'We're doing everything we can, son. Please try not to worry.'

He sipped his tea in silence, staring into space.

'How was Robert after I left last night?' Helen asked, changing the subject. She took a mouthful of tea and flinched as she burnt her lip. She really needed to get going.

'Wouldn't come out of his room.'

Helen hitched a breath. She couldn't see a resolution to this. But it was what Matthew said next that shocked her more.

'Honestly, I don't know what his problem is. This Stephen Chilli Franks guy, he's bad news. Drugs, kidnapping, firearms. The police can't have fabricated everything. They ought to lock him up and throw away the key.'

Helen stared at her eldest son, gobsmacked. 'You know about Franks?'

'I read the news feeds. Sounds like a right shit.'

Goodness. She had to face it, her boys were growing up, and with the help of the internet, Matthew had delved far deeper than she had given him credit for. 'It's complicated.'

'What because Franks is related to Zac? I don't see why. Just because Zac's uncle is a gangster, doesn't mean Zac's done anything wrong, or the rest of the family are involved. Robert needs to get over himself.'

Helen wanted to say more, so much more. To comment on the intelligence about Davy Boyd, his continued association with the criminal fraternity. But it was intelligence not to be shared with the public, and that included families. She couldn't break the police duty of confidentiality, as tempting as it might be.

'He's an idiot,' Matthew said. 'Gran and I, we tried talking to him last night. He won't listen to us. He won't listen to anyone.'

'He'll come round.' Although, deep down, Helen couldn't

be sure he would. The one thing Robert had inherited from his father was his stubborn streak. When he got his teeth into something, something he really believed in, he wouldn't budge. It was all such a mess.

'He needs to.' Matthew rose. 'Anyway, I'm going back to bed. Good luck on the case today.'

A choke caught in Helen's throat as Matthew disappeared. Out of her two children, Matthew had always been the independent, headstrong one. The all-action hero she imagined would be travelling the world when he grew up, occasionally calling her from distant lands. Robert was the family-oriented one. Always chatting, confiding in his mother. Always close by. How things changed…

Helen rubbed her eyes, digging her knuckles deep into the sockets. Perhaps Robert would calm down after sleeping on it. Give her a chance to explain properly later. Otherwise, as much as it pained her, she was going to have to let this play out. Wait for the court case. Let the media coverage fill in the gaps. She only hoped it wouldn't push her son further away.

CHAPTER 53

Ashleigh awoke to a blindingly bright light. She lifted her head, shielding her eyes. She was in her bedroom. Beside her, Noah's chest rose and fell rhythmically as he slept. Realising she'd been lying in a slice of light, seeping in from where the curtains hadn't quite met in the middle, she inched across the pillow and rested back. Waiting for her vision to adjust to the new day dawning.

Her bedside clock read 6.02 am. It was Friday morning. She recalled getting ready to turn in last night. Waiting for Noah to clean his teeth before she showered and climbed into bed. Then nothing. She must have fallen into an exhausted slumber. The lack of sleep and restless nights since the shooting had finally caught up with her.

Her mouth felt like she'd eaten a handful of sand. She swallowed twice, reached over, and switched on her phone. There was a text from the detective, asking her to call back. Lots of activity on the WhatsApp group, she'd read those later, but no new emails. Thank God.

Sliding out of the bed, slowly so as not to disturb Noah, Ashleigh's toes curled as she recalled the excruciating Zoom meeting last night. Trying to appear positive, upbeat with other survivors in the support group. Listening to their worries, their woes, individuals revealing their innermost fears, while this burgeoning secret pressed down on her shoulders. Someone had contacted her claiming to be the killer and she'd been gagged. A gag that made her writhe with guilt.

At least they hadn't responded to her reply. Almost twelve hours had passed since she'd pressed send, and it was, as others had suggested, starting to feel like a hoax, and she couldn't be more relieved. Perhaps, now, with the help of the group, she could focus on the culpability of those arrested.

She pulled her robe off the back of the door and crept out of the bedroom, avoiding the squeaky floorboard beside the entrance. The low babble of a television seeped up from the flat below: Johnny was awake early too. She heard the gush of a shower starting, the sounds heightened in the early morning.

Ashleigh was in the kitchen, flicking the switch on the kettle, when she reread the detective's message. *Could you call me as soon as you get this, please? I need to speak with you about something. Helen.*

The message had been sent at 1 am, when her phone was on silent. Odd. She wasn't expecting to hear from the detective. The arrangement was that Ashleigh would call her if she received further contact from the person claiming to be the shooter. Perhaps they'd had a breakthrough... She leaned up against the kitchen surface, called back and listened to the phone ring out. When the voicemail kicked in, she left a brief message and clicked off. Maybe they'd finally traced the email sender, or the counter-terror unit had charged the suspects and were ready to release more information. She desperately hoped so.

While the kettle boiled, she padded into the front room and switched on the television. A newsreader was talking about the upcoming election. Ashleigh rolled her eyes, backtracked to the kitchen, and made herself a coffee. The message from the detective niggled her. She glanced at her phone again. Maybe she should call the incident room. It was 6.10 am. Would they even be there at this time? She was just working this through in her mind when a voice on the television pulled her back to the front room. The presenter was talking about a shooting.

A crime scene filled the screen. A stray strand of blue

and white police tape flapping in the breeze. A reporter with a jacket zipped to her chin, dark hair blowing behind her in the wind, spoke into a fluffy microphone. But it wasn't Swan Street behind her. It was a Georgian stone building, sash windows. Ashleigh peered closer. If she wasn't mistaken, that was the front of Hampton University.

'Less than a week since a sniper opened fire on young men and women in Swan Street, another shooting has occurred, this time at Hampton University during their annual summer school week.'

What? Ashleigh jolted, flinching as hot coffee sloshed down her front, penetrating the thin cotton of her robe. She pulled the fabric away from her burnt chest. *Another shooting?* She grabbed the remote control, hiked up the volume, and stared at the television as the reporter talked about a student interrupting the killer. Two dead, three casualties. All aged between sixteen and eighteen. So young…

Ashleigh could barely breathe. It was like a bad dream, that at any moment Noah might wake her, just as he had the other morning. But she wasn't asleep now, she was very much awake.

Do not show this to the police the email had said. And she'd ignored it. A wave of nausea enveloped her. The very idea that she could be partly responsible for this attack, that something in her email response might have sparked this second killing spree, made bile rise in her throat.

Her phone rang in her hand, making her jump. It was Helen.

'Ashleigh?' The detective's voice was cool, calm. 'I'm sorry I missed your call.'

'I've just seen the news,' Ashleigh cut in.

'I'm sorry, I wanted to speak with you first, before the press release, hence my earlier message, but we couldn't wait any longer. Is Noah there with you?'

'Yes.' She didn't mention he was asleep.

'Good. As I said, we needed to get the appeal for witnesses out as soon as possible.'

Appeal for witnesses. They'd done that after the O'Malley's shooting. Several times. And yet, whatever they'd done, whoever they'd arrested, they hadn't stopped it happening again. 'Do you think this was prompted by the email response we sent yesterday?' she asked.

'I'm not sure. It could be a coincidence.'

'Some coincidence. I get a bloody email from someone claiming to be the killer and then this happens!'

'We still can't be sure they're connected, and you didn't ignore the message. You opened the lines of communication. Listen, try not to worry. We are investigating every eventuality. I take it you've heard nothing more?'

'No.'

'Good.' Ashleigh could hear voices in the background, all talking at once. 'I've got to go. We've a press conference at 7, I'll call you afterwards.'

'Detective?'

'Yes?'

'I thought you had the right people in custody.'

'So did I. Stay home for now and call me if you hear anything, anything at all. I'll be in touch again when I know more.'

CHAPTER 54

Helen stood in the corridor outside the celebrant room of the Guildhall, listening to the scraping of chairs, the sound of chattering voices, the din of the congregated press. Minutes earlier, she'd had to fight through a tight knot of reporters on the steps outside. BBC, CNN, Reuters, SKY, ITV, all jostling shoulders with local reporters. The second mass shooting in less than a week, in a small English provincial town, had regained the attention of the world media, and they refused to be silenced a second time.

After her exchange with Matthew, she'd quickly changed, dashed in from home, spoken with Ashleigh, and then Dark and Spencer – apprising them of the new incident, the heightened urgency – on the way. Shortly, Dark and Spencer would be starting their day in Northumbria. She desperately hoped they'd uncover something significant.

Helen switched her weight from foot to foot. She couldn't help feeling she'd got off lightly with the chief earlier. Thankfully, her covert investigation had come at just the right time to provide a lifeline: something with which to work, to tell the press, and he hadn't mentioned their conversation yesterday.

She looked at her phone. No new messages. It was 6.26. Kendrick and the chief should be there any minute. They were due to meet at 6.30 to discuss their media strategy. She fidgeted again and stared at the double doors leading out to the landing, trepidation building like air in a balloon as the seconds ticked past. Once again, she found herself missing the presence of Superintendent Jenkins. Ever since she'd joined homicide and major crime, Jenkins had preferred to handle press conferences and, she had to admit, he was adept at managing them. He nurtured contacts, knew who the troublesome journalists were, pinpointed those he needed to get on side to sway the crowd. Since these exercises took her away from the roots of the investigation, she'd happily left him to it. Only now, standing here, listening to the din in the room beyond, did she realise the enormity of the task in front of her.

Six twenty-nine. She looked around at the wood-panelled walls. The lack of natural light in the corridor made the space feel tight, stuffy. And still, the din clattered on the other side of the door. Journalists and reporters who'd arrived early, keen to secure their seat in what was undoubtedly Hampton's most high-profile conference to date. She was searching through her contacts, about to ring Vicki, the press officer, when the door to the corridor swung open and Adams appeared, the pips on his lapels gleaming under the artificial lighting. Vicki scurried alongside carrying a folder. She was dressed in a red trouser suit, immaculate as usual, her blonde hair tied into a plait that rested over her right shoulder.

'Helen,' Adams nodded, his face tight. 'Where's Kendrick?'

'Not here yet.'

'Good,' he said. 'Because I need a quick word with you.' He glanced over his shoulder to make sure they hadn't been followed. 'Half an hour ago, the Prime Minister declared the situation in Hampton a national emergency. The Home Secretary has called for SO15, Counter Terrorism Command, to take over the investigation. Commander Marcus Quinn is flying down this morning from a network meeting in Glasgow.'

Helen had heard the name before, mentioned in briefings and on intelligence, but never worked with Quinn. 'Do you know him?'

Adams tugged at his cuffs. 'I worked with him for a short time in the Met. He's… efficient.'

'And?' By the look on Adams's face, there was clearly a lot more to add.

'Let's just say he's very focused, ambitious. And he's retiring next year. He'll be looking for stories, anecdotes for his after-dinner speech appointments.'

'Which includes coming down here, emerging as the hero of the moment.'

'I didn't say that.'

He didn't need to. Helen knew the sort; she'd worked with enough of them over the years. Rising through the ranks, not caring who they crushed beneath their boots to get there. 'What about Kendrick?'

'I'm not sure. He'll probably be working with them, at least for a while.' His eyes locked onto hers. 'It goes without saying, I expect you to give SO15 your full cooperation.'

'Of course,' Helen said. Though it galled her to pass the investigation over to someone else when they'd done so much groundwork. 'I presume we'll still be involved?'

'We'll be supporting SO15 initially. As I said, they will be taking over the investigation. I expect you to turn everything you have over to them, and I mean everything this time.'

'But, sir—'

Adams placed up a flat hand. 'This is political, Helen. We're down on staff as it is, without an assistant chief constable, and now a superintendent, not to mention you have an inspector role on your team to be filled. They're drafting in officers from all over.' A tenderness filled his eyes. 'Look, this investigation is too big for us. It probably always was.' He glanced towards the door as reporters continued to clatter about in the room beyond. 'We just need to do what we can to pacify everyone until they arrive.'

Before Helen could respond, the doors flapped open, and Kendrick appeared. He nodded at Helen, gave the chief a smile that didn't reach his eyes. It was difficult to read him.

Vicki ushered them into a side room with a low table surrounded by a handful of chairs, twittering about a list of questions she'd obtained from the nationals.

'Right,' Adams said. 'Let's get this over with.'

CHAPTER 55

Ashleigh sat on the sofa beside Noah, an untouched glass of water in her hand, and stared at the television screen where the chief constable of Hamptonshire was lifting his hands, appealing for calm. But his strong words did nothing to mollify the journalists shouting over him as he spoke, some of them on their feet. *Who the hell have you got in custody? What are you doing to protect the people of Hampton? What do you know about the killer?*

The chief was sitting on the stage of the celebrant room at the Guildhall, a room usually reserved for ceremonies – weddings, civil ceremonies – and flanked by two detectives: Helen on one side, a colleague from counter-terror on the other. Cameras flashed. More questions were shouted from the crowd. The chief repeated his earlier statement, that senior officers from Counter Terrorism Command were on their way to assist, and Ashleigh's gaze switched to an enlarged Photofit behind him – the face of man the press were calling The Sniper Killer.

Slim. Dark hair peeping from beneath a hood. Intense, wolf-like eyes. A shiver ran down her spine.

For the last couple of hours, Ashleigh and Noah had checked the news channels incessantly, flipping from one to another, a ball of nausea curdling within her as she desperately tried to find out more information on the latest shooting. And this news conference did nothing to allay her fears.

'We are advising residents to avoid public gatherings,' the chief said, 'and that includes the candlelit vigil tonight.' He went on to talk about extra officers deployed on town centre streets, increased stop and search powers. Ashleigh zoned out. It was the third time she'd viewed the footage; she could almost quote it verbatim.

Not once did the police admit they were wrong with the first shooting. The killer was still out there. And emailing her.

'What time is Zuri coming?' Noah said, interrupting her thoughts.

It wasn't that she'd forgotten about Nia's mum's visit, she hadn't, but with everything that had happened this morning, she'd pushed it to the side of her mind. She looked up at the clock. Almost 9 am. 'She's due in an hour. I doubt she'll come now. Not after what's happened. I mean, it's a bloody debacle.'

'We have to try not to panic,' Noah said soothingly.

'How can we not? The police stopped the investigation, allowed more people to be killed.' Her phone beeped beside her. The WhatsApp group of survivors. The thread had been going mad all morning, speculating about the implications of last night's shooting, the motive, those responsible, what it meant. Ashleigh's mind whirled. She couldn't deal with this.

'You don't know that.'

'Well, what's the alternative? Two different gunmen in a week in the same town? I don't think so, Noah.'

'I'm just saying, we need to wait, find out the facts.'

'Wait? You've got to be kidding me. We waited last time and were told those responsible were in custody. Then nothing. Radio Silence. And what about the email I received?'

'We can't be sure it's related.'

Ashleigh exhaled in exasperation. 'Listen to yourself. You've no idea.'

'Ash, please. Why don't we call the detective again?'

'I've spoken with her, I told you!'

Silence fell upon them. Loaded, uncomfortable. Ashleigh wriggled irritably. She didn't want to argue with Noah. He was only trying to help, but the knot in her chest was so tight, she didn't know what to do, who to turn to.

'Look, why don't I go for a run?' Noah said. 'Give you some time to think.'

'Oh, that's right. You go for a run. Leave me on my own.' She folded her arms across her chest.

'I can stay if you want.'

'I don't need babysitting!' She dropped her voice an octave, anger burning her veins. 'Anyway, you heard the police chief, you can't go out.'

'He's advised against mass gatherings. We haven't been told to stay inside.'

'For Christ's sake, Noah, there's a gunman on the loose.'

'The shootings are planned. Directed at large crowds, not someone running around the park alone.'

'How do you know he won't change up, start taking a pop at anyone.'

'I'll be fine.'

'I think you're mad.'

'Then I'll stay.'

She rounded on him, the anger inside her burning to a fireball. 'Why, because I want you to? Because, quite honestly, I don't need you here.' She was being irrational, she knew that – this wasn't her – but deep inside, her heart was bleeding, her nerves twisted up. She'd lost Nia and Cass. She couldn't lose Noah too. Though she didn't want him to stay either.

'Oh, come on. Don't be like that.'

'Like what?'

'I'm happy to look after you.'

'Look after me?' Suddenly, something inside snapped. The fears, the worries, the secrets and lies breaking into shards within her. 'I'm not a bloody ten-year-old!'

'Ash, please, let's not do this.'

He reached out. Soft, tender eyes, and she shrugged him off. She didn't want to hurt Noah, but everything was coalescing, and she was hurting so bad, she didn't know which way to turn. 'No. Go. Take some time away. Get some air. You clearly need it.'

She turned away to avoid the hurt in his face as he rose for the door, heard him rustling about in the bedroom, getting changed. Seconds later, the front door banged shut. And he was gone.

CHAPTER 56

Back in her office, Helen's back grew uncomfortably hot as she stared at the Photofit of The Sniper Killer. She loathed the media's habit of labelling killers. A hook for people to hold on to, not to mention giving the murderer notoriety. It didn't help that the image, dark eyes staring up from beneath a hood, looked more like a poster from a horror film. If that wasn't bad enough, the phone line from the public appeal had been disappointingly quiet all morning.

She was waiting for an update from Dark and Spencer but, given the urgency, they'd have called if they'd found anything significant and she had to face facts – they were running around the country chasing the ghost of a dead man. So far, they hadn't found Shaw's half-brother or identified TopBoy, and they had no suspect they could link directly to either shooting. She pulled out her hair tie and dragged a hand through her hair, snagging a knot at the back. Wincing as she tugged her fingers through the tangle. Perhaps the chief was right, this case was too big for them to deal with.

She raked another hand through her hair. If she closed her eyes, she could still see the grim faces of the world's media staring back at her earlier. Hear their fractious questioning, their dissent. Adams had gone into the press conference mob-handed, hoping to bring the reporters on side, dilute the public's fears, and the plan had backfired in his face. Even his assurances about armed officers walking the streets didn't help. They wanted answers.

But it wasn't only the media that was bothering Helen. It was day eight and there was still no explanation for either of the shootings. Which could only mean one thing. The Sniper Killer, whoever he was, hadn't finished his campaign.

A single knock on her office door. She lifted her eyes as Pemberton wandered in. 'Three things,' he said. 'First, the organisers are talking about going ahead with the candlelit vigil tonight.'

'What?' Helen stared at him in disbelief. Were these people mad? She could only imagine what a logistical nightmare it would be to police. 'You're not serious?'

'They are saying they won't be beaten, won't be terrorised. Can't see many turning up, though.'

'Oh, Christ.'

'Also, ballistics have confirmed the AK-47 recovered from the canal was the one used in the O'Malley's shooting.'

If both shootings were committed by the same killer, why dump the first rifle? It didn't make sense. 'What's the other news?'

Pemberton's face tightened. 'One of the victims of last night's shooting was a witness at Franks's upcoming trial.'

'You are joking.'

'Afraid not. Jordan Ward. He was one of Chilli Franks's former runners. Apparently, he'd turned his life around. Was planning to start a college course in September.'

Helen stilled. 'First, someone with links to Chilli's rival gang was present at the O'Malley's shooting, and now a witness at his upcoming trial was killed at the university.'

'Could just be a coincidence.'

She pulled a face. She'd been a detective long enough to know that coincidences in policing were rare.

A phone rang in the main office. Pemberton excused himself and wandered out, closing the door behind him, leaving Helen reeling. She'd thought they'd bottomed out any potential involvement by Chilli Franks in the shootings, discounted him. The fact that he now had links with both incidents left her with a deep sense of disquiet.

CHAPTER 57

'Oh, look at that one!' Zuri said, pointing a chubby finger at the screen and elbowing Ashleigh.

Ashleigh stared at the photo of Nia holding up a G&T in a plastic cup, her dark skin glistening under the monochromatic lighting. White teeth sparkling as she gave her usual winning smile. She hadn't been sure about going through old photos with Nia's mother, but the woman had cajoled her to the point of insistence from the minute she'd arrived. It was as if she wanted to soak up, absorb, every second of her late daughter's life. 'That was when we went to see Bon Jovi at the Ricoh stadium,' she said. 'Do you remember she sprained her ankle, climbing across the seats to get closer to the front?'

'Oh, yes. It swelled like a melon. She had to go for physio for months to put it right.'

'That's because she danced on it all night afterwards.'

Laughter gurgled from the bottom of Zuri's stomach. 'Oh, that child. Always so accident prone.'

Zuri had looked drawn when she'd arrived on Ashleigh's doorstep earlier, as if she hadn't slept in a week. But instead of taking Ashleigh aside, asking her about the police investigation, probing her about the suspects or what she might have heard from the newspaper, talking about the second shooting, or even mentioning Nia, she'd merely asked after Noah, then joked that he ran so much, he'd wear his legs down. No tears, no drama as she hugged Ashleigh, cupped her face in her hands, checked she was okay. Then she'd shed her jacket and bustled into the flat, flicking the switch on the kettle and making them both drinks in her usual inimitable way.

Zuri pulled up another photo, this time of Ashleigh and Nia on London Bridge, the night they did the Moonwalk in bras decorated with fairy lights to raise money for breast cancer research, and Ashleigh's chest ached. While Zuri clearly took comfort from the memories, Ashleigh felt like her heart was bleeding all over again.

But she couldn't deny it was comforting to have Zuri there. Her soothing voice. Her easiness. Her amazing spirit in the face of such incredible adversity. Nia had often talked about the struggles her mother had faced in life. Immigrating to the UK twenty years ago, fleeing the civil war in their native Somalia, with three young children. Witnessing shocking, horrifying events most people never faced in a lifetime. Perhaps that had toughened her reserve, made her deal with things differently.

But Zuri still hadn't raised the issue she wanted to talk to her about, and uneasiness tugged at Ashleigh.

They searched through more photos. Of old-school discos, nights out, the school ski trip in Year 9, Ashleigh's eighteenth birthday party. All the while, Ashleigh squirming in her seat, searching for the right moment to interject.

'It was good of you to come,' she said eventually. 'I wasn't sure after…' She couldn't quite bring herself to say the words. 'This morning's news.'

Zuri didn't take her eyes off the screen. Instead, she scrolled down further, to Ashleigh's graduation photos. 'I refuse to kowtow to a man with a gun,' she said. 'Nia wouldn't have wanted that.' She clicked out of the file. Opened another. 'Not that I'm going to the vigil tonight. If you ask me, the organisers are crazy to even contemplate going ahead with it.'

Ashleigh was about to speak again when Zuri tapped the screen and pointed at a picture of Cass, Nia and Ashleigh in Crete, the holiday they'd taken the summer after A levels.

Just before they'd all parted for university. 'Those crop tops,' she said, shaking her head. The girls were dressed for a night out: Nia in shorts, Cass and Ashleigh in mini-skirts, sun-kissed skin glowing. 'They never suited her.' Ashleigh expected her to scroll on, but the woman couldn't take her eyes off the photo. Suddenly, her chin quivered. A tremor travelled through her shoulders. Her eyes filled and she started to cry.

Ashleigh took the laptop from Zuri, rested it on the floor and wrapped her arms around her, holding the woman tight as her tears descended into sobs. She cried and cried. And Ashleigh cried with her. Rubbing her back. Holding her close.

Ashleigh wasn't sure how long they sat there. Eventually, Zuri pulled back, reached into her bag, and pulled out a packet of tissue, passing a bunch across. And still they sat there, staring into nothingness. The morning sun streaming through the window, bouncing off Zuri's dark skin. Until Ashleigh could bear it no longer. 'What did you want to talk to me about?' she asked.

'I'm sorry?'

'You said there was something you wanted to discuss.' Ashleigh held the older woman's gaze. *Here it comes. Her doubts about the investigation. Her suspicions about the arrest.*

'Oh.' Zuri's face folded. She paused a moment, and when she spoke, a croak coated her voice. 'We've arranged Nia's funeral.' A fresh tear trickled down her cheek. She swiped it away with the back of her hand. 'I wondered if you would write a piece for the eulogy. Nia was always a big fan of your column.'

A wave of scrabbled emotions. Honoured to be asked to write something special for her best friend. Disappointment that they weren't about to set off on a crusade for justice together. Ashleigh was sorely tempted to ask about the enquiry, to raise the issue again, but the woman looked so sad, and she couldn't bear the thought of pouring more grief onto an already brimming pile, so she simply nodded.

'Thank you,' Zuri said. 'That means a lot.' She grabbed her bag, stood. 'Right. I'd better go. Will you be okay?'

Ashleigh nodded again, though inside she was still twisted up. She wanted to tell Zuri about the email she'd received but even if she hadn't been gagged by the police, this wasn't the time.

'I'm sorry I missed Noah. Give him my love.' Zuri brushed another tear from her cheek, and engulfed Ashleigh in a fresh hug. 'Promise me something?' she said, pulling back. Large brown eyes staring into Ashleigh's. 'You will hold onto that boy, won't you? He's one of the good ones.'

Ashleigh cringed, the guilt of their earlier argument pinching her hard. Zuri was right, Noah was one of the good ones. She needed to make it up to him. She mustn't let this come between them.

She saw Zuri out, wandered back into the lounge and looked out of the window. The park was quiet this morning, the bench in the corner empty. She watched Johnny cross the road, carrying a guitar case. He must be going for a lesson. He caught her eye, gave a polite backwards nod, which she returned. Still no sign of Noah... She grabbed her phone, texted her fiancé. *So sorry for everything. Love you x*

Ashleigh reread the message. The old her, before the shooting, before life had changed irrevocably, would have regarded that as soppy, soft. She and Noah usually exchanged shallow texts, banter, teasing each other. But Noah hated arguments, and she'd been so overwhelmed she'd been mean, taken it out on him. Soppy was what was needed right now.

She pressed send, switched on the sound so that she'd hear his reply, then tossed the phone aside. Willing a quick response, anything to ease the pain in her chest. The flat was quiet this morning, all her neighbours out, and suddenly, she felt fatigue wash over her. She was resting back into the sofa, about to close her eyes a second when her phone buzzed. That was quick.

She leapt forward, reached for her phone, and froze. It wasn't a text, it was an email.

BITCH!
You went to the police, didn't you? I told you not to, I told you I'd know if you did. I know exactly who you've been speaking to.

I've seen the detectives visit and your neighbours come and go. You think you are safe, sitting at your first-floor window, watching the world go by, cooped up there with your boyfriend. You're wrong.

Last night was on YOU. You should have listened when you had the chance. Now you are going to pay.

CHAPTER 58

Helen wandered out into the incident room, filled a cup from the water dispenser and stared across at their murder wall. Photos of the new victims had been added. Smiley, happy photos beside covered lumps on the ground from the crime scene. It was a pitiful sight.

'Ma'am?' She turned to face Kerry, one of her admin staff: a short, squat woman in a trouser suit, chestnut curls framing a kind face. She was holding out an envelope file. 'This was dropped off at reception for you.'

'Thanks.' Helen flipped it open, immediately recognising the sharp italics of Brandon Eriksen. 'Ah, the pathologist's report.'

'Yeah. Don't know why he didn't come up to the office, he was only in here yesterday.'

'The pathologist was here in the incident room? When?'

'When you were at the canal. Someone must have let him in. He was looking for you, I left a message on your desk.'

Helen frowned. She was reminded of their awkward conversation last night. *Something personal.* 'I didn't see anything.'

The young woman followed her into her office. 'I left it there,' she said, pointing to a space between two piles of paperwork. 'Wait! Here it is.' Kerry bent down, pulled a yellow Post-it note from the floor and handed it over. *Sorry I missed you. Give me a call when you are free. Brandon.*

Helen frowned again – what was he after? She thanked Kerry, waited for her to retreat to the incident room, then opened the file. Sliding out the typed sheets of the autopsy reports from the second shooting. There was another Post-it attached to the front. *Nothing significant to report, give me a call if you have any queries. Or if you just fancy a coffee sometime.*

A coffee sometime… Helen smoothed out the first Post-it and reread it. Then rolled her eyes. Oh, God. She had hoped that Pemberton was wrong and the new pathologist hadn't taken a shine to her. Even if she was in the market, which she most definitely wasn't, she wouldn't exactly be an enticing candidate for a relationship.

She pictured Dean: the tall, dark detective. The one man she'd seriously dated since John had died. The one man she'd taken into her heart, introduced to her kids. But Dean had betrayed her, then passed away soon afterwards. Both the men she'd let into her life now six feet under. Helen sat back, allowing herself a wry smile as she looked again at the note. Based on her track record, any prospective partner would never be a welcome candidate for life insurance.

Pemberton stepped into her office, shaking her back to the present. 'We've heard from Births, Deaths, and Marriages. Ivan Shaw's birth certificate only gives his mother's details. No father is mentioned. No luck with Memington Hall either. Shaw had only worked there a week or so when the incident with Eugene Grant happened. Didn't go back afterwards.' It was almost midday, over fourteen hours since the second shooting, and still their enquiries were leading nowhere. 'The guys from Northumbria are on line two,' he continued, closing the door, then nodding at the phone. 'I've filled them in on our enquiries at the university.'

Helen indicated for him to take a seat, picked up her phone and placed it on speaker. 'How are you both?' she asked.

'We're fine,' Dark said. 'Looks like you've got your work cut out down there.'

'You can say that again. Any news?'

'Not much. We managed to speak with the neighbour this morning.'

'And?'

'An elderly woman called Ellen Granger. She's been away visiting her granddaughter in Durham. Seems to have been the closest person to Shaw. She was a good friend of his Nan's, took him under her wing when the old woman died. Pretty scathing about the girlfriend, called her a good-for-nothing user. After she left, Ellen cooked him the odd meal, looked out for him.'

'Could she tell you anything about friends, other family, associations?'

'Not really. She was the main beneficiary of the will. She said he was an awkward character. The sort that struggles to make friends. He rarely had visitors. She was amazed when he left everything to her when he died, it was totally unexpected.'

'Any news on his computer?'

'Afraid not. She gave away most of his possessions, including the computer, to charity. Just kept a tea set that had belonged to his nan.'

Helen stared at Pemberton. Another potential lead dashed.

'It was Ellen who organised the funeral,' Dark added. 'There was hardly anyone there, just a few work colleagues and the copper that dealt with his case. It was all a bit sad.'

'What about the half-brother?'

'Shaw had mentioned him to her, but she was away when he visited. Didn't give a name though and he wasn't included in the will. There was a man sitting at the back of the crematorium at the funeral, she wondered if it might be him. She looked out for him after the service, but he'd already left.'

'Did she get a look at him?'

'I asked that. She gave us a rough description – slim build, medium height, looked about thirtyish. Dark features, clean shaven. She only saw him briefly.'

'Right. Anything else?'

'I don't think so. Nobody knows who this TopBoy is. We're going to try Shaw's GP next.'

'Okay. Give me a call if the doctor comes up with anything.'

Helen rang off. Finding the brother was key to this line of enquiry, yet they were facing a dead end at every juncture. It was as if he didn't want to be found.

She'd no sooner put her phone down when her mobile rang. It was Ashleigh Urquhart.

'He's been in touch again.' Stuttered words that splintered into a sob.

'Ashleigh, are you okay?' Helen asked. 'Is Noah with you?'

'No, he went out,' she squawked. 'I've had another email.'

Helen asked her to forward it. Within seconds, her email pinged. She scanned it quickly. 'Listen, we're on our way. Don't answer the door to anyone until we get there.'

Pemberton scooted round to Helen's side of the desk, peering over her shoulder as she ended the call. Within seconds, Helen turned to face him.

'Are you thinking what I'm thinking?' he said.

She raised a concerned brow, then looked back at the screen. Their reply had been sent from the columnist's address. Yes, they had visited Ashleigh, but they were plainclothes officers. There had been no liveried police cars at Portland Grove, no obvious presence of police. If Ashleigh had kept her silence, the only way the sender would know she had gone to the police was if they were connected to the inquiry. A feeling of dread twisted her gut as she recalled the speculation over leaks with the first email. Kendrick, discounting the detail of thirty rounds fired at O'Malley's as generic. But nothing about this was generic. 'We've got a leak.'

CHAPTER 59

'He's been watching me,' Ashleigh muttered.

It had taken an age to settle the woman when Helen and Pemberton had arrived at her flat and, even now, as Ashleigh sat on her sofa, a mug of sweet tea in her trembling hands, she looked like she'd seen a ghost.

Helen took the mug from her and placed it on the coffee table. 'Is there anyone you've argued with, or upset recently?'

'No! Not that I know of anyway.' Ashleigh shook her head. 'You don't understand. I've never made any secret of where I live in my column. I wrote a piece about urban regeneration only last month, mentioned Portland Grove in it.'

Helen hid her grimace. That widened the field of suspects somewhat. 'Have you spoken to anyone else about the emails or the case? Friends, family…'

'Only Noah, and he's sworn to secrecy.' Ashleigh sniffed into a tissue. 'I think it's time I tell my editor at *The Hampton Herald*.'

'I'm not sure that's a good idea.'

'You said that last time.' Another sob juddered out. 'And look what's happened. People need to know. The newspaper needs to know in case he contacts them. I'm not keeping quiet about this. Not again.'

Helen suppressed a sigh. Printing the emails in the newspaper, raising more question marks over the killer, was the last thing the investigation needed, the public were panicked enough. But, right now, she couldn't care less about the press. Her priority was to keep the young woman safe. 'Where is Noah?' she asked, changing the subject.

'He went out this morning. I haven't heard from him since.'

Helen and Pemberton exchanged a glance. The couple had seemed close on their previous visits. Noah, the doting fiancé. It seemed odd that he'd leave her, especially the morning after a second shooting. 'When was this?' she asked.

'About nine. Before I got the message. We had… a bit of an argument. Now he won't return my calls or messages.'

'What did you argue about?'

'The shooting. Him going out.' She sniffed. 'We've been stuck in the flat for too long. It's been brewing awhile.'

'Is it usual for Noah to ignore your calls and messages when you have a falling out?'

'Not really. Noah doesn't like to argue.' She met Helen's gaze. 'You don't think anything's happened to him, do you?'

'I have no reason to believe that.' Though his absence did instil a sense of disquiet. 'Did he happen to mention where he was going?'

'He talked about going for a run and then left suddenly.' Her face pained. 'I've phoned his mum. Tried a few friends. Nobody knows where he is.'

Ordinarily, a twenty-three-year-old adult disappearing wouldn't be a prime concern, especially in the middle of a major investigation. People took themselves off all the time, particularly if they argued with loved ones. But nothing was ordinary about this case, and something about Noah's disappearance sat uncomfortably.

Dark's comments about Ivan Shaw, his threats to 'pull a Columbine' skipped into Helen's mind. If the killer was someone close to Shaw, if he'd known them since school, maybe Ashleigh might be able to shed some light. She pressed her lips together, leaned forward. 'Ashleigh, do you recall the name Ivan Shaw?'

Ashleigh frowned. 'Ivan?' She broke off a second. 'He was in my class at school. I haven't seen him in years.'

'He hasn't attended any of the reunions?'

'No. Ivan wasn't one for joining in. Cass thought he was strange. I just felt a bit sorry for him. He was always on his own.' She looked up, met Helen's gaze. 'Why are you asking about him?'

'We understand there was an incident between him and another former pupil from your class,' Helen said, ignoring the question. Watching the young woman's reaction carefully.

'Yes. With Eugene. Ivan went to prison. It's no secret.' Recognition fluttered across her brow. 'You're not suggesting Ivan had anything to do with the O'Malley's shooting? I mean, I know he pulled a weapon on Eugene, but it was only a pretend gun. Nothing real.'

'Ivan is dead,' Helen said. 'He passed away earlier this year.'

'What?' She looked genuinely shocked. 'I had no idea. We went to the same college after school. Hampton College. It was on the old site, where the university is now.' She gasped, pressed a hand to her face. 'But if he's dead, I don't see how he could be involved.'

'We're not sure he is,' Helen said, playing it down. 'It's just a line of enquiry we're checking. We're looking to speak with anyone with links to either of the shootings.' She asked Ashleigh if she had any idea who Shaw mixed with, and she said she didn't.

'Okay,' Helen said. She didn't want to frighten Ashleigh any more than necessary. 'We need to talk about some basic safeguarding for you. We can put you up in a hotel–'

'No!' Ashleigh looked from one to another, fearful eyes wide.

'If the email sender has been watching you, it might be better to move you out for a while.'

'You think this is the killer, don't you?'

'We can't be sure of that. But, until we track him down, I need to protect you.'

'I'm safe here in the flat, I've got my neighbours around me. I'm not moving.'

'Okay.' Helen lifted her hands in surrender. 'If you wish

to remain here, I'll try to make that happen. Stay away from the window and keep your phone with you.'

Ashleigh stared at her.

'Listen, I need to pop out and make a couple of calls. Why don't you give the sergeant Noah's details – what he was wearing, what car he drives,' Helen said gently. 'We'll put out a trace, set your mind at rest.'

'Detective, do you really think I'm in danger?' Her tone was quiet, mouse-like.

'I'm not sure. As I say, I'll feel better when we've tracked down whoever is doing this. We will catch them.'

'You said that last time.'

Helen had no answer for that. She excused herself, blood pulsing through her veins as she moved out of Ashleigh's flat, onto the landing.

The link between Ashleigh and these killings was undeniable, and her priority was to keep the young woman safe, even if it wasn't her investigation. But personal protection wasn't easy to organise.

Helen pulled her phone out of her pocket and tried Kendrick. Listening to the line ring out. Clenching her teeth as the voicemail kicked in. Why was he never available when needed? Well, she wasn't about to wait around for him, or Counter Terrorism Command for that matter. She clicked off and dialled another number. It was time to take the matter into her own hands.

CHAPTER 60

'Who the hell's been talking?' Pemberton said, his face taut as they descended the stairs from Ashleigh's flat.

'It's not just a case of who has been talking,' Helen said. 'It's who they've been talking to.' It was bad enough when the public shared things after they were advised to keep quiet. Loose lips from a fellow colleague, especially someone within your team, someone you worked with day in, day out... The very notion lodged like a fishbone in the back of her throat. 'We kept our enquiries in Northumbria quiet, but the email was a part of the live investigation.' She considered the incident room: the noticeboards littered with information about the attacks, the enlarged version of the email to Ashleigh on the DMI's screen, clear for all to see. Though for the life of her, she couldn't imagine any of the individuals in her department giving out information. 'There is one possibility we haven't discussed...'

Pemberton gave her a knowing look, his face grave. 'I can't believe the killer's one of us.'

Helen couldn't either, but she couldn't deny whoever sent those emails to Ashleigh had the inside track on the investigation. They arrived in the entrance hall and stepped out into the afternoon sunshine. 'Let's keep this second email close until SO15 take over. Only you, me, and the chief for now.'

A nasty thought crept in as he nodded.

'Do me a favour, will you?' she said, grabbing his elbow, stopping him in his tracks. 'Do a bit of quiet digging, find out where the new pathologist came from, what his background is?'

Pemberton stared at her. 'Brandon? You don't suspect him?'

'I don't know. I don't know anything about him.' She hated doing this, singling people out, suspecting those she worked alongside. But Brandon had happened upon their conversation outside the office the other day. His presence at the university after the second shooting was unusual, he should have known from the nature of the deaths it wouldn't be worth attending, and him visiting the incident room... Pemberton had joked his interest was romantic. She'd even considered the idea herself. What if they were wrong, and he had an ulterior motive for getting so close?

Pemberton's phone rang. He dug it out of his pocket, answered.

Helen nodded at the officer in the plainclothes car opposite as they trudged down to their vehicle. Chief Constable Adams had initially sounded irritated when she'd called him earlier. It wasn't until Helen explained the situation that his tone had softened – clearly, he wasn't a fan of Kendrick's persistent unavailability either – and he'd proved surprisingly helpful. Authorising two armed officers to be stationed outside Ashleigh's flat in a plain vehicle, a trace to be put out for Noah's car. After much persuasion, Ashleigh had reluctantly agreed to keep the emails to herself, at least for the rest of the day – one small blessing – and to remain in the building and call immediately if she received any further contact. The young woman couldn't continue like this for long, though.

Helen climbed into her car and looked out across the park as she fastened her seatbelt. It was quiet this afternoon: the bench beside the entrance, the bandstand, empty. The leaves of a willow feathered through the railings, blowing in the soft breeze.

'Sounds like SO15 have arrived,' Pemberton said, finishing his call and joining her in the car.

'Commander Quinn?'

'No. He's stuck at Glasgow airport. His plane is delayed. He's sent his second-in-command, someone named Mike Walker, to get things started. Walker is with Kendrick now. He wants to see you and me for a debrief afterwards.'

Helen squirmed in her seat. The prison visit was in an hour, and her team were tied up, interviewing and following leads from the second shooting. Everybody was busy. Dark and Spencer's earlier feedback, their stalled enquiries, snuck into her mind. This could be her final opportunity to find something before she lost the reins for good.

She passed Pemberton a sideways look. 'How do you feel about covering for me?'

He stared at her, as if he was second-guessing her thoughts. 'In what way?'

'Say I've been caught up, play for time. Give SO15 a rundown on the investigation to date, pass them my policy log if you must.' Unique to each case, the policy log was a senior investigating officer's diary where they recorded their innermost thoughts on the enquiry, worked through their suppositions and theories, justified their investigative strategy and actions taken. Helen didn't part with it readily, though needs must here, anything to squeeze out an extra hour or so.

'You're still going to the prison?' he said, the trace of a smile on his lips. 'Won't be a popular move.'

'Probably not. But'– she drew in a long breath – 'you know what, this is our patch, our town. I'm not ready to abandon it yet.'

His smile widened. 'I'm sure I can delay them a while.'

'Thanks.' She gave him a wink. 'I'll drop you at head-quarters on the way.'

CHAPTER 61

Ashleigh stood to the side of her front window, peering around the edge of the curtain as the detectives drove off, the bony hand of fear and worry pressing down on her. Fear at the empty street outside, the unmarked police car the only vehicle, parked diagonally opposite. Fear that The Sniper Killer had singled her out. Worry that she still hadn't heard from Noah.

The killer said last night was on her. No. No way. She wasn't about to shoulder the burden of a psychopathic killer, whatever his warped mind told him. Because that's what he was. Nobody fires at a group of innocent individuals for nothing. But what did concern her was that he hadn't imparted his message.

He hadn't finished yet.

Another glance at the park. She was beginning to feel like an actor, at the side of the stage, watching a play she wasn't part of while The Sniper Killer roamed free. Hovering in the shadows. She dropped the curtain, backed away from the window.

The clock on her mantel read 1.30 pm. She should be preparing to film her Instagram live, *Recipe for the weekend*. In a normal week, she'd have spent hours practising. Honing her ingredients. Perfecting her recipe, step by step. Ordinarily, she'd be in the kitchen now, preparing everything to go live this evening. Poised to write up her food blog afterwards. She never missed it. Even if she was away, or busy like last

Friday, she recorded in advance. But nothing about this week had been normal.

Maybe she should break her promise to the detective, contact Jason, share the killer's emails with him. Jason would undoubtedly print them – it would be the scoop of the year for *The Herald*. But what good would that do apart from feed his editorial ego? It's not like she had any fresh information to add.

Anger gnawed at her, colliding with her frustrations with the inquiry. She didn't want to do this, she didn't want to play ball. She didn't owe the police anything. But she couldn't deny, she liked the female detective, she really did. The woman seemed to empathise, to care, and she'd seemed conflicted too.

Plus, there was the WhatsApp support group to consider. She'd ignored all the messages today. Speculation over the second shooting, over those in custody. Constant notes and opinions. They'd had no idea she was in neck-deep when she'd chaired that meeting yesterday and, if they found out now, she'd lose all integrity.

The best she could do was to locate Noah. Her nerves performed a jig as she grabbed her phone and typed out another text. *Noah, where are you? Please call as soon as you get this. I'm scared now.*

CHAPTER 62

Situated on the edge of the county of Northamptonshire, HMP Five Wells, a sprawling conglomeration of grey new-build units erected on the site of the demolished former HM Prison Wellingborough, was no less imposing than its previous structure. Recently opened, it was one of the government's new 'smart prisons', designed with workshops on site to focus on retraining and rehabilitating prisoners for release. But locals who lived less than a stone's throw from its gates were reminded of the dangerous inmates it contained, from violent criminals to sex offenders, by the grim network of high-wired perimeter fencing.

It was the first time Helen had visited the prison in its new incarnation, and she was surprised at how quickly she was processed through the system. Although she had made it easy, leaving her bag and phone in the car so that she didn't need a locker, and she took no notebook or pen with her.

Before she knew it, she was directed to an interview room with a small table in the middle surrounded by four chairs, all bolted to the floor. A camera in the corner spun round as she entered.

She'd no sooner settled herself into her chair when a prison guard led in a man dressed in a grey T-shirt and black jogging bottoms. Oliver Stanton was the image of the mugshot held on his file. A thick-set man, with a square jaw, greying hair cropped to number two, and hooded brows. He slumped into the chair opposite Helen, folded his nicotine-yellow hands in his lap and eyed her suspiciously.

'You're not in any trouble,' Helen said once she'd introduced herself. 'I'm here to talk about a former cellmate of yours. Ivan Shaw.'

He continued to stare, unspeaking.

'I understand you shared a cell with Ivan for almost eleven months, up until his release last year.'

Again, Stanton didn't answer. The prison guard shifted his position beside the door.

'Did you hear from Ivan after he was released?' Helen asked.

The prisoner sat back in his chair and stared at her through pale grey eyes. If he was aware Shaw was dead, he wasn't giving anything away. 'Why?'

'We're looking into his associations in connection with a case we're working on.'

'What case?'

'I'm afraid I can't divulge the details.'

'Then I can't tell you anything.' He folded his arms across his chest defiantly.

Helen reined in her annoyance. She hadn't expected Stanton to be immediately cooperative. Prisoners tended to keep quiet, protect each other. But it only served to ramp up her frustration. 'I understand you have a parole hearing coming up?'

Stanton looked from the guard to Helen. 'What's that supposed to mean?'

'It means that any help you give me will be documented on your file. I'm sure the board will look upon it favourably,' she added, pleased she'd ask Pemberton to check out Stanton's case. If ever she needed leverage, it was now. 'So.' She leaned forward. 'What did you and Ivan talk about?'

'What?'

'What was your daily conversation? I imagine you were banged up together for long periods.'

He shot another hard look at the guard. 'Too long.'

The guard ignored him. The stark increase in the UK prison population over recent years had resulted in staff shortages, overcrowding and extended lockdown, something the new Five Wells, with its firm focus on rehabilitation to break the cycle of reoffending, hoped to address.

'Right,' Helen said. She let the silence linger until he responded.

Stanton blew out a long breath. 'We talked about dinner, what time exercise was, when the gym was open. It's always the same in these places, we live to a routine.'

Helen took a second to clasp her hands together on the table. 'I understand you had a disagreement.'

'I don't know what you're talking about.'

'Really? It's well documented in your file. You received a stitch beside your left eye.'

Oliver met her gaze. 'It was nothing. A misunderstanding.'

'Ivan's prison record states others struggled to share with him. Do you know why?'

He looked away, shrugged. 'That's an issue for them.'

'Did Ivan ever talk about his crime?' she asked, changing tack.

'Sometimes.' Another shrug. 'He was angry about it, incensed. Ivan was angry about everything.'

'What do you mean?'

'He raged at the injustice of the world. Kept saying he shouldn't be here. He was only teaching the guy a lesson. Though...' He broke off, looked away, as if he'd already broken a confidence.

'Go on.'

'I tended to change the subject.'

'Why?'

'Because he was unhinged. You share with some oddballs in these places, it's the luck of the draw who you are placed with. Most of us don't feel the need to talk about why we're here. Ivan couldn't stop himself. He enjoyed talking about his crime, joked about how scared the guy was at the prospect of facing the barrel of a gun. Yet if anyone in here had a go at him, he backed down. He was no fighter.' He shook his head, grimaced. 'But he had the ability to get under your skin. And he was obsessed with weapons and war. Always on about different world conflicts. He talked about taking driving trips through Europe to Serbia and Herzegovina. Said you could pick up guns easily there, smuggle them across the border.'

Helen recalled the firearm officer's comments about the AK-47 possibly coming from the Balkans, left over from the war. It was almost as if Shaw had set everything up before he died.

Stanton stared at her. 'Is that what you're here about. Has he attacked someone else?'

The complete unsurprise in Stanton's eyes made Helen shudder inwardly. He clearly didn't know Shaw was dead either. 'As I said, I can't talk about the case, but we would like to speak with anyone he was close to. Was there anybody he spent time with?'

'No. Most people avoided him. Oh, he knew how to speak to the guards, the counsellors, what to say to anyone with authority. He'd learned to turn on the charm when he needed to. With everyone else, he was his strange self.'

'What about friends, family. Did he ever mention anybody?'

'He had a mother. They didn't get along, he refused to talk about her.'

'What about other family?'

'Not that he spoke about. No friends either, as far as I'm aware. He was funny about most people. Insisted on watching those reality shows like *Love Island* on television, then jeered at them – the men and the women. Called them manipulative. Honestly, he had a screw loose. I wasn't sorry when he left.'

CHAPTER 63

Helen took a slow drive back from Five Wells amid a patchwork of rolling countryside. Ivan Shaw's motive couldn't be stronger – he harboured a hatred of young men and women and talked about sourcing the right weapons, smuggling them in from war-torn countries – yet he was dead, and they'd failed to trace his half-brother or anyone else close to him. Now, despite the long hours, dedication, and hard work of her team, she had to hand over a case to SO15 with no hope and no sense of direction.

She was just crossing the border into Hamptonshire when her phone rang, and *Pemberton* flashed up on the screen. She clicked on her hands-free.

'Hey. Any news?'

The optimism in his voice made her chest ache. 'Nothing substantial.' She gave him the rundown on her discussion with Stanton. 'What about there?'

'Noah Gardner's car has been spotted, parked up in Durham Street.'

'Really?' Durham Street was a side road leading to Hampton High Street. 'Do we know how long it's been there?'

'Sadly not. It was first noted at 3.03 pm. Could have been there for hours.'

'Anything from Noah himself?'

'Afraid not. I've spoken with Ashleigh, told her we found the car. She has no idea what he was doing in town, he certainly hadn't mentioned anything. He hasn't contacted any of his family either. She's started phoning round the rest of his friends. I've called him myself, left a message on his voicemail asking him to contact us, in case he's avoiding her.'

Helen considered this. Durham Street was one of the few side roads that didn't require a resident permit and didn't have a time limit; locals often parked there when carrying out chores in town to avoid the high charges in the multi-storey. Noah still might have taken himself off somewhere to cool down. But the timing, on the day Ashleigh received the second email, and the fact that he hadn't spoken with anyone, gave her cause for concern. 'Get a photo of him from Ashleigh, will you? Let's distribute it to everyone on duty.'

'Will do. I've spoken to a mate who works at the mortuary. Our Brandon moved across from Cambridgeshire, he's going to make some discreet enquiries with colleagues there.'

'Okay, thanks.' A part of her still couldn't believe that Brandon had anything to do with the killings, she desperately hoped she was wrong, but she couldn't ignore the fact that he'd spent more time at headquarters in the past week than Charles, their regular pathologist, had in a year. 'Anything else?'

'Yeah, Kendrick's gone.'

'Gone?'

'Yup. He's been taken off the case, his suspects charged with Conspiracy to Commit Acts of Terrorism, and, a heads up, SO15 are waiting for you in your office.'

'Quinn's arrived?'

'No, he's still stuck at Glasgow. His second-in-command is here, some self-important knob named Walker. Believe me' – a huff blew down the line – 'Kendrick's got nothing on him. Anyway, he's here, has taken over your desk and is waiting to question you. Well, I say question. Felt more like an interrogation to me.'

Helen could almost see Pemberton standing in the incident room, phone furtively pressed to his ear, looking through the glass into her office at the man who'd commandeered her desk. Quinn clearly surrounded himself with officious people like himself. 'Has he read my policy log?'

'Yup and apparently, it's not enough. He wants more.'

'Like what?'

'Everything. Every date, time, movement, interview. Honestly, you'd have thought we'd never run an investigation. They'll be asking for our bowel movements next. I've done my best to hold him off, but now the clock's ticking.'

* * *

'Let's go through this again,' Walker said, leaning back in his chair. With his grey suit, his long, lean figure, cropped salt and pepper hair, and narrowed razor-sharp eyes, he looked every inch the interrogator. 'Your officers in Northumbria have interviewed…'

'As I said.' Helen listed the names again from memory.

'Right.' He clicked off the end of his pen. 'I'll need update reports from both officers.'

'Of course. Anything else?'

'Yes, as a matter of fact, there is.' The way he tapped his pen on the page a couple of times before he continued irked her. 'I'd like to know more about your history with Chilli Franks.'

Helen frowned. 'I don't see how that's relevant.'

'If you could just fill me in.'

Little itches started. First in her arms, then spreading to her torso. She fought to keep her composure as she talked him through her family history with Franks, all the time her mind working in overdrive. Considering Pemberton's earlier comment, and Franks's connection to both crimes. Had they unearthed something new? 'He's currently on the remand wing at Wakefield,' she finished up, the itches spreading, like an army of insects marching beneath the skin. 'His trial begins the week after next.'

'Right,' Walker said. 'And I understand his nephew has developed a keen interest in your son.'

'Where exactly are you going with this?'

'This afternoon, the person who uploaded the YouTube footage of the first shooting came forward.' He cleared his throat. 'A young woman named Paige Simmons. The girlfriend, or should I say ex-girlfriend, of Trent Bradshaw. I believe that name is familiar to you.'

Helen eyed him warily. 'Yes, I know Trent. He runs Connect 12, the boxing gym in town.'

'And you'll also know that his father was associated with Franks.'

She couldn't work out where he was heading with this line of enquiry. It was all in her policy log. Her visit to Connect 12, her supposition about Franks. Supposition she'd later dismissed. 'What are you suggesting?'

'Do I need to spell it out? Trent asked her to film the people coming out of the pub last Friday. She claims they didn't know there was going to be a shooting, but he still asked her to upload the footage to the internet under a fake account where it received thousands of shares. Also, a witness due to testify against Franks was present at the shooting last night.'

'It's a small town.'

Walker swung his head back. 'Come on, Helen. You can do better than that. Join the dots!'

Helen looked away. Something was bothering her, picking at the side of her brain. 'Why come forward now?' she said, almost to herself.

'What?'

'You said, a friend of Trent's has come forward. We've had public appeals out for whoever filmed that footage for days. Why now?'

'I'm led to believe she's had a falling out with Trent. And with what happened at the university, she felt it was her duty.'

'I don't understand. They were both present at the first

shooting. If you're suggesting what I think you're suggesting – that Trent was behind it, working for Chilli – he could have been injured.'

'He and Paige were standing a good way away from the victims. It's possible the gunman was deliberately avoiding them.'

True. The bullet holes were concentrated down one side of O'Malley's. Trent was standing beside the door at the other end. And he did appear to leave suddenly… 'Counterterror were convinced they had the right people for the first shooting,' she said, playing for time. She needed to think.

'Let's keep to the matter in hand, shall we?' His eyes bore holes into her.

'We spoke with the liaison officer at Franks's prison, and with informants in the field. There's nothing to suggest Franks was involved.'

'Perhaps he or his followers cover their tracks well.'

This was ridiculous. Wasn't it? Though even as the suggestion passed through her mind, a grim voice spoke up from within. What if she was wrong? What if this really was a drugs war, Franks's last show of power, as Jenkins had initially suggested.

Helen's mind raced. Organised crime had Trent linked to Gladstone, Chilli's rival. If he was involved in orchestrating the shooting, why would he film it? Unless Trent was doublecrossing Gladstone, secretly allying himself with the East Side Boys to get information on who they were working with for Chilli. But two mass shootings… that seemed a stretch. Even for someone with an ego the size of the Empire State Building, like Chilli.

'Where are Paige and Trent now?'

'They're…' He cleared his throat again. 'Helping us with our enquiries.'

Police speak for they were being questioned. She imagined Trent ensconced in an interview room somewhere, pressing his knuckles together. 'Why wasn't I informed about this earlier?'

'You, I believe…' He shook his head. 'Were on a prison visit to interview a dead man's cellmate.'

Helen cringed. When he put it like that, it did sound rather lame. It wasn't as if she'd uncovered anything new either, anything she could counter with. Helen gritted her teeth. But she refused to be defeated that easily. 'Ivan Shaw's half-brother has a sound motive for murder, and he's still out there.'

'And, if needs be, we will actively pursue him.'

If needs be! He couldn't be more dismissive. 'What about the emails sent to the columnist?' she said indignantly.

'We're very much viewing that as a side issue,' Walker said. 'It's possible Kendrick was right, it's a hoax.'

'Ashleigh Urquhart was in the same class as Ivan Shaw. The class that held the reunion at O'Malley's last Friday. They also went to the same college.'

'An unhappy coincidence. Unlike the information about Franks. I must tell you that we see his role as significant. We will be looking at every association to Franks, both before his incarceration and after. And that includes family.'

'I'm not with you.'

'Are you not?' He stood and buttoned his suit jacket. 'Let's just say there appears to have been enough information leaked on this case.'

'Excuse me?'

'This is a SO15 investigation now. Pull your detectives back, and pass everything you have over to us. We'll be taking it forward from here.' He turned as he reached the door. 'A word of advice. If I were you, I'd keep my son well away from Franks's family, certainly for the foreseeable future.' And with that, he turned and marched out of Helen's office.

CHAPTER 64

Ashleigh was in the kitchen, making a cup of tea, when the door buzzer sounded. Noah! Maybe he'd forgotten his key again.

She rushed to the intercom, a flutter in her belly, as she answered hopefully, 'Hello?'

'I have parcel.'

The strong Eastern European accent instantly dashed her hopes. It wasn't Noah. And she wasn't expecting a parcel.

'Can you leave it on the step?' she asked. One of the others would collect it, bring it up later. It was probably only from her mum. She often sent things across, especially items she didn't want filling out her luggage on the plane.

'It needs signature.'

'Could you try one of the other numbers?'

'No one is home.'

Ashleigh rolled her eyes. This was all she needed. A flashback: to her dream the other day. The air swirling around her. Her legs like stone. Ashleigh glanced through the open door of her bedroom to the window at the back of the property. A clear blue sky shone back at her. It was Friday. Almost five whole days had passed since she'd ventured out there, and the thought of going out still made her nauseous. Though she wasn't going outside. Not really. Only downstairs to the shared entrance. Sooner or later, she needed to leave the flat, and what better time than when a police officer was sitting outside?

She tiptoed back into the front room and glanced at the police car. It was parked at an angle. The officers inside appeared to be looking down at something, possibly their phones. Surely, they would have checked out the delivery driver.

The door buzzed again. 'Can you come?' The delivery driver was getting restless.

If the officers weren't alarmed, perhaps she shouldn't be either. 'I'll be down in a minute.'

Slowly, she released the lock and opened the door a crack. The landing was clear. She opened the door wider, felt the movement of the air. And stepped out. Her vision blurred. She blinked. Noah was right, she had stayed in too long. But she wouldn't be beaten. She wouldn't give in to this. She focused on her breathing. Deep breaths, in and out. Slowly, she took the stairs. The entrance hall was empty. She reminded herself it was just her here. Her and the delivery driver.

Ashleigh pulled the chain across, opened the door a fraction and peered around the edge. The sunlight was strong, the air sharp. The driver came into view. He was dressed in blue overalls and holding an A4 flat parcel in brown cardboard, the letters FRAGILE – DO NOT BEND written across the top in red.

'You need sign,' the driver said, holding out a device with a small screen lit.

It wasn't until Ashleigh took the parcel that she noticed the address – Mr F Andris, 8E Portland Grove, Hampton. The postcode was faint, barely readable. 'It's not for me,' she said. 'It's for the flat downstairs.'

'I need signature,' the driver repeated.

It was futile to even consider arguing. Ashleigh reached a hand through the gap, signed the screen with her nail. The parcel was light, not at all cumbersome, so she tucked it under her arm and closed the door. Leaning back against it a second, she allowed her heart to slow. That really hadn't been so bad, had it? Perhaps she could muster the energy to leave the building when all this was sorted.

She sighed, pulled the parcel from beneath her arm and looked across at Filip's door. Should she prop it up there, for him to pick up when he came home? What if it was important, valuable? Like a rare painting. She had no idea of Filip's tastes, she barely knew him, they'd only passed the time of day a couple of times, but she'd feel awful if it went astray after she'd signed to say it was delivered safely. Perhaps it would be better to take it up to her flat. Pop a message on the Portland Grove group chat to tell him it was with her. She pulled her phone out of her pocket and typed a quick message.

She glanced back at his door, about to take to the stairs, when something at the edge of Filip's doorframe, just above head height, caught her eye. Ashleigh peered in closer. It was white, the same colour as the painted frame and the wall beside – no wonder she hadn't noticed it before – and tiny, the size of a large grape, but there was definitely a lens. A camera.

Ashleigh froze. Why would Filip need a camera on this inside door? Callers came to the outside door and used the intercom. Unless he was recording movements, in and out. The killer's notes swooped in. She'd believed it to be someone outside, maybe watching from the park. What if, all the time, the killer was inside the house? One of her neighbours.

Suddenly, her hands turned clammy. Could it be that the people she'd considered herself safe with were actually the ones she should be afraid of? Oh, God.

She reached for the banister, knuckles white. She needed to get back upstairs to the safety of her own flat, behind her own front door, and call the detective.

She was just about to dash up when she heard the key being inserted into a lock behind her.

CHAPTER 65

Ashleigh spun round as the door opened to reveal Filip – Filip of all people! – standing on the doorstep. He was wearing one of the dark suits he wore for work, a white open-necked shirt beneath. A thick layer of stubble coated his chin.

A flicker of alarm travelled across his face. His gaze passed from Ashleigh to the camera, back again. 'I—'

The word spurred her into action. She ran up the stairs, taking them two at a time.

'Hey!' he called after her.

How could she not have known? How could she not have realised that the killer lived here, in this very house. Just a flight of stairs away from her.

She thought of Noah yesterday. He'd spoken with Filip in the hallway, and the very next time he'd gone out, he'd disappeared. Did Filip have something to do with that too? Was Filip even his name?

An icy chill slipped between her shoulder blades as she reached the top step, darted into her flat and locked the door, pulling the bolt across fast. She ran to the window, waved, desperately trying to get the officer's attention in the police car across the road. But a sudden ray of sunshine blinded her and she couldn't see the officer, let alone the car.

She pulled her phone out of her pocket, was scrolling down for the detective's number when a bang sounded. Ashleigh jumped. The phone slid out of her hand and crashed to the wooden floor.

Another thump. 'Hey! You have a parcel for me.'

It was him. Ashleigh's heart thudded against her ribcage. In her race to get away from Filip, she'd forgotten all about the parcel. Damn! She should have left it outside. How could she have been so stupid!

She scrabbled about on the floor. Her phone had slipped underneath the armchair. She needed to press her cheek to the floor, lift the chair.

'Hey,' he said. 'What's going on?'

Her fingertips were on her phone now. She was almost there when another thought occurred to her. Did he arrange for a parcel delivery? Pay someone to call when he knew the house was empty, to lure her out of the flat. Sickly bile popped into her throat.

Another bang made her jump. 'Open the door!'

She tugged at the edge of her phone, pulled it out. The screen was cracked but – thank God! – it lit as she turned it on. Her hands were trembling as she scrolled again, selected the DCI's number and pressed call. Please answer, she willed. Please.

CHAPTER 66

Helen sat in her office long after Walker had gone, staring into space. Afternoon rolled into evening. The sun had moved over the building, leaving her office in shade and, despite the warm temperatures outside, it felt like she was sitting in a freezer.

Leaks… She knew exactly where Walker was going with this. He was insinuating her son had been groomed by Franks's family and was feeding back details. How dare he? She'd been careful, hadn't she? Told Robert, her own son, nothing. No more than he could have read in the news feeds.

Though, she couldn't deny, someone was leaking information.

She thought about Davy Boyd's hard face as she talked about Chilli. His clean record. How she'd refused to step in and stop her son's friendship with Zac, despite his extended family's links with the criminal fraternity. Not wishing to tar the Boyds with Chilli's soiled brush, she'd afforded Davy the benefit of doubt. Then she recalled Sofia's mention of Davy's friendship with Trent. And she placed her head in her hands. How could she have been so stupid? She'd allowed this to unfold, right in front of her eyes.

A single knock at the door made her look up. Pemberton entered with two steaming mugs.

'Looks like you could do with one of these,' he said, placing them down on her desk.

'You're not wrong.'

He closed the door behind him. 'That bad, eh?'

Helen nodded and passed along the conversation.

Pemberton gave a long sigh as she finished up. 'Why is it, when we have a prolonged investigation, they're always looking to hang someone out to dry? I thought they'd be satisfied with Kendrick. At least he made mistakes.'

'Apparently not,' she said. 'If they can't get me on this, I'm guessing they'll go for me for disobeying an order, carrying on with my own covert enquiries.' She couldn't help wondering if Adams was in on it too. It was all well and good when they had live enquiries, something to keep the press at bay. Now they'd reached a dead end, everyone was looking for a fall guy.

Helen fought back the tears at the back of her eyes. Her home life was a mess and now her work was too. And all because of one man. At this moment, she couldn't have despised Chilli Franks any more if she'd tried.

'Have you been suspended?'

'No, just removed from the case. I'm guessing they don't know about Davy Boyd's association with Trent yet – that wasn't in my policy log. Though it's only a matter of time. Have you spoken to Dark and Spencer?'

Pemberton nodded. 'They're taking the afternoon to write up their reports, then they'll be heading back.' He was quiet a second. 'I'm really sorry it's turned out like this.'

They were interrupted by Helen's mobile ringing. It was Ashleigh Urquhart.

'Detective, I need your help. The killer's here, trying to get in my door!'

'What?'

'It's Filip from downstairs.' Her voice broke. A bang sounded in the distance.

'Stay in the flat, keep the door locked and move away from it. Is he armed?'

'I don't think so. I was in the lobby. He chased me upstairs.'

'Hold on. I'll alert the officers outside. Do not open the door until they arrive!'

CHAPTER 67

Helen arrived at Portland Grove to find one of the officers from the armed car guarding the front of number eight, the door open.

'Evening, ma'am,' the officer said as she held up her badge. 'Miss Urquhart's in her flat with a colleague.'

'What happened?'

'At precisely 6.22 pm, DHL arrived with a parcel for Mr Andris at 8E that required a signature. We checked both the parcel and the driver out, they seemed fine. We didn't discover until afterwards that he wasn't home, and the driver had called the other flats. Miss Urquhart came down and took it in.'

'She left her flat?'

The officer nodded. 'She left her flat, not the building. Then Mr Andris arrived home from work. Again, we confirmed his ID, had no reason to be suspicious. We weren't alerted to anything untoward until we received your call.'

Helen sighed inwardly. The officers guarding the property had done their job: verified comings and goings while respecting the residents' privacy and keeping everything as normal as possible for Ashleigh. They couldn't be expected to legislate for an altercation between neighbours inside.

'What happened when you entered the property?'

'Mr Andris was banging on Miss Urquhart's door, demanding the parcel. He seemed angry.'

'Where is Filip Andris now?'

'In his flat. Uniform arrived and arrested him for

harassment, but he needed the bathroom. They're just waiting for him to finish before they escort him to the station. I don't think he's well.'

Helen was accustomed to differing reactions to arrest. Shock played games with the human psyche. Those who'd never spent time in a police cell, never set foot in an interview room sometimes felt intimidated, fearful. But to be unwell. That was a new one for her. Though this was a multiple murder investigation, and the killer had taken great steps to cover his tracks and evade capture. Maybe the realisation of the police finally catching up with him had cast his future in stark reality.

'What do we know about him?' she said in a low voice, looking towards Andris's front door. The door she had passed many times during her visits to Ashleigh. The pungent smell of fresh vomit filled the air.

The officer consulted his notes. 'Not much. Filip Andris, thirty-two, originally from Lithuania. Moved to the UK eight and a half years ago. Bought the flat about a year ago. He works for Salz's, a firm of Chartered Accountants on The Strand in London. No previous with us. Checks with Lithuania and overseas are being undertaken by the control room.'

'Right.' Helen stepped past him into the hallway and scanned the area. Filip's black door sat directly opposite the entrance to the other ground floor dwelling. Between them, the stairs rose to the first-floor flats. She was looking at the mock-wood laminate flooring, the pile of junk mail that littered the hallway table, the scuffed doormat below with 'Welcome' written across it in red letters when something caught her eye. She bent down to examine it.

'What's that?' the officer asked.

Peeping from beneath the oversized entrance mat was a brown envelope. Helen pulled a pair of latex gloves from her pocket, fully aware that if Andris was their killer, this area would need to be meticulously examined. She wriggled her hands into the gloves and lifted the envelope. It was a letter addressed to Mr John Valentine.

'I think it's a letter for one of the residents,' she said. 'Looks like it got stuck under the mat and forgotten.' She placed it beside a leaflet from Iceland supermarket on the hall table. But it struck her as she climbed the stairs – Valentine – where had she heard that name before?

Helen checked Ashleigh's door as she knocked. A couple of scratches, a chip beside the handle that didn't look new. It didn't look like Andris had tried particularly hard to force entry.

A female uniformed officer Helen didn't know answered. She showed her badge.

'She's very shaken,' the officer said.

Ashleigh was in the front room on the sofa. She turned as Helen walked in, relief flitting across her face. 'Where is he?' she asked.

'Filip? He's downstairs in his flat with my colleagues.'

'Why aren't you questioning him?'

'We will be taking him to the station to interview him shortly. In the meantime, why don't you tell me exactly what happened?'

Ashleigh talked her through the earlier events. The parcel collection, Filip chasing her up the stairs, him banging on the door. 'He gave me such a fright.'

'I can see that. Did he say anything?'

'He just kept asking me what was wrong. And banging on the door.'

'Right.' Helen stared at the woman, long and hard. 'What makes you think he's the killer?'

'What?'

'On the phone, you said Filip was the killer.'

Ashleigh told Helen about the camera attached to his doorframe downstairs. 'It's so small I didn't notice it before.'

Many people installed CCTV to watch their front doors these days. Some even linked it to their phone so that they could view who was calling when they were out, something that was proving useful when combating residential burglaries. Though if they installed one here, Helen imagined it would be more useful on the main door. But they needed more than a lone camera to indicate guilt.

'You don't understand.' Ashleigh's voice was tremoring now. 'The killer. He's been watching me. He knows who's visited. A camera would record this.'

'How well do you know him?'

'What? What do you mean?'

'Do you socialise together?'

'No.'

'So, you haven't had a disagreement, or an argument over anything?'

'No. But if he is the shooter, or is supporting him, he's in a good position to monitor things. He chatted to Noah yesterday evening. Asked him how I was doing, whether I was still working at the newspaper. I've only spoken to him a couple of times. I might have mentioned my food blog, but I've never talked about *The Herald*. How did he even know about my column?'

Helen narrowed her eyes. 'Have you heard from Noah?'

Ashleigh shook her head. 'No. Nothing. I've tried all his friends. I'm really beginning to worry now.'

CHAPTER 68

Minutes later, Helen was back downstairs. Filip's flat followed a similar layout to Ashleigh's. His living room overlooked the road, the park beyond. Filip emerged from the bathroom as she entered. An officer beside him.

'What's going on?' he said. 'What am I supposed to have done?'

Scrapes and scuffs filtered through from the bedroom where another officer was searching.

'You've been arrested on suspicion of harassment,' Helen said.

'What? I only went up there to collect a parcel. Why's someone going through my flat?'

'I'm afraid I can't discuss it with you now.' Anything said here would never be admissible in court and she wasn't about to jeopardise an arrest. 'My colleagues will take you down to the station. We'll talk there.'

'No! I want to know what's going on.' The officer made to guide him out, but he wrestled off her hold. 'This is an invasion of my privacy. I've got rights.'

Before Helen could answer, the other officer entered the room, caught her eye, and shook his head. He hadn't found anything in the bedroom. Nothing to connect Filip with Ashleigh or the shootings. That didn't mean he wasn't responsible, they still needed to examine his electronic devices, and she was mindful that he could be storing evidence/

weapons elsewhere or have disposed of them, but something about the situation left her uncomfortable.

'Make sure you seize the CCTV footage,' she said to the officer.

'What?' Filip again. 'What footage?'

'The camera attached to your door,' Helen said. 'Where is the footage stored?'

'Huh!' He ran a hand through his hair. 'I don't believe this. The camera doesn't work, there's no battery in it. It's just a box, installed by the previous owner. I keep meaning to take it down.'

CHAPTER 69

Ashleigh heard the engine rev outside, the car pulling away with Filip inside. Was it possible he was the killer? Or assisting the killer, watching her, maybe even sending the emails? He was certainly well positioned to keep track of movements in and out of her flat.

She thought about the times she'd heard floorboards creak and doors bang as her neighbours moved around their flats. Sadhika's loud voice. The discordant beat of Johnny's music. How she'd taken comfort from those sounds. Though she'd never heard much from Filip...

'Why don't I make you another cup of tea?' the officer said, interrupting her thoughts. Collecting her mug from the side table where a dark gelatinous skin had coated the last cup she'd made.

Ashleigh looked up at her. Jen, is that what she'd said her name was? She wanted to tell Jen that she couldn't care less if she never drank tea again. That she just wanted Noah back and for all of this to be over. That she couldn't go on like this and, tomorrow, her mother was due to arrive. But she didn't have the energy. So, she just nodded, watched the woman retreat to the kitchen, then scrutinised her phone again.

Still no message from Noah. He'd been gone over ten hours now. She fired off another text. *Where are you? Call me, please, just to let me know you're okay.*

The police had found his car in town. Maybe he'd taken himself off there to cool down. She thought about him losing his key, then finding it and forgetting it the other night. He was often absent-minded, forgetful, but he'd never stayed away this long without calling.

She couldn't think where he'd go. She'd phoned the snooker hall and the last of his friends. No one knew anything. Which could only mean one thing: wherever he was, he was alone.

CHAPTER 70

Filip Andris's solicitor sat beside his client, adjusted his tie, and faced Helen across the table. Technically, she shouldn't be conducting this interview. She should wait for Walker, who was hotfooting his way back from Wakefield Prison, where he'd obtained an urgent pass to interview Chilli. If Filip was the killer, they couldn't rule out the fact that he might not be working alone and, if he was affiliated to a proscribed group or even Chilli Franks's gang, they needed to coordinate an interview strategy.

But he'd been arrested for harassment at this stage, not murder, and the whole situation seemed off. She wanted to get to the bottom of it before she handed him over so, as soon as Andris had been processed at Cross Keys Station, as soon as his prints had been taken and the duty solicitor had arrived, she'd called in Pemberton and started interviewing. If she was right, the killer was working up to something. Something big. Time wasn't on her side, and God only knew where Noah was. If she was to thwart another incident, or at the very least find out where Noah was, she needed to start questioning now.

Though, as the interview progressed, fresh doubts as to Filip's complicity wriggled in. Overseas enquiries hadn't uncovered any other crimes or intelligence, and the immediate search of Filip's flat had yielded nothing to link him with the attacks, or Ashleigh. He claimed he hadn't seen Ashleigh for weeks and was not only staunch in claiming his innocence, but he was also vociferously cooperative. He'd handed over his phone, told officers where to find his laptop, and then provided passwords to enable them to access them. She found it hard to conceive a killer with a particular message to impart would do this.

Helen ignored the lingering stench of vomit – they'd had to wait for a doctor to confirm Filip was well enough to be interviewed before they commenced – and sat forward. 'Why don't you talk me through what happened today?' she asked.

Filip raised his head. Dark shadows like bruises glowered beneath his eyes in stark contrast to his pasty-white face. 'It was a misunderstanding,' he said.

Pemberton's chair creaked as he adjusted position, pen poised.

Filip sighed. 'I got home from work to find that woman…'

'Ashleigh.'

'Yes, Ashleigh, in the hallway.'

'Let's go back a bit further,' Helen said. If this was the killer sitting in front of her, she needed to find out more about him, his movements, establish other places he'd visited where he may have stored items. 'Where do you work?'

'At Salz's on The Strand. But I don't see what that has to do with anything—'

'How long have you worked there?' Helen interrupted, ignoring his words.

'About' – his eyes darted from side to side – 'two years.'

'What hours do you do?'

'Weekdays, nine to five. Except on a Friday when we finish at three.' He looked perplexed. 'I get the train. It's walking distance from home. Hampton to Euston only takes an hour or so.'

'Are you in the office every day?'

He nodded.

'For the purposes of the recording, the suspect is nodding.' She sat back, eyed him a moment. 'You say, you were at work today.'

'Yes.' His forehead furrowed. 'I left just after three.'

'What did you do then?'

'I went for a drink with colleagues.'

'You didn't go straight to the station?'

'No.'

Helen asked for details of the colleagues he drank with to verify the information, and then the train times. Pemberton jotted them down. 'Go on.'

'I hopped on the 5.02 train. It arrived at Hampton Station at 6.10. It was almost 6.30 when I got home and that's when I found Ashleigh in the entrance hall with my parcel in her hand.'

'Why did you arrange for a parcel to be delivered when you weren't going to be there?'

'That's the thing. I knew I wasn't going to be back until late. Paid a premium rate to have it delivered after seven.' He uttered a curt word in a different language, a look of contempt on his face. 'The parcel was a photo I had done for my parents' anniversary celebration this weekend. I had it sent special delivery to ensure it arrived in time. I can't believe they delivered it early.'

'Okay. What happened when you arrived home?'

He talked her through meeting Ashleigh in the hallway, following her up the stairs. Talking to her through her closed door. 'I was only asking for the parcel,' he said. 'Then she started screaming, telling me to get away, as if I was trying to hurt her. I didn't do anything, apart from follow her upstairs and knock on her door.'

'Are you aware she was a victim in the recent shooting at O'Malley's?'

'Yes. Sadhika told me.' He shook his head. 'Terrible business.'

'She said you banged on her door.'

'Because she wouldn't give me my parcel. For Christ's sake, it cost nearly ninety pounds. It was nothing to her.'

'She was frightened.'

'I didn't know that. I just wanted my parcel.'

Helen sat back, resting her gaze on the suspect. 'Filip, I'm going to ask you something and I need you to think carefully. Where were you on the nights of Friday 10th and Thursday 16th August?'

Filip's eyes bulged. 'I was in Edinburgh at a work conference on the 10th. At home last night. Hey, they were the nights of the shootings. You surely don't think—'

'Detective,' Filip's solicitor, a thin man in a tired black suit, coughed as he interrupted, 'my client has been arrested for harassment. Please keep to the matter in hand.'

'Are you familiar with Noah Gardner?' Helen asked, changing direction.

'If you mean Noah, Ashleigh's boyfriend, then yes. I have met him in the hallway a few times. Seems a nice guy. Likes jogging.'

'When was the last time you spoke with Noah?'

Filip thought for a moment. 'Yesterday evening. He arrived home the same time as me.'

'And what time was that?'

'I'm not sure exactly. He was returning from a jog. About half seven, I think.'

'What did you talk about?'

'I can't remember exactly. I think… I think I asked after Ashleigh.'

'You didn't speak with him again. Maybe today? This is important, Filip.'

'I don't see why…'

'Noah Gardner has been reported missing. He hasn't been seen since this morning.'

'Detective, is this really relevant?' the solicitor cut in.

Filip waved his solicitor silent. 'I had no idea.'

'So, did you speak with him again?'

'No, I didn't. But I did hear him talking outside my door.'

'Oh?' Helen angled her head. 'What time was this?'

'About nine, nine-thirty last night. They were arranging to meet in High Street this morning.'

Helen leaned forward. 'Who was Noah arranging to meet?'

'Jack, Johnny, or whatever the bloody hell they call him. The guy who lives opposite me.'

CHAPTER 71

'What was that about?' Pemberton said, panting. He was struggling to keep up as Helen rushed into the back office after abruptly pausing the interview.

'We've got the wrong guy.'

'What do you mean?'

'I need to call Kendrick.' She checked her pockets for her mobile phone.

'I don't understand,' Pemberton said.

'You heard him. He was in Edinburgh on the night of the first shooting. We can verify that with his work.' She told him about the letter she'd found beside the mat in Ashleigh's shared entrance hall addressed to Mr John Valentine. 'I thought the name was familiar, but it didn't register at first. Not until Filip just said Jack.' She started scrolling through her phone...

'You don't think it's connected to our Jack Valentine...'

'I'm not sure. Think about it, he's a DMI working for counter-terror. Perfectly situated to send those messages and have an insight into the investigation. Shit!' She thought about the brief conversations she'd had with Jack. The first time she'd met him wandering the corridors of headquarters. His late night in the office, in a position of trust with open access to every piece of intelligence they'd collected in the incident room. She listened to the dialling tone ring out. 'I was convinced we had a mole. Maybe he's more than a mole.' The words fell out of her mouth in one breath. 'Call the office, see if Jack is still there.'

* * *

Ten minutes later, Helen replaced the receiver. Kendrick had sounded dismissive when she called, irritated about being taken off the case. All he was able to tell her was that Jack had been recruited eight months earlier as a civilian investigator and he'd been a quiet and model member of the team. It wasn't until she spoke to their human resources department that she discovered the name on his application was John Valentine and he had asked to be known as Jack. And when she asked for Jack's address, her blood chilled: 14, Tavistock House, Hampton. Tavistock House was a block of council flats that had been deemed uninhabitable by the authorities two months ago, and was empty, awaiting demolition so that they could fill the area with new houses. Jack certainly hadn't lived there for some time.

Opposite her, a red-faced Pemberton stroked his shiny scalp, and ended his call. 'I've spoken to Andris's boss. He was in Edinburgh on the night of the first shooting.'

'What about Jack?'

'The office haven't seen or heard from him all day. They assumed counter-terror had pulled him back. No answer on his mobile either.'

Helen's back tensed, every muscle, every sinew locking together. 'Get on to the officer with Ashleigh Urquhart, make sure she's okay.'

'Will do.'

'I'll get a tactical support team to meet us at Portland Grove urgently. I only hope we're not too late.'

CHAPTER 72

The drive across town seemed to take forever. Pemberton wove in and out of the minimal traffic, flatting the accelerator whenever possible. Helen's phone was glued to her ear, liaising with tactical support, then the office to obtain the registration number of Jack Valentine's Nissan Micra and requesting an urgent county-wide search. All the while thinking of that late night Jack had spent in the incident room. The emails sent to Ashleigh he'd been unable to trace. Now he'd gone missing, AWOL. She desperately hoped there was an innocent explanation, that the dirty ache in her gut was wrong because, in the cold light of day, the reality of the killer being one of their own filled her with horror.

The tactical support team were piling out of their van as Helen and Pemberton parked up in the next street along from Portland Grove. She couldn't risk arriving outside Ashleigh's en masse in case the killer was nearby. She wasn't about to alert him to their presence.

Pemberton switched off the engine and turned to her. 'What I don't understand is, why would he choose to be known as Jack? John Valentine doesn't have a previous police record, or any markers on him.'

'It's an old-fashioned thing,' Helen said. 'Goes back to biblical times when sons were named after their fathers. John was a common name, so families nicknamed one of them Jack to distinguish between the two. It happened in my husband's family. He was John, his father was John, and his grandfather, so everyone in the family called his father Jack.' She slipped off her seatbelt. 'I guess that's where the idea came from anyway. He probably played on it here to muddy the waters.'

PS Dez Eldred, the tactical support advisor, approached as she climbed out of her car. All in black, with a helmet on his head and a Heckler and Koch at his side, he looked like a hero from an action movie. 'I've risk-assessed the area,' he said. 'Apart from Miss Urquhart, there's no answer from the other flats at number 8, the immediate neighbours are out too. We'll get the team in place, then go straight in with armed officers.'

Helen thanked him. At least they didn't need to waste precious minutes evacuating the immediate area.

With impressive precision for the short notice given, armed officers in helmets and bulletproof vests piled out of the van and were quickly deployed. Some to the rear of the property, where a small yard was edged with a low wall, forming the boundary to a car park behind. If anyone tried to escape, they weren't getting away out the back. Helen followed the rest around the corner, where they took up positions in Portland Grove. As soon as everyone was in place, she alerted the officer with Ashleigh to open the main door to number 8.

Waiting at the bottom of the stone steps, Helen could see the entrance door to Jack's flat. She watched Eldred bang the door and announce their arrival, then give his colleague a nod to move forward with the red battering ram. The officer drove it forward, hitting the door once, and again. On the third bang, the lock gave way and the door swung back on its hinges, clattering into the wall with a loud crash.

Officers piled inside, shouting a series of instructions as they searched each room. Within seconds, Eldred was back on the street. 'Clear,' he said, looking past her and across to the park opposite, his eyes darting about. 'But believe me, you're gonna want to see what's in there.'

Helen and Pemberton pulled on latex gloves and moved inside, their boots sinking into the deep-pile beige carpet laid throughout the flat. The hallway was clear. They passed the door to the bedroom to find the double bed made, the area pristine. The kitchen was the same. No washing up in the sink, no junk on the side. It wasn't until Helen entered the living room, the room that sat directly beneath Ashleigh's front room, that she realised what the sergeant was referring to.

'Whoa!' Pemberton said, eyes widening as he followed her.

Helen's jaw dropped. Officers were pulling open drawers in the bedroom, closing cupboard doors in the kitchen, searching the property. The noise merged into a low din as Helen looked around her, trying to process.

The room was dimly lit, the cream curtains still drawn, and sparse on furniture – a black, two-seater sofa, a small coffee table, its glass top shiny and clear. There was a television on a pine cabinet in the corner. But it was the walls that really caught her attention. They were covered in photos, news clippings and maps. So many that the geometric style wallpaper beneath was barely visible. The wall directly to her right was filled, floor to ceiling, with photographs of men and women. Walking through the town centre, in the supermarket, sitting outside bars drinking, couples lolling on grassy areas. In every one of them, the eyes blocked out with black marker pen.

Helen peered in closer. In the background of photos, she spotted local landmarks: the Royal Oak pub, the theatre, Victoria Car Park. The bandstand in Oakwall Park, under a blanket of snow.

'He must have been planning this for months,' Pemberton said, incredulous.

The window was surrounded by a series of maps. On the right was an enlarged map of Swan Street showing the entrances and exits of Victoria Car Park and a series of snapshots taken from the top floor. A red biro-ring ran around O'Malley's pub. To the left of the window was the layout of the university campus, hand drawn on white A3 paper, beneath a printed map of Hampton, highlighting its location in town.

The next wall was plastered with photographs of the house raided in Weston earlier in the week, snapshots of the accused, a photo of Ashleigh Urquhart. Printouts of newspaper articles talking about the shooting. He was meticulously following the investigation from both sides.

Diagrams of homemade IED drone bombs followed. An array of pictures of guns, rifles, ammunition. Photographs of Jack holding a rifle, lining it up about to shoot. Of him loading ammunition. Of him proudly showing off his weapon, the backdrop of desert behind.

Their late-night conversation in the incident room nudged Helen again. Jack's sister lived in Nevada, he visited frequently. What was it he said? He loved the desert; there was so much to do there. She thought he'd meant the sunshine, the diners, the casinos in Las Vegas. But she was wrong. This was where he undertook his training. Where he learned how to handle a weapon, to load it, to shoot. Where he'd honed his art.

A loud expletive sounded from the bedroom. Helen dashed out to find an officer on his hands and knees, looking under the bed. She kneeled to join him. Lined up was an array of rifles, gun-cleaning equipment, telescopic sights. The discarded AK-47 in the canal paled in significance when there with this collection to choose from.

She was just asking the officer to bag them up and get them across to forensics urgently when Pemberton's voice exclaimed, 'Oh my!' drawing her back to the front room.

'What is it?'

Pemberton was facing another detailed map of Hampton High Street on the wall behind the sofa, surrounded by photographs of a tired-looking, empty unit – Reed's furniture store before it shut down earlier this year. In two photos, the upstairs of the furniture store was highlighted in yellow marker. 'Looks like he's building up to his grand finale.'

Helen's eyes widened. 'That's around the corner from O'Malley's.' She looked at the surrounding photos. 'Oh, God.'

'What is it?'

'The candlelit vigil. He's planning to strike again. Tonight.'

'You're not serious?'

'Think about it. It all fits. He'll go out with a bang. Literally.'

CHAPTER 73

Ashleigh was sitting on the sofa when Helen entered her flat, hands clasped together in her lap, knuckles shiny white.

She greeted her, was just about to speak, when a thump reached up through the floor, making them all jump. A series of bumps followed. It sounded like the officers, still moving around Johnny's flat below, had knocked something over.

'What's going on?' Ashleigh said.

'We're just taking a look around Johnny's flat.'

'I don't believe this. What about Filip?'

'We're still questioning him.'

'Surely you don't think Johnny's involved too?'

Helen thought of the weapons she'd found under the bed, the wall plastered with pictures, the map of the town centre, the photo of the furniture store. If she was right and he did plan to strike again tonight, they didn't have long. 'I'm not sure yet, we are still figuring it all out. But we do need to speak with Johnny. Do you have any idea where he might be?'

Ashleigh swallowed. 'No. Why would I?'

'Has he ever mentioned friends or family nearby? Perhaps when you've seen him in the entry hall.'

'No. He's not much of a talker. Noah couldn't stand him, he called him Weird Johnny, but I felt sorry for him. I think he's shy.'

Helen didn't like the sound of that. If Noah thought he was odd, it seemed doubtful he'd agree to meet him. 'So, Noah didn't arrange to meet Johnny in town?'

'What? No! Why are you asking?'

'Filip said he overheard a conversation between them yesterday evening in the hall. He couldn't be sure what they'd said,' Helen replied carefully. She didn't want to panic the young woman unduly. Ashleigh's face puckered when Helen asked if she'd ever known Johnny by another name.

'No.'

'Ashleigh, this is important. When did you last see Johnny?'

'I want to know why you're asking. First, your colleagues arrest the wrong people, then you gag the press. Now more people are dead. I'm not going to be silenced. Christ! I wouldn't even be stuck here, unable to leave, if you guys hadn't messed up in the first place.'

'Ashleigh.' Helen lowered her voice a tone, holding her gaze. She had no time for theatrics. 'We're close, closer than we've ever been to ending all this.' She desperately wanted to tell her about another planned incident, that they were racing against the clock, but she couldn't risk her spilling the beans to her editor, jeopardising their chances. 'I just need your help in locating Johnny. When did you last see him?'

'I saw him walking across the park on his own this morning, about half ten, maybe eleven, I'm not sure exactly. He was carrying his guitar. It looked like he had a day off work.'

'What did you say he was carrying?'

'His guitar. Well, I only saw the case. I think he must be having lessons.'

A guitar case – another perfect disguise for transporting a gun. 'Have you heard him play?' Helen asked.

Ashleigh looked taken aback at the question. 'No, not yet. He likes his music though, he's always got some tune or another playing in his flat.'

The location of Noah's car, in Durham Street, just around the corner from the furniture store, struck Helen. The furniture store had been earmarked to reopen as a second-hand music shop later this year, though the date had been put back several times, and there had recently been speculation in the news about whether it was still going ahead. She eased forward. 'Ashleigh. Can you tell me where Noah was on the evenings of the 10th and 16th of August?'

'Wait! They're the nights of the shootings.' Recognition slowly flickered across Ashleigh's face. 'You're not suggesting Noah was involved.'

CHAPTER 74

Ashleigh closed the front door of her flat on the detective and pressed her forehead against the cool wood.

The officer, Jen, was still in her front room. Instead of rejoining her, Ashleigh walked, zombie-like, into her bedroom, closed the curtains and lowered herself onto the edge of the bed. She needed time away from everyone. Time to unravel the million and one questions racing around in her head.

Filip was in custody, and now the police were on a manhunt for Johnny. Was it possible two of her neighbours were involved in the killings together? But what really bothered her was the questioning about Noah. The detective said they needed to check his movements, eliminate him from their enquiries.

A bad taste swilled in her mouth. Why hadn't Noah mentioned his conversation with Johnny? Was Filip lying about the exchange, deflecting blame? But Noah's car was parked in town. He wasn't returning her calls and messages, and the police couldn't trace him...

He couldn't possibly be involved. Could he? No! The idea was ridiculous. What reason could he have? They'd been together since they were fifteen, she knew him inside out. His parents, his extended family, his friends, his work colleagues. Again, she was reminded of Noah's conversation with Johnny. Did Noah help him out and stumble upon something? Noah was a softie, always doing good deeds for others. He'd cut his elderly neighbour's grass all summer even though he couldn't stand the sight of the man.

She was working this through when a sneaky thought occurred to her. The killer's emails. He said she'd pay, and now her fiancé was missing.

This was turning into a nightmare.

CHAPTER 75

'Right, we've commandeered the upstairs of Hayes, the coffee shop opposite,' Walker said. 'Its first-floor window looks directly into the upstairs of Reed's furniture store.'

Helen stood at the side of the room and sipped at a glass of water. The last hour had been manic. Racing back to headquarters, phone pressed to her ear as she fed back to counter-terror, enrolled the tactical support team, requested detailed building plans of Reed's furniture store.

She switched her weight from one foot to another. Her legs ached, her body was tired, exhausted after a crazy day, but she was running on adrenalin. Standing beside an equally twitchy Pemberton in the counter-terror incident room. Walker at the front, the chief beside him, looking out at a sea of faces as they talked them through the operation to catch The Sniper Killer.

Walker had still been on his way back from Wakefield when Helen had called and explained the situation, and he'd proved surprisingly helpful. Organising his team from the road, keeping the line with Helen open as she continued enquiries at her end. There was no warmth in his voice, no gratitude, but the curtness in his tone was tempered. He was efficient, and efficient was what she needed right now. They could sort out their differences later.

She'd established their target and the suspected location and timing of his next incident. But, after confirming Noah was with his parents on the night of the first shooting, and on his way to see them at the time of the second incident, she'd also identified a potential hostage situation.

'The stairs at Reed's lead to a corridor,' Walker continued, clicking a key, bringing up a layout of the building on the screen. 'Two rooms and a toilet lead off. One that looks to have been used as a store cupboard, the other, larger room, has the window.' He tapped the screen twice. 'The window provides a fair view of the street below, and it's only around the corner from Swan Street where the candlelit vigil was planned for tonight.'

Everyone stared at the map in front of them. It was almost 10.15 pm. The candlelit vigil was arranged for eleven. If Helen was right, the killer would be expecting people to arrive soon.

Chief Constable Adams stepped forward. 'So, what's the plan?'

'We've already despatched plainclothes officers to evacuate the buildings nearby. They'll be using the rear exits, ensuring nobody enters the street. Within twenty minutes, the street should be empty and blockaded. We've also got roadblocks set up, stopping anyone coming into town.' He went on to divide the tactical support unit into sub-teams, allocate them to various stationed points along High Street and the street behind, to cover all entrances and exits of Reed's. 'We'll also be stationing armed officers on the roof of Hayes opposite.'

'What about the possible hostage?' Helen asked.

'The team are just setting up at Hayes. Computers, phone links, long-range cameras. But there's already been movement, a blur in front of the window opposite. And we've just had word that Jack Valentine and Noah Gardner's phones are on and have been located in the vicinity.'

It seemed she was right. He did have something planned for tonight. 'They've switched on their phones?' she asked. Her team had tried locating both phones earlier to no avail, indicating they'd been turned off.

'Yes. My guess is that Valentine has noticed the street outside emptying and suspected we are onto him. If I'm right, he'll be expecting contact through one of their phones. He wants something. We need to find out what that is.' He addressed the room. 'Right, our priority is to confirm the identities of those inside and bring them out alive. From Valentine's MO, we anticipate he'll be using a semi-automatic assault rifle, but on his laptop, the techies found searches for homemade IED drone bombs. He was seen leaving with one guitar case. We can't be sure what's inside, so we are not taking any chances. No one, and I mean no one, goes in without my say-so. We'll try to talk him out first, at the very least to establish the situation before we deploy the tactical team with smoke and stun grenades.'

Helen winced. Notoriously dangerous, stun grenades had the propensity to cause permanent hearing damage to those not wearing protective equipment. If Noah was in there, he'd be at risk of serious injury.

'Right,' Walker said, 'everyone has their orders. Confirm when you are all in place. I'm heading over there now to engage with those inside.'

Chairs squeaked and scraped the floor as the meeting ended.

Helen walked across to the map and took another look at the building layout. The open plan ground floor. The location of the stairs. The position of the three rooms on the first floor. 'I'm happy to travel with you,' she called across to Walker who was pulling on a bulletproof vest, deep in conversation with the chief.

Walker cleared his throat and beckoned her closer. 'That won't be necessary. We're grateful for everything you've done to assist this afternoon. We'll take it from here.'

Assist? Helen could barely believe her ears.

Before she could answer, Adams stepped in. 'I'm content for you to take Helen. High street is riddled with back alleys and sidewalks. Her local knowledge will be an asset.'

'We have detailed maps. I think we'll manage.'

Adams raised a brow. 'I didn't ask you if you'd manage.'

'Commander Quinn's plane lands any minute,' Walker said. 'He was insistent, apart from tactical support, it's counter-terror command only in the negotiation room.'

Adams's face hardened. 'Well, he's not here yet, which means I'm the senior officer. You take Helen with you. If Valentine tries to escape, few officers know Hampton better than her.'

CHAPTER 76

Dez Eldred, the tactical support sergeant, was waiting for Walker and Helen in the car park at the rear of Hayes when they arrived. The drive over had been frantic – officers on the ground confirming over the radio when they were in position. Quinn's plane had landed. He was on his way and firing instructions at Walker: he wasn't to wait for the commander, he was to go straight in with negotiation. Thankfully, the roads were quiet, and they had travelled through town quickly.

'We're putting everyone in place,' Eldred said to Helen and Walker. 'And we've managed to get a confirmed sighting in the upstairs room of Reed's.'

'Valentine?' Helen checked.

Eldred nodded.

'What about Noah Gardner?'

'We're pretty sure they're in there together, there's certainly someone in a chair to the right of the window. We can't get a good visual on the other person, though.'

Helen pictured Noah placing his arm protectively around Ashleigh on her first visit to Portland Grove. Ashleigh, now sitting at home, nibbling her nails, waiting for news. 'Any sign of drones?' Following the information on Valentine's wall, they couldn't rule out him using other devices.

He shook his head. 'The helicopter's sitting high, keeping watch. Nothing yet.'

Walker was back on the phone to Quinn as Eldred led them into the staff entrance at the rear and through a surprisingly

303

small kitchen, considering the size of the seating area out front, that reeked of coffee. Helen's knees pained as she climbed the steep back stairs. She followed Eldred into the room they'd commandeered and suppressed a gasp.

The streetlamp outside cast eerie shadows over a stack of tables and chairs to the side. But what struck her was the desk in the middle covered in open laptops. Officers were stationed on either side of a window covered in a thin veil of curtain. More officers were scrabbling about with laptops and wires under low lighting. It was like something from a movie set.

On the middle screen was an enlarged still image of Jack Valentine peering out of a window, a hoody pulled down over his fringe.

Walker ended his call as he entered. An armed officer beside the window immediately addressed him. 'No clear line to fire on the suspect yet, sir.'

He meant his line of fire wasn't clear of hazards – like other people. Helen's chest tightened. Walker moved across to speak with the marksman. 'What else do we know?' she asked Eldred.

'Very little,' he replied. 'We've managed to obtain keys to Reed's from the letting agent. Firearms officers have entered and confirmed the suspect is confined to the main first-floor room. The rest of the building is empty.'

At least he wasn't moving around. Keeping to one area meant they had a better chance of targeting him.

Walker strode to the desk in the middle and fitted an earpiece, then nodded at an officer nearby who pressed a few buttons on his computer. 'Right.' He placed a finger to his lips. 'We're on.' The room hushed as a phone rang out. One, two, three… Several low groans sounded as it went to voicemail.

'Try again,' Walker said. The room quietened a second time. Every pair of ears listening to each jingle as it rang, counting the ringtones. By the time they reached five, Helen was holding her breath. Finally, there was a click. Then silence.

Walker exchanged a glance with Eldred, then pressed his earpiece. 'Jack, this is Assistant Commander Walker from

Counter Terrorism Command. Please don't hang up. The place is surrounded. We know you are in there, and we know you have Noah Gardner with you.'

It was a moment before Jack spoke. 'How did you find me?'

'That's not important. If you surrender yourself, we'll help you. Treat you respectfully, give you a chance to tell your side of the story.'

Helen looked across at the building opposite. The second-floor curtain twitched, then nothing.

'How is Noah?' Walker asked.

Silence.

'We need to know he's okay,' Walker pressed. 'Can you put him on?'

'I don't think that is necessary,' Jack said.

'We want to help you,' Walker said, undeterred. 'Why don't you start by letting Noah go?'

'What, and let you lot gun me down? No way.'

'You don't want to hurt him.'

'You don't know what I want.'

'As I said, I'm here to help. My job is to achieve a safe outcome for all involved, you included.' Walker stared at the window as he spoke, hawk-like eyes watching for any flicker of movement. 'I'm here to find out what it is you want.'

A huff filled the line. 'I'm not talking to you.'

'Jack, I—'

'There's only one person I'm prepared to speak to,' Jack interrupted, 'and that's the detective chief inspector. Helen. I want her over here.'

The room quietened. Walker shot Helen a surprised glance. Clearly, this was the last thing anyone expected. 'That's not possible.'

'If you care about Noah Gardner, you'll make it possible. You've got half an hour.' The line clicked off.

CHAPTER 77

Walker stood stock-still, staring at Helen. 'Why does he want to speak with you?'

'No idea.' Helen didn't care about Valentine. They could give the order, gun him down as far as she was concerned. But she did care about Noah, and Ashleigh. There'd been too much loss on this case, too many false promises. 'I'm happy to go over there, give it a try.'

'It's too dangerous.' He turned to Eldred. 'How long before we're ready with the agreed tactical entry?'

Eldred brought up the building map on his computer. 'We'll need to get more officers in place… We can certainly do it in less than half an hour.'

'Do it in twenty minutes,' Walker said.

'There's no guarantee it'll work. We need to confirm the location of those inside, make sure it's safe.'

'I don't care.' Walker checked his watch again. Quinn was due to arrive any minute. 'Go ahead, get everything in place. I'll give Valentine a couple of minutes, try him again.'

'What about the hostage?' Helen asked. 'If you just give me a chance—'

'This is my operation.' Walker turned his back on her. 'We'll play it my way.'

Helen stared at him aghast as Eldred left the room, speaking into his phone. The chief was listening in from headquarters, Quinn from the road. Neither had overridden Walker's decision and every second taunted her. She couldn't risk anything happening to Noah, she wasn't about to lose an open line of communication and, since there was no way Walker was about to give her the phone, as far as she was concerned, there was only one option left.

She cast one last glance at Walker, poring over the plans and sidled towards the door. No one noticed Helen slide out and make for the stairs.

CHAPTER 78

Helen slipped out of the back entrance of Hayes under the cover of darkness. It wasn't until she entered the car park that she noticed Eldred, twenty metres or so away, talking into his phone. She ducked behind the tactical support van, waited a second. Only when she was sure he hadn't seen her did she move around the van and start down Severn Street. Keeping to the shadows, checking over her shoulder for Eldred. It wasn't long before he disappeared, and Helen quickened her step.

The fastest route to Reed's was Forten Alley, which ran down the side of Hayes to High Street. Though that put her in the sniper's visual, not to mention counter-terror operatives. No. Severn Street ran parallel to High Street. She sped into a jog. She needed to travel further up the street to Hitcher's Jitty, a narrow aperture between the bank and the One Stop shop. That should bring her out far enough down to miss the cordon guards and allow her to slip across the road before the roadblocks.

It wasn't a pitch-black night, the blanket of sky punctuated by tiny stars, a crisp crescent moon. Her feet pounded the pavement. Soft thumps the only sounds filling the air. By the time she reached the entrance to the jitty, her breaths were coming hard and fast. She turned into the narrow, bricked passage, slowing to pass a row of overflowing wheelie bins. It was darker down here. A thick scent of moss filled the air. She switched on her phone torch, illuminating a leaky drainage pipe ahead. Stepping over a puddle beneath. Rounding a corner, then another until a streetlight illuminated the road out front. Almost through.

It wasn't until she emerged that she spotted the two armed officers standing beside liveried cars parked across the road. Damn! She'd anticipated the roadblock would be further down, closer to Cross Keys roundabout and the edge of town. She stepped back, made to retreat. But it was too late. She'd been spotted.

'Hey!' one of the officers called. Turning towards her, lifting his rifle.

Helen immediately held up her arms in surrender. 'Police!' she shouted.

The officer angled his head, squinting at her bulletproof jacket. They stared at one another for a moment. 'Ma'am?' he called, an air of familiarity in his voice.

His partner, rifle still cocked, looked quizzically at them both. 'It's Nathan Broadhurst.' He lifted his helmet to expose blue eyes, a shaven head, and approached. 'You spoke at my passing out ceremony.'

'Ah,' Helen said, lowering her arms, thankful for a friendly face. 'I see you've done well for yourself.'

He patted his gun. 'All I ever wanted to do.' He looked past her down the jitty. 'What are you up to out here?'

'Using the side alleys to make my way across the road out of view of the suspect. I need to get into the back entrance of the furniture store to speak with him.'

Nathan's frown deepened.

'We didn't want to alert anyone,' Helen said, looking at the cars, desperately thinking on her feet. 'There's a chance the suspect might be monitoring our channels, hence me creeping around. I don't have long.'

'Right.' A short, sharp nod. He rushed back to his colleague, spoke in his ear for several seconds, then returned. 'I'll escort you across the road and down through the back street behind Reed's. You don't want to be moving around out here, especially unannounced. There's Old Bill everywhere.'

He gave a brief wink, replaced his helmet. 'Most of them have guns.'

Helen laughed, more out of relief than humour. They moved across the road and sped up. In less than a minute, she was in Secombe Street, racing towards the back entrance to Reed's.

Nathan signalled to another officer standing at the goods entrance to the old furniture store. Helen winced inwardly as he explained the situation in a low voice, gave her a single nod and the thumbs up, then retreated to his post. She hadn't wanted to rope anyone into her covert action, but at least she was the senior officer. Saying the killer was monitoring their channels meant they wouldn't report her presence immediately, and by the time Walker realised what she was doing, she'd be in situ.

The other officer didn't remove his helmet or introduce himself. He turned and led her silently through the side door and into an area of the furniture store used for deliveries and storage, then through another door and into the old showroom. The room was in darkness, save pale moonlight leaking in through dusty windows. Cobwebs stroked her hair as they navigated by torchlight, out of another door and up a staircase.

Another officer stood at the top of the stairs. He stared at Helen as his colleague whispered the situation and left.

'PC Seth Morgan,' he said, introducing himself quietly, indicating for her to switch off her torch. 'Call me Seth. I'll be here, watching you. Anytime you feel uncomfortable, or you think something's going down, you give me the nod, okay?'

Helen agreed.

Quietly, he let her into a corridor, hooking her gaze as he pointed to the third door along. 'Be careful,' he mouthed.

Helen moved down the corridor gingerly, grateful for the carpeted floor, soaking up her footfalls. It was stuffier up here, a thick heat filling the air, and pitch-dark without her torch. By the time she reached the first door, her eyes were adjusting to the poor light. From the plans, the first door was the toilet. The second, the stockroom. She moved along further and stopped where she anticipated the dividing wall between the rooms would be. The officer was right. It wasn't wise to get too close to Valentine's room, just in case he decided to take a potshot.

Helen angled her head, listened hard. Nothing. She took another look at Seth, standing in the doorway, and said, 'Jack? Jack, it's Helen. I'm outside.'

CHAPTER 79

Several seconds passed before Helen's answer came and when it did, it was short, to the point. 'I'll unlock the door.'

'I can't come inside, Jack. Not while you're armed, and you have Noah.'

'Then why come over?'

'It's not too late, you know. You can give up your weapons, hand over Noah.'

'I think we both know that's not going to happen.'

'Look, if you want me to help you, I need confirmation that Noah is okay. I need to speak with him.'

Quiet fell upon them. Helen was beginning to worry, to work out what to say next, when she heard a rip, like the tear of tape, followed by a groggy voice. 'Hello!'

'Noah,' Helen said, 'are you hurt?'

'Get me out—'

'That's enough.' Jack again. His voice tight.

A scuffle. The sound of Jack replacing the tape. He clearly had no intention of giving up.

'Why did you ask for me, Jack?' Helen said.

'Because most people give me a wide berth. You're the only one who ever showed any kindness. If I'm going to speak to someone, it's going to be someone who gives a shit.'

Several seconds passed. 'We can still speak, Jack, through the door,' Helen said.

'Jack is the nickname my mother gave me. I used it when

I joined the force. John is my name. That idiot, Sadhika, told everyone at Portland Grove my name is Johnny. I prefer John.'

'Okay,' Helen said, pulling her phone out of her pocket, quietly switching it to record. Any conversation or revelation here wouldn't be admissible in court, but whatever she gleaned might, at least, give the case a springboard. She glanced at Seth. 'Talk to me, John, I want to understand.'

'Ivan Shaw was my half-brother. He didn't deserve to die.'

Shaw's brother was in her office, under her nose all the time! Helen battled to keep her cool. 'I'm so sorry. I know how difficult it is to lose someone you love.'

'Do you? Do you really?' There was a sneer in his tone. 'I bet your loved one wasn't subjected to years of bullying and mental abuse, let down by those who were supposed to support him. Ivan didn't stand a chance.'

'Suicide is a tragedy.'

A derisive snort. 'You have no idea.'

'Then tell me. Come on, John. Like I said, I want to understand.' Helen slid down the wall to the floor, the coarse carpet prickling her legs through her trousers.

Her phone vibrated. A text message from an unknown number. Helen opened it and froze: *This is Quinn. I know exactly where you are. Respond to confirm receipt and that you are safe to converse.* Helen glanced again at Seth. Commander Quinn had arrived. And what's more, he'd discovered her activity faster than she'd hoped. She quickly typed, *10.14*, to confirm she wasn't free to speak, then, *can SMS*. Quinn hadn't even tried to order her to retreat. Which could only mean one thing, Walker's negotiation had failed. 'I'm not going anywhere,' she said to John.

'It was my sister, Becky, that found out about Ivan first,' he said. 'An old sickly aunt told her about him on her deathbed. Becky and I had no other family, we were moved from one foster home to another when we were kids. Becky was sociable, a good mixer. Always had friends. One of those strong, confident people. I couldn't find my way. At school, she looked out for me, stepped in when kids called me names. Threatened them when they teased me. Even in adulthood, she fought my battles. Called the bank when I had a problem. Returned faulty goods to shops. She was always there. Then she got married and moved to America, and I had no one.'

Another message lit Helen's phone, *Is the hostage okay?*

Yes. Made contact. The hostage, Noah, is alive.

Okay, Helen, you have ten minutes to talk him down. Keep in touch.

Ten minutes, then what? A stun grenade? Helen pressed the back of her head against the wall hard. Stun grenades were notoriously unreliable. If she didn't get John on side, this could end in carnage. It was 10.46. 'That must have been tough,' she said to John.

'It was. Then Becky found out about Ivan. It wasn't difficult to trace him through Facebook, we were told he had a gran in Sunderland, on our father's side. Becky didn't want to know, she was married, looking forward to having her own family one day, but I couldn't wait to meet him.' He sniffed. 'I'll never forget that first time. He wasn't what I imagined. He'd just come out of a relationship, was pale, thin, brittle. We met in a café in Jarrow, a proper greasy spoon.' He snorted. 'It wasn't until afterwards that he told me it was miles from where he lived, he'd never been there before. We ended up laughing about the coffee, he used that term you used – of it tasting like wood smoke.' A brief pause and when he continued, his tone was soft, wistful. 'Me and Ivan hit it off straight away. We had so much in common. We liked the same bands – the Foo Fighters, Green Day.'

Helen waited. He clearly wanted to talk it out. Then a thump sounded. 'John?'

'It's okay. Nothing's happened. Not yet.'

She imagined him sitting down, pressing his back against the other side of the wall, further up the corridor. It was 10.48. 'Please, tell me more about Ivan.'

'For the first time in ages, I felt alive. With Ivan, I was

part of something. I've never had parents – mine were both addicts, they died when we were young. I never fitted in. Now I had someone to visit, someone like me, to spend time with. A family of sorts. I used to hate it when people at work asked what I was doing for Christmas. Ever since Becky left, I'd been on my own. I wouldn't be anymore.'

'Sounds like you and Ivan became close.'

'We didn't have long, but I felt like I'd known him forever. The weekends I visited, we talked and played video games and talked again. Back home, we emailed all the time.'

10.49. 'Emailed?'

'Ivan was suspicious about phones, social media. He only used email.'

'You were TopBoy.'

'I was. It was a means for us to stay in touch when we weren't together. A private email address, exclusive to him, enabled him to open up. The similarities between us were uncanny. He'd struggled in school, had a rough time fitting in, like I did. The guys teased him, the girls messed him about, and he didn't have a Becky to help him along. I guess I was... sort of protective towards him.'

Protective. She couldn't help wondering if he knew about Shaw's previous conviction. 'I can understand that.'

'He'd moved up to Sunderland to be with his gran, the only person he cared about, and then she died shortly afterwards. He was vulnerable, I guess that's why he was so easily taken in by Cheryl.'

'Cheryl?'

'The ex-girlfriend. He'd thought she was the answer to turning his life around. He finally let down his guard, welcomed her into his home. And she repaid him by taking him to the cleaners and clearing off with someone else.' His voice turned venomous. 'You don't know how hard I tried to find her, to teach her a lesson after he died. But that's the thing with manipulative people, they're clever. They know how to disappear.'

Helen recalled Dark's comment about Cheryl moving several times. Whatever the reason, it had probably saved her life. Her eyes slid to the clock on her phone. 10.51. Only five minutes left. 'What happened before he died?' she asked gently.

'He received an eviction notice. The bitch was supposed to be paying the rent when she lived there. She'd defaulted for the last two months while she carried on with some other guy, left him in arrears.'

'That must have made him angry.'

'Angry? He kicked his house to pieces. Started regressing. Harping on about his school days. How he was marginalised, badly treated. How invites went out every year for a reunion, and he was never invited. Then there was the stuff online.'

'What sort of stuff?'

'Online forums. Where they hate men and women and feel marginalised. He became obsessed with this guy called Elliot Rodger who gunned down young people who he believed ignored people like him, made society unfair. Talked about doing something similar to his schoolmates.'

'The incel network,' Helen said quietly, closing her eyes. 'Did you join him on those sites?'

'For a while. I quickly got disillusioned. Most people on there are all bluff, and woe is me. They spout a lot of hot air. Talk about scaring women, following them at night, drugging their drinks. Nothing constructive. Nothing that's going to change the way things are.'

'What about Ivan?'

'He got angrier. Focused on this Rodger guy, kept reading the manifesto he wrote before he died. Talked about the next school reunion – reckoned he could pull off a shooting, teach them a lesson, without getting caught. I didn't realise how serious he was until he showed me his weapon collection. Rifles, handguns, you name it. I spent a whole weekend trying to talk him out of it, even took his weapons back to my place to keep him safe.' He sucked his teeth. 'I'll never forget that drive home, I was paranoid I'd get caught.'

Helen visualised him cruising down the motorway with a host of illegal weapons in the boot. Parking outside the flat in Portland Grove, waiting for darkness to fall before he unloaded.

When John spoke again, his voice dropped an octave. 'Then he died.' A strange sound seeped through the wall, like a strangled choke. 'And everything changed.'

CHAPTER 80

'John?' Helen glanced at the clock. 10.54. Only two minutes left. 'John, are you there?

She was just about to signal to Seth when he answered, 'I'm here.'

For a second, she thought she'd lost him. 'I know you're hurting. I know it's hard. But I need to ask you to let Noah go. We can still talk afterwards.'

'I'm talking now.'

Her gaze moved from her watch to the door. He needed to be quick.

'In the short months we knew each other, I lived for Ivan. Looked forward to seeing him, to talking to him. It wasn't until he was gone that I realised. Everything he'd been talking about, everything he was planning, had been crucial to his existence. A means to put his past behind him, set the record straight. I talked him out of that. If I hadn't, he'd still be here now.

'So, you carried out the shootings in his name.'

'It seemed like a crazy idea at first. Then the more I thought about it, the more I realised that Ivan was right. If nobody stuck their neck out, made a stand, nothing would ever change. We're the forgotten people. We're not cool, wealthy, sporty, so we get pushed aside. Denied a normal life, a loving relationship.'

Helen sat forward. 'I don't understand. Why didn't you come forward, tell your story after the incident at O'Malley's?'

'I wanted to, but that bitch reporter wouldn't help me.

And those arrests – they were all wrong. Nothing was going to change.'

'The people at the university were youngsters, John. They weren't around when Ivan was at college there.'

'It's the institution, what it represents. The Chad and Stacy behaviour it breeds.'

His words were changing. Becoming pithier, barbed, as if he was spitting them out one by one. He was not only acting out his brother's wishes, but he'd adopted the beliefs himself. 'So why here, now?' Helen said, glaring at her phone. 10.55. 'Why another shooting? You've made your point, John. You can walk out with me, explain your reasons to the world.'

Another message. *We're going in.*

What? It was still only 10.55. She scrabbled to respond. *Need more time.*

We don't have it. Drone overhead. Thirty seconds until we go in.

Bodies appeared from nowhere, lining the corridor, the carpet muffling their footfalls. Seth handed Helen a helmet.

She was just pulling down her eyepiece, checking the ear defenders, when John answered her question.

'The vigil. Celebrating the lives of those people who rode roughshod over Ivan's. I can't let them do that. Ivan and me, we're brothers. We stand together.'

The crash of the forced door drowned out his words. A high-pitched, piercing sound followed. Even behind the protective eyewear, the light was blinding, disorientating, brilliant white in the ruckus of bodies.

Then out of it all came the distinctive blast of a gunshot.

CHAPTER 81

John Valentine stood with his head high, handcuffed to a uniformed officer at Cross Keys custody desk. Granite eyes glued to Helen as she read out the multiple murder charges.

It had been a crazy night. Both Noah and John had been rushed to hospital after police stormed the hideout at Reed's. The gunshot – believed to have been meant for Noah – hit the wall behind him in the melee. Thankfully, officers watching opposite had eventually been able to position the bodies in the room, enabling tactical support to hurl the stun grenade sufficiently away from the suspect and hostage, resulting in shock to both, temporary hearing impairment to Noah, but no permanent injury.

Poor Noah. He'd looked dishevelled when she'd visited earlier. Sitting up in his hospital bed, pale as ice, dark shadows beneath his eyes. Desperate to share his conversation with John Valentine the evening before. How John had asked him to meet him at Reed's, to help him carry in some old decks for the new music store. How Noah had been reluctant at first, hesitant to exchange telephone numbers. He didn't like the guy, didn't want to leave Ashleigh. But after the argument with Ashleigh the following morning, John had messaged, pressing him, saying he didn't have anyone else to assist, and Noah had acquiesced. Unaware he would be knocked out by a deranged killer when his back was turned and then, later, wake to find himself strapped to a chair, facing the barrel of a gun while John manically shared his plan of a third shooting. A

shooting Noah was to witness before he took a bullet himself
– John's punishment to Ashleigh for betraying him.

Following his admission to Helen at the scene, John
Valentine had admitted to both shootings back at the station,
keen to provide intricate details for each and, even now, his
intentions were imprinted firmly onto his contorted face. On
an iPad recovered from his flat, they'd found evidence of
his presence on incel forums, footage of each crime scene,
but no suicide video to be shown in the event of his death.
He'd never planned to martyr himself. He wanted to stay
alive, his presence a beacon on his brother's story. This was
a backlash at everyone in society who he believed had let them
both down, and he was going to make sure the message was
imparted, loud and clear.

A draught passed through the custody block, lifting the
goose bumps on Helen's arms. The drone at the scene had
later been identified as a false alarm – a curious resident
trying to get photos of the blockaded town centre. But in the
boot of John's car, they found an IED device, a drone and a
handset. Helen shivered. If he'd pulled this one off, what he
had planned next didn't bear thinking about. 'Is there anything
you'd like to add?' she asked.

John Valentine sucked in his cheeks and gave a single
head shake.

She handed him the charge sheet and waited while he
squiggled his signature, taking care to dot the i and cross the
t before he passed it back.

It was a surreal moment, standing beside Pemberton,
watching him being led back to his cell. The man who'd
murdered seven people in cold blood and waged terror on
so many, scuffing his trainers on the floor, the police-issue
jogging suit hanging off his hunched shoulders.

'We need a drink,' Pemberton said.

'I think you might be right.' They walked side by side
down the corridor and out into the cool morning. It was just
after 8 am. Chief Constable Adams and Commander Quinn

would be on the stage at the Guildhall carrying out their press conference now, basking in the glory of thwarting another shooting, the triumph of making the streets safe again. The earlier arrests, the media silence, brushed under the carpet as part of a wider terror operation. No mention of Kendrick or Helen, who were now subjects of an internal inquiry. Him for lines of enquiry overlooked. Her for countermanding a major operation by going solo to speak with the suspect at Reed's. In view of the result, the chief was putting in a word for her. Even Quinn, satisfied with another solved case to add to his bright CV, had agreed that her engagement with John Valentine had appeased the killer, elongating the life of the hostage and setting them up for a successful intervention. Perhaps that would make a difference. All Helen knew was that, after today, she would be desk-bound until Complaints and Discipline had completed their investigation.

They were crossing the car park, Pemberton loosening his tie, when Helen's phone rang. It was Spencer.

'All done?' he asked.

'Yes.' Helen smiled at the excitement in his voice. 'Tell everyone to pack up and meet us at Wetherspoons. We'll have a liquid breakfast.'

'Great! I have more news. Just in. Chilli Franks has decided to plead.'

Helen stopped dead in her tracks. 'What?'

'Yup. His solicitor called. He's pleading on all counts. No trial after all.'

Helen lowered her phone as Spencer rang off, her heart thumping her ribcage. 'Did you hear that?' she said to Pemberton.

Pemberton nodded. 'Clearly, he's hoping for a lesser sentence for cooperation. A glimmer of hope that he'll see the outside again before he starts dribbling into his soup.'

It wasn't the sentence that bothered Helen; it was the timing. She'd been banking on the media coverage of the trial to raise Chilli's profile. For Robert to see him for the monster he really was. Any coverage now would be limited, tucked away behind the capture of The Sniper Killer. No massive headlines, no front-page spread. Robert probably wouldn't even see it.

They reached Helen's car. 'Are you coming back to the office first or heading straight to the pub?' Pemberton asked.

'I might drop in at home, meet you later,' she said. She needed time to let this development sink in, work out what it meant for her family.

Pemberton threw her a knowing look. 'Okay. I'm sure we'll be in the pub all day. See you later.'

CHAPTER 82

Ashleigh gripped the banister rail, the wood cold against her clammy fingers.

'You're going to be fine,' Sadhika said, holding her elbow firmly.

Ashleigh stood resolute. She could do this. It was Saturday morning. Noah was home from hospital, her mother was due to arrive shortly. Ashleigh's bags were packed and in Sadhika's car ready for her to join them all at Noah's parents' house.

The edge of an envelope in her pocket scratched her thigh as she lifted her foot. The letter from the local health authority, which had ironically arrived this morning, inviting her to a counselling session on Monday. She would go to the session in person. No more Zoom meetings. She needed to take control, and she was starting today by leaving the flat. Though, for all her brave intentions, it was proving trickier than expected.

'Come on,' Sadhika encouraged. 'Try another step.'

Ashleigh edged her foot forward. It hadn't been like this last night when the detective arrived to tell her they'd found Noah. She'd still felt shaky, nauseous descending the stairs. Stepping outside the front door into the darkness. Streetlights whirling around her as they drove across town. But adrenalin had swept her along then. That and the screaming desire to finally see Noah.

She forced another step. Thinking of the hospital, only hours earlier. The whirlpool of life, the assault on her senses as she was guided along the corridor. For the first time in a week, she'd felt safe. The Sniper Killer was finally behind bars.

An image of Noah, his face lighting up when she reached his hospital bedside, branded itself on her brain. Her thoughtful, lovely Noah. Whose good deed for their neighbour had been his downfall. She'd had to raise her voice for him to hear, could still see him squinting up at her, blinking away the white spots he said lingered in his vision from the stun grenade.

Ashleigh took another step and then another.

Guilt. Its knobbly fingers had picked away at her all night with thoughts of what might have been. Of the different route her life might be taking this morning, without Noah. Analysing every single action. If only she hadn't written that piece in the newspaper. If only she hadn't argued with Noah and sent him away. It wasn't until dawn struck this morning, lighting her front room in shades of rich amber while she pressed her fingers to her temples, that she managed to reconcile her mind. She couldn't be held responsible for the actions of a deranged killer. She couldn't have known that Johnny was Ivan Shaw's half-brother. Ivan Shaw – the quiet boy at school that nobody bothered with. She had no idea what had been going on in his head, what he'd been planning. Nobody did, apart from his half-brother.

The buzz of her phone broke her thoughts. The WhatsApp group. That was something else she needed to deal with.

They reached the bottom step and glanced across at the police tape stretched diagonally across Johnny's door. She could still hear the jaunty beats of his music seeping through the floor, still recall rolling her eyes when his curtains were drawn in the daytime, thinking him tardy, idle. When all the time he'd been using the space as a hideaway, to plot and kill.

A click to the side. Both Sadhika and Ashleigh jumped as Filip appeared, his brown hair limp, his face pallid and drawn. He stared at them both and then across at his neighbour's door.

A second flicked past. For once, even Sadhika was lost for words. Ashleigh stared at Filip. His eyes met hers, and in that moment, an understanding passed between them. He tipped his head, retreated, and closed the door.

'Come on, let's get you into the car,' Sadhika said.

Ashleigh's phone rang. She pulled it out of her pocket, expecting it to be her mother saying she'd arrived at Noah's parents. But it wasn't her mother calling, it was Jason. He'd been messaging since dawn. Looking for a survivor's reaction, a soundbite now the killer was behind bars. Ashleigh stared at the phone a second, buzzing in her hand. The last thing she needed today was to be quoted in a news piece. She switched it off and placed it in her pocket.

Crisp air rushed in as they opened the front door to number 8 Portland Grove. The road outside was empty, a police car parked at the top, keeping the press at bay. But it didn't stop the faces pressed to the railings of the park opposite, watching the neighbours of The Sniper Killer leave their home.

Ashleigh released herself from Sadhika's hold, stood tall and walked down the steps. Ignoring the flashes of cameras, the eyes boring into them. She thought of Cass and Nia, her steely friends. Channelled their strength and climbed into the car, staring straight ahead. She *was* one of the lucky ones, and so was Noah. Unlike the poor victims, they had a bright future ahead of them, and she would never let anyone, or anything, stand in their way again.

CHAPTER 83

Helen could hear low voices when she arrived home. She heeled the door closed, angled her head, but couldn't be sure where they were coming from.

'Hello!' she called.

'In the kitchen,' her mother said.

She kicked off her shoes, was almost at the kitchen door, when her mobile announced a text. It was from Brandon. *Fantastic result. Well done! Fancy a drink to celebrate?* Helen stared at her phone screen, unable to resist a wry smile. Thankfully, she'd been wrong about his involvement in the shootings. Just as Walker was wrong about Chilli. She was still staring at her phone when the door was flung open.

She looked up to face Matthew. He was dressed in jeans that hung low on his hips. A plaid shirt. 'Hey!' Helen said. 'You're up early.'

Matthew ignored her statement, his eyes gleaming. 'It was you, wasn't it, who helped catch The Sniper Killer?'

'I don't know what you're talking about.'

'Yes, you do. We've just watched the press conference. The chief said, "his senior homicide officer went beyond the call of duty to reach out to the killer. Their courage almost certainly saved lives." I know it was you. A reporter asked who it was, and he said, "She's resting today."'

Helen was dumbfounded at Adams's public commendation. The one senior female officer on the case, it could only be her. 'It was a joint operation,' she said, waving her hand dismissively.

Matthew's mouth stretched into a wide smile. 'That was a cool thing to do, Mum.'

Helen could see her mother beam at her from behind him and felt herself glow with pride. For once, she didn't feel guilty for doing her job. 'Thank you.'

It wasn't until Matthew moved aside and she wandered in further that Helen saw Robert tucked behind the door. He was sitting at the table, red-faced, as if he'd been crying.

'Robert has something to say to you,' Jane Lavery said.

Helen looked from her mother to her son warily. 'Oh?'

Jane gave the lad a nod. A tuft of hair was sticking up awkwardly on the side of his head, and when he gazed up at her, eyes wide, he looked young again. Vulnerable.

'We'll leave you to it.' She ushered Matthew out of the room.

'What is it, son?'

'You did good with The Sniper,' Robert said, tears glittering his lashes.

'Thank you.' But the way he dropped his eyes to the floor told her that wasn't all he had to say. She pulled out the chair beside him, lowered herself into it.

'I spoke to Zac's dad,' Robert said. 'He told me everything.'

Helen's stomach flipped. What had Davy Boyd said this time? She wanted to slide in first, to explain about Chilli's case, but a lump crept into her throat, expanding by the second.

Robert hung his head. 'He was upset about the trial, visited Chilli to find out more.' A tear dropped to the floor with a plop, and Helen's heart bled. She couldn't remember the last time Robert had cried, and seeing him in pain, like this, crucified her. She wanted to reach out, to embrace him, to hold him tight, to make everything better, just as she had when he was little and he'd grazed his legs playing on the patio with his brother. But he wasn't young anymore, he was a teenager. There were fewer hugs these days and, after the past week, she imagined a hug was the last thing on his mind. 'He told me Chilli kidnapped an officer. They had to go to hospital afterwards. It was you, wasn't it?'

This was information that formed part of the court case, specific details that hadn't been reported in the press. The lump in Helen's throat expanded further. 'I was just doing my job.'

'He said you didn't tell us because you didn't want to frighten us. You were trying to protect us, just like he was trying to protect his kids. He said that's what parents do.'

'Yes.'

'He also told us about Grandad's history with Chilli.'

Davy had been thorough.

Robert looked up and met her gaze, eyes watery. 'You should have told us, Mum. We're not children anymore.'

Helen tried to swallow back the lump in her throat, but it was wedged so tightly it refused to move. 'You're right.'

He blinked, her agreement catching him off balance. 'Gran's told us everything now. Matt and I know exactly what happened.'

'I'm sorry, son. It was difficult. I lived a large part of my life in the shadow of Franks and his threats. They terrified me when I was young. I didn't want you both to go through that too. And when you and Zac became friends... Well, he seems like a nice lad. I didn't want to mess anything up.'

Robert sniffed. 'I don't want you to hate them.'

'Who?'

'Zac's family. They're good people. His dad knew we weren't speaking, he was trying to help. That's why he got Zac and me together and told us.'

'Oh, love, I don't hate them.' Davy's questionable acquaintances felt like a splinter beneath her skin. She wasn't happy about the father of her son's best friend keeping criminal associations, but she had no proof he was involved in anything illegal himself. Trent and his former partner had been sent home that morning, without charge, and Davy had put himself on the line here. Visiting his brother, enlightening the kids.

Knowing Chilli's ruthless nature, it was difficult to believe that Davy's visit had tugged on the familial heartstrings and swayed him to plea. With the trial around the corner, did the reality of the strong evidence against Chilli push him to plea for a reduced sentence, as Pemberton had suggested, or was there another reason for the change of heart? She pictured their beady eyes, the hard stare. Two men, so similar, and yet so different.

Robert leaned forward and enveloped her, his embrace vice-like.

Helen wasn't sure how long they stayed there. The pair of them, holding on to each other, as if nothing else in the world mattered. Slowly her breath evened, she opened her eyes and looked out into the sun-drenched garden.

Robert pulled back. 'Can we put all this behind us?' he said. 'Carry on like before.'

Helen gave a gentle smile. 'I'd like nothing better.'

At that moment, Matthew and her mother rejoined them. Helen caught Jane giving her grandson a sly wink. 'Right, anyone for a drink?' she asked.

'I think we should go out,' Helen said. 'Celebrate.'

'Celebrate what?' It was Matthew.

'The end of my case. Your upcoming GCSE results.' She looked at Robert. 'Do we need an excuse?'

'Don't you like have to do that boring paperwork you always talk about,' Robert said. 'You know, at the end of a case.' He'd slid back into teenage speak, and for once, she couldn't have been more grateful.

'That can wait until tomorrow. Come on, let's go out to eat. What do you fancy? My treat!'

'Pizza!' The boys laughed as they spoke in unison.

Helen caught her mother rolling her eyes at the prospect of pizza for breakfast. 'I tell you what, there's a new Italian brasserie in town. I'm sure they'll have pizza on the menu. Let's try there.'

Her mother laughed at the compromise and disappeared to get her jacket while the boys trudged out to the hallway.

Helen listened to her sons' excited chatter as they pulled on their shoes. She couldn't be sure what Davy Boyd's future intentions were, but, for now, she had her son back and he was happy. If her job had taught her anything, it was to savour these moments.

She reached for her phone, typed out a quick text to Pemberton. *Raincheck on the pub, I'm taking my family out for breakfast.* She pressed send and then reread the message from Brandon. While his persistence was flattering, the idea of going on a date was daunting, especially after spending so long on her own. Though at the same time, she couldn't deny she did harbour a hankering to share that closeness with someone again, and he was handsome.

Jane Lavery returned to clutching her handbag, a jacket over her arm. 'Everything okay?'

Helen switched off her phone and placed it in her pocket. That was a thought for another day. 'Yes, absolutely fine,' she said. Then she rose and followed her mother out of the door.

ACKNOWLEDGEMENTS

I say this every time and it couldn't be truer: There are so many people involved in bringing a book to fruition.

First, I must mention Philip Bouch, my dear friend and huge supporter, who sadly passed away before this one was finished. We miss you every single day and carry your words of wisdom with us.

I'd like to thank Iain Brown for sharing his knowledge on semi-automatic rifles. As usual, any errors or discrepancies in the story are my own.

Also, to Ella, for advising on all things culinary.

To my agent, Caroline Montgomery at Rupert Crew – working with you is always a joy.

Gratitude to my editor, Lauren Parsons, whom I've had the pleasure of working with for many years; your positive approach and sharp eye make every novel better. Also, to Tom Chalmers and all the gang at Legend Press for believing in this, the fifth in the DCI Helen Lavery series, and championing it, and to Rose for designing the fabulous cover.

The continuous support from the online writing and reading community keeps me sane. (I've said this many times because it means so much!) Wonderful author friends like Rebecca Bradley and Ian Robinson who are always at the end of the phone and whose presence is cherished in such an isolated job. The incredibly supportive book clubs: Anne Cater and all at Book Connectors; Shell Baker and Lainy Swanson at Crime Book Club; Tracy Fenton, Helen Boyce, and all at The Book

Club (TBC); David Gilchrist and Caroline Maston at UK Crime Book Club; Susan Hunter and the guys at Crime Fiction Addict; Wendy Clarke and the gang at The Fiction Café Book Club. Also, to the amazing reviewers and book bloggers, including the lovely Teresa Nikolic, who work tirelessly to spread the word about new books. I'm truly privileged to be part of such a fabulous world.

So many friends have listened to my musings, supported with reading, and offered a shoulder to lean on. Most notably, Colin Williams, Martin Sargeant, Abi Bouch and Nicky Peacock.

To my lovely family, who listen to ideas, discuss character names, and generally keep me in tea, wine and good humour. I'll always be grateful for your support.

Finally, to you, the reader. I couldn't do this without you – thank you from the bottom of my heart.